For Paul

The Year of the Mad Jag

Jonathan

on the Rio Grande

Thanksgiving

'24

"With this roisterous novel based on a real story, Jonathan Slator joins that rare rank of writers who can shift without a clutch between delicious sex scenes, cliff-hanging chases in Arizona canyons, and the slang of Brits and 1980s marijuana growers in love, fear, or disgust. He is equally erudite in quoting lines from Lewis Carroll, Tolkien, and Dylan while never leaving out wise nods and belly-laughs for his readers. For fans of Southwestern U.S. canyonlands, the bonds of friendship, Seventies promiscuity, and cannabis cultivation long before legalization, this is a masterpiece."
—Stephen Fox, author of *Odyssey: Love and Terror in Greece 1969*

"This book is indescribable in the most hypnotic sense: from breathtaking jeep chases to cross-border smuggling, all couched in prurient poetry, Slator delivers an endless stream of transatlantic argot. A unique literary style backed by a driving narrative and a cursed menage à trois make this a fiercely compelling read."
—Lara Santoro, author of *Mercy* and *The Boy*

"Here is the *Shantaram* of the American West. At once lyrical and prosaic, *The Year of the Mad Jag* is a nostalgic hymn to the aphrodisiacs of criminality, drugs, and, of course, sex."
—Alex Dryden, author of *Death in Siberia*

"*The Year of the Mad Jag* is a rollicking yarn about illegal marijuana growing in the counterculture of the 1970s—and it's also an acutely observed account of a bemused, confused love triangle: three English people loosed into the hippie freedom of the desert Southwest, yawing between adventure and recklessness, love and irresolvable torment. In this extraordinary novel, Slator combines a poet's gift for describing the natural world with a memoirist's unsparing honesty in portraying the obsessions of lust and love."
—Allegra Huston, author of *Love Child: A Memoir of Family Lost and Found* and *Write What You Don't Know: 10 Steps to Writing with Confidence, Energy, and Flow*

"I've read a lot of books in my life. This one I would read every day if I could erase my memory. The novel is incredible."
—Suzanne Romero, early reader

"I find it quite ironic that the most dangerous thing about weed is getting caught with it."
—Bill Murray, actor

The Year of the Mad Jag

"I'll Sleep by the Creek"

A Novel
Based on a True Story

Jonathan Slator

HOOPERN PUBLISHING
TAOS

Copyright ©2023 Jonathan Slator

All rights reserved. No part of this book may be reproduced in any form or by any electronic or mechanical means, including information storage and retrieval systems, without permission in writing from the publisher except by a reviewer, who may quote brief passages in a review. Scanning, uploading, or electronic distribution of this book or the facilitation of such without the permission of the publisher is prohibited. Please purchase only authorized electronic editions, and do not participate in or encourage electronic piracy of copyrighted materials. Your support of the author's rights is appreciated. Any member of an educational institution wishing to photocopy part or all of the work for classroom use or anthology should send inquiries to:

Hoopern Publishing
127 Lorenzo Circle
Taos NM 87571

ISBN 979-8-9878568-0-2 (paperback)
ISBN 979-8-9878568-1-9 (ebook)

Book design by Dan Kuehn
Cover art direction by Richard Johnson
Cover graphic design by Tina Charad

This story is dedicated to the memory of Geoffrey King Green, Michelle Glass, and Martin Tomlinson, and Frank and Paddy Slator, who I hope would have forgiven me.

The Year of the Mad Jag 1

Acknowledgments 279

Glossary: Cockney Rhyming Slang. 280

In my first thirty years of life
I roamed hundreds and thousands of miles.
Walked by rivers through deep green grass
Entered cities of boiling red dust.
Tried drugs, but couldn't make Immortal;
Read books and wrote poems on history.
Today I'm back at Cold Mountain:
I'll sleep by the creek and purify my ears.

"Cold Mountain Poems, #12," by the eighth-century Chinese recluse Han-shan, translated by Gary Snyder

Mad
adj. 1: disordered in mind; **2 a:** completely unrestrained by reason and judgment, **b:** incapable of being explained or accounted for; **3:** carried away by intense anger; **4:** carried away by enthusiasm or desire; **5:** marked by wild gaiety and merriment; **6:** intensely excited; **7:** marked by intense and often chaotic activity.
—*Merriam–Webster Dictionary*

Jag
n. (informal) **1:** period of intoxication by drugs or alcohol; **2:** the state of being intoxicated by drugs or alcohol; **3:** a binge, a prolonged period of intoxication. (Late 16th century, origin unknown.) —*Encarta World English Dictionary*

Mad jag
1: Rogue jaguar inhabiting the Mazatzal Wilderness of central Arizona. Most northerly sighting of the largest cat of the Americas. **2:** (cap.) Strain of sinsemilla (seedless cannabis) cultivated in the Mazatzal Wilderness of central Arizona, awarded Best Domestic Sinsemilla by *High Times* magazine, December 1980.

Part One

Into the Canyon

I

Twenty-one years after we rode out that jag, I checked in on Geoff at the QE hospital in Birmingham, that filthy, fabulous nub of our once sceptred isle, as he lay dying. The emphysema had savaged him such that the 210 of his rugby days were now a withered 140, the broad visage now a Dachau mask.

"Eh-up, Stylor, you old sod." His words rattled from froth-corrupted lungs.

"Eh-up, Geoffrey. How you feeling? You look like dog shite."

"Count on you to gild the lily."

"Actually, it's 'paint the lily.'"

"Ever the pedant." He strained to raise himself. I hoisted him by the armpits, flinching at the soggy flaps of skin under the pecs. "Come back from New Mexico to get a grip of my wife again?" he gasped.

"If she's willing. How's she look these days?"

"Bollocks." He groped for his fags on the nightstand, knocking them to the floor.

I picked up the pack, shook one loose, lit it, handed it to him.

"So, you chanced flying even though those loonies just knocked down the moneylenders' temples in New York?" He locked me with a glare.

"They've got enough infidels to kill in Afghanistan right now."

"Shame you didn't book a flight on September 11th." He held my gaze.

He took a long drag; his chest heaved feebly as a bout of coughing wracked him.

"Puffing yourself into an early grave?"

"Doctor says they make no difference. Emphysema is too well set. Basically, I'm fucked. Pretty soon you'll have Emma all to yourself. Haven't the strength to get between you two nowadays." The listless eyes searched out mine. "Ever get the cactus out of your arse?"

The memory of the last night I'd seen him, twenty-one years previous, midwinter '80, '81, was vivid yet. I'd just made the long drive to Arizona from Oaxaca, where, in the southern Mexican highlands and in the company of Geoff's wanton wife, Emma, I'd delivered fifteen thousand cannabis indica seeds to a cabal of Mexican marijuana smugglers and where I'd just got out of a rat's arse of a Mexican jail and where his wife had left me after a lust-lined odyssey through some of the loveliest coastline on earth. Back in Arizona, I had found Emma at Michèle's little wooden house in the arroyo outside Jerome, the ramshackle mining town where we'd all lived and loved and fought, and where we'd all changed forever.

"*Jean, Jean, tu arrives trop tard. Geoff vient d'arriver de l'Oregon.*" Michèle had leaped up and down in her excitement. Only the French could take such delight in a *scandale*. How this darling spirit could, twelve years later, drive out to a spit of land above the Verde River, jam a hose in the exhaust, and choke off her life is another story. That night, thrumming with life, she urged us, in scrambled *franglais*, to flee to Old Mexico, New Mexico, Tahiti ("Oh, those *plages noires*, so wonderful for the making love") as I glanced up the gulch for headlights.

The headlights came; I walked out to meet them. Geoff slewed the pickup to a halt and came fast through the cactus-strewn yard.

"Don't think you're fucking off with my missus, Stylor," he barked, and came on hard, swinging wildly, backing me against the porch rail. I ducked under a haymaker and scarpered away. But he crushed me into the hard desert dirt with a kidney-bruising tackle. I twisted to fend off the fists.

"Don't do this, Geoff, please." Emma ran from the house.

Geoff, fist high, turned to his wife. We staggered to our feet, chests heaving. "It's no good, Geoff. I've decided," Emma said. "I'm going with Jem."

He slumped, spent with the effort of the brawl and the realization of his wife's infidelity. When Emma turned toward the house, his gaze followed her for a second before he came at me again and I went down under a hail of fists and crashed into a cholla cactus. Yelling with rage and pain, the chunks of cactus swinging from my back, I hurled myself at him and forced him down before Emma ran back to us.

"It took a while to get all the spines out, yeah." I settled into the bedside chair. "But I had some help."

"You don't have to remind me, ya wanker. The missus had a soft spot for you even before you slipped her a length." Geoff glanced over my shoulder. A doctor approached. The grimness of this dullard's expression was not lost on Geoff.

"Morning, doctor. Looks like you've come to tell me I'll soon be buying the farm."

The doctor looked at me. "Good afternoon. Jonathan Parkin, pulmonary specialist for the QE." No hand was outheld.

"This is Jeremy Stylor, Dr. Parkin. General ne'er-do-well and back-door man," Geoff said. "You can speak freely in front of him."

"I'd rather do this in private, Geoffrey," the doctor pleaded.

"I'll wait outside."

"No, Style. I'd sooner have you here. Better you than no one." He reached for my hand; his was cold, skeletal.

"Very well." The specialist wrung his pale fingers. "I have to tell you that the disease is too far advanced for us to treat it further with any expectation of success. The antibiotic is not proving effective. We have advanced the dosage as far as we dare."

"How long do I have?" Geoff's hand had the strength and urgency of a frightened child's.

"Not long, I'm afraid. A week at best." The doctor, in his mid-forties, younger than both of us, was clearly not inured to this aspect of his duty. He shuffled edgily. "We're all extremely sorry. We've done all we can and you've been a model patient, an absolute brick . . ."

"Yeah, yeah." Geoff's hand clenched mine. I knew that the flannel from the doc would piss him off at the best of times. "Thanks, doctor, for all you've done."

The doctor, eager to take his cue, fled.

"Where's Ems?" I said. "Should I get her?"

"She went to have a bath. She's been here for days. Give her a bell, would you mate? And send the kids in." He had sunk into the pillows and seemed scrawnier yet.

I scuttled out of the ward to the corridor where Geoff's kids occupied themselves next to the nurse's station.

Tessa, sixteen and surly, who would suffer most from her father's death, threw me a withering glance before turning back to her books. Matthew, a stout twenty, who had his mother's resilience, looked up at me as I approached.

"I saw the doctor go in," he said, studying my face. "Is my dad dying?"

There was a snarky edge to his tone; I wondered if his mother had ever mentioned me.

"Your dad would like to see you both." I avoided his eyes.

"How is he?" Matthew fixed me again.

"You'd better ask him yourself." I tried to sound conciliatory, but I'd always been hopeless when called upon for sympathy and compassion; it seemed to elicit the antithesis: callousness, indifference.

They grabbed their things and slunk away to the ward. I moved to the pay phone and fumbled the unfamiliar coins into the slot.

While I waited for Emma to pick up, it dawned on me with horror that I was about to speak, for the first time in over two decades, to the woman who had cracked my heart; who had caused me the keenest pleasure, the greatest longing, and the longest agony; and against whom the conversation, the touch of the lips both upper and nether, the laugh and cry of every woman with whom I had had an affair since and any with whom I would, all would be compared, judged, stood against this woman and the profound bliss and deep misery I had experienced through, and after, my affair with her.

"Jem?" Her soft Yorkshire vowels stabbed across the years. "What on earth are you doing there?"

"I came over to check on my mum." I felt my voice waver. "Thought I'd look in on Geoff."

"That's nice of you," she said, and I searched for but found no trace of sarcasm. "And how is he?"

"Not so good, Emma. The doctor came while I was there." I heard the snatch of breath. "I think you'd better come."

"I'll get dressed," she said, and the pause that followed was rich. "Don't leave. I'd love to see you. It's been a while."

"Yes, Emma. Twenty-one years."

"My God. That long?" But I knew she knew.

I prowled the hall while I waited, tempted to flee, unsure where to meet her: just the two of us, here in the corridor, with the nurse glancing at us from her reports, or at the bedside amidst the family tableau, a family I'd almost fucked up before it started, and with my old mate ready to croak. Why in Christ's name had I come?

If I stayed here in the corridor, could I trust myself not to collapse, a gibbering wreck, at her feet, or worse, to fling myself on her, gasping, ripping her clothes aside as I had in the past, a violation she had not merely condoned but abetted, many times, during our affair, her own urgency palpable. How the fuck were you supposed to reacquaint yourself with the lust of your life?

I opted for the bedside and skulked there like a spare prick at a wedding as Tessa wept and clung to her dad and Matthew rocked, back and forth, in the bedside chair. I prayed that their mum had aged appallingly and now was as ugly as a box of frogs, eye-bags hanging like a terrier's testicles, a rake of fat warping that once sculpted arse into a slack cellulite sack.

The double doors swung wide and, despite myself, my head whipped round like a hawk's. "Damn you," I heard myself muttering, "damn you." In over twenty years, she hadn't had the decency to gain more than a couple of pounds. That gorgeous ballerina's five foot four, eight stone, was identical to the one that had lain naked before me on many Mexican beaches and Arizona creeksides in that warm winter. Not until she approached the bed did I notice some extra lines on her face and an added puffiness to her neck and cheeks. She hugged me quickly and turned away. Tessa, she, and Geoff were immediately entwined, wracked with sobs.

I crossed the ward to a chair at an empty bedside, where I tried but failed to force a recollection from my mind. As I stared across that hospital ward at the deathbed of my life's best friend, as his family wept in misery for the conclusion of a hideous five-year disease, all that came to mind was this: that the last time I had seen the woman, the wife, the mother, she had led me from the Spirit Room in Jerome, Arizona, to her marital bed. It was early spring 1981 and the husband Geoff was then in the depths of a jagged canyon seventy miles due east of town, tilling an infamous garden for another planting of a famous strain of weed, the incomparable, the mystical, the *High Times* award-winning, the *Newsweek*-featured Mad Jag sinsemilla of Mad Jag Canyon, grown, marketed, and sold at a gob-smacking profit, sweat equity excluded, of about 10,000 percent the previous year by yours truly and the brilliant, crazed Wiz, the original Wizard of the Mogollon Rim.

Emma had led me through the starlit streets and up the rickety stairs, her normally stunning figure swollen to a quivering voluptuousness by the onset of her pregnancy with the young man who now self-consciously stroked her shoulders. Oozing libido, as most women do when first pregnant, she had dragged my clothes aside and with those articulate lips honed the steel of a willing old chap and then rode me confidently and urgently, abandoning herself to ecstasy, clenching my neck so hard in the crook of her arm that I was forced to free myself to avoid choking. As she lifted her chin from my shoulder, I watched rapt as her face contorted in a rictus of lust capped by a last keen of quietus that rang through the silent streets and out over the broad desert valley to the red rock cliffs above Sedona and beyond. I'd always loved the strength of her orgasms, but this one, perhaps heightened by the realization that this was her last time astride me, dwarfed any previous. She toppled as if pole-axed and lay panting beside me, her body arched away, leaving us connected like farmyard dogs until finally, with a delightful queef, she disengaged.

"Jem . . . JEREMY!" Emma's voice snapped me across the ward. "I'm taking the kids home. Geoff wants you to stay with him. Can you hang on for another hour or . . . ?"

"Yeah, sure. Of course." I spotted the lines of strain on her brow. The mascara of one eye had run into an LA gangster's tear, the crow's feet fanning from her eye sockets had furrowed—but goddamn, she was still gorgeous. Her strong mouth sought a smile but formed a pout and her turquoise eyes held my gaze again for the first time in twenty-one years. I'd always expected a tense reaction to this moment, but I wasn't prepared for the surge of disquiet and desire, like the after-rush of a close call in traffic with the danger passed and the adrenaline raking your hamstrings. I watched her walk away and try as I might could not stop my stare.

"You're a twat, Style. A randy twat." Geoff's gravel snatched my eyes away from her arse. He hauled himself up from the pillows. "I don't know why we were always such mates, you and I. I know you always thought of me as a Brummy yobbo."

"Which you were. And you had me pegged as a public school pillock."

"Which no fookin' doubt you were. A little alliteration and a bucket of bullshit make a public-school ponce." A ghost of a grin crossed his mouth. "We had some times, though. People always rave about the sixties," he said, "but you know it really kicked off here, in Brum, in England, in the seventies."

"As Lennon said, 'The sixties were just breakfast time.'"

"Think of the bands we saw in the Brumagham boozers before they hit it big." His chin came up and I glimpsed through the death mask the old fire. "Band of Joy, who became Led Zepp. ELO. Judas Priest. UB40 in the Hare and Hounds."

"I remember Chicken Shack in the Arch Club under the railway track in Aston. With Stan Webb and Christine Perfect."

"I'd rather go blind, boy, than to see you walk away . . ." His attempt at the song trailed off.

"Don't give up your day job."

"Bollocks." He suffered a smirk to cross his face. "And they went on to form Fleetwood Mac."

"Spencer Davis Group in the Elbow Room," I remembered.

"Aaah, the Elbow Room, what a beltin' club that was. Christ, did we pull some totty out of that joint, eh mate." The jaundiced cheeks gained a hint of color. "What about Ozzy Osbourne and Black Sabbath belting it out up in some West Brom pub for a couple of bob. Aye, the Midlands had the fookin' bands in those days. Now it's all Manchester or the Smoke."

He tailed off and welled up, and a tear started across his cheek. I reached for his shoulder and tried to clench it comfortingly. He shrugged me off.

"You know, I tried to forgive you, Style. But I could'na." He grimaced with the pain of the words. "I know Emma went willingly, but at the time it was you I wanted to kill. I wanted to winkle-pick your goolies into the middle of next week. I wanted to . . ." He began to retch and flung the bile away with the back of his hand and reached toward me, guttering.

"Jesus, Geoff. Nurse! Oh Christ. Doctor," I yelled over my shoulder as Geoff grabbed my wrists, babbling like a drowning man while his blazing eyes rolled upward.

2

The repetitive shriek of the stall horn in a Cessna cockpit is as welcome as the wail of an alley cat snatching you from deep REM.

"What does that noise mean, Wiz?" I shouted over the drone of the turbo engine.

"It means if it wasn't me flying we would be auguring in!" The pilot grinned as his hands flickered over the controls, tweaking the pitch of the prop, angling the flaps to slow the plane as we hammered past the canyon walls. "Get that sack out there."

Squatting in the spot from which we had removed the passenger seat and taking care not to foul the dual-control yoke with my back, I jammed my shoulder against the door and forced it open against the rush of warm Arizona air. The contents of the package, tools and grub for the crew, who would soon be pruning—i.e., trimming—the marijuana buds, were tightly lashed in canvas and rope. I forced the package out on to the wing strut, fighting the slipstream, struggling to hang on to the bag and avoid pitching through the door myself.

"You set, man?" Wiz yelled.

"Set!" I shouted back and tried to reassure myself that, as I was hurtling at treetop height through a remote canyon in the desert mountains of central Arizona to drop supplies into a garden now blooming with over seven hundred mature female marijuana plants, there were few pilots in the world I'd rather have at the controls. With over five thousand logged hours, and god knows how many more left unrecorded flying dubious loads across the borders and deserts and oceans of Central America and the Caribbean, Wiz, my newfound partner, was the guy I wanted in the left seat.

"Hold it . . . hold it . . . okay, GO!"

I loosed my grip and leaned out to watch the bag drop, forgetting that the door, which had been held by the breadth of the bag, was now at the mercy of the slipstream. It slammed into my left temple and fired me across the narrow fuselage into Wiz's elbow. My shoulder clipped the dual controls and I felt the plane lurch before he flung me back against the flapping door.

"What the fuck!" screamed Wiz, wrestling the plane, his face creased with concentration. "You dipshit. You want us to wreck down here? In our canyon."

"Terribly sorry." I tried my best Oxbridge and jammed the door handle down. Craning back as the plane yawed through the narrows and Wiz gunned the turbo to climb us into safe airspace, I caught a glimpse of a tall figure clinging to the branches of the white pine that marked our garden. This was Stilt, Wiz's partner from the previous crop.

Wiz kept the yoke pulled in and we climbed toward the canyon rim. I looked across at the charming madman who had brought this sea change to my life. Thick lips pursed into a moue of concentration as he peered through the Perspex bubble; the dark mustache and pointed goatee jutting forward; the keen hazel eyes betraying the compassionate nature of perhaps the softest crook to ever grace the trade.

It didn't seem like less than a year since we'd met in Phoenix, a few days before Christmas 1979, when the only people I knew in the States were Dali and his wife, Fiona.

The Year of the Mad Jag

In '73 I'd flogged seats in a van from England to Greece and the beautiful Fiona and Geoff, then her main squeeze and my main mate, had grabbed the last couple of spots. The van had broken down a couple times before we even made Dover. It took us ten days to reach Athens, by which time the paying passengers were ready to crush my knackers in a vise, Fiona and Geoff had split up for good, he having left the group late one night in Austria on the neighborhood postman's bike. On the volcanic island of Santorini, Fiona had met Dali and a couple of years later they got hitched.

Dali had a lovely adobe house in the oldest section of Phoenix, not far from Camelback Mountain, with a studio in back. Had he realized when I pitched up that winter morning that his house was about to become the major hangout for a stream of overeducated trans-Atlantic yobbos and tarts, he would probably have slammed the door in my grinning boat race. But in keeping with the generosity of his countrymen he threw wide the portal and I moved into the studio.

Dali's paintings, which adorned every wall, were an exuberant concoction of Rousseau, Courbet, Kandinsky, and Hieronymus Bosch elaborated by the influence of early Disney cartoons and heavy metal mags, and tempered with the occasionally sobering touch of Thomas Hart Benton or John James Audubon. The style of his painting and the extravagance of his mustache gave him his moniker.

"This one doesn't seem typical of your style," I suggested one day as we whiled away the hours in the studio. "Is it unfinished?"

"No," he said, grinning at the painting of a rampant jaguar, jaws flared, fangs bared, massive front paws held menacingly. "That's a graphic job I did for the Wizards of the Rim."

"Wizards of what?"

"Wizards of the Rim. The Mogollon Rim."

"Why are they called wizards?"

"They've built a scene around their adventures in the canyons of the Rim, the Carlos Castaneda gig, the growing trip."

"The growing trip?" I asked disingenuously.

"I'm sworn to a code of silence here." He daubed paint lavishly onto a new canvas. "But what the fuck. You're getting savvy to the scene. I've got a label somewhere. Here."

The bumper sticker had the jaguar leaping from the left corner. Dominating the right side were the words "Mad Jag" and below, "Wizards of the Rim, Mad Jag Canyon, Arizona."

"Rather vague," I said. "What's their business?"

"They grow sinsemilla."

"What the hell's that?"

"Seedless grass. The labels go with each bag. And the Mad Jag is the tits, man, primo."

"Let's puff some."

"I'm fresh out. Tomorrow, though, the Wizards'll be in town. We'll be awash in bud. And you'll be picking your brains off the rooftop."

Next morning, a couple of characters strolled into the backyard and my life took the path less traveled by.

Stilt stood six seven and a half in his socks. A dentist by profession, laconic, soft-spoken, sharp-witted, and dry-humored, he soon became a favorite of our group of English expats. A head of tightly curled black hair framed the lean cheeks. Full eyebrows arched over lucid green eyes.

At six one, Wiz was dwarfed by comparison. Raven shoulders above a compact waist gave him a classic cowboy profile. Unlike the others, his clothes were pressed: a crisp green T-shirt and pale creases on his jeans, a throwback to his military days. Faced with the delights of the draft and a tour of grunt duty in the jungles of Nam, Wiz had taken the shortcut to a flyboy life through the warrant officer's option and within six months was flying out of bases near Da Trang. Having fulfilled his obligation to flag and country by savaging the Asian natives from the skies, he'd parlayed the experience into a lucrative if dicey living flying bales of grass across the southern border. A wife and two daughters had put the mockers on the cavalier lifestyle and he was grounded, for the foreseeable future, to a more pastoral illegal existence: growing sinsemilla.

We shook hands and I studied the square face. Slightly flared nostrils gave him the keen, restless look of a man constantly intent on some pressing scheme. Warm eyes had the purple tint of split juniper and darted among the three of us as we talked. Often he punctuated a comment to one of the party with a brief staccato burst of laughter and then caught another's eye with a mischievous glint. His hair had developed from the close military cut but retained that order. The 'tache was tightly shorn but the goatee had been allowed to flourish and was clipped into a roguish point.

Dali, a lean Dave Crosby at six two and 220, brought a solid third arm to this striking triumvirate. A receding hairline had left a widow's peak and shiny temples; gray-green eyes; a loosely curled afro framed the sun-beaten cheeks.

Often I look back to that warm Phoenix morning and regret accepting the demon weed and Wiz's offer of a partnership a few days later. The grass we smoked in Dali's backyard that December in 1979 was by no means the first taste I'd had of the product of the cannabis plant. But the smoking of hash, ganja, hash oil, and grass in England in the seventies was chiefly a late-night habit. Geoff and I would spend our evenings on a swing through the wine bars, downing a few bottles of plonk and laying the cursory hard word on a few bits of skirt, and then stagger back to the flat to tune in to John Peel, *The Old Grey Whistle Test*, and a five-skinned spliff of baccy and Lebanese. Occasionally we laid our mitts on some Afghani black, laced with white streaks of opium, and would become so fabulously stoned that if Murphy was there with his wisecracks, and fat Eric was up from the Smoke, and we had anything left in the Johnnie Walker bottle, we would get so wound up we risked hernia from laughter.

To smoke some gear straight after breakfast in the blinding Arizona sunlight was a new one on me. But I felt compelled to adhere to the local custom and took a few puffs on the wretched excuse for a joint rolled by the wild-looking Yank next to me. Christ, I had smoked Gauloises streaked with hash oil in Amsterdam, pulled on a chillum behind the blue mosque in Mazar I Sharif, and sampled the kif in Marrakesh. This little twist of dried grass shared between the four of us would barely cop a buzz for a high school jerk. Once the joint was passed, Dali doused the hot tip in saliva pooled in the curl of his tongue and tucked the roach in the hem of his cap. Then he, Wiz, and Stilt rose, grabbed a football, and trotted across the road to the park.

A few minutes or maybe a few hours later—to this day, I haven't a bloody clue which—a shout from across the street snapped me away from the vitally important study of the dimples on the rind of a grapefruit that I had plucked from Dali's backyard tree. It was then that I realized I had just been introduced to new realm of indulgence. This wasn't the soporific high/low that I later learned came from oxidized cannabis and hash, but a brilliant, coruscating stimulus that called for action.

As I jogged across the street to join the game, all my drug experience convinced me that I could not remain upright for long, that in a couple of strides I would be sprawled in the grass creased with laughter. But the Mad Jag held a further surprise. Far from stumbling to the ground, I felt light on my feet, an illusion no doubt but no less delightful for that. As I made the grassy area of the park, the ball spiralled lazily in my direction from Dali's practiced arm, seeming to hang forever in the harsh desert sunlight. I accelerated under the parabola, deer-swift, goat-sure, arms extended, fingers splayed to cradle the ball, and continued the dream run into the end zone, little pigskin held ostentatiously aloft.

We flung the ball around the park for what might have been a minute or a day. Finally, we abandoned the game and lay in bliss under the shade of the locust trees. I squinted up through the leaves at the fierce, refracted light and tried to make mental notes, but of course it all faded away in slackness, overstimulus, and the terror and the ecstasy, the misery and the brilliance of the following "annus mysticalus," the year of the Mad Jag.

"Whaddaya reckon to this 'erb, Style?" Dali asked.

"Not bad," I said.

"Not bad, he says!" Dali exploded. "Only a damn Limey could come up with such condescending bullshit about the best grass he ever smoked. You know who grew this righteous gear? Why, these two dudes right here. Up in Mad Jag Canyon. Under the Mogollon Rim."

"The Wizards of the Rim," I said.

"I wish you'd keep our business shit classified." Wiz glanced across at Dali.

"The man does have a tendency toward a loose tongue." Stilt chewed thoughtfully on a blade of grass. As the one among us holding the highest academic distinction, he often strove, tongue in cheek, to confirm the fact in Conan Doyle idiom.

"And this year he's looking for a new partner. Stilt's been forced into early retirement. That's the case, eh boys?" Dali peeled a grapefruit.

"Maybe." Wiz shifted his gaze my way.

"Well, Jeremy Stylor here's got nothing better to do with his summer," Dali went on.

"Hang on a mo," I jumped in. "I'm headed back to London. I've got a new contract starting in March."

"I sincerely doubt the veracity of such a statement." Stilt stared up into the branches of the locust. "I understand you're partial to the boons of our part of the world: the climate, the mountains, the young maidens."

"Not met many maidens," I quipped, but I knew I was caught.

"He's a backcountry man. Climber, sailor, traveler. Just the ticket for our game." Dali handed round grapefruit wedges.

"How 'bout we take a hike in the Superstitions. I'll show you where the crow roosts," Wiz said, nodding rather too eagerly. "You can start on the way of the warrior." I knew little of his Carlos Castaneda influences back then and wondered what the hell he was on about.

The previous February, Wiz and Stilt had parked at the hot springs in the then unspoilt Verde Valley and set off downstream. After a couple of days' hard trek, they had turned away from the main drainage and found themselves in the lower reaches of an east–west canyon that showed intermittent water on the maps. Their speculation that the surface water in this canyon would hold up year-round was proven, and it was here that they first encountered the deranged old cat that would leave his stamp on all our lives over the next years.

They had celebrated finding their spot in true Southwestern bohemian style—by imbibing some strong hallucinogens. As they sprawled around the fire chuckling, anthropomorphizing constellations, a nerve-splitting shriek rang out from the crag above them. They had stared into the darkness, jumping in paranoia at the slightest rustle or firefly glow, until exhaustion overcame their terror. No sooner had they bedded down when another roar, this time from the very edge of the clearing, had them scrambling for weapons. Their subsequent study of animal cries convinced them of the presence of an unlikely jaguar in the area, and thus the canyon, the grass, their whole operation got its name.

On a broad ledge above the stream, they prepared a garden and planted seed from the finest grass they'd smoked: a glorious sativa strain from the mountains of Oaxaca. Once they'd got the crop out safely, their success fueled plans for a coup the following year. Stilt, however, faced a not insignificant problem.

The stork-like fellow's wife, the tall, elegant Emily, was a U.S. Forestry Ranger. This held considerable advantages for the wilderness grower: prior knowledge of activity in the backcountry, such as raptor studies, boreal data gathering, and multi-agency busts of dope growers. When Stilt proposed a second year of his weekend trade, his wife welcomed the idea so long as it was accompanied by his signature on the divorce papers. Thus it was that my moons aligned and I alit in the Sonoran Desert in my thirtieth year to fill a job vacancy in the Mad Jag operation.

Over the next few days, I considered Wiz's offer and wrestled nominally with my conscience. The element that gave me most pause was the effect that failure and its consequences would have on my family. My father had worked like an ant on his beloved Devonshire farm. He abhorred even the concept of middlemen: estate agents, brokers, dealers taking a percentage of his hard-earned harvests. What he thought of downright criminals was unprintable. He shared none of his countrymen's love of the "decent rogue."

If I was nabbed, the treatment meted out by local law enforcement would pale in comparison to the slagging and ostracizing I would receive from him. But time would heal, I reasoned weakly; and we weren't going to get caught, were we?

In the end, the lure of the adventure in this amazing terrain, the chance to make some serious dosh, the arguably harmless euphoria of cannabis, and the pusillanimous thought that I might even be able to convince my dad that I was following his profession outweighed any nagging doubts. A couple of days later, I drove up to Jerome and, over a bevvy in the Spirit Room, pitched in my lot with the Wizards of the Rim.

3

"Scratch me out a line." Wiz spoke crisply into the microphone as he banked the little plane out over the mesa. "Need something to calm me down after you damn near put us into the canyon wall."

I grabbed the thick navigation mirror and pulled the coke vial from my jeans pocket. Kneeling on the floor, I balanced the mirror with difficulty as the plane rode a stiffening breeze, and spread out four snowbanks with my clasp knife. I held the mirror up to Wiz's chin and offered the rolled bill. He hoovered a line into each nostril and snapped his head back as the powder bit.

"How many more bags do we got to drop?"

"Two."

"Good. I don't want to be buzzing this canyon much longer or we might get some company out here."

I snorted my dose from the mirror, savoring the pineapple flavor of the cocaine that had been flown directly from Colombia to the Verde Valley of Arizona only days before and for an ounce of which we had traded our first pound of the early indica. And as it coursed through me and my heart started to race and sweat began to bead my brow and my spirits rose and dipped with the little plane, I cursed my inability to reject a drug that I'd always swore I would never touch, a drug that would fool and divide and fuck us all by the end of the jag.

We approached the rim and Wiz slid the Cessna over the piñons and down past the basalt cliffs into the upper canyon. I could see where the spring burst from the hard rock of the dry creekbed and from there the sweet water turned the canyon bottom to a lush serpentine copse of sycamores and cottonwoods and brought life to bird and mammal and reptile and provided the source for our wicked, victimless crime.

Our next two runs were uneventful. We climbed out of our canyon toward the little town that stood in the pines at the top of the Mogollon Rim, the huge escarpment that runs from northern Arizona to central New Mexico and hides hundreds of live-stream canyons like ours. We swept out over the shallow head of Mad Jag Canyon (we always called it that and never used its map name, even in private), and my heart took a belt as I saw the plume of dust and the vehicle crashing across the spit of land between our canyon and the next one east.

"Holy shit," said Wiz through the headphones. "What the frig's he doing out here?"

"Who is it?" I stared hard at the gas-guzzling four-by working hard along the bad road.

"The Gila County sheriff. And he seems to be heading somewhere fast."

"Fuck me."

"We better stay away." Wiz wristed the yoke to yaw the Cessna north.

"What in Christ's name is the sheriff doing out here?" I stared at Wiz.

"Who knows, man?" The ploughed-field brow of the seasoned smuggler did little to ease my fears.

"Think he saw us flying out of the canyon?"

"Doubt it. He's too far back on the mesa. Bow season starts

in a couple of days. Probably just making sure nobody's getting a jump on the best bucks."

I could see the truck clearly now, parked, and a large man walking through the junipers, going east toward the rim of the canyon next to ours. He stopped and looked up at the plane. Wiz cursed. The man pressed on and I watched him stand at the rim for a while. I saw him turn and walk back from the edge before he disappeared under the fuselage. Was he going to walk over to the rim of Mad Jag Canyon?

"Jeez, Jem. Pretty spooky seeing ol' Willard out here." His jaw was set.

It was sobering to think that someone of Wiz's vast criminal experience would share my concern.

"Yeah, mate." My stomach churned. "I hear he can be a bit rough on those he gets in custody."

"No shit. Three Hawks and some of his Apache buddies ended up in the Globe lockup once after a drunk. He beat the crap out of them. Three Hawks lost a couple of teeth and one guy got a busted arm."

"Let's make a pass south of the mesa. Make sure he doesn't drive across to Mad Jag Canyon," I said.

"Sounds boring. Got a better idea." The cheeks rose. The goatee, which was that day woven into a Hell's Angel's French braid, darted toward me; the mahogany eye glistened ominously beyond the ostrich-egg headphone.

I sighed into the microphone; only too well did I know of Wiz's antics at the helm of a skiff of the sky. The man loved to fly and, like all wild pilots, loved to have someone alongside him when he had a chance to show his skills, particularly when not burdened by a fuselage full of gage.

With a firm pull on the yoke and a kick of the rudder, he swung the plane into a tight bank over the Verde River. Craning our necks, we were able to spot the sheriff's Blazer over the port wing as it worked up the dirt road along the eastern edge of the mesa.

"Looks like he's heading back toward the highway," Wiz said.

"Excellent. Let's head home then."

"Let's just give him a goodbye wave." The grin was terrifying.

"Are we okay on fuel?" I tried one last ploy to avoid the inevitable.

Wiz glanced at the instrument panel. "Sweet. Just."

"Too bad." I tried to find a way to brace myself between the door and his seat.

In answer, Wiz tilted the yoke forward and we pitched into the great rift to the east of our garden home.

"The Narrows." Wiz pointed to his left. "A fine place to bid our fat friend a fond farewell."

I looked across and cursed. The place of my partner's choosing was a tight ravine formed by a huge volcanic dyke which jutted vertically from the rim and a secondary cliff on the mesa. The dirt road skirted the edge of the abyss before slipping through the constricted throat of the Narrows for maybe a hundred yards.

"What's the wingspan of a 182?" I asked.

"Thirty-six feet." He flung the little plane into a tight turn that had me lurching against the door.

"Least you're strapped into a seat," I whined as I realized that the slot holding the road, which we had often driven, was appreciably less than the wingspan of a Cessna 182.

The sheriff's truck clattered along the jeep trail heading inexorably toward the little cleft. Gunning the Lycoming 240 HP power plant to an ear-trembling pitch, Wiz ripped the Cessna up to maximum speed. We flashed into the Narrows and, at the last instant, when it seemed both wings would be clipped by the sides of the ravine, the crazy bastard flung the plane perpendicular to the horizon and we hammered sideways through the tiny canyon, the echoed shriek of the tortured engine and the scream I was unable to restrain abetting the terror.

With all my weight slammed down on the pilot's shoulder by the plane's radical attitude, I strained to peer ahead. Just as we seemed to have escaped the confines of the rock walls, our exit was blocked by the sheriff's Blazer, tires spewing gravel as it skidded to a halt.

"Fuuuuck!" I shrieked and felt Wiz's triceps harden as he hauled the yoke back and the port wing bisected the gap between the bonnet of the lawman's truck and the cliff. The wing tip tore through a mesquite bush; the plane lurched. In the instant before the Cessna spiraled into the void, I caught a glimpse of the sheriff's enamel-splintering stare.

"Whoa, baby!" Wiz yelled, wrestling the controls as we pitched headlong into the canyon. I don't have much of a clue what he did in those next few seconds that saved us from a fiery end in the rocks below. At one point, I had the view to the rim and clearly saw the sheriff training binoculars on me. When it seemed we were out of airspace and could not avert a cataclysmic meeting with the canyon floor, I felt the Cessna stabilize into a more or less controlled dive, and we hurtled out over the canopy of sycamores.

"He's got glasses. Think he can read the wing numbers?" I gasped through the spanking surge of adrenaline.

"Doubt it. Anyway, it's Crisp's registration." The goatee turned toward me and the great roaring laugh assailed me through the headphones.

"You're a complete wanker, you know that. A complete and utter wanker." But I couldn't suppress a pursed grin as the laugh reverberated and Wiz guided the plane into the welcome safety of the Verde Valley.

We had borrowed the plane from the most revered of all this coterie of Arizona villains, the reserved and mysterious Crisp. At the back of his house near Cornville, this godfather of the Verde Valley had improved a dirt road into a makeshift landing strip for his turbocharged Cessna. With studied and uncharacteristic restraint, Wiz made a standard approach and touchdown. We taxied to a worn clearing and scrambled from the cockpit.

Two men who represented the opposite ends of the criminal spectrum, Crisp and Norbert, joined us to inspect the damaged wing. As an international smuggler who owned the Cottonwood airport, Crisp was held in high regard by all the villains I'd met during my year in the Southwest. Our relationship was strained at first and guarded at best. He hadn't forged a successful career in his uncertain trade by opening his arms to every wannabe who turned up. But by the end of the year, having proved myself a competent crook, he warmed to me in his reserved manner.

The other bloke, Nobby, we'd met in the Spirit Room in Jerome one spring evening as we slaked our thirst from the grueling hike out of the canyon. A cultured Swiss traveling through to who knew where, he'd blagged a job behind the bar. As it was Sunday, the Phoenix bikers were in town, many of whom holstered weapons, which, in any Arizona bar back then, had to be handed over. I watched in amusement as they unbuckled Smith and Wessons and Glocks and tossed them across the bar to the Swiss, who caught them cautiously and shelved them.

"Where to next?" I leaned on the bar as he tilted the glass to pour my draft.

"*Où souffle le vent.*"

Maybe the wind can blow in our direction, I thought.

The intense manner of the stocky Swiss with the professorial look had amused us. Glaring at us through pebble-lens specs, he'd told us about his background in the Zurich art world and how he'd come to the West to see "zee vide spaces through new eyes." Within a fortnight we'd signed him up and he had joined us on the hard trek into the canyon.

Crisp shook my hand. He had the rugged face of a good-looking bloke in his early forties who'd been around the block as far as any and farther than most. His skin was pockmarked and leathery, a tad Redfordesque. From the left eye socket to the bottom of his earlobe a livid scar creased his cheek. His eyes had a yellowish cast, the legacy of a tropical illness.

"Steady flight?" he asked as we walked in front of the plane. He stroked the damaged leading edge.

"Bit of a wobble here and there."

"No shit." He and Wiz checked out the buckled wing.

"We'll take care of the repairs," Wiz said.

"We will?" I began my usual banter but added, after Wiz's scolding glance and an even more sobering flick of Crisp's eyes in my direction, "Course we will. Trade or cash?"

"I'll take some of that fine bud of yours. Top colas, yeah?"

"Top colas it is," I replied.

"Vee keep the best vur you, pal," Nobby said to Crisp without a trace of sycophancy; the two had become unlikely friends and remain so. "Sativa or Kush?"

"I could go for some of the Mad Jag for sure."

"The sveet-smelling sativa for a man ov taste." Nobby flicked the tip of his nose with his forefinger. "Can we vly zis crate to San Francisco?"

"Sure." The master smuggler showed his usual brevity. "You guys fix the seats. Wiz, help me get the Leb."

As Nobby and I finished bolting down the seats the others came back, laid two suitcases on a wing, and flipped the catches. We all gave grunts of admiration at the serried array of kilo bricks of blond Lebanese hash, each embossed with a stamp in Arabic. The cases, along with a satchel containing a couple of pounds of our recently harvested skunk, were stowed in the luggage compartment at the rear of the Cessna. Ten minutes later, Crisp roared the little plane down the dirt track and up into the cobalt Arizona sky, and as we watched the plane I reflected again on the unlikely concoction of our gang of crooks: Wiz, the former military pilot; Stilt, the reluctant dentist; Crisp, the career smuggler; Dali, the eccentric artist; and Nobby, a literate and urbane boulevardier from the sophisticated quarter of Zurich.

4

The drive in the old International Scout back to Jerome was plagued by worries. Why was that fat fart of a sheriff creeping around our canyon on the day we dropped supplies for the final phase? Had he heard the plane and driven out to check? Were we under surveillance? Was a posse combed from multiple agencies waiting for us all to hike in before springing the trap?

As I crossed the Verde River, I span the radio dials and picked up an FM station out of Phoenix. The jock spieled the news.

"National Security adviser Zbigniew Brzezinski today argued against President Carter's decision to use his brother, Billy Carter, to enlist the help of the Libyan government in securing the release of the Iranian hostages. Fifty-two Americans have been held in captivity for more than three hundred days after Islamic militants seized the US embassy.

"President Carter's rival in the upcoming presidential election, the GOP nominee Ronald Reagan, took a break from the rigors of campaigning to visit Henry Kissinger at a Virginia estate. The former Secretary of State denied the talks had anything to do with a job in a Reagan administration.

"A Delta Airlines jet carrying 81 passengers and seven crew was diverted to Cuba last night. This was the third such incident in a week.

"In what is described as 'the largest one-time seizure in the Western U.S.,' DEA agents seized twenty tons of marijuana and two boats in San Francisco on Thursday.

"U.S. crude oil supplies reached a record 391.4 million barrels, more than 100 million barrels above the accepted minimum level. The average price of gas in August was $1.23 a gallon.

"In sports, John McEnroe outlasted Björn Borg in a five-set thriller to retain his U.S. Open crown."

I shut off the radio and my thoughts returned to a personal conundrum: how the hell was my affair with Molly and the increasingly intolerable tension between Geoff, Emma, and myself going to be resolved?

Our lives had been agonizingly intertwined since 1975. That year, for three thousand quid and change, Geoff and I had bought a two-up-two-down in Moseley, a suburb of Birmingham destined to become trendy. At the end of our road stood the Moseley Arms. One evening we strolled down to said pub for a couple of pints of the landlord's finest and ran into two girls from the local college. It was my round so I bought the drinks while Geoff homed in on the gorgeous Emma like a rat up a drainpipe and I was left with her charming but plain pal. A couple of months later, I asked Geoff when he was going to put Emma back on the open market so the rest of us could take a crack at her. He replied, pretty testily, that they were going to get married. Geoff, married? Christ, I was appalled. We'd been best mates for years. We shared the house. Who was I to go out on the piss with?

But married they were, with me as a last-minute best man, and Emma moved in. I had the back room upstairs, which adjoined the bathroom. I would lie there at night cuffing a guiltless tumescence to a coughed anticlimax while they gasped their way to satiation. Often on her return trip from the bathroom she would whisper good-night and I would fake sleep. Emma and I would often spend nights around the coal fire discussing Chaucer, quoting Wilfred Owen or slagging Melville. She was the first and last woman in my life I fell in love with before I shagged. Perhaps it was the strain of leaving their jobs in England, perhaps it was the worry of the project, whatever, something had clouded their marriage since I had encouraged them to come out to the Southwest; and I sensed Emma drifting away from Geoff, and closer to me.

Once I was through the shopping mall and lines of tract homes that passed for the town of Cottonwood and made the turn up the hill, my paranoia, as always, started to ease. Soon the tumble of houses on the mountainside which formed the town of Jerome hove into view.

At the bottom of town, I glanced across at the little treehouse where I had lived for my first spell in Jerome. It was up in those branches that I discovered that the hippie girls of the warm climes of Arizona had the morals of the sluttiest British barmaids but were wonderfully lacking any of that Anglo-Saxon guilt. Unlike their sisters across the pond, they were not content with a wild thrash under the sheets in the darkness but preferred to cast aside their clothes in the bright sunlight. One in particular who helped me rock the paradise trees was Annette; she climbed to the nest with me one spring night and we read from *The Rubaiyat of Omar Khayyam* before elbowing poetry for more prosaic matters. She joined me several times in the hot spring days to discuss Sufism, solipsism, and Shepherd's Bush, to serve psilocybin mushroom omelets, and to demonstrate consummate oral skills. It was not until I was confronted one afternoon by her husband ordering me into his pickup, one arm stretched back to finger the stock of the racked hunting rifle, that I had the slightest clue she was married, but that's another . . .

Turning the hairpin and driving back along the hillside opened up the view to the Verde Valley laid out two thousand feet below, to the crimson sandstone cliffs of the Mogollon Rim and beyond, floating like a white-sailed schooner in the pellucid sky, the snow-dusted domes of the San Francisco Peaks, sacred to Hopi and Navajo, skier and snowboarder alike. Up here in Jerome, where the chief of police accepted a couple of top colas from the local growers for his silence every fall, where the mayor wore a ponytail down his back and where the town hovered like a hawk above the maddening crowds of blue-rinse, superannuated dolts choking the gorgeous valley, I felt safe.

My shoulders seemed to lift as I entered the town and some of the old lightness of living returned. The lightness that had swept me and the lads through our twenties, through those roaring years of exciting work and travel and climbs and almost uninterrupted inebriation—that lightness was now tempered by the weight of our project, the celebration of my thirtieth year, and the delight and strain of living with a smart, beautiful, decent, educated, demanding young woman.

I parked and walked to the head of the steps that led down to the house I shared with Molly. I paused as I heard the steady beat of Steel Pulse and leaned over the rail to see her work through her yoga asanas. Watching her pretzel that lithe figure did wonders for my mood.

I trotted down the wooden stairs into the yard—a poor word the Americans use for, in this case, a delightful lawn and flower and veggie terrace that commanded a fabulous view from the bulk of Mingus Mountain to the San Francisco Peaks.

"Welcome home," she said when she heard me, and held the Cobra, back arched severely, head tilted to touch the soles of her feet, and waited for attention. Deluded by Valentino pretensions, I started below the Adam's apple and kissed up across the stretched skin to the chin and lingered at her mouth.

"D'you bring me a prezzie?' she asked, switching to the Eagle, balanced on one leg.

"Two," I said, pulling *Zen and the Art of Motorcycle Maintenance* from the pocket of my backpack.

"I hear that's a great read." She slowly unwound and arched into a backward bow, her entire weight resting on her pelvis, legs held high behind her head. "And what's the second?"

Against her feet I was able to ease the swell at my crotch that the kiss had aroused.

"Ooh, lovely. I'll get into that as soon as I've finished my stretch," she said, wiggling her toes against me. "Wanna go up to the disco tonight?"

"Sure. Saturday night's alright for dancing."

"Wiz and Peggy are going. And Geoff and Emma said they'd be back from Phoenix."

"What are they doing in that hellhole?"

"Looking for a van. And dealing with some visa problems."

"Really?" I tried to keep a neutral tone. "Are they planning to stay in the States?"

"I haven't a clue," she said testily.

I settled into the swing seat in the corner of the garden and watched Molly run through her poses. The bell of black hair shifted across her face as she changed poses. A white halter top clung to her slim, modestly breasted torso. The perfect hips and fine thigh muscles were partially covered by baggy and torn khaki shorts. Aah, beautiful, complicated Molly. Why couldn't I accept her and her eccentricities, why didn't I marry her and settle here in Jerome for a spell? Her shop could provide a steady living; all being well I would have a few bucks from the crop; I could attempt to write the great Anglo-American novel; the marriage would solve the residency problem; I had fallen for the American Southwest, its land, its skies, the warmth of people and climate; and, despite claims to the contrary, I knew I wasn't going back to the sycophantic turmoil of the London TV world. But restlessness still tormented me, and Emma's shadow passed across my future; in a few hours the die would be cast.

"Jem, honey." Molly joined me on the bench. "Your friends from England have been here awhile now. Almost a month."

"Yes, love."

"Well, I was wondering . . ."

"Yes, darling?" God, that public school upbringing makes such disdainful twats of its products.

"You know things haven't been quite the same in our house since they moved in."

"It has been a little crowded."

"I mean, between you and I. We had such a wonderful summer. Just the two of us hanging out here. Lately you've been distant, spaced out."

"I've been a bit preoccupied with the crop."

"Things just haven't been copacetic for me. I think it's time they found their own space."

I knew she was right. We had put them up for a while. And things had been different. I was distant because I was beginning to fixate on Emma. The last thing I wanted was for her and Geoff to move out.

"You're right, love," I said, which wasn't a lie. "I will talk to them about it tonight," I said, which was. "It was brilliant being here, just the two of us, these last couple of months."

"Oh, Jem, thank you. I knew you'd understand." She turned her face to me and we kissed in the languid fashion she liked to begin a session.

"Do you have any of that awesome grass of yours?"

"It's not even noon," I said, consciously adopting the American usage.

"It's not for me as much as you. You know you stay up forever on that stuff."

The aphrodisiac properties of the Mad Jag were becoming legend in our circle. I slipped a joint from my wallet and we shared a few draws. The foreplay resumed.

"This swing seat is goddamn dangerous for this," she said, leading me to the hidden niche of the garden between the bougainvillea and the fence above the drop. "I've always wanted to do it here. I have the best things in life: sunshine, a view, and a wonderful penis."

She leaned against the railing and arched her bottom toward me. I reached to the crotch of her shorts and discovered a rip in the seam. Sensing I wanted to get them off, she started to unbuckle them.

"Hang on," I said. "I've got a better idea." And I grabbed the legs of the shorts and wrenched outward. They gave easily, in a rasping tear.

"You asshole! Those are my favorites."

"I'll sew them up."

"Liar. You know I'll have . . . Aah."

Her protests subsided into a moan. Despite the staying power the Mad Jag endowed me with, I was soon moving happily toward a climax. Molly sensed it.

"Be careful," she gasped. "It's not safe. The other place."

"We haven't got the jelly. It'll hurt—both of us."

"Over there," she said, "Aloe vera. Well known for its emollient and lubricant qualities."

I reached for the succulent in the pot beside the swing seat, broke off a leaf and handed it to her. She slid a fingernail down its length, scooped a full gob and reached back to gel the head of John Thomas.

"Now you lube me," Molly said, and offered the splayed leaf. I dug out a generous blob and slid my fingers between her cheeks. She giggled, leaning her shoulders on the fence, and clutched her buttocks. I applied the gel generously and inched forward. Molly let out a squeal of delight as a vulture swept up the canyon on the rising afternoon air and banked near the fence to check out the source of the cries of the oddly melded humans.

5

That evening, as we sat on the deck, worked on a jug of margaritas, and counted cloud-to-cloud lightning strikes between the thunderheads towering over the Mogollon Rim, Geoff and Emma turned up.

"Eh up, Style," Geoff called as he came down the stairs.

Molly leaned over to me and whispered, "You know, he is a very handsome man. I'll miss having him around to look at."

"He's just average for an Englishman," I joked, and was about to comment on Emma's looks but thought better of it. No doubt Geoff was a handsome git: five eleven, broad-shouldered, and now slim-waisted thanks to the Arizona living, sandy hair bleached blond by the desert sun, and the fair complexion, which had not always been perfect, now tanned and clear.

"Care for a margarita?" Molly asked.

"Twist my arm," said Geoff.

"Emma?"

"A small one, thank you." She stooped to put her bags down. I studied her face as she joined us. It wasn't perfect, not

Liz-Taylor-in-*Giant* gorgeous, but Christ it was marvelous. A halo of deep blond hair framed the angular face. Her turquoise eyes had a delightfully intelligent sheen. An off-kilter tooth was hidden by the swell of lips that would never need collagen. And her ballerina's body—oh lord, I'll never be able to describe that figure in sane language.

"Productive trip?" I asked.

"Not too sure," said Emma. "You know what it's like dealing with immigration."

"Actually, my dealings have been confined to border crossings," I said.

"Coming back from Mexico?" She lit a cigarette.

"The last time I told 'em I wanted to be the first Englishman to hike the Pacific Crest Trail."

"What?" said Emma.

"Bollocks," said Geoff.

Molly merely raised her eyes to heaven.

"What's the Pacific Crest Trail?" asked Emma.

"The PCT, as us long-distance hikers like to call it, runs from the Sonoran Desert of the Mexican border through the Sierra Nevada of California and up through the coastal ranges of the Pacific Northwest to the Canadian border, spanning the continent . . ."

"Okay, Style, spare us the slaver," Geoff said. "How long is it supposed to take?"

"Well, the keen hiker could make it in five or six months. But as I shall be the first Brit, I'm expecting some press along the way. You know, the odd journo coming out from England to struggle along beside me here and there."

"Yes, yes." Emma feigned a yawn. "So how long did they give you?"

"Ten months."

"Ten months!" Geoff and Emma burst out together.

"They fell for that line of crap?" said Geoff.

"Precisely," I said. "They bought it."

"Now you're here committing a felony." Emma laughed, the turquoise eyes sparkling.

"And living off the local populace," said Molly.

I shot Molly a look. "There's another three months before my visa's up. By then we should have a couple of bob stashed away and we'll all be in Mexico for Christmas on our way down to Peru. Right, love?"

"I sure hope so," said Molly. "Say, can we have a little taste of that pineapple to go with the margies?"

"Certainly." I dug out the coke vial and scratched out four hearty lines. I offered Emma the straw and she took it reluctantly. I heard Molly sniff at the perceived snub.

"You know, I've never really tried this stuff." Emma examined the rolled fifty-dollar bill. She poked at the powder and attempted a little sniff. But she exhaled and the rest of the line and part of the others disappeared into the ether. Molly gasped and Emma cried out, "Oh lord, what have I done? And this stuff is so expensive! I'm so sorry."

"No worries. Tell you what. We'll take our lines, then you can have your own on the mirror. You can practice." I handed the bill to Molly, and she inhaled skilfully. Geoff and I followed.

"I've got some ribs marinating. Would you guys light the grill?" Molly went to the kitchen, Geoff sparked the barbie, I set out a line for Emma.

"You don't have to do this, you know," I said.

"Why do you say that?" She studied my face.

"Well." I thought about it for a moment as I held her gaze. "Some say it's a rather insidious drug. That it's very moreish."

"Addictive?" The proximity of her face was terrifying.

"Not physiologically. But the buzz is wonderful but short. You soon fancy another."

"Are you recommending I do not try it?" Again, she turned her face intently to mine, her eyes bright with anticipation and concern.

"Well, Emma, as well as you know me, do you think I would deter anyone from attempting something adventurous?" I asked feebly.

"No, Jeremy, I do not." She leaned forward, tilted the bill to the cocaine, and inhaled gently. In a couple of attempts she had cleared the mirror and sat back, twitching her nostrils.

"What happens now? I don't feel anything. Just a runny nose."

"Patience, Emma. It's a subtle high and takes a moment to come on."

"How did the supply drop go?" Geoff turned to me.

"A bit hair-raising." I lowered my voice and threw a quick glance up to the street. "That Wiz is some pilot. But he can put the fear of God in you."

"Did you stay with Dali and Fiona in Phoenix?" Molly reached through the kitchen window to hand Geoff the ribs.

"Yep," said Geoff, and there was a pause punctuated by a glance from Emma. Of course it was a strain for Emma to stay at their place, Fiona being Geoff's ex and all. The handsome sod had a checkered history. It wasn't that he'd been that much of a Casanova—just a good-looking bloke in the seventies in the cities of England—and, like any of us who had not too ugly of a boat race and a passable line of chat, he had in his time charmed the knickers off his share of crumpet.

"I'm going to have a shower," said Geoff quickly, to excuse himself.

"I'll do the ribs." Emma stood up and moved to the grill with a little sway. "Ooh, Jem! I do feel a little funny." She giggled. "That stuff is . . . amusing." She lifted the lid of the barbecue, picked a rib from the bowl, and put it on the metal rack. She watched it sizzle and thoughtfully licked the sauce from her fingertips. She placed more ribs until her concentration lapsed and she touched the hot metal.

She let out a little cry.

"What happened?" I jumped forward.

"Burnt my finger." She shook her hand.

"That looks like it'll blister." I held her hand. And then, as it lay in mine, she slowly wrapped the uninjured fingers around my thumb and squeezed. The action confused me. I checked her face but she held it turned down. Behind her in the kitchen, I saw Molly look up at us from the veggie-cutting as she prepared a salad.

"I know a herbal remedy for that," I said.

"You do, Stylor?" She looked at me quizzically, her eyes watery, as she sucked the burnt finger. "I never heard you show interest in more than one herb."

"You'd be surprised at the changes in me since I came to the States. I've been doing yoga, meditating, and studying Zen," I said as I walked over to the aloe vera plant.

I broke off a leaf and carried it back to the grill. With the razor from the cocaine mirror, I slit it, then, taking Emma's hand in mine, I gently slid the sticky sleeve down the length of her finger so it fit like the finger of a glove.

"Aloe vera," I said. "Well known for its emollient and lubricant qualities." And from the kitchen I heard the stab of a knife in wood and looked up to meet Molly's glare as the knife swayed upright in the butcher's block.

After dinner, which began frostily but thawed as the Shiraz flowed, I led the way uptown, through the steep streets and narrow paths and stairways. I felt Geoff pressing in behind me and knew him too well not to miss the signal for some idiotic competition. I capered up a flight of stairs, tore across a street, and climbed hard up another twisted path. As I headed up toward the yard of the old school, thinking I'd done him, I felt myself hauled back by the belt as the bastard flung me into a spiky hedge and drove by me to lean on the schoolyard wall, gasping and chuckling.

"Spawny git." I flopped against the railing beside him. We stared out over the gigantic valley as our chests settled.

"Some place you've found here, Style."

"Beats Birmingham, eh? Think you'll stay?"

"See how your harvest goes first."

"You and Stilt growing next year?"

"Happen."

"What does Ems have to say?"

He turned to me for a beat, then away. "She's okay with the idea. She's taken to it here."

"Suits her."

"Maybe more than me." A long sigh. "Jerome, the Southwest, has changed her."

"Did me," I said. "No fucking doubt."

"Not me yet. Not as quick as Ems, anyways."

"She looks great on it. Fit as a butcher's dog."

Another look, but this one studied. I looked away, regretting the statement.

"You can be an aggravating twat sometimes." He shook his head.

"Pardon?" My turn to stare at him.

"Spare me the bollocks, Stylor." He spat into the void. "Don't do anything you might . . ." He broke off as Emma and Molly panted up the steps toward us. He wheeled away and we trooped into the schoolhouse.

The house music that was invading the disco scene didn't do much for me, so I went to the DJ station and shouted for some Robert Palmer, Mark Knopfler, or, god forbid, some Motown. The DJ nodded and I returned to our table where Geoff and Emma, Molly, Wiz and his missus, Peggy, and Dick and Kathy, the local dope dealer and his old lady, sat, talking animatedly or twitching to the tunes.

"What'd you ask for, Mott the Hoople?" said Wiz, his big eyebrows arching into the comma of dark hair and the array of pearly teeth flashing above the goatee.

"Before my time," I lied. "I s'pose you actually like this house crap."

"It'll get the heart beating," he said. "You know, before we step out on the parquet, we ought to get the business done."

"Okay." I turned to Molly. "'Scuse us, darlin'. We have to slip outside and take care of business."

"I've heard that one before," said Molly, smiling at Emma.

Wiz, Dick, and I went outside and leaned on the wall. We were comfortable in shirtsleeves on a fine autumn evening, the most glorious time of the year in the high desert. The summer heat had passed, the nights were cool, and the harvest was underway. A new moon hung in the west and the constellations flamed from the arched ceiling of stars. Orion wheeled south, the Seven Sisters shone overhead, and the Big Dipper pointed out the polar stasis.

"Fancy a bump?" I said superfluously, pulling the toot vial from my jeans pocket. The lean, jockey-like dealer with the drawn cheeks and wispy beard clenched his fist, and I tapped out a generous snort onto the upturned muscle at the heel of his thumb.

"Okay, Dick," said Wiz, taking out a film canister and pouring a bud into Dick's hand. "We've got about sixteen pounds of this indica pruned and ready to go."

The dealer broke off a little of the bud, crumbled it into his palm, and sniffed.

"Nice," he conceded.

"Top grade. Primo," said Wiz. "Great seed that Crisp brought in from Afghanistan with his lapis last year. First time it's been grown seedless."

Dick took his keys from his pocket and shone a tiny flashlight onto the bud. "Good resin. Hairs not too long. Might be a bit immature. Is it all like this?"

"It's ready, man." Wiz flicked his hair back. "It's strong, skunky. People will go ape for this gear, man. You can't lose on it."

"That depends on how much I pay for it," said Dick, taking a Rizla packet from his wallet and crumbling the dope into a New York needle.

"What's your offer?" I asked, and Wiz shot me a look. Obviously he felt I was busting in on his territory, but I didn't like this Dick character much and I'd heard some stories around the Valley that didn't improve his standing in my eyes. There was talk that some other local dealers had got mysteriously busted. Perhaps Dick had had his collar felt a few years back and he'd avoided a stretch in the pokey by squealing on the competition.

"I'll have to give it the two-toke test." Dick lit the joint, took two long draws.

"It'll pass, guaranteed," I said. "Soon you'll be seeing stars and your missus'll look like Stevie Nicks. So, what's the offer?"

"Fifteen."

"Fifteen hundred a pound! For some of the best indica ever grown in this country." I turned away in disgust, playing the hand heavy.

"Easy Jem," said Wiz. "Dick, that won't meet muster man. I know this shit will go for two hundred bucks an ounce in Phoenix."

"I can't be sure it's gonna move easy," said Dick. "I could go sixteen."

"Cash?" asked Wiz.

"No way," I said. "I won't let my share go for less than eighteen."

"Can you cash us out or do we have to front you some?" said Wiz.

"Fifty-fifty," said the dealer, and picked shiftily at a nostril.

"How about this, Dick." Wiz was leaning in between us, trying hard to find compromise. "Give us seventeen a pound and you come to the woods and get it. Save us the risk of driving it to town. Jem? You in on that deal?"

"Okay, I'll go for that. But it has to be a total cash out," I added, giving Dick a straight stare as my jaws ground on the cocaine buzz.

"Can't do that." Dick caught my eye briefly, before a streetlight glinted off the glasses and one eye disappeared. I felt a shiver. "I don't have that kind of cash in hand. It's a lot of scoots. Half up front and half when I've moved the rest."

"Then it's no dice," I said, and realized that I was not only talking like some film noir gunsel but that I was diving headlong, again, into a situation which was way out of my depth, driving a hard bargain with a man who had survived many years in a criminal demimonde.

Earlier in the season, I had felt drawn by the justness of the adventure. I'd even duped myself into thinking that the Mad Jag was so righteous that we might change the world with its purity. Growing this fine grass with its exquisite smell and unique high in a beautiful rugged canyon had seemed hardly a crime. Now, as we charged into the last phase of the project, events seemed to be racing ahead of us and we were barely able to throw the track down ahead of the train.

"Let's figure the math." Wiz pulled a calculator from his pocket. "And then we can see if it pans out. Sixteen at seventeen hundred..."

My mind ran ahead: six sevens are forty-two, etc. I wanted to beat them and took a stab at it.

"Twenty-seven thousand two hundred dollars." A second later, Wiz confirmed it.

"He's right."

"How about twenty thou up front and the rest within a fortnight?" I said, knowing the word would start a digression.

"What the fuck's a fortnight?" asked Dick, and I thought I glimpsed a trace of humor.

"Fourteen nights. Two weeks," said Wiz. "I've had to learn a new language working with this damn foreigner."

"No, I've had to learn the new language," I said. "You've had to learn the old."

And there was a chuckle from all three of us.

"Are we on, then?" asked Wiz. "Twenty grand down and you come to the mesa to pick it up. The balance in two weeks."

"If it has a good high, okay, we're on." Dick looked at us in turn, held his hand out to Wiz first, then turned to me. "Good doing business with you." I felt a spinal uncertainty as I shook the small hand.

The wee feller walked inside. Wiz and I soaked up the quiet.

"Pulling in this moola will help us finance a couple more missions, eh?" The bearded face grinned at me and I felt the surge of anxiety that often accompanied such announcements, and such sly grins.

"What do you have in mind now?" I asked cautiously.

"I've always said this growing game is just for raising capital, man." He fixed me with that manic stare. "Now we can really start to turn some profit."

"Doing what exactly?"

"I've been looking into Crisp's Oaxaca contacts."

"Don't expect me to be part of some hare-brained smuggling scheme," I told him. "I'm taking this crop out of the canyon and then it's 'Home, James, and don't spare the . . .'"

"You can't book back to England now."

"Don't bet against it." I tried to sound convincing, knowing full well he had me down.

"Whatever, man." He pressed on. "The Mexicans don't have a clue how to take care of their weed, right? They soak it in Coke to hide the smell, then smash it into burlap sacks and by the time it gets north of the line it looks like a compost heap, smells like a treatment plant, and you're lucky if it gives you a headache."

"It's not that bad," I said, having puffed a few reasonable reefers from south of the border. "Remember the Mad Jag's from Oaxaca."

"My point exactly. The Mexicanos have great seed, they just don't know how to cure it. They don't know about sinsemilla and how the dudes up here go for the green."

"You want me to go to Mexico and supervise a harvest." I shook my head.

"You just need to go down a couple of times. And you'll never have to transport the stuff. Also, the Mexes don't grow the indica yet—four months in the ground not seven, stronger buzz. We can bring back planeloads of top-grade skunk buds that cost us say a couple hundred bucks a pound and flip 'em for over a grand apiece. Smoke the competition. What do you say?"

"Last time I was in Mexico I ended up in the Hermosillo jail," I said, recalling a bad night when my traveling partner was beaten senseless beside the road by the Federales.

"Think about it. I plan to use the cash to bankroll some scams. Remember, pal, money's round . . ."

". . . meant to roll. That's what makes America great." I said, repeating one of his favorite lines.

"You got it." He chuckled. "But listen, man. It's not just about making some solid dough. Cannabis has been grown and used for thousands of years, and not just to get high. The goddamn government calls it a Class A drug along with heroin to justify the billions they spend on the DEA."

"The War on Drugs. Nixon's baby." I snorted.

"Exactly. The crook himself." Wiz shook his head. "No one ever talks about the medical qualities of weed, the CBD, the cannabidiol that doesn't get you ripped, that can be extracted to treat people for all sorts of conditions: it's an analgesic, lowers blood pressure, treats glaucoma, all sorts of health shit. Maybe one day it will be sold on Main Street and people won't be locked up for years 'cos they smoked a jay on the porch." He hawked and spat over the schoolhouse wall.

"Don't hold your breath." I turned. "Let's shake a leg,"

Back inside, we all hit the dance floor. I sidled between Peggy and Molly and did my best Joe Cocker while my mind wandered to the conversation with Wiz. Despite my best efforts to dispel it, I could feel that fatalistic side of my character beginning to prevail. Could we get away with smuggling some weed from southern Mexico?

As to the stigma if we were caught: what country doesn't have a guilty love of the brigand, the bandit, the train robber? Wasn't there a universal fascination with the big-hearted crook, the villain who snubs his nose at authority and pulls off the big blag, as long as he doesn't kill or maim someone in the process?

We swayed around in a loose group until I was paired with Emma. I concentrated on the daft moves of the solo dancer fancying his chances: arms aloft, body arched, the pathetic sidle in behind the turned figure. To my surprise and mild terror, Emma responded. Soon we were whirling in unison and I felt electricity crackle between us. When she smiled up at me and pivoted to angle her bottom in my direction, I felt the first pang of doom.

We hung on until the death and then wandered out and down through the steep stairways of Jerome. An unblemished vault of stars toppled overhead, sweaters were flung over shoulders, voices rang through the autumn air. Molly took my arm as I stared up into the night sky and I knew I could never again live in a place where I didn't welcome clouds.

At the kitchen table Molly poured some bourbon and without invitation dug into my jeans pocket for the coke vial, pausing at my old man for a quick placatory clench.

"Ooh," said Emma as she watched Molly chop some lines, "I'd like another stab at that stuff. I felt wonderful on the dance floor."

"You looked wonderful," I added, suffered withering glances from Molly and Geoff, and swiftly changed subject. "Now, you two are planning to come down into the canyon to help with pruning the harvest, yeah?" I looked at Geoff and Emma.

"Pruning?" said Geoff, lighting a cigarette. "Will we be using secateurs?"

"Manicure scissors work best."

"My god, it must take ages. How many plants did you grow?" said Emma.

"Roughly seven hundred," I replied with a smirk.

"Seven hundred. Jesus wept!" said Geoff. "We'll be there till Christmas."

"We reckon with ten of us in the canyon working steadily it should take about a fortnight."

"And we'll stay down there all the while?" asked Emma, a grin conveying her excitement. "Just like Girl Guides camp."

"Except that if you get caught at Girl Scout camp you're not risking a couple of decades in the state penitentiary," said Molly.

"Twenty years! You're joking?"

"Regularly it wouldn't be that much, but these guys chose to grow in the most redneck Mormon county in Arizona." Molly punctuated the statement with a swift snort of her line and pushed the tray to Emma.

"Not to mention," said Geoff, "there'll be plenty of cocaine and guns about just to make sure we get our collars felt for a felony."

"No guns," I said firmly. "Absolutely no firearms. I've insisted on that since the beginning. I had a problem with one of Wiz's mates and it nearly came to blows."

"Hey, it's Arizona. No gun, no Harley, no vote." Molly pushed the mirror toward me and gave a start of surprise when I held my hand up.

"You aren't doing any?" She clocked me in amazement.

"I'm sick of the stuff."

"C'mon, don't be a party pooper."

"I'm not enjoying it. It feels weird. My ticker especially." Ten years later, when he diagnosed me with bundle branch block, the MD would ask me if I had used cocaine in the past.

"Honey, you're as strong as a bull. Let's just finish this gram and then you can think about quitting."

"Okay, okay. I just don't like the, uh, vibe of this gear." I snorted.

"You really think we'd be in serious trouble if we were caught, Molly?" Geoff sucked deep on a fag and chomped his jaws together.

"The DEA are going to screw with the weight count. They'll pile the full plants on the scale, call it a couple of thousand pounds and say they've busted a major ring." Molly tilted the bourbon bottle, laughed mirthlessly, and topped up the shot glasses.

"Thanks for helping me recruit a crew, darling." I turned to Geoff and Emma. "It's up to you lot. You just have to sit in a beautiful canyon in the lovely autumn weather and snip away at a few buds. The chances of getting copped down there are very slim. Day rate, two hundred a day, room and board on the house."

"Baked beans and a bear-trashed tent." Molly laughed. "But it is a gorgeous piece of real estate. Too bad there isn't a road in there, we could sell creekside lots for . . ."

"Over my dead body." I rose and turned to the English. "Let me know in the morning." I picked up the coke vial and headed for the bedroom.

"Couldn't you leave that here, sweetheart?" said Molly. "I just want one more. And you did say you were quitting."

I looked at her, noticed her eyes were watery and her skin was drawn back against the tight lips.

"It's all yours," I said. "But do be careful with this stuff, love. It can easily get the better of you."

"I will."

In bed I gave Edward Abbey a crack but finally found myself listening to the chat in the kitchen as the coke worked its insidious hold on me, and them. The shower was running and I realized Emma was bathing. There was only one bathroom in Molly's place and I needed to clean my teeth, desperately! I slipped from the bed and into the bathroom.

"Okay if I brush my teeth?" I asked disingenuously.

"Of course," she answered without hesitation.

Sadly, the heat steamed the shower curtain, but behind it I could see, in the mirror, that the profile of Emma's fabulous figure was still discernible.

The bathroom door swung open. "Jem, Emma is in the shower. You shouldn't be in here." Molly's voice had a barbed edge.

"Two days ago we were all skinny-dipping in the Verde."

"Big deal," she snapped.

"Why?" I knew I was looking for an argument.

"Jeremy. I need you to quit this bathroom right now." Molly's tone was absolute.

I returned to bed. A few minutes later Emma came through our room to reach hers—a route that could be avoided—and I knew, delightedly, that something was up. She held the towel wrapped above her breasts but as she reached for the door handle she let the towel fall so that I could see her naked back slip through the doorway. I lay there feeling a madness well up from somewhere deep as Molly and Geoff flapped the lip at the kitchen table.

The lunacy took me and I made, or did not make, a decision that would affect the rest of my life. Pulling on a pair of jeans but omitting to zip the fly, I strode into the kitchen. Geoff and Molly looked up.

"Why don't you two sleep together and I'll crash in the back with Emma." I heard the words but barely grasped that they came from my mouth. I was in limbo—at once detached, dispassionate, yet tense, taut, like one's first time speaking in public. Geoff and Molly stared at me, appalled, slack-jawed, dumbstruck. I zipped up my fly, a gesture I would later claim was incidental—which always fell on cloth ears—and returned to the bedroom to await the fallout.

It came fast.

"You think you're sleeping in my bed!" Molly's anger flooded the room. "Dream on, buddy. It's the back porch for you. And hit the road in the morning." She snatched the sheets off me.

"Molly I was just . . ."

"Save it, Jeremy. Just get the fuck out of my bed."

I slipped by her and made my way out to the porch. I trod lightly past the window of Geoff and Emma's room, eased Molly's calico cat to one side, resisted the urge to cuff it, and slumped on the couch.

My cautious approach had not tipped off the English couple to my arrival outside their window. I was soon eavesdropping on an intense row.

"What the hell was all that about?" Geoff snapped.

"I've no idea." Emma's voice was calm yet defiant, almost thrilled.

"Give over, Ems." Pain underscored his tone, like deep water in a stream. "Don't tell me you haven't encouraged Style."

"I haven't done any such thing!" Her turn to snap.

"Cobblers." Geoff snorted. "You two have been playing footsie since we came to Arizona."

"That's simply not true."

"I'm not blind, Emma." His voice rose an octave. "You certainly haven't had a lot of time for me recently."

"And you've been tearing my clothes off every night, I suppose." I imagined her glaring across the room.

A weighty silence.

"Look." Geoff groped for words. "I know I've been a bit tense since we came over here."

"Maybe we should think about going into therapy." Emma's voice was quieter.

"Therapy! Jesus! I wanna go to therapy like I wanna beat my old man with a steak mallet. We've only been in this hippy-dippy backwater for a couple of weeks and you're already talking like one of 'em. Soon you'll be suggesting aromatherapy or numerology or some other New Age wank." Geoff drew a tired breath. "Sometimes I wish we'd stayed back home."

"Perhaps *you* should think about that, then." Her voice was firm, but there was an underlying tinge of fear.

"Emma!" I heard his feet pound across the room, followed by her gasp as she sat back on the bed. "Emma. If I ever hear you make a fucking suggestion like that again I won't be responsible for . . ." Her shriek was shrill for a second, then muted. I sat up, wondering if I should rush into their room. Instead, I stood firmly on the floorboards and walked heavily to the rail.

Geoff's volume dropped to a fierce whisper. "We're man and wife, Emma. And that's the way I intend it to stay. So don't ever make a fookin' suggestion like that again."

I gazed out over the enormous, moonlit valley, and cursed and cursed.

6

"Dick, sorry about this, mate, but I'm going to have to put the blinders on you for the last stretch."

It seemed absurd, but Wiz had insisted that I blindfold Dick for the last dozen miles of the drive to the canyon rim, so I followed orders. When we reached the pass on the General Crook Trail that led from the oven of the Verde Valley to the cool pine country, I pulled the Scout onto a dirt road among the ponderosas.

"Jeez. This is a pain in the ass," Dick complained. "Like I'm gonna tell people where you guys have your crop."

"The less you know, the less you can tell if you're ever in a bind."

I tied the scarf around his head, recoiling as a shower of exfoliated scurf rose from his thinning pate. I put him in the back seat and made him lie down. It might seem a bit odd to a passing driver to see a blindfolded man sitting bolt upright in the back of an old truck.

I drove back to the highway and a couple of miles later dipped down through the switchbacks that marked the beginning of the Mogollon Rim.

"Want to listen to the radio, Dick?"

"Whatever!" was the muffled reply.

I found some Boz Scaggs on an AM station from somewhere in the vast Midwest. The song ended and the Associated Press news came on.

"The war between Iran and Iraq has escalated, according to sources in the Persian Gulf. Iranian rocket attacks have destroyed a power plant near Basra, while in Baghdad state-sponsored television claims Iraqi troops have made significant advances into enemy territory.

"Representative Michael Myers was expelled Thursday from the House on a 376 to 30 vote. Myers was convicted in August for his involvement in the Abscam scandal. He was found guilty of accepting bribes from FBI agents who claimed to represent an Arab consortium seeking congressional favors.

"Billy Carter says he isn't apologizing for 'a damn thing' in his dealings with Libya. Appearing on *The Phil Donahue Show*, the president's brother claimed he did not act improperly in accepting a $220,000 unconditional loan.

"Iran's parliament has chosen the mullah who led the assault on the U.S. Embassy to head its commission on the fate of the fifty-two hostages."

A thousand feet lower, where the pines thinned, I turned through the little town we'd code-named Fruitown and followed the road toward Relic Canyon. A few cabins and trailers lined the road. After a mile the asphalt turned to dirt and the flora changed almost at once to high desert scrubland.

The road took a wide curve as the enormous gash of Relic Canyon came into view. I hit the washboards too fast and felt the old Scout cut loose as it juddered through the corner.

At the next bend I was surprised to see two men ducking into the roadside trees. I slowed to check them out as they scrabbled up the bank and was relieved to see scruffy jeans and sweatshirts and pathetic bundles of belongings. Illegals. Wetbacks, working their way up from the border for a chance at the Yankee dollar. I looked at the two wiry men, their gaunt features betraying the desperate nature of their lives; hollow eyes stared down at me, as nervous as deer. I reflected ruefully on my own immigration status and how one wag in the group had dubbed me the fogback. But the wry grin was wiped in a scrotum-wrinkling second as, barreling round the hairpin a mere hundred yards shy of the jeep trail we took east to the Mad Jag mesa, was Sheriff Farr's Blazer. I swung the Scout into the bar ditch.

"Get down, Dick. On the floor!" I snatched my faded serape from the passenger seat and flung it over the huddled figure.

The sheriff slowed on the narrow road and, as he stopped, I stared in horrified fascination as his window lowered. My chest pounded and my mouth felt as if it had just been scraped with steel wool.

"Howdy, sheriff." I nodded at his pinkish, broad visage. A thick tuft of nostril hair jutted from each side of the red septum, and one carried a fleck of dried snot. But it was the eyes that were most riveting, deep blue and with all the icy cold that that color metaphorically holds. He ground the lower incisors against the back of yellowed uppers before he spoke. A bulge beneath the lower lip betrayed the wad of chew.

"Howdy." His eyes flickered over the inside of the vehicle. "Goin' huntin' today?"

"No. Going for a swim. By the bridge in Relic Creek." I tried to half-mumble the words, hoping to disguise my accent, but merely succeeded in sounding more nervous.

"A swim, eh?" His steel-blue eyes bored into mine and the fair pyramid brows arched. "Little late in the year for swimmin', ain't it?"

"Uh, maybe so." I edged the clutch out.

"Say, feller." He leaned and spat a black ball of phlegm on my rear tire. "Keep a sharp eye out. There's all sort of strange parties out here this time of year." He swept his eyes across the back seat as I jerked the Scout forward.

With one eye on his vehicle in my wing mirror and half my ticker in my esophagus, I drove slowly round the bend and then charged forward to a small turnout. I grabbed my binoculars, leaped from the truck and pounded up the steep ridge to its brow.

The sheriff's truck was moving slowly away. What lousy fucking timing. What wretched luck. Was it just coincidence? Had he seen Dick's huddled shape?

I slumped against a rock and waited for my heartbeat to settle and the wave of nausea to ease. I was about to move back from the ridge when I heard the sheriff's truck skid to a halt. I snapped up the Zeiss glasses and watched the huge peace officer exit his vehicle, firearm drawn. His fierce bark rang out.

A few moments later the two *mojados* slunk out of the ditch. The sheriff barked orders and the men spread-eagled against the side of the truck. Cautiously he frisked them, then one of the men turned to speak and the big oaf leaned back, balled his fist, and smashed it into the skinny feller's kidneys. The man doubled forward with a scream and, as the other twisted to see, the sheriff swung the barrel of his .357 Magnum into the haggard face of the Mexican, lifting him off his feet and sending him spinning into the bar ditch.

The lawman stood back as the two men groaned and writhed. He surveyed his handiwork with a smug grin, then slipped handcuffs from his belt, cuffed the first man, and shoved him unceremoniously into the back of the truck. Stepping into the ditch, he reached for the second feller who crawled away in terror, obliging the sheriff to lurch after him. He delivered another vicious slap to the man's head before hauling him by the scruff to the unit.

I lowered the binoculars and lay with my face in the dust. Christ Almighty! To see proof of Willard Farr's mean streak in the flesh was terrifying.

I drove the truck back and turned hard onto the jeep trail that led to our mesa. After a couple of miles of wrecking shock absorbers, I pulled the truck into the shade of a stout piñon.

"Okay, mate," I said. "It's shanks' pony from here."

"I suppose that means we're walking," whined the dealer, climbing from the truck and stretching. "You guys sure know how to make a guy hurt."

I shouldered the heavy pack of food, clippers, flashlights, stove fuel, and other necessities for the harvest work ahead, locked the truck, hid the keys under a stone, and marked its position carefully. Wiz and Nobby would be driving out of here and I would be going down into the canyon for one last blissful spell alone before the players trooped in for the final act.

I set a brisk pace across the shattered plates of rock and hard clay. Dick stumbled behind and grumbled about the hike, the heat, the bugs. We dipped through a couple of arroyos and skirted an open clearing before weaving through the trees to the rim. We followed it south for a couple of hundred yards before turning away from the edge to a black basalt outcrop.

"Make a fire here at sundown." I said, trying not to sound like John Wayne. "Whatever happens, stay here. Don't wander off."

"When? When do you think you'll make it back by?" Dick said, obviously ill at ease in these surroundings, far from his Phoenix bungalow. "This place is scary."

"Just wait. Don't smoke any weed. Keep your wits about you. There could be all sorts of people about this evening, including DEA agents disguised as bow hunters."

"You're a real comic, you know that."

With a chuckle I turned on my heel and strolled to the rim. Despite the tension of the day, my spirits were high. All being well, we would be splitting Dick's cash in a couple hours. In another fortnight, we would have the bulk of the sativa pruned and bagged and ready for the helicopter to fly it out—yes, a helicopter! Wiz, a fixed-wing pilot in Nam, had added the rotary license and was itching at the chance to drop a Jet Bell Ranger into our canyon.

I ambled along toward the westering sun and gazed up at a great anvil cloud towering over the Verde River. Although the summer heat had fallen off, it was still over eighty degrees in the Valley at noon, warm enough to produce the odd thunderstorm—the fabulous Indian summer of the desert Southwest.

I looked down on the yellowing band of sycamores and cottonwoods that hid the creek. I longed to be down there. Paradise is a much-abused term in these days of hipster travel, but a sweet water year-round stream gurgling through an avenue of broad-leafed trees down a rose-cliffed canyon through hot dry uplands ranked right up there with, IMO, the primo arcadian spots on our lonely planet.

I watched the nighthawks wheeling in the dusk, wings barking like rutting deer as they dove after insect prey, and reflected on my recent suggestion of the wife swap. Within a couple of days Geoff and Emma had found an apartment in the Old Jerome Hotel. I had been forced to spend a couple of nights in the treehouse in the gulch, which had lost much of its early romantic allure. Finally I had returned to Molly's apartment to get my clothes and found her sitting disconsolately on the front porch.

"You're an asshole, Limey!" was her curt opener.

"So I've been told."

"I'm not the only girl you've handed this bullshit, then?"

"That's not quite what I meant."

"Why would you say a thing like that, Jeremy?"

"I don't know, the coke, the late night. I've been feeling pretty tense recently, with the crop coming on." I sat down in the chair next to her.

"We're all stressed out, Jem." She leaned toward me. "Did you think I was putting the hard word on Geoff?"

"You had said you fancied him."

"I had said I thought he was a handsome dude. That doesn't mean I was desperate to jump his bones. I've got one Englishman to handle. That's quite enough." I turned to meet her gaze. Black hair formed a proscenium to the suntanned, freckled face. The dark brown irises glistened, the whites were blood-tinged.

"I'm sorry. It was thoughtless. I don't know what came over me." I put an arm across the back of her chair.

"You're an asshole," she repeated, and laid her head on my shoulder. I sighed with relief, and my cynical self leaped for joy. I'd have a place to stay and, if I played my cards right, a regular squeeze for the last leg of the journey after all.

A movement between the sycamores in the streambed fifteen hundred feet below snapped me away from my recollection. Through the binoculars I saw Wiz and Nobby hopping boulders toward our rendezvous, beside the creek at the base of the wash.

Panting, I made the top of the tumble of rocks which formed the only reasonable access into the canyon. From a stash we'd dug under a tree stump I pulled a stout canvas bag and dragged out our climbing rope. Scrambling into a coffin-like slot at the rim, I threaded the rope through the one-inch belay tape which we'd fixed there in the spring and lobbed the two ends down the cliff. With another loop of tape and the belt in my jeans I was able to fashion a harness. Clipping the doubled rope through the figure of eight, I jumped off the lip and abseiled to the base. I pulled the rope through, shied away as it lashed down, and quickly hid it at the base. Then I started the treacherous descent through the cascade of massive blocks of black igneous, which we called the Salt Mine due to the sweat we'd shed clambering up and down the long, tortuous tumble of hot black boulders all summer.

Thirty minutes later I stood on the canyon side at treetop level, settled my heaving chest, and whistled the call. The response was immediate and I climbed down the last pitch.

"You're late on parade, lieutenant." Wiz was kneeling beside the creek.

"Got held up," I explained quickly.

"Nobody holds up ze English. Ze Battle of Waterloo was won on the playing vields of Exeter, *ja*." I had made the mistake of telling Nobby that I had attended a minor public school and he never missed a chance to wind me up about it. The Swiss was slumped against the bole of a tree smoking a fag, wearing shorts as always, his wedding tackle flopping out of one ragged leg.

I dropped to my haunches and drank deeply from the delicious, crisp water of our creek, which pulsed from between strata of limestone a stone's throw up-canyon from where I crouched.

I had thought Wiz was also drinking but when I looked I saw him crouched over the water and heard him singing softly, Lennon and McCartney's "Yesterday."

"I know you love this creek, but . . ." I glanced at him.

"According to this Japanese guy, water responds to positive rhythms to produce beautiful shapes when it freezes." He crooned the chestnut before finishing the explanation. "I've been working on this pool all year. I'm coming back in the winter to check it out." He gave me a neutral glance and I reflected again on the mysterious nature of the man.

I doused my face from the stream, swept back my hair, and looked at Nobby to get his take on Wiz's latest eccentricity. Nobby grinned and shook his head. I noticed the slightly jaundiced cast to his face.

"You okay?"

"Nobby took a spill in the creek." Wiz pursed his lips in an attempt to avoid creasing up. The Swiss had spent long spells in the canyon that summer and every time we came in to relieve him, he seemed to have suffered some accident.

"What've you done now?"

"Aah, vuck me, Chem." He groaned. "A vew days ago I vell onto a rock in the creek." He rubbed his back and stretched. "I am pizzing blood vur days. Aah vuck."

Nobby had claimed to be on a fast, a prolonged meditation while in the canyon, but knowing his love of cannabis it was not unreasonable to presume that he had been stoned out of his skull from first light until night. His insistence on wearing shorts or a wraparound skirt and sandals the entire time as part of his "discipline" meant that Wiz or I often came into the canyon to find him in some state of medical malaise: lacerated shins, his back pitted with bug bites, a scorpion sting, a stab from an agave bayonet. The seriousness of this latest mishap was not lost on us, but the humor of it was too much. Wiz caught my eye again and cracked up, and I let out a laugh.

"Ach, vuck youz guys," Nobby yelled, but his eyes sparkled and he gave a rueful, tight-lipped grin.

It was harvest time and the three of us who'd worked and sweated and worried through the year together were now about to reap reward. I looked around at my cohorts in crime, at the gorgeous creekside that had been our home for three seasons, and the boxes of lovingly cared for and cured herb ready to be carried out and sold, and I smiled.

"We better get going. Sun's over the rim," I said. "Which one's mine?"

"Take your pick." Wiz held a palm out to the three packs.

I hefted a couple of the loads. "This one seems lightest."

"Tote the other, then." His tight goatee angled challengingly toward me; big eyebrows arched into the questioning frown. I knew the source of his needle. As a guy who'd been through officer training in the U.S. military, he had done his share of "rucks," fast hikes with heavy loads, and he could certainly take me on the flats. But for some reason my simian rib cage gave me the edge on the climbs.

We shouldered the loads.

"Here we go, boys." Wiz looked around at us and grinned. "If the Great Spirit smiles on us, it's time to cash in. No more scrimping and scraping." He loved the Beatles. "It's fat city from now on." He held his palm back, like a relay runner waiting for the baton, and we two undemonstrative Europeans were happy to slap the American low five.

"Let's go. Rendezvous at the Stellar's Perch." Wiz strode across the boulders and started on the steep, brutal climb away from the stream toward the western rim, already deep in shade.

Throat scalded, chest wracked, quads twitching, I squatted under the piñon at the Stellar's Perch, so named by us after the Stellar's jay that often squawked down at us when we rested there.

Wiz came up next and slumped against his pack. I passed him the water bottle. We looked out over the canyon as he calmed his lungs; the shadow line was just edging up the Anasazi ruin on the eastern cliff; the pewter-gray thunderhead loomed over the canyon from the south; a keen breeze chattered through the shrubs and dried our sweat.

"So, what held you up?" Wiz slipped his arms into a pile vest.

I told him of the chance meeting with Willard Farr, and described the sheriff busting the wetbacks.

"That asshole's a disgrace to his uniform." Wiz, the military vet, hawked and spat. Then he turned to face across canyon, the eyebrows angled in concentration.

"Is that him? Is that the jag?" His voice was gravelly with excitement.

I swiveled my head to match his eyeline. "Where?"

"There in the saddle, above the Anasazi ruin."

I followed his outstretched arm and noticed the bright shape. I scrabbled for my binoculars, fingered them into focus, and caught a flash of a large cat form before it disappeared from the skyline.

I spun my head to Wiz, who continued to stare ahead. Since his first hike into the canyon with Stilt, Wiz had speculated constantly on the presence of the jaguar. Though he'd seen multiple tracks and heard many terrifying nighttime shrieks, he'd never seen the creature.

"Damn, man," I said. "Whatever it was had the shape. Cougar? Bobcat?"

"Maybe it was a nagual."

"A what?"

"Don Juan tests Carlos in the ways of the warrior." Wiz turned to me. "One day a jaguar stalks them. Don Juan tells Carlos he has to keep his cool. It may be the real thing or it may be a nagual. An enemy magician, who can take the form of an animal. To do evil."

I smiled at him. At first, I had dismissed Wiz's Castaneda lore as dubious at best. But so much had happened during my time in the canyons and so many layers of reality had been separated and melded that my inbred skepticism had given way to a reluctant acquiescence.

"Willard Farr in jaguar form? He'd have to shed a few pounds."

"Not so many. They've recorded jaguars at over three hundred pounds."

"'Bout right." We both laughed.

Nobby hauled himself in beside us and flopped down.

"All right, mate?" I helped him pull off the pack and looked at his face. His cheeks were hollowed and his eyes watery.

"I'll make it, Chem," he said, but without conviction.

Wiz and I started up the last pitch, pushing each other hard up to the caprock.

I reached the bottom of the cliff and tied in to the rope. I'd made a couple of moves before my partner arrived and slung the rope behind his waist to offer a belay. I soon knocked off the climb, clipping to the bolts we had placed in the spring and then painted black to blend with the basalt.

Wiz tied the packs to the rope and I hauled up the two very valuable loads.

"You know, I could just head off with this gear now." I grinned down at him.

"You can run, buddy, but you can't hide." Wiz looked and up and shook his head. Then he took off back down toward the Swiss, who struggled gamely up.

Ten minutes later, I was hauling the third pack to the rim. I tossed down the rope, put a bight around my waist and stood back from the lip.

Nobby came first. Having done some climbing in his native Alps, he usually made light work of this pitch. But, weak from his infection, he struggled mightily and shouted a couple of times for me to hold his weight. The rope sawed into the small of my back and I wished for a harness and a belay device. Nobby crawled over the lip and lay panting on the rock, face twisted in exhaustion, his glasses steamed up.

I lobbed the rope to Wiz, who tied in and swarmed up. Nobby dragged himself to his feet and we pressed on along the rim in deepening dusk until we could see the light of Dick's fire reflected from the rock.

"I'll go in and check that all's well. Then I'll give you the whistle."

I took great care over the couple of hundred feet to the fire, remembering the stories I'd read of Apache warriors taking hours to cover short distances before they leaped on their quarry. Once I had a visual on Dick, I circled toward the little cliff and waited again. Finally satisfied that I had done all I could to check for an ambush, I crept forward toward the figure hunched over the blaze and was extremely pleased with myself to be able to whisper in Dick's ear.

"All safe here, mate?"

The wiry bloke leaped from his haunches and staggered a couple of paces before gaining his footing.

"Asshole." He stared daggers at me. "Scared the crap outta me."

"I told you to keep your eyes skinned. Everything kosher round here?"

"Everything's cool."

I whistled. Wiz hurried into the firelight, slung two packs down. Nobby stumbled in and warmed his hands by the fire. Wiz pulled one of the large Ziplocs that contained a quarter pound of the early blooming Hindu Kush buds; we called it skunk back then and I gather people still do. He handed it to Dick, who broke the seal and lifted a couple of the flowers.

"Looks good. Sure it's fully dry?" Dick crumbled a bud in his fingers and sniffed.

"Cured for four days in the shade," Wiz snapped.

"Got a real strong smell," said Dick.

"Skunk. The heavy-duty smokers love it."

"Okay, I'll take it. But if it dries out and loses weight, we'll have to make an adjustment on the balance."

"No way," I chimed in firmly. "It's a deal at twenty-seven two hundred or not at all. We're already fronting you a fair bit."

Wiz looked like he was about to say something to mediate the tension, but he held his tongue.

"Okay, okay. Since I've come clear up to Bumfuck Egypt for it." The little dealer opened the pocket on his backpack, pulled out rolls of bills, and placed them on a boulder close to the fire.

I gave a little involuntary hiss of breath. The bundles of twenties and fifties looked sweet. I almost grabbed one but restrained myself, picking it up casually and tossing it across the fire to Nobby. The Swiss flicked a thumb across the end of the notes, making a neat staccato rattle, like a conjuror with a deck of cards. He grinned across the flames at me.

The bills felt crisp to the touch, and I was soon lost in the tactile rhythm of the count. Twenty, forty sixty, eighty, one hundred, twenty, forty, sixty, eighty, two, twenty . . . The fire crackled, the breeze from the nearby storm rattled the piñon branches, a whippoorwill called from the ridge. I felt a surge of bliss, not just because we were about to score but simply from realizing that this was one of those unique moments in one's life, a high point, one that I would look back on in my old age.

"It's all there. Twenty grand," said Wiz, and threw me a grin.

"Course it is." Dick looked aggrieved. "Now let's go. I gotta drive back to Phoenix tonight."

Nobby slung one of the packs and he and Dick started away.

Wiz stashed his loot in the side pockets of his pack, shouldered the load, and stood facing me.

"It's a good start." He grinned across the firelight, the thick mustache bristling from the upper lip, keen brown eyes reflecting the light and his obvious satisfaction with the train of events.

"Certainly is." I grinned back. "Now I can buy some decent shoes." I held one of the old huaraches up to the firelight. We both stared at the tatty sandals with the tire-rubber soles and burst into roars of laughter.

"I can't believe you haven't busted your ankle hiking in those half-assed Mexican boots." He chuckled again, and again we caught each other's eyes and simply nodded with satisfaction at our success. I expected a slap of hands, a hug even, but my partner turned from the fire.

"See you in a few days," he said, and strode away.

I watched him disappear and wondered again if it was my fault that we didn't have a tighter rapport. Why couldn't I shake my disdain for his Carlos Castaneda musings, his New Age ways, his thoroughly ingenuous American decency?

But nothing could mar my simpering delight at the initial success of our venture. I strolled through the moonlit high desert with more money in my pack then I'd ever seen at one time in my life and made camp under the overhang of a basalt outcrop as the first sheets of rain lashed into the arroyo.

7

The last, moist tendrils from the forty-thousand-foot tower of cumulonimbus settled on the top bills of the nests of notes set in the light of the juniper fire. A billion-kilowatt light show backlit the massive cloud as it toppled south, teasing the barren uplands with sparse showers. I cut a disk from the beef tenderloin on the light grill I always carried in my pack, scooped the blackened onions from the skillet, and while I ate pondered the fate of my companions, the ten-thousand-dollar wads warming themselves beside the blaze.

At long fucking last we had some payback. Here was the first tangible evidence that this madcap wilderness blag might actually bear fruit; here finally was reward for the shoulder-scarring carries of gear in the late winter, the staggering agony of schlepping the hundred-pound Briggs and Stratton pump through the mountain terrain; the nauseating paranoia that had dogged many waking and sleeping hours of the last eight months. Here at last was solid proof that we were about to make some serious spondulicks. I settled back against the basalt, drew sparingly on a slender spliff of as fine a sinsemilla as was to be found in those times, and allowed my mind to wander over the pleasures of spending the loot.

I had in hand ten thousand bucks. That would make a handy down payment on a terraced house in Hammersmith or Chiswick, but who was I trying to con? There was not a snowball's chance of me going back to the Big Smoke and picking up my career. If I'd learned anything from this mad year, it was this: that despite the delightful urban abuse I'd enjoyed since leaving the farm a decade earlier I was truly my father's son, a countryman at heart, and I could never again live happily in a city.

How much more could we realistically expect to get from the crop? After the usual culling of male plants and the attrition of deer, drought, molybdenum deficiency, etc., we had brought to maturity seventy indica females and about seven hundred sativas. The indica had produced seventeen pounds of bud, which we had just sold for a tad over twenty-seven thousand dollars. Seventy divided by seventeen equals four and change, call it a quarter pound a plant. Down in the canyon the remaining sativa plants, by the same reckoning, would produce . . . I wrestled with the math. Seven hundred by four equals one hundred and seventy-five. One hundred and seventy-five pounds of killer grass at roughly eighteen hundred a pound. Good god! We were looking at making three hundred and fifteen thousand dollars, put twenty-five aside for Nobby and expenses leaves a hundred and forty grand apiece for Wiz and me. Not bad!

Also, despite my misgivings about Dick's character and dodgy reputation, he could probably move all our crop, given time. Of course, at that time, we had only an inkling of his troubles with his old lady and never expected his untimely kicking of the bucket. A week after our done deal at the fire on the mesa that Dick was cooking up his freebase when he and Kathy fell into one of those awful domestic arguments that escalate swiftly to vitriol. The row rose another notch and Kathy, fearing for her safety, ran out to their pickup. As she jumped in, Dick ran from the house with his Magnum and lay on the bonnet pumping lead through the windscreen while Kathy screamed and hunched over the wheel and drove four blocks before she slammed to a halt and fell sobbing across the bench seat.

Dick's body, mutilated, mangled, and dismembered as a result of its peristaltic passage through a narrow sphincter framed by the undercarriage of a solidly forged American steel automobile and an asphalt road, was discovered by a resident taking his dog for an early morning crap. Wiz and I were out seven grand and change and we'd lost the best dealing contact we had.

But right now, I had some real cash and still eluded the law. Enough cash, maybe, in that wonderfully unjust system of world justice and one particularly prevalent in the great and corrupt U.S. of A., enough dough to buy myself out of trouble should we get nabbed before the gig was done. I grabbed three of the bundles of notes and skipped around the fire attempting a juggle, but succeeded only, in my stoned and deliriously happy state, in dropping one into the embers. I collapsed in a fit of giggles, frantically brushing the sparks from my hard-earned lucre.

The moon rose. I climbed the little scarp, settled into the simplest asana, the half lotus, and made a lame attempt at meditation. Fingers and thumbs forming the circle, drawing deeply on the pungent post-storm air, I began my mantra. But the elimination of desire was impossible and *Om mani padme om* was soon interspersed with *Oh the money pat me om*, then *O me o my what fun* it will be to spend it and finally *Oooh mama paddle my tum*, how long will it be before Emma's fair nether thatch slips down my muscled gut to guide the shameless manifestation of my inability to suppress desire into her moist nirvana.

Next morning, I cocooned in my North Face down bag till the sun rose, brewed tea, packed leisurely, and strolled to the rim. The air was cerulean in the wake of the storm. In the Apache plumes on the canyon slope a covey of mountain chickadees whistled. Gliding effortlessly along the rim cliffs, a pair of ravens banked away with a startled cackle when they saw me, their plumage iridescent in the early light.

Down canyon a small flock of birds worked the warming air. I swung the glasses up and was pleased to see the female Harris's hawk and her harem of three tercels, the only polyandrous hawk in the Americas.

I threw my pack down to the base of the cliff, well aware of the cash stashed in a pocket, and marked carefully where it came to rest. Gingerly I descended the Salt Mine rimrock, eschewing the rope. After the knee-jarring descent, I drank long from the creek. Then I began the familiar schlep downstream, as always hopping the boulders rather than walking the pleasanter sandy streamside areas so as to avoid leaving footprints and thus being able to check for those of intruders. Occasionally I missed my step and turned back to sweep a track from the sand with a branch.

The familiar trail slipped by and after about half an hour I found myself at the junction of the main stream and the dry side canyon that gave a long tough hike to the more remote east rim. I dropped my pack and climbed up this east side route to a lookout. I sat there for perhaps twenty minutes, tuning in to the canyon sounds, scouring the rim for a glint of metal, listening intently for the sound of a motor, or worse yet the distant murmur of voices. All seemed well.

I found myself lured yet again into the simple mystery of this place. If there was a threat to our success in this escapade, I had always felt it came on the outside, on the highway or in town. Here, in the bottom of this gorgeous canyon, where the company came in the form of a phainopepla singing from the mesquite or the grasshoppers scratching a complaint of the heat, I could not convince myself, or perhaps bear to think, that anything violent or arresting could occur.

It was this canyon and this country that had changed my life—not the lust for money, nor the awkward camaraderie with Wiz, nor the fleshy and psychoactive delights of Jerome and its bohemian crowd. No, it was the recuperative and contemplative qualities of a lush streamside habitat and the stunning vistas of these dry, high plateaus that had made the deepest mark on me and had, in some vague, regressive fashion, rekindled values that my mum and dad had instilled in me during my childhood on the farm.

As I strolled back to the creek, I spotted the paw-print and froze. We had seen the cat tracks several times during the year and heard the bone-chilling scream in the night. Though Wiz and Stilt had claimed the presence of the jaguar and had named their strain of grass after it, I always allowed for some hyperbole on their part and reckoned the cat in our canyon was a big tom cougar.

The first time we had hiked in to search out a new garden, we had had a terrifying encounter. Camped in a clearing, warming a can of beans over a small fire, we had been petrified by the ungodly shriek of a very large animal. Wiz had leaped to his feet brandishing a burning branch. "C'mon then, you son of a bitch! Let's see your ass!"

I was caught in a paroxysm of both terror and mirth; it creased me up.

"What's so goddamned funny? That jaguar could eat us alive." The humor was scotched. I had researched the threats of this desert country before I committed to the project: bad-tempered rattlesnakes, jaw-grinding Gila monsters, lance-like agave, scorpions, tarantulas, bears, mountain lions. Despite Wiz's claims to the contrary and his and Stilt's story of their brush with a big cat, I had never truly imagined we would have to contend with a jaguar, the largest cat in the Americas, an immensely powerful beast capable of pulling down a healthy steer.

"Jesus Christ. I thought you guys were joking about the Mad Jag. I thought there were none left in the States. They're all south of the line . . . Aren't they?" I had added hopefully.

"No. They've sighted them recently in the Peloncillos and also in the Chiricahuas. This one may have wandered up here many years ago and been unable to get back south. Trapped by the expansion of Phoenix."

I stooped to examine the huge paw-print. It was about the size of my hand when I bent my fingers a touch. The track was fresh, the edges of the front toe pads crisp. I was no Tonto, but I reckoned the creature had passed through that day, maybe within a few hours, and was certainly in some part of our canyon at that very moment.

What exactly I intended to do if confronted by this enormous predator I really didn't have an effing clue. The advice on the National Forestry noticeboards for encounters with mountain lions offered some crap about making yourself as large as you could, waving your arms and shouting. That might cut the mustard with a cougar, the biggest of which might top a hundred and fifty pounds, whereas the jaguar could reach three hundred—a heavyweight compared to his welterweight cousin.

I spotted three more paw-prints as I rock-hopped the familiar terrain. This was usually my favorite part of the journey. Deep in our own canyon, half a day's hike from the nearest road, in the best shape of my life and with my knowledge of the lay of the land, I figured I was quids ahead of any agency man if he tried to feel my collar.

We'd always considered our best chance was to "book," to use my partner's colloquialism, or "get on our toes and leg it," as Geoff would say. We had explored all the possible exits from the canyon, and although the few we'd found required some brutal scrambling and scary free soloing through the caprock, we fancied our chances to shake off any would-be captors.

As I neared the garden, an extra degree of caution crept into my step. The stream was squeezed into a ravine here, leaving a couple of sandy beaches where we'd had to lob in some stepping stones to avoid leaving prints. But the cat had no such concern and had left a dozen crystal-clear tracks on the beach. My high spirits since the deal the night before were elbowed away by the old fears on approaching the plants and the presence of this huge cat. I sat and pondered and listened.

The garden was just a couple of hundred yards downstream. If we'd been discovered, the agency men were probably crouching in cover close at hand. This was the spot where I always forced myself to wait. I slipped the shoulder straps from the pack and settled in.

Fifteen minutes is a long time to sit still when your nerves are on edge, but I made myself do it. I checked my watch and was about to move on when a movement at the top of the outcrop had my head whipping up and my heart pounding. In that hideous interval between the sighting and the recognition I had to fight the urge to run headlong. Then I saw the great head of the jaguar swing toward me, and a wave of relief and terror and delight swept through me.

I'd humored Wiz's claim of a mad jaguar in our canyon, as I had many of his outlandish theories born of a brilliant imaginative mind, a glut of powerful drugs, a profound and disturbing period in a war zone, and an unhealthy interest in the occult. But he'd been right all along. Here he was, the crazy old jaguar living in the Mazatzal wilderness of central Arizona and hunting our canyon. Jesus fuckin' Christ. How brilliant. How terrifying. Would I ever sleep soundly again down here? Never mind sleep—would I survive the next few minutes?

I slipped the Bowie knife from its sheath on my belt, determined to go down with at least a tussle. How many slashes does it take to stop or kill a wildcat this size? Does a jaguar come at you head on or does he ambush his prey? Will he give me a mortal wound and torture me for hours like a house cat with a cricket, allowing me to crawl close to cover before springing on me again to rake me with those massive claws until I slowly bleed my rich English blood onto this barbed province? "If I should die, think only this of me, that there's some corner of a foreign field . . . in that rich earth a richer dust concealed." What the fuck would Rupert Brooke have done? He didn't have to face a jaguar in the wilderness—no, Jem, he had to fight the Hun in Flanders. Better this death in the clean desert air than a guttering demise in the mud and the gas of the Somme.

I gazed up at the cat, gripped. I could see why the Mayan myth said the rosette markings on his cinnamon coat had been daubed with mud by his own paws. Camera! Camera! Get some evidence. I fumbled the tiny Minox from a side pocket of the pack, all the while keeping my eyes fixed on the jag. I raised the camera, tried to steady it, and snapped off a couple. At the shutter click I saw his ears twitch. I slowly lowered the camera and stared up into his eyes and wondered what to do next, all the while wishing that I was on the Tube, or in the King's Head at Shepherd's Bush, anywhere but here, yet feeling a keen thrill at the discovery of this almost mythical creature and all the while my fool side recognizing that this was a seminal moment. I had sighted and photographed the most northerly incidence of a jaguar in the USA, and I would never be able to tell *National Geographic* or anyone other than Wiz and the rest of our motley crew. Ah, the curse of the outlaw life!

As I sat and stared at the jaguar, my thighs twitching with tension, my shoulders arched and taut, I noticed his head flicking occasionally to the side, as if he had a nervous tic. Drool spilled through his fangs. Was the huge cat suffering from the curse of aging as much as any human might? Was he becoming eccentric and unpredictable in his dotage?

I rose and lifted the backpack over my head, but could not bring myself to shout. We had spent too long keeping quiet in this place. The cat lifted his head. I noticed a raggedness to the dark dapples of his coat, a lack of luster to his eyes. Perhaps he was not so swift on his pins these days; maybe there was hope for me after all.

I threw the pack above my head and caught it again and tried a yell, which emerged from my parched throat more like a grunted greeting than a full-blooded challenge. But it had some effect. The jaguar rose and stretched his limbs as if bored with the whole affair.

In a strange and perhaps totally unjustified manner, I felt an affinity with this beast. America and this escapade in the wilds of Arizona had restored in me a sense of the value of wilderness, and it had also made me an exile, an outcast, a stranger in a stranger land. Much as I loved these Western Yanks for their generosity, their easy acceptance, their lack of judgment, I had not lost the totally unwarranted superiority instilled in me by eight years of English public school. The conflict between the twin loves of society and solitude had polarized in my year in the Southwest, and the bliss I felt while alone in the canyon was tempered by the infuriation I often felt when in the company of my American friends. The jag and I had both adapted to our new environment, but we were both doomed to yearn for the homeland to which we knew we could never return.

The great cat stood and displayed his splendor: the mottled coat, the powerful upper muscles, the large handsome belly. He yawned and the huge incisors and the span of the jaws left me in no doubt of the damage he could inflict on my cranial bones. He stared down at me for several minutes before he turned from the crag and disappeared.

With every nerve ganglion jangling, I approached our patch and the legal point of no return. The sight of a large scorpion arching his stinger toward me as I unwittingly cornered him, normally enough to have me dancing away like a scalded Fred Astaire, caused little concern. My fears were larger: a huge feline springing on me or DEA men rushing out to fling me down and cuff me. I scoured the creekbed for sign and listened intently, but neither adversary was detectable.

I came to the spot where I would climb away from the stream and into our garden—an irrevocable move that would solidify my guilt. The temptation here was to keep going so that if we were apprehended we could claim we were merely hikers exploring the canyon, we had no idea some crooks had a plantation up there, how dreadful, the youth of today, etc. Once we had slipped into the garden and started tending the plants, claims of innocence would be tough to uphold.

In the spring, we had moved a few boulders here, in the lee of a bend in the creek, to make a pool in which to submerge the suction hose. As I cleared some leaves from the pool, the breeze wafted up-canyon in the morning warmth and I caught the unmistakable musk of our flowers. Above me, on the alluvial bench, a meadow of the most seductive and potent sativa females on the continent were using every womanly wile to attract some male seed.

I drew a deep breath and climbed the rocky trail, and froze in my tracks. What the fuck next! The pump, normally stashed in a hole we'd dug in the roots of a sycamore, was out in plain view. Once more that day I felt a cold sweat creep down my spine, and I scoured the surrounding undergrowth. But a closer look brought a flood of relief. Bright scratches on the metal frame and rake marks on the bole of the tree identified the black bear which had caused us so many problems during the year. Not content with stealing our food and ripping the tent walls to shreds, he seemed to have a fascination with our equipment. This was not the first time he had dragged the pump from the stash or thrown the hand tools into the open. Goddamned bear, did he think he owned the place? I walked gingerly into the garden and as I strolled through the swath of swaying plants my fears ebbed away.

They were magnificent, and utterly feminine. Willowy and fibrous, the whole plant gave to the prevailing wind, and often, in the summer, when evening gales hurtled through the canyon narrows, the plant laid itself alarmingly horizontal to ride the squalls. This was cannabis sativa, the strain of the Americas, evolved in the mild climate of the tropics. The tops of most plants were way over my head. I had to reach up to inspect the finest colas, pulling lightly on the stem to gauge the maturity of the bud. As I brushed through the crop, I triggered an overwhelming aroma.

We had nipped the growing tips of the plants extensively throughout the year. This stimulated growth and created a bushier plant with more flowers and higher yield. A bonus was that delta-9-tetrahydrocannabinol—the psychoactive element THC, the gear that got you ripped—was concentrated in the tips of the cannabis plant at any growth stage, and although they made for a rather raspy toke those June and July prunings did offer a buzz. Some of the plants we had left untouched, to allow their tops to grow unchecked. One plant in particular had concentrated all its sublimated desire into the single top cola, which had swollen to outsize a man's forearm; I pulled it gently down and there, clinging to the flower, a pair of mating mantises were well set in their coitus.

Oh god, was I to be a morbid voyeur of this most gory coupling? We'd seen many of this iconic species as the plants had matured; they were attracted to the flowers. But here for the first time was a mating pair. I stared in grim fascination as the unpalatable entomological truth played out.

The female, her legs planted deep in the viscous seed bracts, bore the weight of the smaller male as he clung to her back, his lower abdomen throbbing with passion. She turned her head as if to kiss her lover, but as I watched, both transfixed and appalled, she began biting off chunks of his head, like a child eating an apple. In a few minutes the male was entirely decapitated, yet his nether regions continued to pulse as he gave life and body and seed to propagate his species. Christ! I loosed the plant hoping, as it swung wildly, that this loathsome pair would be flung aloft and apart. But no, as I followed the cola to and fro, I could see the decapitated male still thrusting, driven on, I learned later, by a tiny brain lodged in his lower parts.

I moved away, not without a nod of admiration to the single-mindedness of my fellow male. If the display of distaff amorality held a message for a lust-driven lad, I took no heed—to my eventual cost.

The process of growing seedless marijuana is one of cruelly unrequited lust. The sinsemilla farmer spends the summer months studying his plants as they declare their sex. When the male plants show reproductive elements not dissimilar in appearance to a cock and balls, they are unceremoniously uprooted and thrown away. The virgin female plants continue to produce flowers long into autumn in the vain hope of consummation, which are then dried into buds and sold at a premium to the discerning American smoker, who in the early eighties was elbowing the "all sticks and seeds" imports from Colombia and Mexico for the fresh green from Humboldt County and now Arizona. Not only was seeded weed a pain to clean and smoke, but sinsemilla had the added advantage of a smooth sweet taste and, last but by no means least, a higher potency.

I strolled through the garden, admiring the crop the way my dad had admired the wheat in September fullness in the high meadow. I was as proud of our field of grass as he had been of his.

From a perch on the bank above the southern end I could survey the swaying tips. In just a couple of weeks all the "ladies" would be down and hanging and this gorgeous display of feminine pulchritude would be gone. In a couple of days, the pruning crew would drop in: Three Hawks, Nobby, Stilt, Wiz, and three couples: Dali and Fiona, Geoff and Emma, and Molly and me.

All fears of getting nabbed were now gone. I'd been in the garden for about half an hour, so I felt the danger of discovery had passed. Once again, the bliss of this place and this gig washed over me. I had always felt as if we were doing the world a favor by growing and distributing this brilliant dope. That, of course, was a sanctimonious thought, but the value of any grass, as the rawest rookie grower knows, is in the seed, and the Mad Jag seed was the most potent, most playful, most aphrodisiacal, most psychedelic, most profoundly unforgettable pot in the world and it was being grown for the first time in prime agricultural conditions as pure unadulterated seedless grass.

I walked through the garden, balancing on the little walls we'd built to divide the terraces, and passed the tall plant where, to my appalled astonishment, the male mantis still plied his guillotined duty.

I dropped down the steep trail to the creekbed, and paused on a familiar rock to drink. The trail to the camp showed bear sign. I cursed as I saw that one side of our nicely camouflaged Coleman tent was hanging in tatters from the frame. Once inside, I saw the muster of gear that Wiz always left on my sleeping pad. It never failed to amaze me that the wild drug-running pilot was tidier than a spinster schoolteacher.

Arrayed in perfect order were two AA batteries, a wrench for the pump flange, a can of bear spray, a snakebite kit, spring-loaded manicure scissors, and, most welcome among the utilitarian items, a tiny black glass bottle containing half a dozen Demerol, which were intended for use in an emergency for a sprained ankle or a busted bone but were often washed down with a beer after a hard evening's watering and induced a state of euphoric catalepsy that often lasted into the wee hours.

I spent the afternoon patching the tent and leveling a space for another tent, which would house more of the crew. In the evening I strolled down to the swimming hole below the garden.

I stripped and dove. The water was cool now, in October. I thrashed a few lengths before hauling on to a flat rock to dry.

A flight of cliff swallows flared across the pond, bills gaped to drink. A crimson glimpse in the brush betrayed the lovely vermilion flycatcher, stocking up before the passage south. Near at hand, water bugs skirmished on the invisible surface membrane. I dozed off to dream of a diaphanously clad maenad, remarkably like Emma, beckoning me to a leafy bower, until Molly, with Medusa hair-do and harpy breath, swooped down, talons tensed to rake my wedding tackle, black wings blocking the sun. I was woken by an enormous shadow passing the clearing. The female Harris's hawk, whose nest high on the eastern wall I had watched through the summer, had dropped into the canyon to check out my flesh, only to sheer away when the carrion rose.

I skulked around the camp till the margin of sunlight on the eastern rim shrank to an ocher band. I crossed the creek, not without a glance each way, and hauled the pump to the top of the bank and pitched the thick priming hose into the pool. From the garden I dragged the two-inch heavy-duty hose and attached it to the cast output flange. At the junction of the hoses in the center of the garden I opened the valves and laid the hoses into the upper terraces. Then, while I waited for the light to dim, I took another stroll through our redolent meadow and selected, with mixed emotions, about a dozen plants to cut.

With an eye to both the maturity of the bud and the necessity to thin some crowded areas, I culled a few plants. I carried them upstream to a sycamore copse where we had strung some twine. Anticipating the most heavily shaded spots, I gently draped a leg of each dying lady over the string and carefully stroked the leaves down around her buds. The leaves would help shade the flowers and enhance the curing.

At camera dark I prepared myself for the most damning part of our operation: firing up the pump. Bracing myself with a foot on the frame, I hauled on the drawstring and the four-stroke motor chugged into life. As the water surged, I ran ahead to direct it and make sure the initial thrashing of the hoses didn't damage any plants. This event was always a delightfully chaotic welter as the size of our garden and the power of the pump made it a challenge for one bloke to stay ahead of the water flow. We knew the chances of being busted in the dark were remote. Anyone on the rim could certainly hear the distant engine, but we had convinced ourselves that they would not be able to identify the source in the dark. So, with the pump stroking away, the hoses flailing, and the light fading, and with a perfect "watering" moon cresting the rim, I started the evening's work.

Four hours later, mud-caked to my knees, ankles bruised from stumbles along the terrace walls, every piece of clothing soaked or damp, and muscles rugby-match sore, I happily shut down the goddamned noisy pump. I collected a sack of dead leaves from our stash and squelched through the garden broadcasting the leaves in areas I knew would be exposed in the morning. After a last sniff of my favorite plants, I trudged back to the camp, grabbing the bottle of Sam Smith's from the creek as I passed.

I kindled a fire, chucked the remainder of the steak on the grill, and settled back into the rock seats we had built. This was always a delicious moment, but in the circumstances—ten grand trousered, the rest of the grass ready to harvest, three days of solitude ahead, a certain first shag in the canyon guaranteed with Molly's arrival, and the potential of Emma looming—it was near bliss. Ten minutes later, after a toke of an early plant and a few swigs of the Yorkshire pale ale, it was.

The frogs of summer were gone. The pretty ring-tailed cat made his nightly run across the log seat next to the fire.

As I slumped into a knackered drowse I heard or thought I heard or imagined I heard the soft muffled song that serenaded me every night I spent alone in our camp. Was it confusion with the murmur of the stream or the naiad, nymph of freshwaters, trilling her lullaby, or a siren luring me further into this seductive web of risk?

"I'll sleep by the creek and purify my ears." Ah, Gary Snyder, Kerouac's Japhy, and his beautiful translation of the hermit Han-shan. I must read more of both. Or Yeats, so I may one day muse alone in the weed-flowered glade.

Later, as the foolish and euphoric Mad Jag musings ran capricious courses through the cortex—Ferrari drives down the Amalfi coast, nights with Emma in the Dorchester, climbing El Cap—a blood-stilling shriek boomed off the canyon walls and the thin hairs on my alarmingly balding pate bristled like cholla spines. As I bedded down, I wondered if Coleman guaranteed their tents against exiled and eccentric jaguars.

8

"No shit? You saw the jag?" Wiz's face gleamed with envy and delight. "I told you, man. You disbeliever. And he didn't jump your ass. I told you." He clenched his fists and held his arms up, like a striker celebrating a goal. "He's down here to be our protective spirit. Just like Don Juan says. Far fucking out!"

He looked around to survey the reactions of the group sitting cross-legged around the tarpaulin under the canopy of russet-leaved sycamores. Wiz was just finishing laying out everyone's kit, as was his wont: manicure scissors, knife, pliers, a piece of fruit, one of his beloved tiny black glass bottles, each one filled with a half gram of coke.

It was the evening of the day the pruning crew had straggled down into the canyon. Wiz, Stilt, Nobby, and I were giving tips to Geoff, Emma, Dali, Fiona, and Molly on the finer points of pruning high-quality grass. Three Hawks had also hiked into the canyon. Here was the entire gang: Yanks, Euros, and Natives all under one tree.

"Chroist Almoighty, there is actually a fookin' jaguar down here." Fiona's Brummy accent soured the still autumn air.

"A slightly barmy jaguar, I reckon," I said.

"Barmy?" Molly raised an eyebrow.

"Nuts. Crazy. Losing his mind," Geoff chimed in.

"He's old," I added. "Maybe senile. But still strong."

"Not too many jaguars in England, Fiona?" chuckled Three Hawks. An Apache, born on the San Carlos reservation, he'd got a degree in zoology at Northwestern and returned to the reservation to work as a wildlife biologist.

"Thank god," said Fiona.

"I was sent to the border ranges on a multiple-agency study of the jaguars down there," said the Apache. "Spent weeks tracking 'em in the mountains. Never saw one."

"They're elusive, eh?" Emma looked up.

"Very. It's the most unusual big cat." Three Hawks warmed to his theme. "They kill by crushing the skull of the victim, not by choking like other cats. And they're crazy strong. One was seen dragging a horse carcass a mile."

"Thanks for that vital information," said Geoff. "That'll make us sleep much better down here!"

"Males spend their entire adult life alone," continued the Apache. "The only contact they have with other jags is when they mate."

There was a moment's silence before I could not resist the obvious.

"Sounds like the perfect lifestyle," I said, and was bombarded with abuse and concord from both genders.

The clamor died away and we all settled to the job in hand. Spread across the tarp were enough branches of dried weed to put us all in the state pen for the duration, a walkie-talkie, and a transistor radio now playing the restrained reggae of Gregory Isaacs.

"You've been down here most of the summer, Nobby." Emma looked up from her tentative trimming of the buds. "Have you ever seen the jaguar?"

"No. But him and I talk, most nights in vact."

There was another pause, glances were exchanged, someone snickered, and then the entire crew of unlikely crooks burst into laughter.

When the uproar died down Molly asked, not without guile, "Who's sleeping with who?"

"With whom," corrected Fiona, and suffered a pouted stare from Molly.

"Never had you tagged as a pedant, Fi," I chimed in, in support of the missus. "Now, let's see how you're going here."

"Don't call me that, Style. You know I hate it." The Birmingham beauty offered up her bowl of pruned buds.

"You don't need to clip 'em so close." I showed Fiona another bud. Looking at her bright green eyes and wide mouth, it was easy to understand why she had done some modeling and had been a Playboy Bunny, and why Geoff had chased her halfway across Europe. "A few leaves help it burn better."

"With whom would you *care* to sleep?" Stilt asked, smiling mischievously at Molly.

"We've got the two Coleman tents." Wiz, never really comfortable with suggestive banter, interjected. "I have Fiona and Dali and Geoff and Emma billeted in the big one, Nobby and I in the smaller one. Jem and Molly can have the two-man. Stilt and Three Hawks, you get the fireside."

"You and me, baby." Three Hawks gave a limp wrist to Stilt.

There was general assent to the sleeping arrangement and the group settled quietly to work.

"Wiz, what should I do here?" Emma showed him a stick of weed with a nice top cola and a few smaller buds spaced along the base.

"Guys. This here's a good question." Wiz held up the branch. "We want the long buds to be really tight. These two lower buds that don't wrap against the main stem, snip those off."

"I see," said Emma, and went back to work. After a moment she asked, "What do we do if someone finds us down here, Wiz? Do you and Jem have a plan if we get spotted?" I found myself watching her; hands working deftly on the grass, ridged thigh muscles topped by blue cotton shorts, the tank top clinging to the delightful breasts.

Since my foolish suggestion of a partner exchange three weeks before, the tension had been palpable. Geoff and I had resorted to platitudes and barbed exchanges. Molly had put a brave face on it; she had obviously been hurt by my proposal, but perhaps due to her history in the looser ethics of San Francisco and Jerome in the late '70s, which included rumors of the occasional dalliance with those of her own gender, she felt she could not protest too much. More intriguingly, she had alluded to Geoff's good looks a couple of times recently.

"We've got an escape contingency," Wiz announced confidently. "We have several options for getaway trails."

"Stilt." Emma looked quizzically at the medical man. "Do you think we have a chance to get away if we're spotted?"

"Well, my dear." He straightened his long torso. "I do believe that there will be members of our little band of thieves who will make good their escape."

"In plain English," said Geoff, "when we see the bloody rozzers rushing in with M16s pointed at us, we run like the dickens. And those swiftest on their pins might get away. In other words, if we're rumbled, we're shagged. Right, Style?"

"I would prefer to say if the DEA men do get the drop on us, and down here I think that's very unlikely, there are ways out." I looked around the group. "Tomorrow we'll give you a gander at the escape routes."

"Escape routes may be okay for these dudes who've been down here for the entire year and know every rock." This from Dali, who was twisting a reefer from the buds he was trimming. "How about the rest of us who could barely make it down that goddamn ankle-busting wash? We've got no chance of outrunning those guys."

"Shall we shut this guy off?" Molly reached for the radio, from which Dire Straits rocked along.

"Let's wait to hear the news." said Wiz, as the DJ waffled on to the top of the hour.

"Bomb blasts rocked New York, Los Angeles, and London

today, injuring at least five people. An Armenian anti-Turkish group claimed responsibility.

"Iraq launched a new series of attacks on the battered Iranian city of Abadan yesterday.

"U.S. and Iranian officials have reached an impasse in negotiations over the release of the fifty-two American hostages.

"In opinion polls released today, GOP nominee Ronald Reagan has a slight edge over President Carter in the running for the presidential election. The polls . . ."

"I can't bear to listen," said Stilt, snapping off the radio. "It will be a sorry day indeed for our country if that man is elected to power."

"If the hostages aren't released soon, then Carter is stuffed," said Molly.

"No shit!" said Wiz. "And he's already riding Carter's ass about being soft on drugs. If he wins, they'll be spraying paraquat from the Mexican border to Patagonia."

"And the prisons will be overflowing." Molly sighed. "The next thing you know, they'll be privatizing the prison system."

"Already being discussed, my dear." Stilt emphasized his point with a cola.

"Well, at least it will keep the price of weed up," said Dali, twisting a spliff. "So let's enjoy it while we can." He took a long draw, big chest swelling, receding forehead well furrowed, lips splayed away from the teeth, eyes popping with effort, arms held wide, palms up. He held the pose for some twenty seconds. We all watched the ritual in fascination as a thin plume of smoke faded from his nostrils and, try as he might to avoid the inevitable, he collapsed in a coughing fit, and the rest of us creased up in a fit of giggles.

We whittled away at the rick of weed as the shadow climbed the western rim. There were groans and stretches from those who, unlike us three full-time moonshiners, had made the grueling hike for the first time that day and were feeling the after-effects. I was about to add my ten pennies for an early quit when a noise from the direction of the creek had all faces raised and wide-eyed, the newcomers staring at Wiz and me.

"Stylor, let's go." Wiz was up. "Rest of you hang here. Be ready to haul ass."

We loped quickly and quietly through the sycamores in the manner we'd learned during our time in the canyon. As we approached the creek, Wiz held his hand out and we froze, ears cocked. The sound came from downstream, closer to the garden. Silently we stole to the creek bank and peered through branches. At the start of our hidden trail to camp, the cinnamon black bear was digging in the rocks.

Wiz loosed a long sigh of relief at the lack of human intrusion, and turned to me. "That dude has caused us a lot of grief this year," he said. "Time for payback. Give him a bit of a scare."

"Let digging bears dig, I say."

"We need to let him know there's other large mammals down here. Someone else will be working this garden next year, for sure."

We watched for a spell as the bear clawed rocks aside, intent on getting down to whatever food he sniffed there. His strength was obvious and alarming.

Eventually Wiz made to rise but, before he could, I held him down because another large mammal had turned the bend in the creek: the jaguar! He came on a few steps before he clocked the intruder, lifted the great head, and let rip a gravelly roar. We both gasped and stared, transfixed as the two impressive creatures faced off. Rising to his full height, front paws held wide, the bear gave a shudder that shook his tawny pelt and then cocked his head and gave his own loud cry.

"Holy crap." Wiz's whisper was tense, shrill.

With a few swift bounds the huge cat came up to the bear, who stood stock still; the jag reared high, waved a giant paw; the stand-off was classic, riveting; both ursine and feline animals made short challenging charges; finally, the bear dropped to his normal stance, turned, and ambled up the creekbed toward us, yet throwing a cautious glance back at the cat. We watched, rapt, as he came on. When he was directly below us Wiz made to rise again, but before he could a sharp noise from behind us froze the bear. He glanced up, held his nose high, and then, either scenting us with his keen olfaction or spying us with his dodgy sight, he decided that discretion was the better part of valor and tore up the opposite canyon side and disappeared, an avalanche of rocks and sods of soil splashing down into the creek marking his rapid exit.

"Jesus." I looked at my partner. "Remind me never to run uphill from the bear."

"No shit." Wiz grimaced and stared back down the creek to where the jag stood still. "See how the jag ran the bear off. I told you, man. He takes care of us. Custodian of the canyon!"

We watched the cat pad upstream toward us and then, as if stung by a hornet or simply for joy, he hopped in the air like a spring lamb and then cantered wildly through the creekbed, splashing up showers. As he passed, we sank lower into the bushes and held breathless as he dashed beneath us, gave another jaunty leap, then rounded a bend out of sight.

"Wow," said Wiz. "He's batshit crazy!"

"Second childhood, maybe?" I said.

We turned and were met with bug-eyed stares from the rest of the gang, who'd crept forward to see the source of the commotion.

"Christ, you guys sure got some big scary company down here." Dali, as usual, threw his comments out. The rest simply stared or shook their heads in disbelief. A nervous chatter rattled among the crew as we wandered back to the clearing and Wiz, glowing with delight at finally having seen the creature which had been such a presence of his two years in the canyon, declared work over for the day. We straightened the work space, and we all trooped along the creek toward the camp. I fell in behind Emma and asked, "Fancy a stroll through the garden?" I expected a rebuff but was surprised by the eagerness of her reply.

"I'd love to."

We hopped the stepping stones in the dry part of the creekbed. I offered my hand on the steep path to the garden. Our hands locked and I pulled rather too heartily and we overbalanced for a sec. I had to hold the sycamore trunk with one arm, her waist with the other. There was a moment when flesh was pressed at the hip and her face tilted up. The battle between my anxiety to check for someone watching and the desire to look at her was no contest; I stared down at her until she turned. I released my hold and gestured grandly toward the garden entrance.

"Come into the garden, Maud
For the black bat night hath flown.
Come into the garden, Maud . . ."

I paused to give her a cue, and oh, though I knew she would know the lines, as would any educated English schoolgirl, the ensuing moment was exquisite.

"For I'm here at the gate alone
And the woodbine spices are wafted abroad
And the musk of the rose is blown."

She lingered over the vowels of the last line and then turned and her lucent smile colored much of what had gone before and much of what would come in my life.

She pulled the agave-stalk gate aside and stepped among the plants. I followed, my heart hammering.

"I think your plants might have inspired another line from Tennyson." She slipped a thumb thoughtfully under the strap of her top. "How about, um, 'And the aroma of marijuana is lofted abroad.'"

"And the stench of the stuff gets you stoned."

"A little heavy on the alliteration." She giggled. "But haven't you a romantic bone in your body?"

"You might be surprised."

"I might, might I?" Her glance sent a shock down my spine.

I followed her along the paths, gaze wandering down her back, across the lovely bottom and over the strong quads. She had arrived in Arizona carrying an "English" layer over the lean ballet form; however, the mountain hikes and outdoor life since had restored the taut litheness of her dancing years.

"I love these little terraces you've built." She stooped to repair a damaged rock wall. "Reminds me of northern Thailand."

"A better cash crop than rice." I crouched beside her and our arms brushed as we worked together.

"It must have taken ages to prepare the garden."

"About six weeks."

"Did you have to improve the soil?" She turned her face toward mine and we held for a beat, pregnant with promise. I found myself studying the pronounced flatness of the bridge of her nose.

"We had tests done to check the pH balance and the mineral content. Then we had Wiz drop in supplements to bring it up to par."

"Wiz flew his plane down into the canyon?"

"Yep. I was on board for a couple of flights."

"You were the bomb aimer? I bet that was exciting."

"And how, as they say."

"Show me your prize blooms," she said, waiting for me in one of the little clearings among the plants. I led her along the edge of the garden, where we had to brush between the manzanita limbs and the arching, flower-tipped branches of the sativa. The aroma of the weed, wafted about by our passing, was particularly potent here.

"Does the smell really get you off?" she asked, again disconcertingly locking my gaze.

"Unfortunately not. But it is sweet, eh?"

"Yes. Striking, unique."

We were at the south end of the plantation, furthest from the entrance and hidden from view by the canopy of colas and the steep, oak-covered bank.

"We're working with a perfume company to see if we can catch the essence of this strain." I leaned against a boulder and pulled down a mature bloom, brushed the flower to bring out the scent, and held it for her to smell. Her shoulder came against mine. She let the branch swing back up and leaned beside me; my skin at the point of contact felt on fire.

"It's quite different from the hash we used to smoke back home." She stared out through the plants, lost in thought. "It seems to have dreamlike qualities, but it's also enthralling, stimulating . . . physically."

"People have said that the Mad Jag can make you feel a little . . . frisky."

We stood there, silently absorbing the thought and the evening sounds: the rasping of the cicadas, the breeze soughing in the piñons, the prattle of the creek; the tension between us galvanic, the moment teetering. A fleck of dark and light caught our eye.

"That's the phainopepla. He and his mate raised a brood in the mesquite over there this spring. I thought he might have flown south by now. See him." I put my arm across her shoulders, drew her close, and pointed. "There. In the oak. Do you see his crest?"

"Oh yes. He is handsome. Lovely red eye."

"He's known as the mistletoe flycatcher. They nest in clumps and distribute the seeds."

"Now there's a romantic creature." she said, and seemed to briefly humor my ornithological whimsy. But the purple desert flycatcher, *Phainopepla nitens*, was not, it transpired, at the forefront of her thoughts.

She spun, no, pirouetted into my arms, head back, mouth clamping my lips, tongue immediately probing, her breasts, firm shields with thimble bosses, brushing my chest, pelvis pulsing against an immediately proud John Thomas. I was taken aback in every sense, pinned against the boulder. I'd locked lip with a few lusty women in my time, but nothing approached the intensity, the urgency, the complete sensual encompassing that Emma threw into the clinch. The taste of her saliva, the tang of her breath, the timbre of her gasps, the touch of her hips, all swept aside any doubts my amoral mind might have had and I found myself hurled like a novice surfer to the lip of the wave.

She broke away.

"Oh Christ. What the hell am I doing? What is in this dope of yours?" She held her hands on my chest, while mine stayed locked in the small of her back.

"You can't blame it all on the grass."

"No. I know. We've been close since I married Geoff. But I really only thought of us as friends. Until the other night, that is, when you suggested a . . . a partner swap."

"And did the idea intrigue you?"

"Yes." She held me with that disarming look. "I have to admit it did. And now even more so." And she swooped in on me once more, a tad more cautious this time but nonetheless urgent and utterly engaging. The immediate physicality of her embrace was unique; she seemed to have a hair-trigger libido. The prospect of attempting to match her appetite had my red-blooded side raring to go while the wimp in me held back. God, had I listened to the latter!

I cupped her buttocks to still her hips, fusing her hot bone to mine. She molded against me, a moan warming my throat.

"Emma, this is mazed." I used the Devonshire slang in an attempt to defuse the moment.

"You're right. But something's come over me since coming to America. Giving up my job. Now this crazy adventure, this gorgeous canyon. It's overwhelming. I feel so vulnerable, and at the same time so strong. Oh, I'm just talking crap." She slumped on my shoulder, her body pliant against me.

"I know. That's what happened to me out here. The desert triggers something . . . something feral in you."

"That's the word!" She stared up at me, then leaned in and kissed me languidly, her pelvis pistoning against me the while.

"God, you feel wonderful!" she whispered. "Geoff hasn't been paying me much attention recently. He seems uninterested. I have my own . . ." She tailed off, pulled away, and stared defiantly at me. "I'm going to tell him right this minute."

"Jesus, Emma, don't do that. We've got to keep things together while we finish the crop."

"You just want to have a swift fling with me on the sly?" Her eyes blazed.

"That's not what I meant. But I have to think of the harvest. And Molly."

"But you're not that close. You told me yourself." She gave her head a quick shake. "I'm sorry, that's not fair of me."

"Let's just wait. Not be too hasty. There'll be a time."

"This may be the time, Jem Stylor. Carpe per diem, as we say in Leeds, seize the day and the cash." And she was gone into the jungle of cannabis, her passage discernible only by the top colas swaying as she strode away.

I leaned back against the rock staring up at the western wall, the cliffs raked with magic hour light, the darkening shadows of the junipers pitching off the bluffs; and then I panned, in a torpor of longing and foreboding, the Harris's hawk's evening stoop across the canyon to her roost. She, at least, was content in her polyandry.

9

Sound travels in the still, dawn desert air. In the semi-comatose state of not quite waking, it seemed as if the voices were right outside the tent. I was galvanized into consciousness and scrambled outside, naked.

"What's up?" asked Molly sleepily.

"Shh," I snapped, straining to hear. Wiz was by the fire pit, frantically pulling on his jeans. I caught his eye through the trees and held my finger to my lips.

"Where are they?" he mouthed, and I held my hands out, palms up. I reached back into the tent for clothes and binoculars and froze again when the voices started. I couldn't hear the words, but it seemed inconceivable that they were not below the rim. And anyone who had dropped off the easy country of the flat mesa into the steep, dangerous terrain below the rim could have only sinister intentions—arresting us, or perhaps more threateningly, stealing our crop.

My heart thumped as I crept to Wiz and we crouched against the bole of a pine.

"We should get the others ready to bail," he hissed.

"May be too late," I said, sweeping the canyon sides with the glasses.

Again, the sounds of men talking wafted down. Would they be talking so openly if they wanted to take us by surprise?

"See anything?" Wiz's voice was strained. Was all our hard work coming to naught after all? A movement caught my eye and I swung the glasses to the rim above the amphitheater—a huge cliffed bowl on the eastern wall. There they were!

"On the rim!" I whispered.

Wiz grabbed the binoculars.

"Two men, with rifles. Hunters, I reckon. Here."

I held the glasses as steadily as my twitching arms would allow and sharpened the focus. Two guys in camo, rifles across their chests, walking carefully on the rim edge, peering down into the canyon. All right, all fucking righty.

"Hunters!" I looked at Wiz with relief. Not DEA men, or thieves about to rush in and nab us, or worse.

"How'd you know? Agents could easily get some camo gear." His face was hard. "They sure gotten plenty of files."

Of course he was right. My relief began to ebb and, as I tracked the men along the rim rock, I began to feel an intense yet uncertain terror. There was something ominous about one of the hunters. The man was big, oafish yet nimble in the way big men often are. But what was it about this man, why did his profile alarm me? I watched him bring the telescopic sight up and pan the rifle through the canyon bottom. He moved on and was obscured.

"I've lost him. We have to move."

We slipped to the base of another tree to get a clear view. I scoured the rim for several minutes before I found the hunters again. I flicked the focus knob and, as the men sharpened in frame, I felt a lash of fear jolt the back of my thighs. It was the big man, Sheriff Willard Farr, on the rim of our canyon and staring into it with a telescopic lens. Holy Christ! The Mormon twat. The Latter-day wanker.

"It's him. The fucking sheriff." My voice was strained.

"Fuck." Wiz stared at me, wide-eyed, crease-browed.

Why couldn't Willard Farr leave us alone? There were a hundred canyons he could hunt. Why did he choose this one? Why was he always creeping around our mesas? Was he merely waiting for the right day to coordinate a multi-agency SWAT team descent onto our gang of "violent felons"? Was he up there, right now, mouthing away loudly to show he wasn't on to us while planning the bust all the while?

I had to steel myself from rushing to tell the gang the gig was up and we should all take our best shot at a getaway. With everyone scarpering in different directions, maybe a few of us would slip through the net and could help the others with lawyers, bail, etc. I lay there watching the men, feeling the sweat on my neck, struggling to train the glasses steadily as my chest thumped.

"Do you think we should make a dash for it?" I studied Wiz's face. The strain was etched in the lines. He'd put so much into this deal over the years: exploring the canyon, studying the agriculture, researching seed, investing cash.

His forehead was furrowed, the neatly clipped mustache jutted out from the pursed upper lip, the goatee pointed from the clenched chin, the deep brown eyes shone intensely. We'd never truly gelled as mates—not in the fashion that I had with Geoff and the rest of the lads I'd blundered and bludgeoned around the cities and beaches of England and Europe and Asia with in the seventies. Wiz was too decent, too generous, too ingenuous to command the respect of an English cynic who, as John Fowles said, was "born to act, bred to lie."

"One of us should go on up to the mesa. Check it out." He looked at me. A bone of mild contention existed between us over his inability to out-hike me, especially on the climbs. "Yeah. It had better be you. You've always claimed to be a climber."

"If you insist." I scoured the clifftop again and cursed my exaggertaed stories of climbing adventures. I watched, fear raking my spine, sweat beading my brow despite the dawn chill, as Willard Farr panned his rifle and scope along the canyon bottom until it was trained directly on us, the garden, the strings of hanging plants, our whole secret microcosm. He held for an interminable moment, until with a last upward flourish the rifle tilted away and he and his partner strode from view.

Twenty minutes later, armed with a small pack containing two water bottles, a bag of trail mix, a slab of cheddar, binoculars, the walkie-talkie, and a can of shoeblack, and with Wiz's recurve bow lashed onto it, I was halfway up the canyonside picking my way across a steep, loose shale slope littered with pancake prickly pear, buckhorn cholla, and the evil banana agave, which formed a treacherous path between a two-hundred-foot red rock cliff below and a towering sheer buttress above.

I negotiated the slope and turned into a steep but comparatively solid gully. I scrambled up the couloir without mishap, skittered diagonally across another of the hideously dangerous screes, and was then faced with the major challenge of the dicey route I'd often considered, but never taken, up the eastern wall of Mad Jag Canyon. Above me the final rim cliff, roughly a hundred feet of extruded igneous, was breached by a narrow ramp that appeared from below to offer passage through the wall. As I sat in the cover of a juniper, I could see that the ramp indeed might "go," save for one minor flaw: a short pitch where the ramp was no more than a crease in the face and where the climber—i.e., muggins here, skulking under the tree with the sheriff overhead and evidence enough for half a lifetime in clink beneath—that climber would truly be on his mettle.

I started up. The first section was straightforward: a sloping ledge about three feet wide. I soon realized I was bounding up this easy section and had to force myself into climbing mode: take it easy, don't thrutch, deep breaths, look for the holds, be deliberate, get into an easy rhythm so you're psyched for the thin section.

As I approached the narrow part of the ramp and paused to study the moves ahead, I wished like hell there were someone next to me: a trusted partner handing the rack of hardware, offering encouragement, gently cradling the rope in callused hands, ready to clench safely shut if I peeled. But I was here alone and all the terror of solo climbing and the fear of the fall flooded back.

I couldn't resist a glance down into the canyon to see if I could make out the garden and our pruning crew. I imagined Wiz watching through the binoculars, scolding the rest of them into packing their gear, checking and destroying incriminating clues. The landing zone, should I fall here, was a cactus-strewn pad seventy feet below from which, if I wasn't impaled on a handy Spanish bayonet, I would bounce over the next bluff to a certain and messy demise.

I forced myself to concentrate on the pitch. C'mon, you tosser, I chided. It's only about thirty feet, then you'll be back on easy ground. Just get on with it, for fuck's sake!

I cinched the waistband of the pack, wiped my fingers on my jeans, and started across. Sharp edges offered handholds and a band of quartz gave purchase for the shoe tips. A comparative calm came with progress. A vertical crack halfway across gave perfect hand jams, grist to the gritstone climber, and I paused, hands slotted deep in the crack, thumbs angled across the palms to force the muscle at the thumb's base against the wall of the crack to form a tension hold, any one of which a climber worth his salt can hang his body weight. I glanced upward, tracing the crack, and considered following it. Cracks are the climbers' trails, the weakness in the cliffs that offer a way. But this one steepened and thinned. I knew to pursue it was folly, a distraction from the real route—the rest of the traverse.

The tiny ledge for the feet petered out here and the handholds looked farther between. I longed for the little alloy wedges slung on shoestring Perlon that I'd slotted, and often had fallen on, in my early climbing days.

I felt the eyes trained on me through the binoculars from the creekside, and with a fatalistic sigh I loosed my grip on the snug crack and launched across the rock. The first few moves were thin enough, 5.9 U.S., E1 5b English, but then almost within reach of the ledge I was faced with the curse of the traverse: a hideously difficult hand swap on the same hold. I kept trying the move but felt unable, and certainly unwilling, to remove my right hand in order to place my left on a tiny incut hold. My forearms began to pump, my chest heaved and the blood pounded in my temples. I finally worked my right hand around to the side of the hold, laid my weight back and moved my left toward the hold. But before I could settle the fingertips I experienced the climber's worst fear: because of the opposition nature of the move I had begun the awful "barn door," the hingeing away from the rock that could only spell disaster. My left hand scrabbled uselessly for purchase and I had no choice but to abandon both hands and give the wall a desperate kick and leap for the ledge.

My left hand caught the edge and sheered off. My right snagged a horn at the lip. I crashed a kneecap against a protrusion and swiveled, wrenching my shoulder, but I held on. Gasping with pain and the terror of the near fatal miss, I swung back and mantled on to the narrow ledge, twisted, and sat pinned against the wall, quivering and catatonic.

I massaged my wounds and rocked back and forth until the pain subsided to a tolerable level. Perhaps five minutes later, I was able to go on. The last part of the ramp went with ease, and once I gained the mesa I moved quickly to the cover of a large juniper.

My knee throbbed from the blow and my shoulder socket felt like it had been dislocated as the adrenaline shot of the close call waned. I unstrapped the bow from the pack, opened the tin of shoeblack, and smeared it on my face. Lastly, I switched on the walkie-talkie.

"Wiz, come back." I whispered hoarsely.

The reply barked across the mesa. "Hear you loud and clear." I scrabbled to reduce the volume.

"I'm on the mesa. Keep your voice down!" I hissed.

"Okay. I watched you all the way, man. You looked a little sketchy on the last section." Wiz chuckled. "For a second there, I thought you were going to crater."

"I was just making it look dramatic."

"Yeah, right!"

"I'm going to skirt the edge." I spoke softly, glancing to the south. "Don't call me or you might give me away."

"Will do. Happy hunting."

I turned the walkie down, slung the binocular strap over my neck, gripped the bow, and set off cautiously along the mesa to find Willard Farr, the sheriff of Gila County. After a few minutes stalking through the junipers, a harsh voice froze me to the basalt.

"Where the hell are all these eight-point mulies you said was out here, Willard?"

I had stumbled onto my quarry. The two men, fifty yards ahead, peered into the deep maw of the confluence with Mad Jag Canyon and Sycamore Canyon. I shuffled carefully away from the rim to the cover of a live oak break.

Through the branches I could see the broad back of Willard Farr seated on an outcrop, mopping his temples with a bandanna. On the cliff edge his partner, a slight man, sat drinking from a military canteen. "Thought we would have a shot at any number of bucks by now."

"Seen a bunch of 'em out here all summer." Willard Farr pulled jerky from a pocket and tore off a bite.

"Seems like we'd be better higher up. In them pines."

"Hold your horses. We got a couple days yet."

"What if we see one down in these canyons? Or we get one gut-shot and he hightails over the rim. We're never gonna get the rack."

"There's ways down there."

"You ever been down in this hole?"

"Once. When I was in high school. Me and some buddies packed in from Pinedale. Lord, it was a hard scrabble. But in the bottom, there's some fine places. Clean water straight from springs. Any amount o' game. Wide beaches jus' made for sleepin' on. Made you wonder if the Angel Moroni had sent us there just to see his works." Willard Farr stood and stretched.

"Any one go down there these days?" asked the other man.

"Who knows? Like I say, the water's plenty. I'm sure them wacky baccy growers are all through this country."

"What makes you reckon that?"

"We arrested a couple of 'em on the far side of this mesa last spring."

"How'd you know they were fixin' to grow pot?"

"We watched 'em in the canyon and then we found 'em with a bag o' seed."

I crouched lower in the bushes as I remembered Wiz telling me about his friend Robert getting caught trying to set up an operation in the next canyon. And how pissed off he, Wiz, had been that his pal had jeopardized everyone's chances of pulling off their gigs out in this neck of the woods.

"Seen any sign of 'em this year?"

"No real sightings. Seen plenty of tracks out on these mesas. And seen a few odd boys in town. But right now I'm keeping a weather eye open. It's harvest time and if them growers wants to get their dope outta here they gotta pass through these roads and through town. That's when I'll be waiting for 'em. And we'll have their butts in the county lockup in Globe quicker'n that." The big man clicked his fingers, then shouldered his pack and looked hard at the other man.

"Them fellers think they can get away with growing their dope in my county and corrupting them good kids up in the Payson high school, they reckon without Willard Farr!" And he strode away along the edge.

I watched his partner trail after him and reflected. Okay, so the feds weren't about to swoop down and fling our arses in the pokey any time soon. But fat Farr had a sniff of us, and if we didn't stay on our toes we could get snagged in a trice. But overall, the tension of the last few hours was largely swept away, and in the surge of relief a daft bravado took a fatalistic grip of my collar.

When the men reached the tip of the peninsula and looked down into the spectacular joining of rifts—Sycamore and Mad Jag Canyon in the foreground, Relic slicing grandly into the middle, and the Verde cutting through the deep background—I slipped from cover and darted across the narrow spit of land to arrive at a low outcrop above the rim of Sycamore Canyon. I skulked behind a rock and looked for the men to wander in my direction. When they were close, peering into the gulf, I stepped into plain view and walked toward them along the lip of the higher ground.

The smaller man was first to spot me. I kept my gaze ahead but clocked him jump out of the corner of my eye.

"What the . . .?" he gasped, and I saw Willard Farr swing toward me.

"Well, I'll be," said Farr.

I paused and lifted the bow in acknowledgment. "Spot any whitetails out here, fellers?" I attempted my best redneck.

"None so far," said Farr hesitantly.

"Tarnation. Happen I'll settle for a coney for supper," I said, and before they could reply or I corpsed with laughter I strode on, and as soon as I was sure I was out of their sight I burst into a paroxysm of giggles and at a dead run wheeled around the edge of the promontory and raced along the rim above the amphitheater.

I soon slowed to a brisk walk, letting the rush of the climb and the encounter slacken, and savoring the sweet relief of knowing that the sheriff did not have knowledge of our operation. I allowed my mind to return to the brilliant preoccupation that had absorbed it since the contact with Emma in the garden a couple of evenings past.

She had been cool afterward. The group had spent the daytime hours sitting in a loose circle, trimming the enormous crop. Initially the task had seemed insurmountable, and Wiz and I had worried whether we could complete it before the weather changed.

As the days slipped by, the gang got the hang of the job and the large plastic sacks filled with a sweet-smelling harvest of neatly trimmed buds and the pile of top colas steadily grew, we began to take heart and realized that the brunt of the task could be accomplished by the present workforce.

Apart from the odd eye contact, Emma gave no indication of wishing to continue the flirtation. Nor, mercifully, did I have any sense that she would tell her husband she had determined to have an affair with his best mate. Sitting across from her and studying her face turned down to the work and feeling an overwhelming desire for her, I was reminded of one of the oft-forgotten facts of the sexual revolution of the seventies.

It has always been assumed that the men made out like bandits during that time, that we wallowed in a morass of lust, leaping from bed to bed, and bird to bird, without a backward glance nor troubled by a pang of commitment. I, though, being the product of an all-boys public school and therefore intellectually and emotionally incapable of maintaining a relationship with a member of that alien opposite sex, had prided myself on staying aloof from such human frailties and was convinced I would be able to do so for the rest of "me natural." No doubt it was a fabulous time to be single and employed in a "glam" profession; with a passable phisog and a fair line of bullshit one seldom suffered celibacy long.

However, I doubt I was the only male who, having taken home a girl from pub or club, cranked Robert Plant and the lads out of the eight-track at ninety-six watts, and engaged in a mutually pleasurable exploration of each other's hidden recesses before parting in the dark, did not feel a jolt of deflation when that same girl swept blithely into the club the following evening without a nod of recognition or, worse, sallied into the night on the arm of some other grinning bastard the next. The promiscuity of the time made for as gratifying a ratio of consummation to attraction, arguably, as any era in recent history, yet the emotional waves and troughs were ridden by both sexes.

On her second night in the canyon, Molly had suggested we take our sleeping bags into the garden. We'd made a bed under the white pine and sipped Cuervo from my little flask before launching into the inevitable, delicious sex of practiced partners, fueled by the cool night air on naked skin, a crystalline sky, the scent and high of the sativa.

The next afternoon, we all took a break from the tedious work and sauntered down to the swimming hole. I dove in and tried to swim a flash length before bumping into a boulder. I climbed out and lay back in the sun, one eye open to spy the scene. Molly, darling girl of the hippie haunts of the desert Southwest, dropped her threads without a thought, ducked her willowy figure into the cool stream and dipped her hair in the shallows to shampoo it. Fiona, ex-model and proud of her voluptuous figure, stood prominently near the water's edge and gave a cautious yet obvious display of her disrobe. Wiz and Geoff stood toweling by the creek, fine tall figures framing the dark centers where their tools, shrunken by the cool water, gradually resumed respectability. Stilt's towering angular form topped a boulder as he sawed a T-shirt across his back.

My one open eye was focused on Emma as she stooped between two large boulders, tentatively stripped, and, stepping quickly over the creekside rocks, tried to hide her body in the stream. This was October and the creek water was bloody cool and she came up with a gasp, bowed her back, crossed her arms under her breasts, cleaving them into prominence so the water spilled from the nipples in twin cascades.

10

"Wonderful. Baked beans and toasted cheese sarnies. Again." Fiona opened two cans, shoved them onto the grill, and slumped against the stone seatback. A week had slipped by since the Willard Farr incident, the work and the routine were beginning to lose their novelty, the food supply had run thin, and the booze was low.

"Maybe it's time someone went to town for supplies?" Molly suggested.

"I need to make arrangements to get this stuff outta here." Wiz loved to keep his plans secret, but everyone in the group knew about the chopper.

"Whock, whock, whock, whock." Dali whirled an upright forefinger. Wiz threw him a scowl.

"Perhaps we should all take a break for a couple of days," Geoff suggested. "Have a bath, go out for a meal, get pissed, come back for a last stint."

"I'd prefer to stay down here." The firelight shone in Emma's eyes as she glanced around the clan. "I'm beginning to grow fond of this place."

"I have to return to my practice or my partners will think I've suffered the dentists' fate," said Stilt.

"Dentist's fate?" Emma glanced up.

"For some unknown reason dentists have the highest rate of suicide of any profession." Stilt stood to his enormous height, then crouched over Molly. "Personally, I take nothing but delight in probing the molar regions of my fellow humans." He loomed over her. "Open wide, my lovely."

"Get away from me, you weirdo." Molly twisted her head aside.

"I've had it up to 'ere for now." Fiona held a hand at her throat. "I'm with Geoff. Ready for a manicure and a massage. How 'bout you, husband? Gonna walk me out?"

"So long as these guys don't mind me carrying a little of this righteous 'erb with me." Dali looked quizzically at Wiz.

"Be our guest," said my ever-generous partner.

"If you're going out, Wiz, I better stay down here. Hold the fort, as it were." This is getting interesting, I thought. Just Emma and me down here for a few days, a few nights.

"I s'pose I could last a few more days." Geoff spoke first. "Long as I'm getting paid," he added tamely.

I cussed silently. "How 'bout you, darlin'?" I asked Molly.

"How could a girl refuse such a gracious invitation?" she replied.

"That's the plan, then," said Wiz, looking to keep the peace as always. "Dali, Fiona, Stilt, Nobby, and I will head out in the morning. You four can hang out down here and keep up the good work. I'll be back with supplies in two days. Anything you guys need?"

"Bottle of Herradura," said Geoff.

"Moisturizing cream. My skin's getting like sandpaper." Emma brushed her forearm. "And chocolate. This grass gives me a sweet tooth."

Next morning Wiz, Dali, Stilt, Nobby, and Fiona took off after coffee. Three Hawks had left a few days earlier. The remaining four of us went to work, shrouded in a pall of tension. Platitudes were all we could manage. It was another brilliant

Indian summer day, cloudless, pleasant in the shade, invigorating in the sun. We snipped doggedly at the rank of plants that had been hung upside down on a lattice of strings to dry in the deepest shade available, the direct Arizona sunlight being too harsh. The next phase, 'pruning' as the American growers called the process of preparing cured, cut grass for market, was what we toiled at. Trimming or manicuring would better describe the work of clipping the buds from the branches and a few dried leaves from the colas. Wiz was a perfectionist and rightly figured that quality preparation of our harvest would command the highest price on the street.

Through the treetops a woodpecker flew the queer undulating flight of his kind, landed in a pine and began hammering at the trunk. I lifted the binoculars. The barred back and fawn breast gave the clues as I leafed through the Peterson guide.

"A Gila woodpecker."

"Fascinating!" Geoff sniffed. "Jesus, Stylor, next you'll be wearing pebble-lens specs and an anorak."

"Anorak?" Molly gave Geoff a questioning glance, followed by a smile that would soften the heart of a wounded Cyclops.

"A cheap shitty coat these tossers wear, dweebs you'd say, who go bird- or train-spotting or whatever in England. I've had to put up with Stylor and his odd bird fancy for a decade now." Geoff's wink to Molly from under a Byronic lock draped across the temple, a ploy I'd seen my pal pull successfully with the fair sex many times before, was well received by the clever Molly, who a few years after the jag became a trial lawyer, with whom you didn't cross swords or briefs, in the Bay Area.

"May I?" Emma, ignoring both her husband's scathing opinion of the pursuit and his flirtation, trained the glasses on the bird as it noisily spiraled up the trunk.

"Lively chap. Nice little red cap he has, like a schoolboy. What does it say about him?" She shuffled her bottom toward me and, keeping her hands occupied with a branch of weed and the manicuring scissors, leaned in to read.

"Monogamous. Sometimes hawks for insects." She toppled slightly and laid her forearm on my thigh for balance, sending a charge of electricity through me. "Range, Sonoran Desert, central Arizona and New Mexico. Numbers decreasing." She pushed herself upright but stayed close as she resumed her work. The spot where her arm had lain glowed.

"What does it mean, 'hawks for insects'?"

"Chases, pursues them."

"I see." She looked up at the bird. "Let's see you hawk then."

I saw Molly catch Geoff's eye and raise her forehead mockingly. He smiled broadly back at her.

Silence fell. We snipped and brushed leaves from the buds, then carefully tossed the market-ready product into bags with rolled-down tops. The larger colas were set aside in a smaller bag, our "primo stash," and often I would stoop to admire this cream of the crop, groping my arms gently under the candlestick buds and lifting them up to bring the beauties and the pungent aroma to my face.

Around late morning, as I was thinking of brewing tea for this English and Anglicized gang, we heard the most dreaded sound for the wilderness marijuana grower: the rhythmic thump of a helicopter's rotors. Molly and Geoff scrambled to their feet and ran for cover. Emma made to rise also but I pressed her down by the shoulder; we were essentially invisible under the trees unless the chopper dropped well below the rim, and then it would be time for some drastic action.

The helicopter burst over the rim cliffs just north of the amphitheater. The racket was deafening. I thought I saw the chopper pitch into the canyon and I leaped to my feet. Through the binoculars I watched it hold its line, soar above the Anasazi ruin, and then disappear out of sight to clatter away to the north.

"Fookin' 'ell. What was 'e doing so low?" Geoff's face was pallid. I looked hard at my mate, now here with me in the mountains of Arizona, the two of us who'd shared so many nights out, so many travels, who'd chased so many girls together, who'd shared so much foolishness in our twenties through that shining decade, the roaring seventies. I remembered where I'd seen that pallor before: on our epic trek across Turkey and Iran and Afghanistan in '71, climaxing in Srinagar where we'd settled into a houseboat on Dal Lake puffing happily on the hubbly-bubbly, staring up at the Kashmiri night sky, a basket of hot coals between our thighs and a blanket wrapped tight against the Hindu Kush cold. And how I had felt a sea change in my life; that in pulling off this journey I had convinced myself that the world was there to be grabbed by the goolies, hauled in, and I now grasped *ananda*, Sanskrit for bliss. Yet the experience had been soured by Geoff's quailing before it; it had proved too much for him, it was all too far out in every sense, and despite my attempts to rouse him he never truly caught the thrill, never felt the pulse of excitement, as I had, from the lingering buzz of the journey and the swell of the world's greatest range beckoning from the north and beyond that range the fabulous high plateaus of central Asia, and he had argued for a dash back to Mykonos or Formentera, places where he knew the scene and where the Scandinavian birds would shed their threads after a couple of Cuba libres or a splash of ouzo and there was water skiing and darts and footie on the beach and . . . And now I could sense him paling at this more dangerous game, trying hard but lacking the bottle for it, and watching his wife slide toward his pal who, he knew, would without a twinge of compunction slip her a length and then lob her back in the manner in which we'd lobbed the barmaids and media babes around the Hammersmith gaffs and King's Heath drums for so much of the last stunning decade. The situation was spiraling beyond his control, and he felt those Isfahan fears flood back.

"Christ knows," I said. "Could be the sheriff, the Forestry Service doing logging research, joyriders from Payson checking out the Indian ruins, who knows. Just can't worry about these things." I sat down.

"Don't worry?" Molly was on edge. "That sound was god-damn scary."

"Do they often fly that low?" Emma slipped in beside me and went back to work, outwardly unfazed.

"A couple of times this year." I tried to sound casual. "I know it's pretty frightening but I really don't think it's anything to do with us. I've heard that most of the agencies assigned to bust the growers think we're trigger-happy cutthroats and they don't want confrontations. They generally fly the chopper in low over the patch to let the growers know they're coming, to give them a chance to clear out."

"How do you know they weren't doing just that?" said Geoff.

"Too high, mate. They'd fling that thing right over the tree-tops if they wanted to let us know the infantry was coming in."

"Hmm." He sank reluctantly back to the pruning.

"Too much for me," said Molly. "I need a break. Anyone up for a swim?"

"Maybe a plunge. That water'd freeze the balls off a brass monkey," said Geoff, and rose.

"We wouldn't want that to happen, now, would we." Molly gave Geoff a smile, which he returned—not, I thought, without mischief.

"Coming, Ems?" he asked.

"In a mo," said Emma.

"Go ahead. Got work to do," I added sanctimoniously.

"C'mon then, me old china plate." Molly tried her best Cockney rhyming slang, which I had tried my best to teach her, took Geoff by the arm, and, with a glance at Emma, led him away through the sycamores.

"Tee, tee, tee, tee, tee, teeeah." The lovely song of the canyon wren warbling down the scale broke the awkward silence.

"What a wonderful song. What's that chap's name?" Emma's enthusiasm seemed genuine, but I couldn't suppress the suspicion that I was being stitched up.

"That's the canyon wren. Never knew you had any interest in birds."

"My mum was a bit of a birdwatcher. I used to go up into the Dales with her as a girl. Hoping no one would see us while she had the binoculars out."

"I know that feeling. My father did the same."

"When I went down from uni, I started going out with her a lot. It gave us some common ground."

"And you warmed to her subject?"

"Exactly."

"Which genus do you like?" I asked presumptuously, hoping to test her.

"Don't you mean which order?" Her tone remained even. "The passerines. I love their songs. And it always seemed wonderful and sad that they have to migrate so far."

"Such small creatures surviving such arduous journeys."

"Of course, many don't." She looked at me. There was a pause. Then she drew a deep breath.

"Molly and I have been talking." She kept her head down. "She thinks your suggestion of the other night might not be such a bad idea after all."

"What suggestion?"

"Spare me the guile, Jeremy. It doesn't become you."

"Sorry."

"She says she hoped to develop a relationship with you but she knows it's never going to be reciprocated. You only want an affair. So, as a girl who likes to grab life by the . . . collar, she's warmed to the idea of a fling with Geoff."

I felt myself flushing, intimidated by this turn, blindsided by Emma's grasping of the nettle. Nothing from our years together had hinted at this trait but here she was, taking the initiative in certainly the most significant moment in her married life and, as it might prove, her entire life.

"At least while we're down here, anyway. In the canyon, away from dull cares."

"Just a quick fling then."

"Not necessarily." She bridled at the inference. "Neither of us is taking it lightly. Course, if you don't fancy it . . ."

"Emma Harrison, I've wanted to make love to you since I first set eyes on you in a Birmingham pub." I turned to face her. "If it should happen down here, which, after a certain farm in Devon, is my favorite spot on the planet, that would be unthinkably brilliant."

"It can." For the first time since the helicopter passed, she looked me in the eye. And we held, locked on, silently committing to the knowledge that the longing would be consummated, or dashed.

"What does Geoff have to say about all this?" I broke the mood.

"Nothing yet. Molly's just broaching the idea. Why don't we join them?"

"A quick dip might be refreshing."

"Oh Jeremy Stylor, sometimes I think you would have made a fine village vicar." And she let her laughter peal through the canyon and turned away down the path, gave a neat demi-plié, twirled, caught my eye, and danced away toward the creek where her husband was being propositioned by his best mate's squeeze.

They were sitting naked side by side on the little beach when we arrived. Molly turned and grinned. Geoff did neither. I stripped and stood for a moment bracing myself for the plunge. The pale thirteen stone of blubber accumulated in London had been whittled down to a sharp 160 pounds, the best fettle of my life. I watched Emma undress, felt the old man stirring and dove in before I was further exposed.

I swam to the rocks, turned, made a few strokes underwater, and came up next to Emma as she glided in holding her head up and her hair dry. She brushed against me and we swam alongside one another. At the far end of the pool, I held the rocks and she shivered, wrapped an arm around my waist, and pulled our flanks together.

I felt Geoff's glare, but when I chanced a glance their way, he and Molly were facing each other. I turned back to Emma and she angled her head to kiss and we touched mouths for the first time in public, as it were, and though, this time, I was prepared for it, the palpable pleasure she took in her immediate arousal again caught me on the wrong foot and I had to break off or I would have been unable to leave the pool for half an hour.

We swam back and beached beside the others. Geoff looked at me, a ghost of a smile creasing his mouth, and shook his head as if to say, "What the fook, mate, no point in rowing against the tide." He lifted his shoulders alternately, the practiced signal for the start of a song and I picked up the rhythm with him, waiting on the tune, and he launched quietly into one of our favorites.

"It ain't me, it's the people who say . . ." Robert Palmer, who we'd seen at the Hammersmith Odeon, just a year past.

"The men are leading the women astray."

And we were on our feet, giving it heaps, as we had a thousand times on a hundred different songs at innumerable parties, shebeens, and shindigs, only this time naked on a beach in the bottom of a beautiful canyon in Arizona about to swap partners, about to pull off, we hoped, the perfect crime, and about to blow a decade of friendship. We hit the turn in tandem, shaking our buttocks at the girls.

"That's right, the women are smarter,
Smarter than the men in every way!"

After a reprise of the chorus, the applause tumbled in and we bowed foolishly in three directions, to each of our wives, common law and statutory, and to each other, sharing a genuine grin. The girls stood and with a quick glance between them plunged into the creek and emerged, and then, in their individual ways, smoothed their hair back, tautened their bodies, and made it quite clear to the ne'er-do-well and the husband sat on the sand that these bodies were on offer to be taken in the very near future.

That afternoon, we worked for a few hours in a mood rich with expectation. Geoff was back in form. For all his understandable reluctance, he had enough nous to recognize his wife's firm resolve, enough skepticism to know he couldn't rely on his mate to do the decent thing, and enough *cojones* to wallow in the attention of a lovely woman who'd decided to bed him.

The handling of the grass caused a film of resin to build up on our fingertips. Now and again, we paused to scrape this into little rabbit turds that we then rolled into the main ball of hash, which, now the size of a hawk's egg, was kept in a bowl.

The canyon rang with deliciously nervous laughter and, lacking Wiz's foremanship, we jacked it in around late afternoon when the sun abandoned the clearing. As we strolled over to the camp for tea, Molly pulled me to one side of the path.

"Emma's very determined. We've been bullshitting quite a bit." She put her hands on my chest.

"So I hear."

"I think Geoff's very cute."

"Do you?"

"I think you're pretty cute too. Mighty cute in some areas."

"We all have our cross to bear."

Molly stepped back. "Let's cut the crap, Jeremy. I wouldn't have agreed to all this if I hadn't given up on you. When you first showed up in Jerome, I fell for you. I figured we could have a future. But I'm too New Age for you, too hippie, just too goddamn American . . . whatever. As soon as you've sold your share of this shit, you'll be off like a prom dress. Peru or Thailand or god knows where. So, I don't wanna hurt any more than I already do. Not sure being with Geoff will help." She paused. "Another of you goddamn cold Englishmen . . ." And with that she hurried away.

I tried to bring myself to rush after her, grab her, and pull her to me, to hold her close, to comfort her, to tell her that in my selfish and sublimated way I had truly loved her and that she had changed me for the better and taught me not to be frightened of her fair sisterhood, but my path was blocked by the impassable barrier of a public school education and untold generations of ingrained English reserve.

At the fireside we made tea but soon moved on to the remaining booze, the dregs of a bottle of *añejo*. I passed around a pipe filled with the "finger hash" and Geoff found a decent station out of Tulsa, Oklahoma. Soon we were all jiving round the fire to Dire Straits. Elton John roared in with "Saturday Night's Alright for Fighting," then there was more Robert Palmer, his brilliant cover of Toots and the Maytals' "Pressure Drop."

"We're havin' it large," chuckled Emma. "Just like the Moseley days."

"Havin' it large?" Molly whirled in beside Emma.

"Letting your hair down, going the full Monty. Not giving a toss!"

Molly flung herself alongside Emma and she took the lead as a man does in country and western style in the West, gripping Emma's fingers and playing her like a kid with a yo-yo, and Emma with her professional ballet background was a willing foil, letting herself be flung back and forth, the tie-dye skirt Molly had lent her swirling hip high, the lack of undies delightfully plain. Geoff and I cut down on the cavorting and formed a backing line, clicking fingers and swaying in unison as the girls danced.

"Oh pressure drop oh pressure, yeah eh, Pressure's gonna drop on you."

The girls swung close as the song finished and Molly pulled Emma against her and kissed her firmly on the lips. Emma, taken aback, pulled away, but then, out of curiosity it seemed, responded, angling and opening her mouth and giving herself fully to the contact for a spell as Geoff turned to me with a wide-eyed grin. The girls stepped back, Molly laughing, Emma licking her lips thoughtfully.

The little transistor radio lost the signal and we slumped down on the fireside benches. Quiet descended as Molly stoked the fire and prepped a frugal dinner.

"Lentil soup, anyone?" Molly gripped the saucepan handle with a stained sock and poured us all a serving in our cups. We sipped in silence, catching eyes lit by the firelight.

"We've got bread and cheese." I tried to lighten the mood. "Anyone fancy a cheese toastie?"

Shakes of the head and grunts were the only replies. It seemed as if all present, for reasons unique to each, wanted to get the evening over with. Finally, Molly rose and stretched; immediately Emma stood, strode up the short path to the two-man tent, grabbed my sleeping bag and hers from the other tent, and with a glance in the direction of the fireside said goodnight. I remained, riveted to the rock bench by my fear of and for Geoff.

Molly took Geoff's arm, but he stayed down.

"I'll be there shortly," he said.

Molly came across to me, lifted my chin, and pecked me on the cheek. "Good night, Jem. Sleep well."

"Yes, All right. You too," I stuttered, feeling Geoff's eyes locked on me from across the fire.

We sat in silence for minutes, hearing Molly arrange things in the tent.

"It'll be okay, mate. In the long run." He fingered a nostril and snorted a curl of phlegm into the flames. "But right this minute I'd like to . . ." He broke off.

"Cut my trollies off?"

"For starters."

"Well then, I'll be on me toes before you have the chance."

I stood. So did he.

"It feels as if we're coming to the crux of something, Style."

"I hear you." The American usage slipped out.

"Right. A binge. A mad jag, as Wiz would say." Geoff took a swig of tequila and tossed me the bottle. It came hard and I had to move sharply to snag it.

I drank and we looked at each other again. There was a long moment before he said, "Don't you hurt her, Style."

"Give me some credit, Geoff."

"You know what I mean." And he stared and I tried to hold his eyes but could not and turned on my heel and walked away to find the place his wife had chosen for us to have sex.

I expected to find her in the garden, but it was deserted. I was about to look down by the creek when I heard a sound above me. She had taken the steep deer trail to the outcrop where we often went for an evening toke. I climbed up. The sleeping bags and pads were laid out and two candles flickered from the rocks. She was undressing as I approached and gave a little start. She turned, her arms crossed at the hem of her cheesecloth blouse, paused a beat, then lifted it over her head. She unbuttoned the tie-dye skirt and stepped out of it. She stood, hands on hips, one foot splayed out, *deuxième position*, assured, expectant.

I soaked up the scene. This gorgeous woman, naked, lit by the candlelight and a waning moon, the rocks and desert shrubs forming a sheltered clearing, the canyon walls looming black overhead, then back to Emma, her blond halo catching the light.

The uneasiness which I had tried to expunge reared its ugly head, as another ugly head failed to do so.

"You're absolutely sure about this." I kicked off my shoes, stepped close, and shed my sweater and T-shirt.

"Jem," she scolded me. "Do just get on with it."

"Could you give me a hand with this? I'm having trouble. Must be the tension of the evening." I looked at her as I fumbled with the belt of my jeans.

"Poor boy." She started on the belt, then dropped to her knees and swept my jeans and underdogs to my ankles. She paused, staring at the obvious, and I tensed my thighs hoping for the obvious, as my normally reliable old feller called for some encouragement.

She grinned up at me, ovaled her lips and was about to oblige when there came from below us a rasping growl guaranteed to shrink the member of Achilles. At first, I thought it was Geoff or Molly venting the joy of their lovemaking, but then came a basso profundo growl, followed by the distinctive, sawing cough that distinguishes the jaguar from the cougar.

"That's not . . . Is it?" Emma tilted her face up to me, her mouth wide in disbelief.

I considered conjuring some lie, afraid the truth would ruin my chances for this evening. I opted for the truth.

"Yes. It's the jaguar."

"Christ almighty." She threw herself under the covers, snatched them up to her chin and stared frog-eyed at me. "The mad jag." She gave a throaty chuckle, and I was again amazed at the transition of the timid Yorkshire lass into this passionate creature of the American woods. She reached out. "Come to my arms, my beamish boy, and save me from the jaguar."

I laughed at her quick twist of the Lewis Carroll line and stepped to join her, forgetting I was hobbled, and crashed down. We both cracked up and I flung the bedclothes aside and snuggled in beside her, pulled her to me, searching for her lips, her mouth, her tongue, desperate for the urgency of the garden exchange, longing to discover how the exhilaration of that encounter could carry over into the more complex area of carnality.

She came at me, pressing me down, her thigh flung across my belly, her body tensed against me, the swell of her pubic mound rasping my hip.

I felt overwhelmed, overstimulated, and held her back to look at her face.

She sniffed and turned onto her tummy, but looked over her shoulder and smiled. I drew my fingers slowly down her spine, clawing my hand as I approached the lumbar region, raking the ridged muscles that paralleled her spine with my nails. She took a long breath as I started up the swell of her bottom, her thighs parting, her hips lifting as I angled my hand to find her center. Her gasps shortened as I probed and her body shifted to accommodate my hand and my fingers found her trigger and she pivoted up seeking the stimulus, her spine now canted sharply at the small of the back, nature's loveliest tripod formed by her angled thighs and arched torso, and I sat up to look down at her nether pout, as abandoned, as pink, as hungry as a fledgling's gape. Her breathing became shallow as I worked to deliver her release, my own arousal now painfully taut. As her panting rose in a crescendo and her flailing hand found a twig which she clamped between her teeth, I realized that any pathetic hope I'd had that this would be a quick fling, a fortnight fuck, a brief dalliance, was pure bullshit, and that, even though we'd yet to consummate, I had found the woman of my schemes and that woman was spoken for and I heard Dylan's lines from *Blood on the Tracks* echo through the canyon:

> *I like the smile on your fingertips*
> *I like the way that you move your hips*
> *I like the cool way you look at me*
> *Everything about you is bringing me misery.*

11

The rhythmic clatter of a helicopter pitching into the canyon was on this occasion, three weeks later, welcome. Emma, Geoff, Dali, Nobby, and I were sitting in the trees at the edge of the clearing a couple hundred yards north of the garden, well wrapped against the pre-dawn November chill. Beside us were ricks of boxes, a good percentage of our harvest.

We jumped to our feet and I held the walkie close. Dali and Geoff, nervous as cats, started to jog the boxes from under the trees into the clearing.

"Hang on," I yelled above the increasing din. "Let's make sure it's one of ours."

It sounded a shade dramatic, but Wiz and I had discussed the protocol and we were to wait for his word.

"Molly, do you read me?" Stilt's voice crackled into the morning air, above the din of the chopper as it came into range. I thought of Molly on the rim, raven hair tied back from the high-cheekboned face, deep hazel eyes scouring the mesa, and wondered why I was such a snobby twat and why I didn't realize the end of my pulling years was fast approaching and I'd better settle down soon.

"Read you Stilt, loud and clear." Molly spoke clearly.

"Everything A-OK?"

"Affirmative. The coast is clear on top."

"Copy that." I imagined Stilt nodding across the cockpit to Wiz with a twitch of a grin, and Wiz acknowledging him, stoked to be pulling off the blag in the way he had hoped, whisking the crop out of the canyon in an expensive helicopter before the sheriff had dragged his Mormon lardass out of the sack.

"Stylor, do you read me?" Stilt was now taking charge of the operation as smoothly as he would the removal of a wisdom tooth.

"Affirmative. Got a good copy."

"All set down there?"

"Standing by at the LZ."

"10-4, we're coming in."

I watched the helicopter swing to the north over the Anasazi ruin and thought of Wiz juggling collective and cyclic, the chopper's controls. He brought the Bell Ranger over the clearing from the north and turned a flash 180 up-canyon into the expected breeze, even though the plastic tape I had tied to the crown of a pine hung limp.

The wash from the rotors thrashed the piñons and tore the leaves from the ground. We stood back and protected our eyes. Wiz's face lit up his side of the bubble and I grinned back. As Wiz slid the Bell Ranger down, chaos hit the glade: branches were flung like feathers; the racket from the turbos had us pawing our ears; the top boxes of grass were flung among the trees; Nobby and I mantled over the remaining boxes; the others crouched forward, like sailors in a storm.

As soon as the runners touched, Wiz lowered the revs and the typhoon eased to a gale. Stilt's door burst open and he ran toward us in a crouch, and I knew he saw himself rushing into a hot LZ and reckoned what a loss he was to the great U.S. military machine.

He stopped in front of us and smiled self-consciously. "Good morning, all," he yelled.

"Morning." And we all grinned at one another for a few seconds before Stilt grabbed a box and placed it on the stretcher frame at the side of the chopper.

"Keep 'em coming," he yelled, and we ran back and forth, ducking unnecessarily under the invisible blades of death as Wiz kept the engine idling. When the stacks were three high, we threw shock cords over the load and clipped them to the frame. Finally, two tarps, which Wiz had custom ordered, were draped over each stack and tied down.

"How many more do we got?" Wiz shouted to me.

"Another twenty-five in the garden."

"We'll drop these and be back in an hour." Wiz brought the revs up and we shied away as he whirled the craft through a tight bank, gave us a quick nod, and flung the chopper across the treetops and down the canyon.

We watched the machine race away over the sycamores and then we five set off along the streambed, warm now due to the excitement and the movement. An impromptu race broke out. Dali had a good start and bounded ahead; Geoff and Emma were hot on his tail. I eased in to the rear, passing Nobby, who strolled along, oblivious to such foolishness. Emma's wonderful nimbleness kept her in the running, but the boys laid on the power.

I caught Emma, grabbed her arm, and pointed to the right where the old creekbed cut a direct path through the ox-bow curve of the present watercourse. I led her through the shortcut, boulder-hopping at first, until I realized with delight that this was one of our last times in the canyon; we needn't care about footprints anymore as we were about to fly the last of the crop out. I let out a whoop, and charged up the bank through a narrow ravine, then plunged down again in a long steep slide and ran the last few steps into the manicuring copse as the boys panted up through the sycamores.

"Fucker!" said Dali.

"Twat!" said Geoff, and we all stood gasping and laughing and throwing off our jackets and basking in the thrill of seeing the chopper accomplish this crucial part of the operation without a hitch.

I was stooping to lash the remaining boxes to the pack frames when a rasping growl followed by Emma's shriek of alarm snapped me round. On the rocky outcrop of the ravine above Emma's head, the unmistakable brindled coat of the jag, lit by the first rays of light to crest the eastern rim, stood, tensed to leap. His huge orange eyes blazed, the shoulder muscle rose behind his head, fangs shone as he bellowed, the amber coat glowed in the magic hour light. There was a magnificence to the terror he caused.

"Dali, mate, the fast ball," I hissed, remembering him showing me the "heat" that had earned him a place on the mound for the Air Force Academy in Colorado Springs. But Dali had already scooped up a river rock and with the briefest of knee lifts launched the most important pitch of his life.

The rock whistled past the mad jag's skull to strike a thudding blow against his shoulder, throwing him fractionally to one side as Emma leaped across the slope and tumbled into the streambed. The huge cat stumbled on the bank, regained his footing, and turned, to be met with a barrage of missiles and yells as we pelted him with whatever we could grab and waved sticks in the air and screamed until our throats were hot.

The old jag backed away and stood for a moment staring at us. The stocky pit-bull build, the massive front paws and limbs, were sufficient to deter any advance on our part, but when he displayed the terrifying span of his bite and let go another guttural scream and the tell-tale wheezing bark the three of us froze again. With a dismissive flick of the great head and an almost forlorn backward glance, he limped away.

Geoff dashed over to where Emma lay in the shallows of the creek.

"Christ, love. Are you all right?" He lifted his wife from the shallows.

She stood, painfully raising an arm and rubbing the shoulder joint.

"Christ. I think that big bastard *is* a little mad." And she gave a nervous laugh.

"Goddamn right, he's a crazy fucker. You clock the size of 'im?"

Dali threw a glance back down the creek. "We better stick together. Case he circles back for a shot at one of us."

"But did he actually make to attack?" Emma asked. "I just got the heck away."

"He didn't move till Dali nailed him with the stone," I said. "Maybe Wiz was right. He is our guardian spirit."

"Jesus Christ, Stylor." Geoff spat out the words. "Never thought I'd hear you spouting this New Age sewage."

"Damn straight, Geoffrey man," Dali said firmly. "You heard the fucker growling, Style, and saw him face us down. Some goddamn guardian!"

After a moment, I said, "He looks a little run-down since I last saw him. Wonder if the old feller'll make it through the winter?"

"Let's hope he bites the dust pretty smartish. I may be down here growing next year." Geoff gave me his pained look.

"Keep your eyes skinned." I gathered up the other boxes and stooped to tie them to the pack frames. "Emma, give me a hand, would you?"

Dali climbed the bank from where the jag had leaped, mumbling his customary commentary, selected an arsenal of rocks, and warmed up by flashing a few across the creek. Geoff took a vantage point on the opposite bank.

"Okay?" I looked at Emma and realized the question was wasted. The sheen of her eyes made them lapis-dark, the nostrils had a tensed flare, her lips were drawn back in a blend of incredulity and delight, her rib cage rose and fell, pressing her bra-less breasts against her blouse as she flung off her jacket.

"Okay? Okay?" She almost yelled it, causing the others to twist their heads toward her. "A fookin' jaguar. They'll never bloody believe me back in the Moseley Arms." And she threw her head back and laughed heartily.

I looked across at Geoff and he shook his head, startled by the strange woman his wife had become.

"Hold this for me, please." I balanced the pack frame upright.

"Glad to." She dropped to her knees and grabbed the pack. I worked to strap on the boxes, our faces a foot apart. I felt her eyes following mine, saw her switch her eyeline briefly in Geoff's direction, then she leaned forward to kiss me full on the mouth.

"That's for bringing me to Arizona, to the canyon." Her smile was effulgent. I could only grin back, stupefied.

The night of the "wife swap" had not ended quite as expected—at least, from my point of view. Emma's orgasm had been so startlingly profound that it had replaced the male climax in forming the normal finality of the act. We had spooned closely in the aftermath and though she had made gestures to continue making love, I had happily declined; she had fallen asleep in my arms.

For the first time in my life I had felt some misgivings about getting a grip of a lovely woman. It wasn't that I had never felt any guilt about bedding my best friend's wife; of course I had. It had merely seemed justifiable because of the history. Emma had come into both our lives at the same time; Geoff getting across the pub to her first simply gave him first dibs on her; and the marriage certificate was so much paper. My reluctance, however transitory, was born out of realizing that Emma's unbridled sensuality, not to mention her sharp wit and our shared love of language, would lead me into an affair of which I would lose control. To put it bluntly, I was petrified at the prospect of sliding once more between the sleeping bags with Emma.

As we made it back to the LZ with the last boxes of our crop, Molly's voice startled me from the radio.

"Jem, come back, Jem."

"Go for Jem."

"Honey, there's a truck out on the mesa."

Oh Christ, just as everything seemed blessed.

"What's its twenty?"

"Coming up from the Relic Creek Road."

"Have you seen it?"

"No. But I can hear him getting closer. What shall I do?"

"As soon as you hear the helicopter, start trying to contact Wiz and Stilt. Do you copy?"

"Copy."

"When you've raised them, tell them about the truck and let them decide whether to continue or abort. Do you copy?"

"Copy that. Let Wiz know about the truck and let him decide. Right?"

"Right, darlin'. Exactly. You've done splendidly."

"Thanks, hon. Standing by on top. Where all girls should be!"

"That's my Moll."

We sat in the clearing in silence for several minutes. A light breeze ruffled the branches. The canyon was quiet at this time of year. A few juncos foraged in the bushes. An Abert's squirrel, recognizable by the black tips of his pointed ears, worked the edge of the clearing until the radio barked and he dashed away.

"Stilt, do you copy? Stilt?" Molly's voice betrayed her concern.

We all hunched closer to the radio. We could hear the distant drone of the helicopter.

"Stilt, do you copy? Stilt?"

I pressed the transmit button. "Keep trying, Molly," I said unnecessarily, adding to the tension.

"Stilt, do you copy? Stilt?"

"Go ahead, Molly." Stilt's voice had its usual cheerful tone.

"Stilt, there's a truck driving out on the mesa. Do you copy?"

A pause, then, "Copy that. We got a visual."

"Jem says you should decide whether to continue or abort."

"Copy that. Stand by."

We listened to the Bell Ranger clattering over the mesa. After a couple of minutes, it burst into the airspace above the canyon.

"Jem, Molly, do you both copy?" Stilt's clean enunciation carried over the airwaves.

I let Molly answer first, then responded.

"The truck is heading out on the mesa. He's too close to our canyon. It's too risky to drop in now. We're going to abort. Do you copy?"

"Copy that," said Molly.

"Copy," I said with a sigh. "We'll schlep this last lot out on foot."

"Okay. Take your time. Be safe."

"10-4." I lowered the walkie and looked at the others.

"Bummer." Dali shook his head.

"We'll have to hike the rest of it out to the vehicles ourselves. Course you don't have to. Obviously there's some risk involved."

"Not to mention we have to drive some of it to Stilt's in my van?" Geoff was looking at me intently, a frown shadowing his brow. "You can't get it all in your Scout." Geoff had bought a VW camper van for the trip to Baja we were all planning for Christmas.

"Right. So how about a grand each to you and Emma for driving a few boxes to the stash?"

"Two thousand dollars to risk maybe ten years in the Arizona state penitentiary." Geoff's face was hard.

"What's it worth, then?" I asked, looking from him to Emma.

"What do you think, Ems?" he asked.

"It's a lot of money but a lot of risk. The money would be good for our trip. How about four thousand, Jem, two grand each?"

"Fine." We shook hands. I turned to Dali, great hulking bear of a man, his afro ruffled into a wild halo by the wilderness living.

"How about you, mate? A triple day's pay for hiking the stuff out?"

"Six hundred. Cool." We shook.

Three hours later I was giving Molly a genuinely appreciative hug on the rim. Below us, spread out down the tumble of boulders that formed the brutal path from the creek to the mesa, the others struggled upward. I helped Molly break her little camp, belayed Dali up the cliff, and threw the rope down for Geoff and Emma. Then Nobby climbed up smoothly, without a need for the rope.

Once they were all on top, we took a breather. Dali told Molly about the jag attack. Molly, eyes bulging as the story unfolded, jumped up and gave Emma a tight hug.

"Dammit, sister! That's a hell of a rush for an English gal. Jem's told me about the jag before and I'd like to have seen it. But not that goddamn close."

"What happened to the truck, Molly?" Geoff pulled on a sweater as a November breeze swept the mesa.

"Drove back out as you guys made the climb."

"Just one of those damn crazy coincidences," said Dali. "Fuck. We could've just waited and saved busting our asses hauling the shit up this sorry-assed jumble of rocks. No wonder you call it the Salt Mine!"

"Who knows?" I said. "Anyway, it's too windy now for flying canyons. We need to figure out how to get to the vehicles."

We sat around snacking on Wha-Guru Chew energy bars and pemmican bars bought at the Mount Hope health food store in Cottonwood. There was fruit and Dr. Bronner's cheese puffs and vegetable chips. While we ate, we planned the crossing of the mesa, on which there could be any number of vehicles or, worse, hunters afoot. Our loads, boxes lashed high on pack frames, were miserably conspicuous, and the vehicles were parked across the other side of Relic Creek Road. Molly would run interference ahead and call us on, from cover to cover, on the walkie. I shook hands with Nobby, who was heading back into the canyon to tighten up the camp and garden for winter. The others bid the Swiss farewell and looked anxiously at me to give the word.

"Let's go." I shouldered my load and looked back into the canyon with not a little regret. Had I made my last visit to this unforgettable place, which had played such a crucial role in my recent life? I stared down and thought I heard a guttural roar. Was that the mad jag signaling his delight at our final departure, or offering a valediction?

"Jeremy. C'mon." Emma's voice turned me away from the rim, I thought, for the last time.

The crossing of the mesa was nerve-wracking but, apart from the grinding of a vehicle in the distance, mercifully uneventful and, coupled with the climb from the canyon, unmercifully exhausting. By the time we flopped down under a piñon to wait for Molly to cross the road and check that the coast was clear, the three sherpas were on their chinstraps.

"Damn, man. I'm blown out on the trail," gasped Dali, quoting Dylan, and sprawled star-shaped on the ground against the pack frame, brawny arms still through the shoulder straps. Geoff slugged from his water bottle, grim-faced. Emma staggered in, dropped her pack and, using a branch as a barre, groaned through a few ballet stretches. Even though I'd made this grueling hike some forty times this year, I too was knackered.

"We should pull into the Fruitown café for breakfast," Dali said.

"I don't know about that, man," I said. "Not with these loads on board."

"Jesus, Style," said Geoff. "Bloody slave driver. We need some snap. We've hardly had a bite past our lips today."

"All right, all right. Just don't tell Wiz. It's against orders."

Molly called us forward and we hurried across the Relic Creek Road and down the quarter mile of the Mimbres Canyon jeep trail to the vehicles. Sixteen of the boxes filled the luggage compartment and much of the back seat of my little Scout, to the roof. The remaining nine went on to the bed of Geoff and Emma's camper.

"Jeez, that stuff smells killer." Dali was squeezed into the back seat of the Scout.

"And we sealed it in three layers of poly bags."

We drove up the dirt road and came into the outskirts of Fruitown, glancing at the holiday cabins where some of the owners were sealing them up for the winter. After the disappointment of losing the chopper and the hard work of the hike, my spirits lifted as we cleared the vicinity of the canyon. I began to hope we could make the drive over the General Crook Trail and down to Stilt's without further sweat.

We came onto the paved road, past the oldest schoolhouse in Arizona, a fire station, and a trailer park restricted to "seniors only." We parked in front of the Fruitown Lodge. Once in a while we had stopped at this timber-built café when we emerged from the canyon, but generally Wiz argued against it and we simply grabbed some drinks and snacks from the general store across the road.

I slammed the doors of the Scout and hoped the smell of the grass wouldn't leak. I was worried that we might actually carry the aroma with us into the café. An elderly couple sat in a slatted wooden booth. A guy in a denim shirt and tractor cap hunched over his meal at a counter stool. Molly picked a table near the wood stove. Clichéd Western artwork hung on the walls: a cabin in the aspens; a grizzled mountain man rode through a snowscape, leading a packhorse; a cougar gazed from a crag at distant travelers.

"Still serving breakfast?" Molly asked the old battleaxe of a waitress when she designed to leave her post leaning on the counter next to the cash register and shuffle to our table.

"Yup," she said, twisting her withered boat race to the clock, which, I will remember to my grave, said five to eleven—as the following fifty-three minutes will always rank as the longest of my life. We ordered and, as the crone limped away, I watched Geoff's phisog blanch as he stared lizard-eyed through the window behind me. I turned, in slow motion, and froze. Parked alongside the old Scout was the tan Chevy Blazer emblazoned with the logo of the Gila County Sheriff, and alighting, if such a term can be applied to a bull of a man of 280 pounds, was the sheriff himself, Willard Farr.

He walked around to the back of the Scout, checked out the license plate, peered inside, and, it seemed, from my POV through the dirty window, paused to sniff the air like a dog pointing. He came to the front of the vehicle, looked at the tires, studied Geoff's Veedub, and headed for the café.

We stared at one another in stunned silence as the door swung wide, the wood floor creaking under the sheriff's bulk. He surveyed the room, checked out the other customers, and lumbered toward us.

"Morning, sheriff," said Molly cheerily.

"Morning. Which one o' y'all's drivin' that Scout?" He stood close to the table, his gut cantilevering over the broad leather belt which held a panoply of tools of his trade: spray can, handcuffs, walkie-talkie, and a very large handgun.

I considered attempting my best American accent, but reckoned that if the gig was up I might as well stick with the truth—at least, some of it.

"That's my vehicle, officer." I looked him in the eye and wondered if he remembered me from our previous encounters.

"I am goin' to have to ask you to step outside." A chill ran through my chest.

"What for, if I may ask?" I stood up.

"Just step outside, sir."

I gave the others a lame wave as the huge man held the door and I walked out from the dark room into the Arizona sunshine as reluctantly as any death row inmate on his last dawn.

"I need to see your registration and driver's license." He peered down at me through cheap mirror shades.

"Is there a reason for this?" I blurted out.

"Your license plate expired in September."

First the relief, a huge wave. Then the bitter recrimination. Jesus effin' Christ, if we all got busted because I had forgotten to do the registration, oh god in heaven I would never forgive myself—and nor, more to the point, would the others. I opened the door, groped in the glove compartment for the papers and slammed the door in a vain attempt to stop the lovely incriminating stench of our grass drifting under the sheriff's snot-flecked nostrils. I reckoned that the olfactory perception of a teetotaling, non-smoking Mormon was frighteningly sharp.

"Oh, good lord, officer, I've been meaning to do that for simply ages." David Dimbleby would have been proud of the Sloane Square jive. "To tell the truth, I'm not quite sure how one does those things in this country."

"You ain't from round these parts then?" He looked over the top of the registration form at me and sniffed the air.

"No. Actually I'm from England. Just popped over the pond on a flying visit."

"Is that so." He looked at the strange international diver's license that didn't carry a photo. "So what all are you packin' in this truck? In them boxes?"

To this day I'm convinced my heart stopped beating while I thought of and spoke my response. "I'm just giving the girlfriend a hand to move." I'd lost so much moisture from my mouth I was barely able to croak out the words.

"Where's she moving to?" He peered through the passenger window.

"Jerome," I said before any cogent thinking could suggest caution at mentioning the hippie town on the hill to a Latter-day Shithead sheriff.

"Jerome, eh?" he said, and glared at me for a moment. "You been here but a short spell yet you gotten yourself a girlfriend already?"

Christ, he didn't miss a trick!

"I met her a couple years ago," I stammered. "In Europe. Greece actually." The lies were mounting and I tried, desperately, to keep tabs on my bullshit.

"Awful tidy, your girlfriend."

"Beg your pardon, officer?"

"All her chattels neatly boxed. No furniture. No clothes hanging."

"She is very organized. I get a bollocking if I don't keep her place shipshape." I tried a fake chuckle but only a dry gasp emerged.

Farr stared down at me for a long moment; the sunglasses hiding his eyes added to the terror flooding my senses. "I'm going to have to cite you. If you report to your nearest police station within five days with a new registration there won't be any further charges."

He held out the clipboard and pointed for me to sign. My hand shook like Guy Fawkes signing his confession. He ripped off my copy, handed it to me, and drew a quizzical breath into his nose.

"I'll take care of this right away, officer. So sorry to trouble you." I held the café door open, encouraging the fat bastard away from my truck and the goddamned invidious smell as fast as possible. He paused for a moment before entering the café. I followed him in and slumped down at the table as the guys followed me with riveted stares.

"Registration's run out," I said, and knew that if looks could kill I was suffering four tortured deaths at that moment. Minutes of an excruciating silence followed before I got up and asked the old bag at the cash register for some coins for the newspaper machine. I strolled outside as casually as possible, slotted the quarter for the *Arizona Republic*, and contemplated making a dash for the pine trees just across the side road. I glanced through the window and saw the four faces glaring at me, picked up two papers, and went inside.

I offered sections of the rag around and reckoned that if the cook didn't get the food out here pronto, I would run screaming into the kitchen and beat him to a pulp.

"Christ. Reagan won," said Dali and looked around at us.

"My god, so he did." Geoff shook his head.

"In a landslide," Emma said.

"Poor old Jimmy." Molly pushed out her lower lip. "The Iran hostages sank him."

I said nothing despite my disgust at the news. I didn't want to promote a political discussion among these lefties in front of a man I assumed to be a solidly conservative Reaganomics-loving sheriff glowering at us from the next table, and enough illegal drugs in our vehicles to make the highlight of the sheriff's career if he discovered them.

From his table, Willard Farr continued to size us up. I cursed the cook for a worthless sluggard.

"At least the Suns won. Just." Dali flicked the *Arizona Republic*.

"Close game?" I asked, eager to bring the conversation round to something bland.

"Yeah. 108 to 109. Over the Pacers. Johnson made a couple of free throws at the end to clinch it."

The tension seemed to ease a notch.

"*Honeysuckle Rose* is coming to the Cottonwood theater, Jem." Molly pointed to the entertainment page. "Let's go see it. I love Willie Nelson."

"I'd rather see *Ordinary People*," I said, scanning the page in search of more small talk. "See how Redford measures up as a director."

"They say Donald Sutherland plays a wonderful part." Emma forced a brave smile across the table.

"More coffee, anyone?" The waitress offered the glass jug. Dali held his cup; she poured slowly.

"Strange perfume one of you's wearing," the shrew mused. "Kinda like the smell after my grandson Frankie cuts the grass at my place."

Out of the corner of my eye I saw the sheriff's chin come up. I stared at the gang as their faces registered the tension with chameleon eyes or downcast faces creased with fear at the woman's comment.

"It's new from Estée Lauder," Emma chimed in, as everyone's nerves jarred again. "It's called Autumn Leaves."

"I'll have to get some for my eldest." The woman turned to me. "Where's your friend today?"

"Which friend?" Sweat beaded my brow; disquiet clawed my thighs.

"The feller with the pointy beard. Looks like a carny."

Farr's stubbled skull swiveled toward me.

"Oh, him. Haven't seen him in a while. He left town, I guess." My faltering attempt to brush Wiz out of the picture tailed off, and on the silence that followed, suspense rose like a hawk on a thermal.

Finally, the bell rang on the ledge to the kitchen and the simple statement "Order up" sounded like a governor's reprieve. The old bird reacted like cold honey, slowly folding the pages of her paper, gathering the plates on her arm, and wandering over to our table.

We wolfed the food down.

"Someone cover the tip." I strode to the cash register and waited in an agony of suspense for the crone to add up the figures.

"You c'mon back now." The old dear slowly doled out the change.

"If I'm over this way I sure will," I said, and heard the sheriff shift his bulk in the chair.

"Say, young feller." The massive lantern jaw lifted slowly to punctuate the question. "Didn't I see you in that Scout on Relic Creek Road a week or so back?"

The others stopped in their tracks: Molly, in the doorway; Geoff reaching behind her, hand on door; Emma halfway across the room; Dali, rising, coffee cup twixt table and lip—a frozen tableau.

"Maybe," I croaked. "I did venture out to the hot springs one time."

"Why would you go there?"

"Bad knee, officer. Old rugby injury. I find the waters ease the pain."

"Weren't you going swimming?" Jesus fuckin' Christ, the bastard had the memory of an elephant!

"No . . . no," I stammered. "Water was too cold."

I pressed on toward the door, shepherding the gang ahead of me, feeling the sheriff's glare on my back and expecting his harsh call to "Hold it right there." We made it into the sunshine, barely avoiding the temptation to rush to the vehicles.

I started the engine and was immediately assailed with a torrent of vitriol.

"You lazy-assed fuck," Dali screamed from the back seat.

"You worthless fookin' gobshite," Geoff howled over the walkie.

Molly simply loosed a long primal scream as I drove out of the lot and started up the hill. I said nothing, concentrating on getting the old Scout rolling as fast as I could up into the pine country. I rolled down the window and spat, and guzzled water and spasmed a dry heave, and tried to breathe deeply. Abuse rained down as everyone vented the pressure from the agonizing breakfast in a caff with a life-ruining threat seated across from us and the pungency of the grass permeating every thought.

We groaned up out of the valley through the switchbacks. At a dirt lay-by, which gave a clean shot down to Fruitown, I jumped out, propped my elbows on the hood and trained my binoculars on the front of the café. Dali stood beside me shaking his head and muttering, "Goddamn, goddamn, that was close. Amazing that Mormon oaf didn't sniff the gear. Redneck asshole probably never got close to any . . ."

Through the window I watched the sheriff digging into his biscuits and gravy. The old dear brought over the coffeepot and stood by his table. I watched her hold the officer in conversation for a long while.

Then, as time and action slowed, I saw the huge man splutter coffee and shove back his chair. The woman stepped away as he flung down his napkin and disappeared from view.

Through the magnified frame of the binoculars, I saw Willard Farr burst from the café and snatch open the Blazer door. Then, with a squeal of rubber and a howl of siren, he roared up the road toward us.

12

"Holy goddamn fuckin' Jesus Christ, Stylor!" Dali stared down at me, eyes bulging, gob wide, as the banshee shriek of the siren echoed through the rim country, rising in volume as it approached. "The fat fuck's onto us!"

I stared at the gang of friends I'd brought into this mess and felt a stab of horrified responsibility. Molly's scared brown eyes shone through the windscreen of the Scout. Geoff and Emma gaped from the Volkswagen.

I palmed my temples in a moment of blind panic, then started yelling.

"Molly. Drive the truck down there!" I pointed to an overgrown logging trail into the forest. "Geoff, go after her. Get out of sight!" Molly splashed through a puddle by the cattle grid, Geoff followed, and they soon drew a dreadful scraping noise as they forced the vehicles through pine boughs.

"Grab a branch, man," I yelled at Dali, and we began sweeping away the tracks of the vehicles as the wail from the sheriff's truck grew louder and Dali mumbled and swept and cursed.

"Goddamn you, you Limey loony, you 'n' your dumbass scams. I just wanna do my artwork, screw my old lady, 'n' you drag..."

"Let's go. GO!" And we ran through the trees and flung ourselves down into the brush as Farr's Blazer screamed into view. Peering through live oaks, I saw the truck brake hard alongside the turnout and clearly saw Willard Farr's square, reddened face looking toward us. Would he see the disturbed water of the puddle? Could he make out the tracks we hadn't been able to sweep? Jesus, oh dear fucking Jesus, help us out here! I lowered my face into the dirt and prayed.

A shriek of tire rubber told me my prayers were answered, and I lifted my head and saw the Blazer roar away. Dali and I sprinted to the vehicles and jumped aboard. We crashed back up the road and turned onto the highway heading downhill, back to Fruitown.

"Where the fuck are you taking us?" Molly shouted.

"Just calm down a moment," I shot back. "Let me think."

We raced down through the curves and turned by the Fruitown Lodge back onto the Relic Creek Road. I was ahead of Geoff and, as he slowed to make the turn, I heard the wail of a siren and for an awful moment thought the sheriff had realized we'd doubled back. I grabbed the walkie.

"Geoff. Step on it, mate. Turn on Relic."

"Copy that." It was Emma's voice, sounding crisp.

Another cruiser, presumably summoned by the sheriff over the airwaves to join the pursuit, tore past the junction. I slowed, peering in the wing mirror, expecting Geoff and Emma to get nabbed, but the state trooper's black-and-white raced on up the hill.

I gunned the old truck down the paved road and onto the dirt. A plan was beginning to form in my fried brain. I turned onto a side road and pulled up at the spot where we had loaded the weed less than two hours before, though it seemed like a lifetime. Geoff swung the van in beside me and we all leaped out. They stared at me in various states of agitation.

I tried a smile but it wouldn't form. "I'm going to take this jeep trail. It goes through the headwaters of Relic and comes out at the bottom of the General Crook Trail. We'll put all the gear in my truck."

"We can't get all the boxes in your truck." I saw a cloud lift from Geoff's face, and Emma's lightened.

"We'll take it out of the boxes. Just toss it in there in the Ziplocs," I said.

"Let's do it." Molly flung open the back door of the Scout and began emptying the boxes.

"That's a hell of a trail. Thirty miles and change of bad road. It'll take all night. People say it doesn't go through." Dali stuffed the plastic bags of weed under the seats. "Ever driven it?"

"No. Wiz and I talked about it as an escape route. I'll just have to try it."

"Jeez." Molly's voice was still strained from the terror of the close calls. "You can't go it alone. You'll need help in the washouts, you could get a flat, bust an axle. God knows what."

"It would be nice to have a hand, certainly, but I've got a good set of tools and the winch. I don't want to put you lot at more risk." I looked around this unlikely mob of friends and lovers working to transfer the contraband, and managed a smile. "Don't everyone look so worried. We gave 'im the slip, didn't we?"

"But we nearly ended up in a shitload of bother thanks to your slackness." Geoff dumped the contents of a box into the Scout and stamped the cardboard flat.

"Okay, okay! But look. Clean out the van; make some smudge sticks and burn 'em to kill the smell. Then drive straight down to the hot springs, wash your clothes, wash the van. And if you get stopped by the rozzers, you'll be squeaky clean."

Now a plan was set, the tension eased. The lovely perfume, which had got us dangerously close to a rake of bother, dominated the immediate surroundings as we worked.

"Jeez, man, that was a damn close-run thing back there." Dali kept up a sotto voce commentary. "And that sheriff, what a porker he is. Mean looking sumbitch, wouldn't want to fall foul of . . ."

Soon the Scout was packed to the gills. We flattened out the boxes and slipped them around the outside of the load to disguise the contents of the truck from a cursory glance. Each bag contained a quarter pound of buds and four bumper stickers with Dali's drawing of the jag. Lastly, we spread trash bags on top of the pile and slammed the doors.

"You can't take this back road on your lonesome, Jeremy my boy. You need some backup, man." Dali's face thrust toward me.

"I'll go with you, Jem." I turned to see a brave smile on Emma's face. Of all the gang, she had shown most equanimity during the panic. It seemed she had the head for this daft game, and there would be added pleasures of her company on the gnarly drive ahead.

"Good," I said, and this time my smile was effortless. "Love to have you along."

"You can't go, Emma," said Geoff.

"Why not?"

"You don't know anything about fixing punctures or using winches."

"Oh, and you're the master mechanic? When we get a puncture in Brum you're the first to call the rescue lorry."

"Whoa, whoa." Molly stepped in. "Let's not have a domestic right here. We're all stressed out enough for one day. I think Geoff should go." I wasn't sure if her motive was to recommend a better partner for the journey or to prevent me being alone with Emma overnight.

"Right," said Dali. "Geoff's the dude for this trip."

Geoff looked trapped. He hadn't volunteered, but was now flung into the frame.

"C'mon, mate." I grinned. "How about a little desert sightseeing with your old scuffer here?"

Geoff looked hard at me. His face softened, he cocked his head, and said, "Okay, ya tosser, let's go."

"All right!" Dali yelled, before lowering his voice. "The intrepid hobbit duo departs on its quest through Mordor and all the kingdoms of Middle Earth to deliver the mystical herbal potion of the Mad Jag to the land of Arizona and thus to enlighten its inhabitants, lifting the dark cloud of oppression from the . . ."

"Oo-eh, shoot up, Doyley." Emma laid on the Birmingham brogue with a trowel, in true Fiona fashion, and for the first time in many hours we all smiled. Molly wrapped her arms around me.

"Take care, honey." She looked me in the eye and kissed me quickly on the lips. She turned to Geoff, while Dali grabbed me in a gorilla's embrace.

"Watch out for yourself out there, man. Bring that killer weed back and I'll set about moving some of it for you."

"Right. That'd be great."

Emma stood apart.

"Good luck, Jem." She made no attempt to advance. I went to her and she leaned forward from the waist to kiss my cheek, with all the intimacy of a Russian politician. I was left questioning the coldness: was she angry because I hadn't argued for her company on the drive? Was she saying she didn't want the affair to develop after all?

"Bring those two sleeping bags from the van, Geoff," I said. "Well, cheers everyone. Tell Wiz to meet us an hour before dawn tomorrow morning with his Suburban. Make sure he understands—one hour before sunrise. We'll wait a mile in from the highway by the old corral. Where that dirt track cuts off. He knows the place."

As I opened the driver's door, a siren drifted down from the north and galvanized us into action. A minute later the van was out of sight and I was bouncing along a rugged jeep trail into the Mazatzal Wilderness in a four-by-four jammed to the ceiling with high-grade sinsemilla, and a man riding shotgun who, until his wife had recently cuckolded him with yours truly, had been my best mate and a posse of Arizona's finest on our tail. It wasn't exactly the conclusion I'd hoped for the project, but it would be one for the grandkids—if we pulled through.

We rode in silence for the first few miles. The road dipped and weaved through the juniper country of the mesa. The going was steady and I began to feel better as we put some miles behind us. I'd always loved exploring the backcountry and the little jeep was in its element here. If I had to outrun Willard Farr or one of his boys, I fancied my luck on these four-by-four trails. On the highway? Snowball's chance.

The road dipped through an arroyo, climbed the bank, then turned steeply through a break in the rim. Spread before us was the upper section of Relic Canyon. The road swung back to the north under the rim cliff and clung to the canyonside like a picture rail to a wall.

"Jesus. Quite a view." Geoff craned his head in front of me, peering down into the gulf.

"Wanna stop and take some snaps? Show the lads in the rub-a-dub back home." We'd worked in a West End theater one winter and had to learn Cockney rhyming slang, as the old lags who'd staffed the place for decades deliberately laid on the argot to sort the Londoners from the provincials.

"I think we'll just press on for now. What with the load we have 'n' all." Geoff's face was grim.

I eased the jeep along, well aware of the drop-off to my left. Here and there we had to negotiate boulders that had fallen onto the road, calling for dicey moves where our wheels skirted the edge or having to cant the jeep high on the off-side. The going was fair for a couple of miles and we swung to the west as we neared the headwaters of Relic Creek.

"What about the stream crossing?" Geoff asked.

"There used to be a bridge, but it got washed out in the flood of '65."

"More good news. So, what's your plan, Style? Build a ramp and take a run at it?"

"There's a ford, I believe."

"You believe. And if there isn't one, we can just turn around and go back to meet the sheriff, who's probably setting up the welcoming party right now. Christ, I should've fookin' stayed home."

"Nobody twisted your arm. You could've let Emma come."

"Great idea. Send my wife into the wilderness with my best mate so he can zigzag her brains out at every bend in the road."

"Whatever!" I said, thinking of no better response.

We dropped down toward the creek in tense silence. This was the first time we'd had just each other's company since the exchange of partners. I was prepared for animosity, but the acrimony had hit early. I worried that things might kick off royally before we made it out.

I tried to ease the stress by bringing up one of our craziest adventures. "Bit like that drive we made through Iran in the old Land Rover in '72. Remember?"

"Yeah. You nearly landed us in that Isfahan jail by insisting we buy some Johnny Cash," he snapped. "Those secret police arseholes followed us through the back streets. We barely gave 'em the slip."

That went down well, I thought!

I pulled the Scout to a halt at the remnants of the bridge buttress. We walked down the steep bank where a few faint tire tracks showed the way. The ford was a poor excuse for the word, merely the creekbed with an odd boulder rolled aside.

I pulled a crowbar from under the passenger seat and we hopped across the rocks to check out the steep far bank. There were disconcertingly few signs of other vehicles. We worked on a few of the larger boulders with the bar, standing in the cold water in our bare feet, slipping and struggling to roll them aside and all the while wondering if we were losing too much time and some keen rookie looking to jump a rank up the law enforcement ladder was right now thrashing his county truck down the track toward us.

In maybe twenty minutes we had a path for the jeep. Geoff walked in front, guiding me as I crept forward in low range. The truck tilted and slipped as rocks spat from under the tires, and we were close to the far bank when the old Scout dropped on the passenger side and fetched up against a rock. I backed up and came on again and pressed the hammer down, but only succeeded in digging a hole with the front wheel.

Geoff flailed his arms, shouting. I disengaged the drive train.

"Hang on, Jackie Stewart, for Christ's sake." He lurched under the truck with the crowbar. After a couple minutes he flung a rock out and emerged, his T-shirt and jeans soaked in places.

"Try it now. Easy."

I made it across and crawled slowly up the steep bank. I jumped out and we sat apart on the bank slapping warmth back into our toes and pulling on socks.

"Fookin' great holiday this turned out to be." He'd dropped his Levi's and was wringing them out.

"At least it's warm. Imagine groveling in a stream on Dartmoor in November."

"At least I would be away from you."

I chuckled, and we sat quietly for a moment under the sycamores and alders that formed the usual riverine canopy of the high desert streams. I vowed to return one time and spend a couple of hard days watching flycatchers build nests.

Geoff rose first and strode to a fridge-sized boulder. He tried to prise it loose with the bar, to no avail. We cast about for a better lever. I found an old two-by-four from the wrecked bridge. Using a stone for a fulcrum, we leaned on the timber until the rock gave suddenly and we fell in a heap and the rock bowled gently down the bank and into the stream, nicely blocking another vehicle from exiting the creekbed.

"Let's hope we don't have to come back this way," I said.

"Shouldn't worry you, Style. You were always good at crossing Rubicons." He turned away and walked to the truck. It was going to be a long drive.

We pulled away from the tree-lined creek and into desert terrain: ocotillo cactus arching its thorny fronds, saltbush, desert spoon, and the huge pointed blades of Parry's agave. The road turned south through the broken country that marked the transition between the high plateaus of the Mogollon Rim, whose elevation averaged between six and eight thousand feet, and the Verde River basin, at a little over three.

I kept the truck grinding along in low range as we dipped and rose over the rolling land. Occasionally we had views over the lower parts of Mimbres Canyon and across the vast Verde Valley and the mountain range through which the freeway ran to the urban abomination called Phoenix.

We were coming quietly downhill at one point when a bobcat leaped from the roadside bank and charged across the road and away.

"Christ, startled me for a moment," I said. "I thought it was a lion."

"Seen a mountain lion since you've been out here?"

"No. A couple of bobcats at these lower elevations. And of course, the jag." I tried to keep the conversation alive.

"Right. Wiz was gutted that you had seen the jag first. As you guys call it."

"We knew there was a big cat in our canyon, but I'd always thought it was a lion."

There was a moment's pause while I thought of something more to say.

"Well, this is a quite a situation you've got us in, Jeremy." Geoff broached the first subject of tension using my full name, something he rarely did.

"A wee bit dodgy," I admitted. "But as long as we can get through this road, we should be okay. Wiz'll meet us at the other end and we'll offload the gear to his truck and we'll be home free."

"What about the vehicles? Should we plan on getting rid of them?"

"I'll have to drop this one, right away. But I'd planned on trading it in for our trip to Baja." I looked across at him. "I don't think you need to sell yours."

"You don't think they'll hassle me if I keep it?"

"When we get back from Mexico you might want to think about it."

"Yeah," he said thoughtfully. "After Mexico."

We were dropping down into an arroyo and I had to concentrate as runoff had scarred a deep trench down one side of the road course, which forced the Scout to tilt radically. Some of the stress of the situation had been lifted by Geoff's willingness to chat, taciturn though he remained. Now if I could just find some way to open the subject of Emma, I felt it might be best for both of us in the end; even if there were some aggro at first, it would be good to clear the air.

Before we could broach any other topic, the afternoon was shattered by the distant but still hideous clatter of a helicopter.

I jammed on the brakes, cut the engine. "Damn chopper!"
"Where is it?" Geoff stared.
"South," I said, "and west." I pointed.
"Coming our way?"
"Shh."
We listened. It seemed to be tracking the course of this road. With our recent knowledge of these machines, we soon realized it was approaching, fast.
"Yes, it is." I started the motor.
"You sure it's looking for us? They can't rope in a helicopter to search for small fry like us?" Geoff looked at me.
"Small fry! I wish we were, mate. We're big-time drug dealers to them. We'd be one of the biggest busts ever in Gila County. Sheriff Farr's grinning face would be on the front of all the local rags."
"Christ." His face was dark.
"The arroyo," I yelled. "Maybe there's some cover there." I swung the truck into the bed of the sandy wash and we both jumped out, searching desperately for a place to hide a jeep.
"Up here, by this rock wall," Geoff shouted from the bend. "C'mon!"
I ran the truck hard through the heavy sand to where Geoff was dragging a rock from between a small crag and an old Arizona ash. I jammed the Scout in against the wall, smashing the wing mirror and gouging the front wing and passenger door. The hideous clatter of the chopper increased and we worked frantically to break up the lines of the jeep, ripping up branches of bear grass and tossing them on the roof and hood.
"There's not enough greenery!" I said. "They'll see the white roof."
"The weed! Throw the weed on top."
I balked. Throw our hard-won darling buds of m.j. onto the roof of this old jeep! But he was already scattering buds on the roof and flinging the poly bags down the cliff side of the truck.
"C'mon, you worthless wankstain, pitch in! If they spot us, you can kiss your precious crop goodbye." Reluctantly I joined him, gingerly shaking out the lovely buds till we had a carpet of green covering the horizontal surfaces of the Scout—the most

expensive spray job in the history of automobile manufacture. I stooped to pick a few buds from the sand as the rhythmic row of the cursed helicopter rose another increment of decibels and then, as it cleared the caprock of the little arroyo, screamed its deafening malevolence down on us.

"Get down, ya tosspot! Hide."

We dove against the front of the truck, panting, sweating. The chopper came on and on until finally the racket was so intense that we knew it was dead overhead. My head was on Geoff's chest; at first he seemed to withdraw from the contact, but then he reached around and pulled me to him and I felt his heart pounding against my temple and was overcome with a sense of comfort from our years together and the ease with each other's closeness born of many drunken nights sprawled in the same bed or on the beaches of the islands of the Cyclades, and one freezing brass monkey of a long, long bivvy on a ledge in a storm just above the fissure Brown on the west face of the Blatière in the Alps, or the night we'd huddled together, freezing our knackers off, at the top of the Salang Pass at 4,000 meters just north of Kabul in '72, and just having him there in the midst of all this lunacy as the harpy creature bore down on us and sought to wreck our lives forever. The thunder of the infernal machine shook our bodies and I felt a bud drop off the hood onto my head. I wondered if the wash from the rotors would clear the weed and expose the truck roof.

The racket fell away fractionally as the machine crossed the east rim of the arroyo and we thought we were, for the moment, spared. But the noise didn't decrease.

"Oh Christ. He's circling." Geoff slithered further under the truck and I squeezed in after him. We lay jammed against each other, soaked in sweat, shuddering with fear. The chopper crossed the arroyo to the north of us and I was convinced it would soon land and loud commands would be yelled. But Geoff's idea seemed to have worked; the chopper banked around to the south and the infernal racket died away.

I stayed curled against him, basking in the reassurance of the solidity of his broad chest, unwilling to abandon the fraternal warmth, knowing that I was not as tough as I thought, that this gig was way too much and that I yearned for support, something paternal, and the closest thing to that was my longtime friend. He shoved me away.

We moved cautiously out into the arroyo and climbed a gully to the top of the crag. The chopper was out of sight now in the bowl of Relic Canyon where we'd crossed the creek, and we saw it emerge to follow the road along the cliffside and up over the mesa toward Fruitown. We looked down on the truck and its camouflage net of marijuana. Geoff grinned.

"Nice idea, pal. I knew there was some reason I asked you along." I laughed at the sight and the relief of dodging another bullet.

"If it'd been up to you, you useless whingeing twat, crying about your crop, we'd be bending over now for some redneck lawman." And he came at me and rammed me off the little cliff so I had to leap down on to the roof of the truck and I landed with a cry of dismay, crushing buds underfoot. I skidded onto my arse in a pile of pot on the hood.

"That's what I think of your precious fookin' Bob Hope and all the fookin' trouble it's caused us." And it was his turn to be tickled, roaring his deep natural laugh and pointing down at me and creasing up at the sight of my downcast face. It was worth a few broken buds to see him back at his best.

We bagged up the weed, working together, the tension between us gone for a while at least, and the aftermath of the adrenaline rush leaving us chattery, nervous, high as kites.

"What do you say we jack it in for a while. Get forty winks," I said. It was late afternoon and we were well worked.

"Suits me. Been a bit of a day."

"I doubt the chopper'll come back, but let's camouflage the truck. We'll sleep easier."

I used pliers to rip some black hawthorn and chokecherry branches.

"Sorry," I said quietly to the plants in the way Wiz had done, and I had adopted, when we prepped the garden in the spring.

"Jesus Christ. You're going soft in the head." Geoff kicked and tore at a tough serviceberry bush to emphasize his point.

"It's time you began to realize that the earth is our mother and if we don't treat her well . . ." I laid on the New Age drivel with a trowel to wind him up.

"Cut the crap, will you, you soft git." He gave his shrub a fierce tug, tore up the entire plant, and flung it on the truck, and I creased up again, delighting in the pleasure of scathing abuse, an exclusively English masochism.

We found a broad sandy shelf under an overhang across the arroyo.

"Quick Bo-peep'll be welcome." He tossed down a blanket. "This is all a bit much for a Brummie bloke."

"You and me both." I gulped water and sat on the ledge.

"Never thought growing up in King's Heath, bath bun of a police sergeant, that I'd one day be on the run from the fuzz in Arizona."

"Let's hope we make it out safe and sound. If I remember your dad, he won't be too chuffed if you end up in stir."

"Say that again." Geoff nodded. "His boy in an American clink! Can't see the old man rushing over here to bail me out."

"Did he press you to follow him into the Old Bill?"

"Early doors, yeah. But after he and Mum split the sheets, I went off the rails and he hit the cufflink pretty hard."

"He could be a bit rough on you and your brothers, you once said."

"When he was Scotch mist he could be a right mean twat." My pal shook his head at the memory. Being British, and in spite of our years of friendship, we'd seldom broached that barrier into emotional terrain, but perhaps the risk of this daft endeavor had overcome his usual reserve. "We took to locking the bedroom doors when he came home from the boozer or he'd give us a backhander."

"You were the eldest, of course. Did you ever have to look after your brothers?"

"When I was maybe sixteen and starting to hold my own in the neighborhood I came home once and found him giving our Ian a pasting. I lost it and gave him a sock on the jaw. Knocked him down."

"Did he change his attitude after that?"

"He did." He smiled. "We almost became friends."

"Good on ya." I rose. "Get some shut-eye, me old china. I'll take the first watch."

I climbed to a lookout. It was a cool, blustery evening. High cirrus showed crimson streaks. A huge cumulonimbus soared into the troposphere and threatened a storm. I sat back against a rock, wrapped my faded serape around my shoulders, forced myself into deep yoga breathing, and reflected.

It had been quite a day: three episodes with helicopters, one thrilling, one disappointing, and one terrifying; an exhausting hike; a series of gut-wrenchingly close calls with the law; and a dangerous and knackering drive through a rugged wilderness. Here we were, two English blokes on the run in the wilds of Arizona. How the hell did it turn out like this? But they hadn't nabbed us yet, and in my fool way I allowed a smirk of satisfaction to crease my mouth. In a sense wasn't this the perfect ending to the crim's dream—the law at your heels but not too close, the loot safe for the time being? Wasn't this the wannabe crooks' desire—to follow Pretty Boy Floyd, Butch and Sundance, or Ronald Biggs by pulling off a crime by the skin of the teeth, without killing or maiming some innocent?

I stared out across my beloved Verde Valley, basking in one of those brilliant sunsets that make you swivel your head like an owl on a post, reluctant to miss any shift in shade as the entire sky, east to west, from city of the desert to snow-cowled mountain, bled through the middle spectrum. The tang of rain drifted in from the thunderhead; flashes of light lit its billows.

I pictured Sheriff Farr somewhere in his truck, fuming, barking instructions to his deputies, cussing himself for not nabbing us at the café, growing more frustrated as daylight faded and he realized night would smile on our escape.

I would have to sell the Scout immediately. No big deal, as I needed a camper van for our planned trip down to Baja. I could slip across the border at Ajo and head to Todos Santos alone.

But who would join me down there? Geoff's brother, Stuart, had planned to come over from London to travel with us. And what about Geoff and Emma? If they decided not to come down, would I be mortified or perhaps a little relieved? Spending time with Geoff on this drive had again given me second thoughts about shafting his wife—but god I wasn't growing fond of her, that had happened years ago, no, I was fascinated by more than her sharp wit, her love of language, her raw sexuality, and much as I was reluctant to come between them I knew that if she came my way again well . . . Jesus, was I torn.

I watched the tints on the clouds merge. A muster of nighthawks strafed the nearby ridge. A keen breeze tousled the agave stalks. I huddled deeper in the blanket and shook my head to ward off sleep. I was worked, shagged out, and needed to get a couple of hours' kip before moving on, but Geoff was out like a light and I didn't want to disturb him. I stood and walked to the top of a rise trying to shake the drowsiness, turned, and found something to rivet the attention without prejudice: on the cliff-clinging road that we'd driven that afternoon, a pair of headlights crept forward in the twilight.

13

Mesmerized by the headlights as completely as any beast of the field, I shook off my qualms and ran the possibilities: we must assume it's a lawman. No one in their right mind would set off into the wilderness on this road right after dark unless they were ordered to do so, or were highly motivated, as would be Sheriff Willard Farr. Could he get by the rock we'd rolled into the stream? Would he realize we'd rolled it there, then call ahead and send the harpy beast after us again? Or set up a roadblock at the far end?

Jesus, no peace for the wicked.

"Mate, wake up!" I shook Geoff lightly by the shoulders. "We gotta hit the trail."

"What, what is it?" He sat up, shaking his head.

"A truck back on the frog and toad."

"Fookin' 'ell." He struggled to his feet.

"He's a long way behind us." I handed him water. "I was going to make rosy lea but you'll have to make do with Adam's ale."

"If we ever get outta this mess, it's going to cost you a rake of real ale." He drank.

"No worries. Spirit Room tomorrow night. My shout. Much as you can skull."

I scraped the truck away from the cliff and Geoff guided me in reverse down the arroyo. He wrenched open the damaged passenger door with a grinding shriek of metal and clambered in. We drove on.

I pressed the truck steadily for the better part of a couple hours, pleased with the way the little Scout moved over the trail as it became more rugged. We reached a pass of sorts, cut the engine, and got out to check on the pursuit.

"Hear anything?" I asked.

"Nope. Maybe they're in the streambed trying to move that rock." Geoff lifted his face to the sky; a few raindrops fell. "Shit. It's starting to rain."

"Thought it might. Those clouds at sunset spelt precip."

"Precip! Precip! Now you're the effin' meteorologist! C'mon out to the desert mate, he says. Dry as a bone out here, he says. Christ!"

To the west, a turquoise band clung to the horizon. A fine waxing moon sailed between reefs of cloud and bathed the desert valley in a soft wash. In this light, my binoculars were still useful. I trained them on the ridgelines to the east.

"Let's go. This rain's cold." Geoff moved toward the truck.

"Hang on."

"Hear something?"

"Ssh."

We both saw the bright headlights clear the ridge.

"Jesus. He's got past the rock." We ran back to the truck, shoes slipping as the rain spattered in the desert clay.

"How far behind do you think they are?" Geoff was arched forward, Hampstead Heaths grinding.

"Hour and a half. Maybe an hour."

"So, we're okay if we can keep going."

"Long as the truck doesn't crap out."

"And the road doesn't give out."

"And we don't get a puncture."
"Or break an axle."
"Or get bogged down."
"Bollocks!" I yelled.
"Boolloocks!" yelled Geoff.
"Booooolloooocks!" we both screamed.

At the rim of the lower reach of Mimbres Canyon, I braked and we looked down.

"This is the rough section everyone talks about," I said.
"And what we've just driven is the F1 track at Monza?"
"We've got about fourteen more miles. If all goes well and Wiz is on time, we'll get out of this just fine."
"Course we will." He belted the dashboard. "Let's go."
"As long as they're not waiting for us at the other end."
"Maybe they don't think we're in here as the chopper didn't spot us."
"Maybe the truck behind us is just some other jokers."
"Maybe growers like us coming in at night to pull their crop out."
"Who knows?"
"Who the fook knows," he yelled.
"Fuuuuck knows!"
"Fooooook knows!" The chorused curse seemed to ease the strain.

I drove hard down into the canyon, stopping at basalt ledges where I had to let the weight of the truck slip over the lip. We turned uphill for a section where the rock steps were sometimes over a foot high and the going tortuously slow. The chassis of the old Scout scraped alarmingly. Rain was now drumming on the roof, and the little wipers strained to clear a mere half-moon across the windshield.

"The good thing is they'll be as slow as us," I said.
"Except they've got a government issue vehicle and don't give a damn if they break it up."
"They give a damn about losing us."

As we turned downhill, I felt something off-kilter with the steering.

"What's wrong?" Geoff sensed my concern.

"It's pulling left. Shit. I think we've got a puncture."

We jumped out as a flare of lightning blinded us and a deafening crack of energy pealed through the trees.

"Good Christ, Style. We're in the very heart of your precip! And now a fookin' puncture. Bastard." Geoff kicked the hissing tire with venom.

I stuck a flashlight in my mouth and pulled tools from under the weed. "Here. Loosen the lugs. I'll work the jack."

I dropped into the cold mud and scrabbled under the chassis with the little bottle jack, found the cross member, and started whirling the articulated bar. Geoff flung his weight onto the four-way lug wrench and the nuts cracked loose.

"Get the spare."

He splashed to the rear and set to work on the nuts. Another klieg light lit the clearing and after a slightly longer pause the thunder followed.

"The storm's moving on," I called from under the truck.

"Too bad. I hoped we'd get struck by lightning. Put us out of our misery." He grunted on the lug wrench. "Jesus, these nuts are rusty. They won't give."

"There's WD-40 under my seat."

He sprayed the nuts on the spare. I strained at the jack handle as the weight of the jeep came on.

"She's going up. Finish those nuts."

As he spun the lugs on the front wheel, I lay underneath whirling the jack handle—then noticed that the jack base was tilting in the damp soil.

"Geoff, Geoff! The jack's going over!" I felt the terrible weight of the truck settle across my back, twisted my head sideways and let out a gasp. I saw Geoff's feet splayed away from the wheel housing and heard him groan as he took the strain. One of his feet shot away in the mud before he took another stance and heaved. The pressure on my shoulders eased for a second and I flung myself backward, cracking my skull on something hard, and lay back staring up into the pouring rain, moaning.

"You okay?" He eased the truck down.

"Yeah, yeah. I think so. Fuck, that was kinda frightening." I stretched my back muscles. "Thanks, mate."

"You daft prat. Get back under there and make sure the jack's set properly. More haste, less speed, as me old mum used to say."

I crawled back to work, found a solid plate of basalt, and cranked away at the handle, making sure this time that my torso was clear of the chassis. Sharp pain stabbed across my shoulderblades. Geoff grunted away at the nuts on the spare and I heard them break loose and thanked the lord that he, not Emma, was here.

I got the Scout jacked up and Geoff rolled the spare round as I snatched the wheel off the drum. We flung the spare on and shoved the flat under the bags of grass, and while he tightened the nuts, I lowered the truck off the jack. We listened and looked back along the trail. There was no sign or sound of pursuit.

"Maybe they got stuck. Or broke down." Geoff looked hopefully to the east.

"Wait. I hear it." I peered through the binoculars at the dark ridges—and gasped. I had expected the headlights to appear at the far ridgeline, the one above Relic Creek. Instead, they emerged at the interim crest, as if they had jumped a valley while we wrestled with the wheel change.

"What is it?" demanded Geoff.

"Nothing. It's nothing. Let's go."

"Nothing, he says, as the long arm of the law bears down on us. If you hadn't made a balls-up of setting the jack . . ."

"You took half an hour to loosen the nuts, you weakling."

"Cobblers!" he screamed. "Just drive!"

We jumped in and set off again, shivering in our soaked shirts.

"You got a heater in this jalopy?" Geoff fooled with the controls and soon the fan whirred. He held his hands to the warm air for a mo, then pulled a battered pack of Marlboros from his jeans and lit one.

"You're filling the truck with that stench." I cracked the window. "When you gonna quit those C-sticks?'

"When you quit your griping." He drew deeply, handed it to me. I took a couple hits and passed it back, and soon felt the tobacco rush. We slipped between steep cliffs where the road was barely wide enough for the truck to pass. At the base of the canyon, the road cut across a streambed through a grove of cottonwoods. We stopped the truck and hurried across the shallow stream to check the far side. The rain was steady and cool, but we were hyped from the tension and the effort and stumbled into the stream and stared at the obstacle that, at first glance, appeared to shag us royally.

On the far bank, the flow from many a spring flood had cut into the slope and left a sheer wall, higher than my outstretched arm. Above that, a perilously steep bank, now soaked and slippery, stretched another twenty feet before the grade eased. Obviously, no one had passed through this year.

"What if we hide the truck and let the law pass by?" Geoff turned to me. His hair was streaked with dust and grime and plastered to his scalp by the rain, his pupils were pissholes in the snow, his cheeks gaunt.

"Why, then, he'll catch Wiz. And we'll be stuck between them and never be able to get out."

"Won't they be waiting at the other end?"

"That's why we're meeting Wiz at the corral. There's a side road back to the highway. Rough as dogshit but passable." I swung the door open. "Let's look at this."

In the light of the headlights, we checked out the barrier.

"The winch," said Geoff. "Can it pull us up?"

"We'll have to try." I pulled the Scout forward over the boulders, went to the front, and shone the flashlight at the Warn winch.

"How does this thing work?" Geoff peered in beside me.

I unwound the electric lead and examined the control box.

"How does it work?" he asked again.

"Haven't a clue."

"What? What the fook do you mean?"

"Never used it."

"Oh brilliant. Oh yes infookindeedy, folks." He stood up to his full height, fists clenched at his shoulders, and bellowed into the darkness. "Here we are in the back of befookinyond in the middle of the fookin' night trying escape the law and Stylor tells me he never used his fookin' winch! God give me strength."

I pressed the reverse button and the drum turned, allowing the hook to dangle.

"Take the hook up the bank. And quit your whingeing, as they say in Oz."

"Fook you, as they say in the U.S. of A," he said, and despite everything I couldn't suppress a chuckle. "Get your arse against the wall. We need to use combined tactics." He used the climbers' term for hoisting one's partner over steep rock.

I leaned back against the wet bank and laced my fingers to make a step. He lifted his soaked sneaker on to my hands, grabbed my shoulders, and hauled himself up until his crotch was at my brow.

"Any chance you can get your festivals out of my boat race?"

"Blow me." He stepped on my shoulders and scrabbled at the loose soil above the vertical. I gasped as his shoes dug into my flesh above the collarbones. I grabbed his feet and shoved hard. He disappeared, grunting and clawing his way over the edge.

"Give me a couple more feet."

I pressed the button on the winch control box. He looped the cable end around the base of an old cottonwood and flipped the hook over the wire.

"C'mon down and work this thing." I got back in the truck and craned out the window to line the wheels up squarely with the bank.

"Take up the slack," I said, and Geoff braced himself at the top of the wall, one foot high on the slope, holding the little control box and looking across at the winch and back at the cable as it tautened. I eased the Scout into the vertical dirt. The cable, guitar-string taut, gently lifted the front wheels off the ground.

"Not bad," Geoff said, and kept his finger on the button. I eased the clutch out and the tires bit and started to claw at the soil. The winch continued to coil cable and the truck tilted alarmingly, tires spinning against the gravelly bank.

"Put the rabbit hutch in!" Geoff yelled above the scrabbling tires. "Let the winch do the work!"

I watched the bonnet rise until the Scout was vertical and I was lying back in the seat, an astronaut ready for takeoff. Everything fell to the back of the truck; in the rear-view mirror I could see the bags of Mad Jag piled against the back door. The rear bumper scraped the rocks of the streambed. I worried the fluids would spill from the engine. Now the entire weight of the Scout was suspended on a strand of cable, which in the headlights seemed terrifyingly thin.

"All right." Geoff crouched, watching the tires creep up the cliff. The cable pinged and snapped as it seated on the drum.

"Stand back, mate," I called through the window. "If this cable snaps you'll be cut in half."

"And you'll crash and burn at the bottom of this slope." As if to emphasize his bravado he crouched closer to the front wheels as they crested the vertical. "Let the clutch out. See if you can get some traction."

I engaged the drive train gently; the tires gripped and the truck advanced under the dual pulls of winch and engine. As we crept up the slope the cable angled to the tree, slewing the Scout, forcing Geoff to jump back.

"Stop winding now. Unhook the cable." I felt the truck steady itself on the easier slope. Geoff scrambled up to the cottonwood, slipped the hook from the wire, and threw it round the tree. We made the top of the rise and Geoff let out a whoop and ran to the winch to wrap the cable and control box cord. I switched off the motor, got out, and stretched my back, which was sore from the tension of the drive and having to bear the weight of the truck for a few seconds.

"How you doing, matey?" Geoff stood beside me and I looked up at him. His eyes shone and his mouth was pursed in a satisfied grimace.

"Bit creamed."

"You look ready for an Otis Redding." He lit a fag.

"Makes two of us." I said looking at his bedraggled state. "What time is it?"

He stooped to read his watch in the headlight. "Quarter to three."

"Jesus. Time flies when you're having fun."

"Are we okay to make the meeting with Wiz?"

"Think we'll be right. So long as we don't have any more mishaps."

"Right. One more puncture and we'll be up shit creek."

As if to punctuate his concern, we heard the grind of a V8 motor on the canyonside behind us.

"They're gaining on us. Who the fook are those guys?" The relief flooded from Geoff's face and fear lined it again.

"I bet a few quid it's the sheriff himself." I watched the headlights rise and fall between the trees and reckoned they were less than two miles behind us. "The bastard's going to be stalled here the same as us. Let's go."

"Maybe they don't have a winch." Geoff looked hopefully at me as we climbed aboard. "Do they have winches on the county vehicles?"

"How the fuck should I know?" I gunned the Scout through a dip and Geoff bounced hard.

"Take it easy! Don't be a cunt all your life, take a day off."

We pressed on. At first the road was bad and the ruts filled with rain, but the terrain eased and we started to splash along nicely. We mounted a rise and looked down on the lights of Camp Verde and the headlights of a vehicle on the highway; only a couple of miles separated us from the end of this ordeal!

"Alfookinrighty!" Geoff shouted.

"Let's check on our friends." I shut off the motor and we stood on the slope looking back to the east. A faint trace of gray on the horizon betrayed the coming dawn. Then we saw the headlights coming on inexorably toward us and we groaned again and hauled ourselves back into the truck and started on the last leg, exhausted, beat, soaked, cold, worn down by this pursuit.

"Evidently they do have winches on the county trucks," said Geoff.

"So it would seem." I drove hard, praying that Wiz was on time. The rain eased and across the valley we saw headlights turn from the highway and my heart lifted.

"Dig out the walkie."

Geoff fumbled in the glovebox.

"Wiz, come back, Wiz."

A beat.

"Wiz, come back, Wiz."

"This is the Wizard of the Rim." Never had I been so glad to hear the mad Yank's voice.

"Yes. All right, mate. Yes," Geoff roared into the mike.

"Steady on there, boys. Had a tough trip?"

"Yes." Geoff steadied his voice. "Do you see our lights?"

Silence, then:

"Yep. I've got a visual."

"Good. About ten minutes behind us is another truck."

Silence again, then:

"Okay. We'll just to have hurry the transfer."

"Right. We'll meet you at the corral."

"Copy that. At the corral."

Geoff slumped back in his seat with a long, deep sigh. I felt relief flooding into me as my strength ebbed. I wanted to say something, I wanted to slap a high five with Geoff, I wanted to hug him, but knew such blatant shows of gratitude would seem crass and American to him. Still, I couldn't leave it alone.

"Thanks for coming along, Geoffrey old son. I couldn't have done it without you."

"My pleasure." He stared ahead. "Doubt if Ems would've been quite so much help."

"Got that right."

"You might have had the odd nice stop with her," he added and I thought, here we go.

"Mate, you know . . ." I tried to measure my words. "I haven't exactly chased after your missus."

"You haven't exactly laid off her either."

"She and Molly had the whole deal planned. What was I supposed to do? After all, you slept with my missus."

"You two aren't married."

"Spare me that line."

"It's not so much the shagging that worries me, Stylor. You

and I have certainly swapped a few bints in the past. And Emma and I have never really shaken the treetops . . ." His voice tailed off, as any man's might at such an admission. "I just want her to be happy. And if it makes her happy having a fling with you, well, it hurts like hell but I can handle it." His hands clenched the dashboard.

"But if you ever try to take her away from me . . ." He turned to glare at me and I was only able to look at him briefly, cowed by the pain and passion in his eyes.

"She's the sun and moon to me. I'd be lost without her. Shattered. Gutted. Done in." He grabbed me by the shoulder and twisted me toward him and shoved his face forward. "If you break up my marriage . . . well, I would definitely think about killing you. Or her. Or myself. Or maybe all fookin' three of us."

I considered telling him that I hadn't actually shagged her, but I knew the argument was specious.

We drove on in thick silence, the two of us absorbing his words. Despite the tension, I felt a sense of relief. Geoff had poured his guts out at no little cost. His confession that he and Emma didn't move the earth in the sack must have hurt, and certainly threw some light on her desire for an affair. Was my best mate, the tough rugby flanker, the talented if reluctant rock climber, the hard-drinking wild-driving rake about town, was he not quite Casanova between the sheets? I quickly scotched that idea as I recalled the several times I had slept close enough to hear him giving a lass a good thraping and seen the contented glaze in her eyes the morning after. Or did the lusty Emma demand more than one mere mortal could provide? The truth, of course, lay somewhere in between. They'd been married three years now; that was a long time. Passions subside. Eyes wander. Familiarity breeds . . .

A clanking sounded from beneath the truck.

"Now what? Jesus H. Christ!" I braked and climbed out, sore and weary. We dropped reluctantly into the mud once again and lay under the jeep. The driveshaft was hanging by one bolt from the rear U-joint.

"What the fook next?" Geoff grabbed the shaft and snatched it back and forth in frustration. In the valley to the east, we could hear the other truck coming on. "Got any spare bolts?" he asked.

"No." I lashed a kick at the U-joint and merely succeeded in grazing my shin on the undercarriage. "Aaah! Bollocks!"

"Course not," he shouted. "Stylor be prepared? No fookin' chance!"

"Who d'you think I am? The effin' Automobile Association?"

"Well, you better come up with something sharpish or I'm off like a robber's dog among those cactuses."

"Cacti," I corrected foolishly.

"That's it. You fookin' worthless pedantic twat." His spittle hit my cheeks. "I'm on my toes." He rolled away.

"Hang on. Hang on a mo." I grabbed his arm. "We can take the rear shaft off, leave it in four-wheel, and we can make the last mile with just the front axle driving."

He rolled back and looked at me, lying in the damp dirt, his face inches from mine, bright in the flashlight. "Right, RIGHT! Sometimes you are a clever cunt. Well, get the fookin' tools then."

I jumped back, scraping my cheek on a chassis member.

We got the remaining bolt off the rear connection and swung round under the truck and worked on the three bolts of the front U-joint, against a discordant background track of the other vehicle grinding through the desert toward us.

I thought one of our Warren Zevon favorites might ease the strain.

"I'm between a rock and hard place," I sang through a gravelly throat.

"And I'm down on my luck," Geoff joined, and we finished together:

"Send lawyers, guns and money, oh, The shit has hit the fan."

As we worked on the last bolt, Geoff holding one end with a pair of mole grips while I tortuously removed the nut with an adjustable wrench, the lights of the pursuing truck briefly lit up the trees around us.

"Get a move on, man!"

"I'm trying, damn it."

"Next time bring a socket set, you wally."

"Like there'll be a next time," I said, and we pulled the last bolt through and scrambled out.

"Stop talking like a fookin' Yank." Geoff hurled the driveshaft into the desert with a discus thrower's twirl.

"I needed that shaft for the trade in."

"Bollocks. And turn the lights off so the sheriff can't clock us."

I killed the brights and gingerly let the clutch engage. The front-wheel drive seemed to work fine and we breathed again, pitching through a couple of arroyos and down toward Wiz and salvation. We climbed up a little rise past a rusty, silent windmill and a stagnant pond and into the corral and there was the big red Suburban and we swung in and backed up to his rear door.

"A truck's followed us the whole fucking way." I started flinging bags into his vehicle.

"The law?" Wiz crouched in the luggage compartment and packed the Ziplocs as best he could.

"Must be." Geoff flung bags from the Scout. "We've got a couple of minutes. See his lights?"

Wiz glanced up for a second.

"Holy shit. What d'you do to get the sheriff so fired up?"

"What do you mean?"

"He's hotter'n a bull's ass in fly season. There's cops everywhere. And they pulled in the state helicopter." Behind us the noise of the truck engine rose noticeably. "Did you see the chopper?"

"Yeah. We had a brush with it yesterday afternoon."

"There's a cop at the turn to Relic Road, a couple down by the hot springs, a state trooper up at the pass and one at the end of this road."

"Oh Christ. How did you get in?" I asked.

"Cut the fence on the highway and hauled ass cross country."

"How are we going to get out?"

Wiz was savagely tearing trash bags and flinging them over the stack of grass.

"You're going to have draw him off." Wiz shoved the last bags under the heap, slammed the rear door, and ran for the driver's seat.

"Draw him off? They're looking for my truck. I'll end up in the slammer for sure." I looked at Geoff and we both gasped from exhaustion and the relentless stress of this escapade. Behind us the truck was climbing the rise toward the corral.

"You're clean now. Bullshit your way through. It's either that or lose a slew of our crop," he yelled from the window, and slammed the Suburban into gear.

"He'll see you've taken this road and radio ahead."

"Have to chance it," Wiz shouted as he gunned the big engine and shot down an indistinct track to the south.

I leaned against the Scout and watched the big red Chevy crash among the mesquites and disappear from view.

"Here comes the sheriff, Style. Let's make a dash for it!" Geoff was staring to the east and backing away from the Scout.

"No, Geoff. Don't give him a reason to shoot. You'll be all right, mate. It's Wiz and me they're after."

The truck rattled down the cactus-lined road and turned in a blaze of light that Sergio Leone couldn't have bettered: headlights shone, a spotlight burned into us from the light bar on the roof, and the hydrogen ball, which had crested the horizon as they approached, backlit the truck into a stark silhouette. Slumped against the hood of the Scout, completely knackered, I shaded my eyes and peered in misery into the rosy-clawed dawn. The driver's door opened.

"You guys set a harsh pace through those canyons." The man was indistinguishable in a halo of light.

"We didn't reckon we'd ever catch up to you," the second fellow said, opening the passenger door and stepping out.

I squinted into the brilliance. There was something odd about their vehicle; it was squarer and smaller than the usual Arizona sheriff's late-model four-by.

"Are you dudes trying to set a time for the Mimbres Canyon run as well?" The driver walked toward us and I saw he was not in uniform and a glimmer of hope shone again in my shattered psyche.

"Uh, maybe," I stuttered, and glanced at Geoff.

"Aren't you part of the NAU four-by club? Why else would you be hauling ass along that road at night?" The strapping young guy, dressed in shorts, a sweatshirt, and high-laced logging boots, had now reached us.

"The Mimbres Canyon run?" I asked, looking at his ruddy, tired face.

"It's like a hazing into the Lumberjack Off-Road Club." He drained a Bud and crushed the can underfoot. "What *are* you dudes doing out here?" He looked to the south, where we could all hear Wiz's vehicle grinding away.

The second guy brushed his partner's shoulder with the back of his hand. "Maybe best if we book, brother."

"No worries, mate." I held my palms up. "It's all good. Tell us about this Mimbres Canyon deal."

They glanced at each other for a moment before the driver spoke hesitatingly. "You leave Flagstaff after class in the evening, drive the highway to Strawberry, run the Mimbres Canyon Road, and have to make Flag before classes the next morning."

"And you have to down suds all the way." The other guy laughed uneasily, and we two exhausted and very relieved outlaws chuckled along.

"We were trying to catch up to you to see if you had a light. We wanted to burn a doobie but lost the matches." The driver looked at us and then down the road, where Wiz's vehicle was crashing through the desert, and back to us with a quizzical tilt to his face. He shuffled back a pace.

"I've got a light," I said, my mind wrapping around this development and seeing an exit from the cul-de-sac. "In fact, I've got a puff of weed here myself. If you care to try something fresh." I pulled a reefer from my wallet.

"Fresh, eh? Local?" said the second guy nervously.

"Matter of fact it is," I said.

"Grown maybes not so far away?" The driver pointed back along the road we'd both taken and nodded to his pal.

"Not so far away, no," I said, and suffered a withering look from Geoff. There was an awkward silence while I lit up and passed a joint of the Mad Jag. The sharing of the grass eased the tension and we chatted about the drive and Geoff and I lied about how tough it was getting round the rock in Relic Creek and didn't lie about winching out of the Mimbres streambed and laughed about the roughness of the trail as the sun arched over the Verde Valley and a deputy sheriff waited on the highway to arrest us.

"What time is it?" the driver asked. Geoff told him.

"Jesus!" he said. "We gotta hit it or we won't get the record. Thanks for the jay."

We shook hands all around and they backed away hurriedly and took off in their Willy's Jeep.

"What the fook are you thinking of, Stylor?" Geoff spat the words. "You might as well take those blokes over to the rim of the canyon and show 'em the garden!"

I slumped against the old Scout as Geoff lit into me.

"I can't fookin' believe you sometimes. What the hell would Wiz say . . ."

"Fuck off, will ya." I was at the end of my tether. "I'm shagged, knackered, not thinking straight. Anyway, those guys are harmless. And we're finished down there."

"I'm not. I could be down there next year." He scraped the passenger door wide and climbed wearily aboard. "And let's hope those blokes *are* harmless."

I pulled the truck out of the corral and set off toward the highway.

"Shouldn't we follow Wiz through the desert? Won't the cops be waiting for us at the highway?" Geoff asked.

"We don't want draw attention to Wiz. We have to chance it this way."

"They'll have the description and the plate of your vehicle. The sheriff's sure to have sent out all that guff after you nearly got us collared at the caff."

"They can't bust us on suspicion. We're clean now."

"They'll throw us in the slammer for the night at least." He shook his head. "I'm not going out to the main road with the Arizona Sweeney Todd lining up to book us."

"You're not serious?"

"Fookin' am. Let me out."

I saw sense. I pointed to a little mesa. "We'll pull up on that ridge. Watch what happens to the frat boys."

The trail was in fair shape up to a low saddle where a rough two-track made by ranch hands cut north. I dropped the Scout into low range and we skidded through the deep bar ditch and followed the faint trail. Below the ridgeline I stopped, and we loped up to where we had a view of the highway. Just a couple hundred yards north of us a sheriff's pickup was parked on the highway behind the Willy's, lights flashing. Through the binoculars I saw the deputy, firearm held out in both hands, questioning the NAU lads, who had their arms high on the vehicle, legs akimbo. The cop gestured with the gun and the driver walked to the rear, swung the doors open, and pulled out a satchel of tools, a backpack, and other gear. After a long look into the vehicle, the officer's body posture eased, and the gun was lowered a little as they all spoke. Then, as my heart sank and my exhausted limbs ached for relief, we were thrown under the bus for the second time in twenty-four hours by Arizonans. The driver and passenger were both nodding and pointing in the direction of the corral and I could hear the excited voices but could not make out the words. I didn't need to. The deputy dashed back to his pickup, threw a U-turn, siren wailing, and raced down the highway, turn signal blinking, toward the corral road.

"Harmless, are they, those blokes?" Geoff's head sank.

"The tracks in the ditch. He'll see where we turned." I dragged myself to my feet. "We have to brush 'em out. C'mon."

I started down through the mesquite at a trot until Geoff rushed by.

"I'm gonna fry your fookin' cream crackers for breakfast if we get out of this, Stylor," he hissed as he sprinted away, and I gathered the dregs of my energy and dashed after him and we pounded down the track at full tilt as we had on a thousand rugby runs in our life before.

As we neared the junction, we tore branches from a piñon and I leaped into the bar ditch as Geoff worked on the curved tire marks in the middle of the road. We swept furiously as the siren howled closer and then Geoff ran by me and I turned to follow but lost my footing on the ditch bank and fell headlong and felt him grab my shirt collar and haul me bodily up the slope. We ran into the trees and threw ourselves down, chests heaving, as the deputy barreled past in a pall of dust.

"I'll get the Scout," I gasped.

"Why don't we just stay here? Lie low for a spell." His haggard face turned to me.

"The cop will come back when he sees we're not at the corral. Take up his post again at the highway, shut off our escape." I dragged myself to my feet.

"Maybe I'll take my chances out here." Geoff's head slumped to the dirt.

"Your choice." I looked at him. "You got a couple minutes to decide."

I staggered back up to the ridge, jumped into the Scout, and drove down, window open, listening to the siren, which I reckoned still came from the corral. I braked and looked for Geoff, but he was nowhere to be seen. Had he bottled it at the last hurdle? Or made the wise choice and was slipping back to the nearest water, Mimbres Creek, for a couple days?

"Geoff!" I whispered as loud as I dared through the passenger window. "Mate. What the . . ." The siren came stronger from the corral.

"Bollocks!" I dropped the clutch in, slewed through the bar ditch, sank to a halt to switch to high range, and set off. As I thrashed the tired old Scout up to a decent rate a form burst from the piñons, leaped the bar ditch, and snatched the door open.

"Fookin' 'ell, Stylor, you sniveling gobshite." He grabbed the truck frame and the door handle and scrambled up. "You'd have left me."

"You said you'd chance it out here." I ripped his T-shirt hauling him in. "I thought you were on your toes."

"I was having a slash." He fumbled his fly closed. "Who needs enemies . . ."

"With friends like us," we both chanted.

I rattled the short run to the highway, crossed the cattle guard, and stopped and waited, even though there was little traffic.

"What the hell, Stylor, let's go!" Geoff shouted. "We've got a deputy sheriff up our arse."

"Hang on. We need cover." I panned a look up and down the road.

"Cover? What the hell are you talking about?"

I saw what I needed, checked both ways again, and turned south, driving against traffic in the northbound lane, which was clear. I gunned the Scout, and once a big duelly pickup passed to our right in the southbound lane, the driver staring hard at us through wraparound shades, I swung into the narrow gap between his Ford and the cattle truck behind him.

"Fuuu . . ." Geoff's shout was drowned out by the blaring klaxon from the semi, which was rollicking along at considerably more than the forty-five miles per hour I was managing to coax out of the clapped-out Scout. I heard the shriek of tortured rubber and in the rear-view mirror watched the Kenworth grille fill the frame. Geoff's fists, braced against the dashboard, had pale shiny knuckles; the single fist, in the wing mirror image, thrust from the semi driver's window was steepled by a jutting middle finger, and the horn continued to defile the still desert morning.

"You crazy pillock," Geoff groaned. I stomped the right foot down until we were tucked tight against the duelly, and no sooner had I done so than we heard the siren hurtling north from town. The state trooper flashed by.

A mile further down the road, I swung into the turn lane and as the cowboy driving the semi leaned on his horn again and flung a bottle onto the roof of the Scout and shouted down a litany of curses, I turned down the dirt road to Stilt's house.

14

A U.S. Forestry house in Wet Beaver Creek Station occupied by Stilt and his wife, Emily, as a perk of her job, provided as unlikely and safe a safe house as we could have hoped to secure. I drove in under the Arizona ash and cottonwoods, the latter still draped in an amber mantle, parked in front of the clapboard house, and sagged forward onto the steering wheel. Beside me, Geoff was twisted tortuously, sound asleep.

"Mate. We're there."

He stirred. I walked around to his door, opened it carefully. He slumped across my shoulders and I supported him over the first few steps until he came to.

"I can walk on my own, you daft twat." But he tempered the scolding with a pat on my shoulder.

Stilt and Wiz were at work in the garage. Wiz had set up the Ohaus jeweler's scale and was checking the weight of the bags.

"You two take a nap on some of these precious flowers?" Stilt held up a flattened specimen as we dragged ourselves into the garage and slumped down in folding chairs.

"Yeah." I smiled at him as he did quality control on the weed and handed the bags to Wiz. "We had a lot of time for kip out there."

"Judging by your appearance, gentlemen, I doubt that very much."

"Dali and the girls make it out okay?" Geoff asked.

"They got stopped. Twice, man, twice." Wiz looked up from the scale. "But they were clean and they were able to talk their way through. That was a good plan you had. Give us the full story?"

So while they weighed, bagged, and boxed our crop, Geoff and I recounted our blunders and heroics and we all laughed and shook our heads at the close scrape in the café and the closer call on the highway, and our desperate all-night off-road drive, which, if ever enshrined on the screen, would rank as the slowest car chase in history, our manic drive to stay ahead of a sheriff who turned out to be a pair of off-roaders heaven-sent to distract the law and allow the safe passage of the Mad Jag.

"Time for a strategic retreat, old chap. Overseas I'd recommend. Allow the hue and cry to die down." Stilt locked down the arms of the scale and lowered it into its case.

"You gonna have to lie low for a while. Or get the hell out of Dodge," said Wiz.

"Really?" I had thought of this, of course, but was sobered to hear my outlaw friends confirm it so gravely. "But without any evidence they can't get any charges to stick, surely?"

"Don't bet on it." Wiz lifted the last box onto the stack. "You've pissed off the sheriff something rotten. He missed a career bust back there. If he gets you in custody no telling what he might pull to get a conviction."

"I would concur. If our obese officer of the law incarcerates you in his dubious accommodations, you'll be ruing your lapsed subscription to Amnesty International," said Stilt.

"That's not so bad, Style." Geoff stood and yawned. "You can sod off down to Mexico. We'll meet you down there."

"I suppose I will." I was quite sure Geoff wished to get me as far away from his wife as possible.

We moved into the ranger's kitchen and while Stilt cooked waffles, sausage links, eggs over, and coffee, he, Wiz, and I figured a fair price for the provision of the safe house and for him to transport the odd few pounds down to Dali in Phoenix. I threw in a few hundred bucks to leave the Scout there for a few days and borrow his old pickup. We finished breakfast and I lurched outside, wrapped myself in the serape, and crashed out on the porch couch.

That evening we met the girls in Paul and Jerry's bar in Jerome. They were sitting in a booth next to each other, facing the entrance. When Geoff and I stepped through the glass doors they tumbled over each other in their haste and met us at the pool table, brushing aside the local players who stood back, amazed at the passion of the embraces.

"Oh god, we were so worried! Why the hell didn't you call?" Molly held my shoulders after the first crushing embrace.

"Sorry, darlin'. Fell asleep. Wee bit shagged after the night out."

She looked me in the eye again, kissed me on both cheeks, and turned to Geoff, leaving Emma and me caught in an awkward moment before I held her hips and she came against me and kissed me hard on the lips and stared up at me and said, "I'm quite glad you're safe."

"Not half as glad as I am." And I looked down at her and all was right in the galaxy again.

We sat in the booth and told our story yet again, this time with guiltless exaggeration, and made the girls collapse with laughter and stare with mock terror. And they told us their tale of thoroughly cleaning the van and sweating bullets when the deputy stopped them near the hot springs. I kept casting glances at the door, nervous of the sheriff making a routine check of the bars of the hippie town on the hill, or, indeed, looking specifically for me up there.

Wiz, Stilt, and Dali lobbed in and Geoff called for a party at his new gaff. We reeled into the cool dry air, all of us variously intertwined, down the center of the street, past the ruin of the Bartlett Hotel and the police station, and we lurched down the steep street passing the narrow flatiron and Tracy's pottery store and up the creaking wooden stairs of the Old Jerome Hotel.

Word of the party flew as it only can in a town of, give or take, five hundred. The wooden floor of the old hotel groaned as a rager took off, and we were all soon havin' it large. I lurched ecstatically between groups: Curt and Sharon, the lovely couple of gold jewelers; Craig, the mastodon ivory carver, whose auburn hair hung to his haunches, coupled at that time with the ill-fated Michèle; Walrus Lee, from the gulch; Guy, of course, drunk as a deacon; the gorgeous lesbians Irene and Karen, who'd now become Sage and Quinoa; and Katie Lee, the famous folk singer and environmentalist, who'd been the last to run the Colorado River through Glen Canyon before the flood and who, with Edward Abbey, had fought for the removal of the dam decades before it was cool to do so.

Wiz lured Molly onto the dance floor. When the chance came, I cut in and led her out on the deck, with its view over the vast valley under an interminable ceiling of pearled velvet.

We danced awkwardly for a mo before I spoke. "I'm going to have to head for Baja early."

"So I heard."

"Things are a little hot around here just now."

"For you, yeah."

"You can travel down with Geoff and Ems. We'll have Christmas on the beach. Just as we planned. My treat. Right?"

She kept her eyes averted, one hand on my shoulder, the other in my palm: two acquaintances at a dance class in a church hall.

"I'm not coming to Mexico." She looked up. "I've put the shop up for sale."

I stepped back, broadsided.

"But darlin', Jesus. We've chatted about it for ages."

"We talked about a lot of things, Jem. Traveling. Living together. Starting a business. Very few of them lead anywhere. There's no future with you. You've got your mind set on Emma right now, but you'll drop her as soon as you've had your fling. And as soon as you've sold your crop, you'll be off like a robber's dog, to steal your line."

"But, but . . ." I was speechless. This wasn't the way I had planned it at all. Sure, I still hoped there might be a chance to pursue the affair with Emma, but I hadn't reckoned with losing Molly completely. I had hoped to keep my bread buttered on both sides and Molly wasn't having any of it. "What are you going to do? Where are you going to live?"

"I've been in Jerome a couple of years now. I need a change. I'm going back to Stanford. Finish my law degree." She stared out to the cliffs on the eastern side of the valley. "I love this place. But it gets old sometimes. Too many people hanging out, going nowhere." She welled up and buried her head in her hands. I reached for her but she sprang back.

"Don't. I can't bear it. I would have loved you, Jem. But you don't want me. You don't want anyone. Sometimes you can be so . . . so fucking cold." She glared at me. "Sometimes I come home to you and see your face, it's like . . . like stepping into a cold shower. And then you turn on the hot. I don't know where I am."

She tried to push past me.

"Please, Molly." I held her. "I've been so very fond . . ."

"Oh, for Christ's sake, spare me that patronizing bullshit." She pulled my hand off her arm and ran along the porch past the door to Geoff and Emma's place and down the stairs and out into the dark streets of Jerome. I slumped against the rail, astounded at how hard I was taking this, even though I'd largely expected and precipitated it. I stared out at the brilliant land and sky that had won my heart more than anything or anybody in my life and was overcome by a deep-seated aloneness, and thought of the passages of Kerouac's, those that talk of the great vast sadness of the American West, and of Thomas Wolfe struggling to convey the incomprehensibility of the land and those living there, passages I'd swept aside in my wild and unshakeable twenties as so much existentialist drivel, but now their meaning seared into my vulnerable brain and I sensed that, despite the present success of our scam, a blackness loomed ahead.

Two people came out on the porch and I stayed, out of sight, in a threadbare winged armchair.

"It's top-grade shit, man." I recognized Monkey, the barman

at the Spirit Room, better known as the town coke dealer.

"How much a gram?" It was Wiz.

"A C-note."

"Let me try a pinch."

"Sure."

I came out of my chair with a red blaze in front of my eyes. I strode to them and tore the bindle of cheap coke from the dealer's hand, opened it, and threw it over the rail into the night air.

"What the fuck are you doing, man?" The tall, wiry bloke came at me and I was happy to have him come at me. I brushed his hands aside, grabbed him by the lapels, and slammed him up against the wall with a fury born of all the suppressed tension of this year, this scheme, this jag, this idiotic dangerous drug, this awful parting from a woman I had loved but was too stupid, too arrogant, too goddamned fond of myself to admit it. His head bounced forward and he groaned and swore.

"Stylor! What the hell are you doing?" Wiz tried to pull me off, holding back my raised fist.

"Cocaine is bad news, Wiz. Especially this cut crap."

"Mellow out, man. It's not so bad."

"You always said you'd stay away from the powders."

"A little toot won't kill you." Wiz eased his grip as the tension ebbed.

I loosed my hand from Monkey's throat.

"That's a hundred bucks down the crapper." The dealer slid up the wall away from me.

I pulled two Grants from my wallet, stepped toward him as he shied away and stuffed the notes in his shirt pocket.

"There's your C-note. Now fuck off out of town."

"You'll regret this, English. There's rumors in town about what you've been cooking up this summer."

"If I want any more of your lip, I'll scrape it off my zipper," I snapped back. He turned and hurried down the stairs.

I fell back in the chair, breathing hard, and stared up at the porch roof.

"What in god's name was all that about?" Wiz leaned against the rail, facing me.

"Cocaine is bad for you, mate."

"What makes you say that?"

"I think it's damaged my heart."

"What? Why do you think that?"

"I've been having palpitations. My heart's been fluttering."

"No shit."

"I've been reading a book on drugs. There's a chapter on dangerous interactions. Weed and coke aren't good for your ticker."

"But you're strong, dude. You can out-hike anyone in this valley." He came and sat on the coffee table beside me. I slumped forward, palms on forehead, elbows on knees, and a thin cry escaped my lips before I could suppress it.

"Man, you need to chill out for a while." He reached over and kneaded my shoulder muscles. "Three Hawks is having a sweat in the morning on Oak Creek. You should come. You need a good cleansing."

I let him work the muscles for a while then straightened up, pressing back in the chair to shrug off his hands, still uneasy with the contact.

"I will. I'll sleep down there tonight."

"Good idea." He looked down at me. "Hey, man, I wanna thank you for bringing the crop through safe. That was a ballsy drive."

"Piece o' cake," I lied, and managed a trace of a grin.

"You gonna be okay?"

"Of course. Right as rain," I said. "I've had enough party for a while. It's been a pretty hectic couple of days. I'll see you at the sweat."

"Good. We need to talk."

"Oh yeah?" I smelt a rat. "About what?"

"It'll wait. Hasta mañana."

I stumbled down the rickety stairs and across the street and leaned against the fence to gather my wits. The noise of the party drifted down. I looked down over the rooftops of the ramshackle town that clung to the mountainside like a wasp's nest to a tree trunk. It certainly wouldn't be the same place with Molly gone—even if I could ever come back.

I was still driven by the same hubris that had compelled me to hitch to Spain at fifteen; to lead the lads, pissed as farts, on a runner out of the curry house in the wee hours; to drag Geoff to Srinagar and pull him up those cold faces in the Alps; to jump on this jag when Wiz had mooted the idea; and to bollock down any drug that came my way. I'd never thought of myself as much of a poet, but nonetheless, like Rimbaud, felt the "poet became seer through a long, immense and reasoned derangement of all the senses. He searches himself, he exhausts all poisons in himself, to keep only the quintessences . . ." My body was getting tired of the poisons and the dhukha was beginning to outweigh the bliss, as Ginsberg might have put it. If we pulled off this blag, what was next? A couple hundred grand in hand, and would I be setting up a bar in Phuket, a club in Ibiza, a trekking company in Kathmandu?

"Jem? Is that you?" Emma's voice lilted down from the balcony.

I thought of slipping away down the footpath close at hand.

"Are you all right?"

"I'm okay."

"Fancy some company or . . .?"

"Of course." If I could stomach anyone's company just now, Emma's came top of the list. She joined me at the fence. We stared out in silence for a while.

"Will you go back to England after this?" She knew the answer but asked anyway.

"Will you?"

"Geoff and I have enjoyed helping you in the canyon. And we love Jerome, the people, the climate." She looked at me. "Geoff's talking to Stilt about growing with him next year."

"You're here for a while, then?"

"For a while, yes."

"Wanna walk me to the truck?" I stood up from the fence.

"Love to."

We set off up the street on the lower side of the flatiron, toward the sign of the House of Joy restaurant, a fishnet-hosed leg creaking in the November wind.

"You weren't put off by our recent scrapes?"

"I wouldn't go through that again by choice. But I guess we would be a bit more cautious next time. Learn from your mistakes, as it were."

"Glad to be of service." I laid the sarcasm on a little more heavily than I'd intended.

"Oh, Jem." Her reprimand was justified and I smiled at her and slipped my arm around her waist and she turned and pulled me into the dark entryway under the sign. With a gasp we angled mouths and buried our fears in a fervent, searching kiss.

"When are you leaving for Mexico?" She held my cheeks in her hands when we came up for air.

"Couple of days. Molly's not coming, you know."

"She told me. We've grown close. I shall miss her."

"And you?"

"Absobloodylutely." Her hand snaked down between us to palm my old man. "Wouldn't miss it for the world."

"Really?" I choked. "Why's that?"

"The fact that you're hung like Dean Moriarty has nothing to do with it." She giggled and slid her face into mine so the dual glow of her eyes became one.

"After our night in the canyon, you have the advantage over me, sir. And I intend to reciprocate." She ran her fingers up and down my groin. "Once or often. And however you choose."

She kissed me again and the little cry that always escaped her lips after the first contact again acted as a potent stimulant and she folded her hips firmly against me and I slid one hand up to cup her breast, teasing the thimble nipple between thumb and forefinger, before she held me back.

"We'll see you in Todos Santos."

"I'll have the ceviche marinating."

I drove down the switchbacks, through the valley, and out toward the lower portion of Oak Creek, where Three Hawks had built the sweat lodge on Crisp's desert creekside. Thoughts assailed me. Should I dash back to Molly and try to patch things up? My heart fibrillations nagged at me: had I fucked up my ticker through my own indulgence? The dope was stashed—but it had been a damn close-run thing and I had to leave town or risk a serious bust. My friendship with Geoff teetered on a knife edge: whether I slept with his wife again or not, the damage was done. And Emma, oh Emma! I had tried to rationalize letting her go, just shutting her off next time she made an overture, but knew I couldn't tie myself to the mast and sail on,—and, after the last kiss under the sign and her promise of a full-service consummation once we got to Mexico, well, it would have been a shame to miss out on a true closure when everyone thought we had already done the deed!

I was stirred next morning by the soft tones of Three Hawks's chants as he shoveled red-hot stones from the base of the dying bonfire into the sweat lodge, which was built on a shelf above the creek among some mesquites. A couple of ancient cottonwoods arched overhead. I bailed out of my sleeping bag, stretched, shivered in the cool dawn, and hurried into my threads.

There was a coffeepot half buried in the coals. I poured a cup of cowboy coffee and squatted by the warmth. Three Hawks, a deerskin loincloth covering his Jockeys, raked embers from the stones and lifted them with the shovel.

"Had a good finish last night," he said.

"Oh yeah? What d'you have left?"

"Hundred and fourteen."

"Bull, bull, double seven?"

"Wise guy." He faked to spill the hot rocks on me. "Triple top, double top, double seven."

"Not bad."

Wiz's truck came down the dirt road.

"Here come the *jefes*. Better put the show back on." His sharp eye winked at me from the oxblood face, and he resumed his chanting.

"Morning." Wiz and Crisp swung in beside me and sat on a log.

"Good morning." I realized the presence of the renowned smuggler was not coincidental.

"*Yataheh*," said Three Hawks, emerging through the low door of the lodge and reaching back to drop the blanket behind him.

"*Yataheh*, bro," said Crisp, and gave the almost naked Apache a snug embrace.

"*Yataheh*, man," Wiz said. "Anyone else showing up?'

"*Quién sabe?*" Like many of the Indians raised in the Southwest, Three Hawks had better than basic Spanish.

"The fewer the better." Wiz rose and began to doff his clothes. "We gotta couple of favors to ask you."

"Sounds dodgy." I began to strip.

This sweat lodge, a low structure of cedar poles intertwined with brush and sealed with dried mud, was fairly permanent by sweat lodge standards. We'd come down here a few times during the year, often after a jag to sweat out the poisons. Three Hawks would conduct the ceremonies, which seemed to vary in gravity with the nature of the attendees: trust-fund crystal gazers from Sedona and the proceedings were long and drawn-out; a couple of the local old-timers and formalities were light. Three Hawks had helped Crisp with his operations many times in the past, and I now knew why the meeting had been called at the sweat.

We stripped naked. Crisp called the Apache greeting and on Three Hawks's word ducked into the lodge. Wiz followed suit. I came last, ducking through the east-facing door. The heat assailed me and my hangover increased to an intolerable throbbing. I bumped into Wiz's haunches in the darkness and was softly chastised. I squatted to escape the fiercest heat, dropped my head into my hands, and allowed my pupils to dilate. After a moment I could make out the figures sitting cross-legged on the shelf and the basalt stones glowing in the pit in the center of the hovel. Three Hawks beckoned me to sit between him and Wiz.

The Apache handed us each a sprig of sagebrush, then he passed a small drum clockwise round the group. When the drum came back to him, he began a solemn rhythmic beat to accompany a song dedicated to each of the four cardinal points, sung in his native tongue then repeated in ours. To the east a hymn of new beginnings, to the south one of desire, to the west healing, and to the north a lilting panegyric of old age, wisdom, and asceticism.

Three Hawks ladled water onto the stones with a cut gourd, and the intensity of the heat rose with the humidity; he then held an earthen bowl and offered further prayers before passing the bowl, which took the place of the conch in *Lord of the Flies*: if you held it, you could speak. We each gave a salutation or expressed a desire, and then the bowl was passed back to the Apache and we all took in the heat in our various ways for a long while, perhaps half an hour, while he chanted in a strong baritone.

"I hear you had some fun with our friend Farr." Crisp spoke at last, catching my eye across the gloom. Three Hawks lowered his voice and continued, sotto voce.

"Fun may not be quite the right word."

"But you got clear, and with you guys's harvest, man. That was huge."

It seemed as if my exploits of the previous couple of days had increased my stock in the eyes of the Verde Valley's most highly regarded crook.

"When are you headed to Mexico?" he continued.

"Phoenix tomorrow, hang around for a couple of days with Dali, then head south at the weekend."

"How long you plan to be south of the border?"

"Till the new year, at least. Maybe drive on to the Yucatán and Belize."

In the half-light I saw Wiz's head turn toward Crisp. "That may turn out sweet," he said.

"Oh yes?" I replied cagily.

"There's a crop being harvested in Oaxaca soon. It's from the same seed as the Mad Jag."

"We need someone to head down there to supervise the curing and boxing of the grass," Crisp said. "Our friends aren't savvy to the new methods."

"They're liable to trash it," said Wiz. "Not hang it right. Ram it into the sacks. We want to get it back here in the best shape possible so as to get the best price."

"Who's flying it back?" I looked at Crisp.

"You got it."

"Why can't one of you two go down now?"

"I got another flight planned. Jamaica, mon," said Crisp.

"And I got the girls," Wiz said, referring to his two daughters.

"If I spend any more time away, especially over Christmas, the old lady'll have me in the stockade."

"And what, if I may be so forward, is it in for me?" I asked

"My Cessna 414 has a payload of about fifteen hundred pounds, chock-a-block," Crisp said. "But if we prepare the weed properly it takes up more space, so we reckon we can load a thousand pounds. We're lookin' at buyin' it for two hundred a pound."

"The shitty brown Mexican sells right now for maybe three fifty, four hundred." Wiz was getting animated. "But if we bring it green and pristine, dude, we can get maybe a grand a pound for it. Nobody needs to know it's Mexican. It'll look and smell and smoke like the home-grown sins, if you do the job right."

"So we're offerin' you a chance to come in as a partner." Crisp nodded across the coals. "We need to raise sixty grand cash up front."

"We each ante up twenty. And we each put in our side of the work," Wiz said. "Crisp flies, you oversee the curing and the packing, I get the buyer. We all unload the plane. Including Three Hawks here, who's also our driver."

"That's me," said the Apache. "Let's step outside. Take some of that good Arizona dirt."

I gratefully led the way through the blanket door. The air and the atmosphere of the dealmaking had become stifling. I stood in the blinding light, eyes closed, enjoying the cool air. Three Hawks took my arm and led me to a shallow trough in the ground.

"Lie down," he said.

"Looks like a shallow grave," I said as I obeyed.

"Right. I'm gonna bury you alive, white eyes. Then put honey in your nostrils and watch the ants chew your face off." He grinned and shoveled the ocher dust onto me as I squirmed. "That's it, *ponsai*. Get that dirt into your skin. Get those poisons out."

I spread the sandy soil over my body, climbed out of the trough and stood letting the mud dry into a patina of dust and sweat while Wiz rolled in the dirt bath.

"You really know someone who'll buy a thousand pounds? At a grand a pound that's a million bucks, right?" I asked Wiz.

"Right, a million. Old college pal in Chi-town."

"Why doesn't he buy our current crop?"

"He might yet. But he's into real bulk. He doesn't usually trouble with less than half a ton."

"These Mexican friends of mine down there are really kosher." Crisp lay down in the dirt trough; Three Hawks coated him. "You'll have a blast. They'll look after you, man. You don't even have to go far out of your way. You can drive the coast through Michoacán, stop off and catch a few waves. And Oaxaca's beautiful. Ever been there?"

"No," I said with a smile. Being invited to join a smuggling ring by a big-time crook as he lay naked in a dirt bath while an Apache shoveled pale Southwestern dust over him, on the edge of a creek, at sunrise in the Arizona desert, didn't happen every day.

"We'll make a quarter million apiece." Wiz's voice lifted an octave. "We can do a bunch of loads. And you can take the indica seed with you. And we'll grow it down there, seedless of course, and make a massive killing next year. Whad'ya say, man?" Wiz's wide-eyed, pearly white grin shining through his mud-caked face topped it, and I burst out in peals of raucous laughter. After all that had gone down these last couple days, this took the biscuit.

Finally, I calmed down. "I'll have to think about it." I grabbed the shovel. "Get in there, you pesky redskin. My turn to bury you alive."

"No fucking way." Three Hawks laughed, threw off his few clothes. "You reckon I'd lie in a shallow grave with three *billiganas* surrounding me?" And we all laughed and ran to the creek, bare-arsed and bollock-naked, and plunged into the cool waters of another of those beautiful, year-round streams that in 1980 channeled fresh waters from the cold, high Colorado Plateau into the warm desert reaches of the Verde Valley and many of which, over the ensuing decades, have been drained to a trickle or worse by drought, greed, and unfettered construction.

Part Two

Over the Border

15

There wasn't much to Todos Santos in 1980, but that suited me just fine. I doubt I could have found a better spot on the continent to meditate, surf, study bird life, and try not to cuff the carrot too often. A couple miles south of the village, via the sandy jeep track that would soon be made into an asphalt highway and contribute splendidly to the ruin of the last gorgeous stretch of North Pacific coastline not yet raped by developers, I found a huge crescent of sand, unsullied by human hand or presence and with a point break curling sharp and clean off the northern headland.

A small palapa I built there, of driftwood and palm fronds made, in a brake of lush brush, a stone's throw from high water. I built a firepit, watched pelicans glide at the lip of twelve-footers, considered the perspicacity of the decision I'd made to smuggle half a ton of marijuana into the United States, and lived alone in the sea-loud shade.

Crisp had offered to take my ten pounds of the primo Mad Jag colas as collateral against my twenty grand stake. Thus, the only commitment required to snag a quick quarter mill was to travel down to Oaxaca to serve as consultant on the curing, manicuring, and packing of the weed, and to help unload the plane back in AZ. Also, in the bottom of the little fridge in the camper was an unusual six-pack of Budweiser. The beer cans, which had plastic inserts and threaded bases, contained approximately fifteen thousand indica seeds culled from our most productive and robust Hindu Kush plants.

It was the Oaxaca trip that was worrisome. What the hell was I going to encounter down there? What stripe of dodgy hombres was I going to have to persuade that their method of preparing grass was outdated and they needed to restructure their operation to please some pushy gringo *inglés*? And what about the whole *mordida* conundrum: the bite, the bribe, the backhander, the oil to grease the squeaky wheel? I had never really been comfortable with those sorts of deals, and now I had to learn on the fly and hope to Jesus I didn't cross the wrong *mano* with the right *plata*.

Another dark memory dogged me: the breakup with Molly, which had left me colder and more regretful than I could ever recall.

I had swung by her place after the sweat to check in and, truth be told, check out. On the deck an unfastened duffel bag spilled my things. Through the window I saw Molly sorting clothes in the bedroom, a room where we had spent so much. I had paused in the doorway, sobered by the bareness of the stripped room, watching her work, feeling the hostility of her turned back.

"When are you taking off?" My adoption of the U.S. usage was craven.

"Tomorrow. And you?" She didn't turn.

"Tomorrow also."

"Don't forget your books. They're in that box, right there." She pointed, but still wouldn't catch my eye.

"Thanks for packing them." I picked up the box. "Will you let me know where I can reach you? I'd like to stay in . . ."

"I'll write Emma with my address." She turned and swept her eyes across my face and on further: a lens whip-panning across a *mise en scene*, her dark curtain of hair wiping the frame in a fade to black.

"Molly, I . . ."

"Jem, I'm very busy." She reached into the top of the closet. "If you've got something to say, why don't you write me? You always said you were going to write about this year. Not that I've seen much evidence."

"I will write."

"Send me the galley proofs. I'd be a good editor . . . especially as I've never had more than a bit part in your plot."

"Molly, you know that's not . . ."

"Jeremy." She spoke to the closet. "Just get your shit and go!"

Finally, I turned away. When I stooped to scoop the duffel bag from the deck, her hands still held the shelf, chin on chest.

Grim thoughts were still nagging me as I took off down the face of the first of a clean-up set early one evening in Baja, and as I kicked back into the head-high wall and held my battered twin-fin Skip Fry on the lip for a second, I caught movement on the shore. I carved back into the trough, attempted a flash bottom turn, looked up in excitement to see if it was she, wiped out immediately, and got thrashed inside.

Ten minutes later, worked, I paddled in through the soup trying vainly to look cool as Geoff and Emma waited on the sand with Geoff's brother, Stuart, and Wally, an English pal who'd come over the pond to visit and had hooked up with Michèle, our friend from Jerome. There was also a photographer, Greg, whom they'd met whale-watching at Scammon's Lagoon.

"Hard at it, Robinson Crusoe?" Geoff had his usual sardonic tone. The others laughed and we all shook hands and embraced and I led them up the beach to the palapa.

"Anyone fancy a drink?"

"Does the pope crap in the woods?" Wally grinned.

I offered beer from the cooler and squeezed limes for margaritas.

"I started to clear a space for you lot." I gestured to a half-hacked area next door. "Needs a bit more work. Been busy."

"Busy surfing and skiving!" Emma smiled and our eyes met and I wanted to leap up and grab her and stare into her eyes for a day or so. I handed out the drinks and built a fire of cactus ribs.

"I've got oysters. The oyster fishermen came in the other day and anchored outside the break. I paddled over and dived down with them." I dragged a sack of oysters from the cooler and started to shuck them while they all plied me with questions.

Geoff: "How's the point break?"

"The dog's bollocks."

Wally: "How's the tequila?'

"*Fuerte.*"

Michèle: "*Il n'y a personne à cette plage?*"

"Not a soul."

Emma: "How's the bird-spotting?"

"There's a lagoon to the north with egrets, ibises, ospreys, stilts, and loads of hummingbirds."

"Will you take me there some time?"

"Of course." I passed around oysters and limes.

"I caught some great fish from shore this morning; the locals call it *huachinango*. I'll stoke the fire up and we'll chuck it on the grill."

The sun was nudging the horizon, its fire waning to an amber glow as it slipped beyond the sea. A great stratum of convective cumulus caught the westering light and produced a stunning finale to the day. The travelers settled in after the long drive, sitting on deck chairs or sprawling on the rug, tuning in to the elements of this lovely spot: the boom of the surf, the crackle of the cactus fire, the smell of salt and smoke, the soft light.

We spent the next couple of days pretty much naked. We read, fished, surfed, tossed the pigskin and the Frisbee. The boys learned that a sprint could slap one's knackers around quite painfully. Both genders learned to their cost the discomfort of baring too much pale buttock to the tropical sun.

One evening a weathered *viejo* strolled down the beach with half a *cabrito*, a kid goat, for which we traded a small saucepan and a couple knives, and then slow-roasted it. All was calm, tranquil, idyllic. But such a state could not last.

We drove down to Cabo San Lucas for supplies. The road was nothing more than a jeep track winding along the cactus-strewn shore, and it took us most of the day to make the sixty miles. We stopped frequently to admire the beaches and had lunch with a lovely old German lady who had built a hut on the shoreline and was "studying life forms." The closer we got to the town, the worse the state of the road, and we had to dig ourselves out of some deep sand in an arroyo. We made Cabo San Lucas by late afternoon.

There was one modern hotel up on the west headland, the Finistere. The rest of the town comprised a variety of whitewashed motels, a couple of taco stands where the expats met for breakfast, and a few restaurants on the beach. Some small yachts sat anchored in the harbor, sheltered by the long headland featuring the now famous arch. We congregated at the Cabo San Lucas Yacht Club, and it was there that it all went to pieces.

"I'm going to have to head down to Oaxaca in a couple of days." I was leaning against the corner of the bar; Emma sat on the stool next to me, Wally next to her, the rest at a table nearby.

"What you gannin' doon there for?" Wally piled on his native Geordie when he'd had a few, which on that jag was generally any time after the sun was over the yardarm.

"Business, lad." I gave him a smirk.

"No names, no pack drills." Emma sipped her piña colada, trying in vain to keep from stabbing herself in the cheek with the paper umbrella.

"No harm done telling you lot. I'm going down to show some growers how to cure and prune a rather large crop of grass. Then my partners, who shall remain nameless," I gave Emma's elbow a nudge and Wally a grimaced wink, "are going to fly it back to Arizona. We all unload it and I make a shedload of dosh."

"Ow'weir, mon. What's this 'we' business?" Wally drained a Dos Equis and tapped the bottle on the bar. "Divn't count on me tappy-lappin' along on your dodgy schemes."

"Don't you want to make a couple of thousand bucks for twenty minutes' work?"

"A couple of thousand bucks or a couple of decades in the pokey. No fookin' way." He started on another Dos Equis. "This beer's canny, mon, but I could murder a pint of Federation."

I laughed and turned to Emma. "How about you, Ems? Fancy unloading a planeload of pot? Could be a laugh."

"Aye, 'appen it could." The company of another northerner, it seemed, had revived her Yorkshire patter. "But tell me more about the trip to Oaxaca. You start with the ferry to Puerto Vallarta?'

"Right. Then, if you have time, you spend a couple of days in Yelapa."

"Yelapa? That's the place you can only reach by boat?"

"Precisely. One hotel, a few houses to rent, waterfalls, a disco, mind-boggling *raicilla*."

"What in heaven's name is *raicilla*?"

"A pulque drink made from cactus. Mildly hallucinogenic."

"Sounds great." Wally perked up.

"And after Yelapa?" Emma dragged the chat back to the journey.

"I haven't been farther south than Yelapa. But you head on down through Michoacán and Guerrero. There you're in the true tropics, lush vegetation, humidity . . ."

"Oh god." Emma's eyes shone. "I've never been to the tropics."

"You're in them now, ya silly cow." Wally and Emma had that sort of relationship.

"Yes, but this is desert. I want that steamy heat, vines, monkeys chattering in the palms, brightly-colored parrots."

"Snearkes, mosquitos, fevers." Wally sensed trouble. "I thought we were going wheel-watchin'?"

"Sod the whales. I'm going with Jem." She fixed me with that look that I remembered from the canyon. "That's if he wants company."

"Uh, well . . . Yes, it would be nice to have someone along."

"Good. That's settled then. I'll tell the others." And before I had a chance to protest, she strode over to the table.

"Fookin' 'ell, Style. What've you done now?" Wally shook his head slowly.

"What've *I* done?" I stared at him wide-eyed and turned to see the others glaring at me past Emma's animated back.

Stuart came over, ordered a beer, and said, "Trust you to ruin my fucking holiday, Stylor."

"What've I done?" I tried again.

"Don't give me that crap. You've been after Emma since Geoff first met her." And he turned away.

Wally and I drank in silence for a while till he ordered some shots.

"You might as well get palatic. So when Geoff gives you a pearsting you won't feel the pearn." And we slugged the tequila without clinking.

"Why don't you come along, mate? You'd really get to see a lot of Mexico."

"Oh why, aye mon. Be a spear prick at a wedding while you give Ems a threarpin'. Then dive in with you and your iffy drug-runnin' chums. No thanks." He kept his head down and I sensed his condemnation and embarrassment with the scandal, and that I'd put the mockers on his trip.

"Bring Michèle along."

"She's got to be back, mon. The teachin'."

Michèle came and sat next to him. She looked past him at me.

"Jeremy, Jeremy. ¿Qu'est-ce que tu as fait?"

"*Rien.*" I gave my best attempt at a Gallic shrug. She snuggled up to Wally and the two of them stared at me: Wally, stern, mustachioed, stolid, northern English working-class, and Michèle, pretty, angular, mischievous, from privileged southern French stock. Michèle gave a twitch of her head and the trace of a smile and I couldn't help smiling back at the sight of these strange bedfellows, and, yes, at the thought of having Emma, just Emma, finally just Emma, with me on a long drive along a gorgeous coastline to a great adventure.

"Divn't teark it so lightly, ya gobshite." Wally scowled. "The two of yous'll breark Geoffrey's heart."

I was going to make some reply in my defense, tell him that Geoff and I had talked about it, that we had already swapped partners down in the canyon, that he was sort of okay with it, but I was groping for the right words when Geoff shouldered his broad back between us, looked at me, and said, "Your round, I believe." It was twenty-one years, at his deathbed, before we again exchanged a civil word.

Drunk, palatic, legless, we stumbled from the yacht club and drove the vans until we bogged down in the beach and everyone passed out. I awoke before dawn with a throat as foul as a vulture's armpit and lurched away for a slash. As I passed the other van, I could hear Geoff and Emma arguing, and in the agony of the hangover I felt my eyes smart and tried to force myself to start up the motor and drive away from it all. But I lacked the decency and the backbone and crawled back to bed to await my fate.

We dug out the vans and shared a tense late breakfast at the taco stand on the main street, which in 1980 was still dirt. As we finished, Emma walked to their camper, climbed inside, and emerged a few minutes later with her bag, which she put into my vehicle. She returned to the table and Geoff and Stuart rose without a word and boarded their Volkswagen, followed by Greg, the unfortunate traveler caught in this ill-tempered English soap. Wally and Michèle stood awkwardly for a moment.

"Reckon the breakfast tab is yourn, Style," Wally said, then turned to Emma, of whom he was especially fond.

"I hope you know what you're doin', lass." They hugged.

Michèle held me, then Emma, and then with a quick "*Au 'voir*" grabbed Wally's hand. The van rattled out of town and Emma and I sat in silence, staring at the quiet bustle of the little town and wondering what the hell we'd done.

We spent the morning shopping and booking passage on the ferry to Puerto Vallarta. Conversation was stilted and strained. Around mid-afternoon we set off north toward the palapa. I drove slowly, warier than usual of damaging the van or getting stuck, but even so we sank into soft sand in a wash and piled out, grumbling. I had silly thoughts about our trip being ill-fated, and shoveled wildly. Emma pitched in.

"Try it now, Jem." She stooped to watch the wheels as I engaged the clutch. "Stop, it's just digging in."

"I've got an old rug in the back. We'll put it under the tire."

I shoveled hard to make a rut and Emma knelt beside me and between us we pushed the rug against the rubber. Our arms, sweaty from the work, were pressed together, and I turned toward her and our mouths met and she toppled back and I fell across her, snatching her head to me, searching for her tongue. But she twisted away and my head snapped up.

"What's wrong? Have you changed your mind after all?" I stared down at her in real concern.

"No." She giggled, arching her back off the ground. "I have a shovel digging into my spine!"

We laughed and laughed and kissed deeply again until she held me away.

"After all this time, waiting for this," she said, brushing her shorts clean. "I don't fancy screwing you in the middle of a dirt road beside a bogged-down van. I want to make love to you in your little hut, in the firelight, with those frightening waves booming in and stars overhead."

So that evening, after a meal of freshly caught lobster, we did just that. And though I didn't feel the earth move, the roof of the palapa certainly rocked when she reached her arms high to hold a crossbeam and kneeled astride me for the first time, and her rasping cries of climax drowned out the crash of the surf and the spasms at the heart of her hips sent such unforgettable tremors through mine that I was moved beyond any level of pleasure hitherto experienced and realized that all my lewdest dreams and profoundest fears of this affair were proven that night on that beach.

16

The coastal road along the nexus of the steep, *madroño*-covered hills of the province of Michoacán and the warm Pacific waters was unpaved in late 1980, and we could have camped, stayed, and surfed for weeks at any one of a hundred deserted beaches on that fabulous shore and not seen a soul. As we left the flintier desert and traveled south the humidity rose, the flora broadened, and the sharper edges of our affair fell softly away.

One afternoon a pickup truck approached as we drove slowly along a rut-ridden track, lined with house-high greenery.

"Looking for someplace to spend the night?" A thick Texas accent came from the leathery Anthony Perkins face.

"Perhaps," I said cautiously.

"Hang a right just down aways. We got a little ree-sort down there. We're frying *cabrilla* tonight."

"All right. Maybe we'll pull in."

We found the ree-sort, a few shabby huts and two dilapidated restaurants, after a tortuous drive. I noticed a dirt track leading to a headland and we drove out to a point overlooking the sheltered bay. We made camp, which, with the wonderful Veedub camper, merely entailed popping the canvas roof and pulling out the bed linens on the high bunk, a tedious task that was usually followed by Emma and me clambering up to interweave limb and torso, lip and labia, prose and poetry, palate and penis, before the kettle had boiled.

This evening we showed restraint and sat in our deck chairs, sipping tea. Moored in the bay were a couple of small yachts; from one of them a sailor paddled out to ride the point break. A brace of osprey hung, delta-winged, above us in the fresh afternoon breeze.

"Emma?" I seldom used her full name. She replied in kind.

"Yes, Jeremy?"

"Why did you decide to come with me?"

"That's an odd question."

"Not so odd." I stared at the ospreys. "You've left your husband to join his best mate on a criminal enterprise and to share his bed."

She paused. "I only went steady once before I met Geoff, and it hardly matched *Dr. Zhivago* in the romance stakes. There were a couple of flings while I was on tour with the ballet. Geoff and I do all right in that area, but I wanted to be with another man."

"I'm honoured to be the chosen one!" My sarcasm was thinly disguised.

"Jem." She was looking intently at me. "It's not as if I picked up a stranger at the pub and dragged him into the sack. I've always loved our times together. Sitting by the coal fire in our little house, chatting about books we'd read, listening to Geoff and you tell hair-raising stories of climbs and travels—I know you both so well. Is it so terrible if I sleep with you both?"

"As long as he doesn't take it too badly. He can be a sensitive lad," I said, but I knew that the sensitive one might well prove to be me. "What about prepping the harvest in Oaxaca? You going to lend a hand?"

"If you say it's pretty safe, absolutely."

"We're going into the villain's lair. There's bound to be risks."

"I'm ready for that. It fits my new M.O."

"Seizing the moment? Grasping the nettle?"

"Exactly." She fell silent for a moment before she went on. "Growing up in that semi-detached in Leeds, I could tell my folks weren't happy. Mum claimed she liked her job at the library but I sensed that she was less than chuffed with her structured life, the modest house, a decent man for a husband but hardly D'Artagnan. Dad soldiered on at the local council but I knew he longed for something more challenging, more engrossing."

"You were young when he died."

"Eleven. Mum and I became really close then. She pushed me to take more chances in life—she had so many regrets."

"So you became a teacher."

"Bollocks," she scolded. "I was a dancer for many years before I wrecked my knee. I chased that dust devil."

"Fair play."

"Teaching isn't the spunkiest profession, I grant you. That's why I jumped at this chance to come to America. Geoff wanted to stay in Brum, stick with his career, start a family. But I felt trapped. I was terrified of repeating my parents' life."

"Did you talk to your mum about quitting teaching, going to the U.S.?"

"I did, and she said, 'Go, lass.' Don't think twice."

"It's all right." I tried to sing the Dylan line. "And sleeping with me—more 'carping per diem'?"

She giggled, recalling our first intimacy in the garden. "Remember when you took Christina to Scotland? She and I had drinks when she got back. She gave a glowing report!"

I smiled at the memory of the brilliant computer programmer who'd charted a successful path through the misogynistic seventies' barriers of her profession by eschewing any man who attempted to remove her glasses. Nonetheless, her inhibitions and underwear had dwindled inversely to the mileage logged north of the border on that fine week prowling the Highland glens.

"I've been intrigued since, to see if you matched your reputation."

"And?"

"I need to conduct further tests." She gave a chuckle, came to me, and straddled my lap.

Later, we walked down to the beach bar and were greeted by the Texan.

"Welcome. Welcome to Bahía de San Gerónimo," he said, and ushered us to a rickety table. "¿*Cerveza*, ma'am?"

"If I may."

"Okay. And I'll bring you an hors d'oeuvre just to sharpen your appetite. It's the specialty of the house."

Emma gave me a quizzical glance and I shrugged my shoulders. We watched the two yachtsmen row to shore in a tiny dinghy and walk up to the café. With a cursory nod to us, the only other diners, they took a distant table. I thought their behavior European—in the standoffish, supposedly urbane manner one would expect to encounter on a similarly unpopulated Greek island or French beach.

The Texan emerged with the beer and the "hors d'oeuvre," which cast some light on the sailors' reserve—American brothers, it transpired—and why they were anchored in this particular bay. He set the bottles on the table and slipped an enormous spliff between the condiments.

"That might improve one's appetite," I said, nodding my thanks, and ran the joint under my nose.

"Plenty more where that came from."

"Is that right? Locally grown?" I realized immediately that I might have been too forward, but he had, after all, piqued my interest.

"That's for me to know and you to find out." He trotted out the cliché, then softened. "You interested in grass?"

"Somewhat."

"Wanna see some primo product?" He leered down at me and his head shook. I felt a jolt of fear. Was this guy playing with a full deck?

"Don't go to any trouble."

"No trouble. C'mon."

We rose, and he led us back through the tables. I felt the stares of the brothers. We passed through a disheveled kitchen to an undecorated room. He pulled a box from under the bed, set it on the covers, and opened it, standing proudly beside it.

"You ever seen shit that fine?" He pulled a branch from the box and held it out.

Emma was closest to him. I gave her a little nudge and she examined the grass.

"It's a little brown for the American market. Looks like it could have done with a little longer in the ground, too. See the seed bracts." She held the stick of buds under the bare lightbulb. "They aren't as full as they should be."

"Oh yeah?" He looked at the weed and frowned at Emma.

She gave a little sniff of the branch. "Mmm. Nice aroma but would have been a lot better if it had been cured in the shade. And you'll need to prune it tighter to get top dollar for it in the States. You can't leave this much stick showing." She put the branch back in the box while I tried to avoid creasing up.

"What the hell? You a contributing editor to *High Times*?" The Texan glared at her.

"Easy mate. You offered to show us," I said.

"I didn't mean to offend," Emma said.

"Okay. No offense taken." His face lightened. "I see you guys know your grass."

"We've got a working knowledge," said Emma.

"We've got over two hundred boxes like this one." He nodded his head maniacally and began to grin again. "And we've got a way to get it back to the States."

"By land or by sea?" I jerked my head toward the front of the joint, where the two sailors drank.

The Texan narrowed his eyes at me and leaned his crook-nosed face into mine. I felt another stab of disquiet. Were all dope smugglers except my partners as unhinged as this madman?

"That's for me to know and you . . ." He stopped as if suddenly remembering something. I wondered how much of his stash he smoked each day. "But I need to find a buyer back there. You guys wouldn't know . . ." He tailed off.

"It's possible," I said. "Check us out if you get to Arizona."

"You got a card?"

I pulled out a Mad Jag sticker that I kept folded in my wallet.

He looked at the sticker and his eyes bulged like organ stops. "Mad Jag! Mad Jag!" Emma slipped in behind me and held my wrist. "You guys grew the Mad Jag?"

"You've heard of it?" It was my turn to be bewildered.

"Heard of it? Course I've heard of it." He turned to a desk, wrist-deep in scattered papers, and scrabbled through them. "Where's that goddamn magazine? I have it sent down so I can follow price trends. Good sins fetches three K a pound in Alaska. We're thinking of sail . . . sending ours up there. Aah, here it is. Yes. You guys just won *High Times*'s award for Best Domestic Sinsemilla of the Year."

"No way." I looked at Emma and she laughed.

He leafed through the pages. "There it is, see? 'Best domestic sinsemilla of the year. A smooth yet powerful stimulating high, has psychedelic qualities.'" He turned the magazine over like a teacher showing the class and moved it back and forth under our noses, making it hard to read. But there it was: a picture of one of our buds and Dali's jaguar, rampant, leaping off the page.

"Well, I'm buggered." I smiled at Emma.

"How on earth?" She shook her head.

"Wiz sent in the bud and the label just before I left."

The Texan's face poked over the page. "See, what did I tell ya? Hey, boys!" he yelled to the restaurant. "These guys are far out. They grew the Mad Jag grass. Come and meet my partners." He waved us into the kitchen. "Oh, I gotta prep the grill for the fish. You'll eat with us, yeah? On the house."

A pile of coconuts lay on a thin cutting board. He grabbed a machete from a hook and began slashing at them. Shards of coconut husk shot across the room. He flung the mess under a filthy grill iron, reached for a can, and doused the fuel with a liquid that smelled remarkably like petrol. He struck a match and tossed it in one motion. A fireball sprang from the grill and for a second the man's startled aquiline profile was frozen in backlight as he reared back from the heat as if betrayed. Several small fires caught on the underside of the thatched roof and he leaped spastically to slap them out with the flat of the machete.

Emma was firmly tugging me toward the door, urging us as far as possible from this deranged creature. He swept past and beckoned us toward the young men.

"This is Spencer and Randy, from La Jolla."

As we introduced ourselves, I noticed a glow at the next restaurant, less than a hundred metres away. In a trice, flames had engulfed the tinder-dry structure.

"Christ! That place is on fire," I said, and they turned slowly to watch. No one moved a muscle toward the blaze.

"Shouldn't we help?" Emma looked at the three men and then at me in amazement. Silence was the terse reply. We watched the restaurant burn, catching glimpses of men silhouetted against the flames vainly fighting the fire.

Here we were, in a remote village in Michoacán in the company of a lunatic wanna-be smuggler and his two henchmen, whose taciturnity was probably quite justifiably based on the eccentricity of their crazy partner, watching the competition's premises burn to the ground. And none of our acquaintances lifted a finger to help. Yet we had just learned from this eccentric that our grass had been awarded the highest accolade from the accepted arbiter in these matters, *High Times*. I grinned, watching the rafters of the restaurant crash into the inferno and send a shower of sparks into the night, and wondered if we could raise the price of our crop. But no, I'd made a deal with Dali and the price per pound was set. The upside of the award would mean he could probably move the weed a lot quicker.

Some days later, we awoke on a strip of sand somewhere near the border of Michoacán and Guerrero. After our usual cups of PG Tips, I prepared an unusual breakfast. Emma sat across from me, as naked as I, while I spread out half a dozen peyote buttons, each about the size of a hamburger bun, on the cutting board.

"What is your pleasure, madam?" I asked.

She held up one of the little dark green cacti, closed her eyes, and attempted a mild piss-take of the Buddhist's "om."

"I think this one and I have a deep bond."

"Okay." I began pulling at the pale tufts of fiber that stuck out of the cap.

"Why do you do that?"

"This stuff has strychnine in it."

"Oh, great. We're going to ingest a strong hallucinogen that contains a deadly poison. Are you sure you know what you're doing?"

"Absolutely."

"How many times have you taken peyote?"

"Once."

"Did you prepare it?"

"No. But I watched Wiz very closely."

"Then I'm sure we'll be just fine." She smiled to offset the sarcasm.

I chose another cactus, pulled the hairs from it, and began slicing the pulpy flesh. Emma picked a morsel and put it in her mouth.

"Ugh!" She gagged. "It tastes awful. How are we supposed to eat enough to get the effect?"

"Well, normally you mix it with orange juice in a blender. The citric acid neutralizes the alkaline of the cactus."

"But we don't have a blender, do we?'

"I thought I'd chop up some fruit and make a sort of fruit cactus salad."

"That should do it." We both chuckled nervously. It seemed ironic that we had brought this little cactus, *Laphophora williamsii*, from Arizona, when it had been grown in northwestern Mexico and smuggled into the States. Peyote produces mescaline; mescaline produces a dissociate state, visual hallucinations, and, we hoped, heightened sensory perception and insight.

I chopped the cactus finely and mixed in the fruit and we sat cross-legged around a bowl forcing down the acrid pulp.

"Now, you might feel a bit dodgy at first."

"You don't say." She grimaced as she swallowed.

"You might throw up. It acts as an emetic. The whole process is supposed to be cathartic, cleansing."

"Great." She contorted her face again and I couldn't help grinning at her. It was marvelous to have her along to share this venture, to see her adventurous side come to life. The quiet young teacher who'd sat by the coal fire in the Birmingham terrace house was now squatting cross-legged, naked and totally tanned, on a Pacific beach and about to experiment with an exotic hallucinogen.

An hour later I groveled on my hands and knees in the surf, my guts dry-heaving until I thought my ribs would crack and I wondered, in all seriousness, if I was going to make it. A few feet away, Emma sprawled on her back in the shallow water, groaning.

"Jesus, Stylor. What've you done to me? I think I'm going to die." She gagged again and turned her head to spit bile.

"Hang on a bit. It'll soon pass." I tried to sound reassuring, but my own retching belied my confidence.

We crawled about in misery for a while longer before the puking stopped and we managed to stagger to our feet and realized we might live after all. I brewed some chamomile tea and persuaded Emma to eat some dry toast. Then began a day that we both still look back on and find hard to express.

Much of the day was euphoric. I watched Emma for eons as she waded in the surf, spread-eagled on the sand, or sat in the shade under the palms. Her emergence at one point from the water was absurdly classical, Venus birthing from the waves.

Time and visual perception became distorted. Colors became so luminous that I found myself mooning at a flower or cactus in interminable incomprehension.

At one point I stood waist-deep in the sea and watched a drop of water fall from my hand like molten metal bleeding from a crucible, then waft like a feather to splash into the ocean, scattering droplets like mercury hitting steel. Later, I lay with a latticed sun hat across my eyes, for hours perhaps, delighted by the kaleidoscope of light and color exploding and diffusing through weft and warp.

The hallucinations began around mid-morning. I saw my father walking along the shore with his usual brisk step; but he became protean, swerved into the water, and morphed into a red kite, and then morphed again into a hideous creature, a winged insect with an enormous raptor's beak which swept down on me. Was this Father's way of condemning me for jeopardizing the good name of his family? I writhed face down in the sand in Promethean agony as the creature gorged on my offal, until Emma, seeing my distress, ran over and shooed away the phantom.

"What was it?"

"My father. Death. A harpy. God knows." I gazed at her face, and my paranoia eased as I studied the fair eyebrows, the slightly chapped full lips, the down beneath her septum, the dilated pupils and bright irises that bled between malachite, turquoise, and mother-of-pearl as I stared into them, transfixed.

"And you? Seen any ghosts?"

"No ghosts. Lots of very strange visuals." Her expression remained neutral, distant.

"Nice or nasty?"

"Fascinating, more. One minute it's Magritte."

"Bowler hats on the waves?"

"Suspended above them. Some Kandinsky, as you would imagine."

"Point and plane out of whack?"

"Compositional cockups. Then Bruegel, Max Ernst, Even Joan Miró got a look in." She rolled closer to me and angled her thigh to brush mine lightly.

"I thought you read English lit?"

"Thank you. I will take that as a compliment. I will have to reread Crowley one of these days," she said, lifting her leg gently. The point of contact burned. "And Lewis Carroll or Huxley."

"Have you passed through the doors of perception?"

"I think I might be slipping through the keyhole." She giggled and turned very slowly, or so it seemed, so that the length of her body wrapped me like hot clay. She looked down at the arousal her touch had caused. "At the moment I'm reminded of Aubrey Beardsley's banned etchings."

"Ink drawings, I believe."

"Pedant."

We walked the beach, locked together in a trance, a mystique of wonder, stimulation and desire, on and on until one of us stumbled on driftwood or snagged a toe in the sand. At the end of the beach, we swam around a rock formation and found a tiny comma of sand.

"I'd like to dance," she said, limbering up. "Any requests?"

"When I was at uni I worked the spotlight at the Birmingham rep for Prokofiev's *Romeo and Juliet*. Do you know that one?"

"Jem." She gave me a pained glance. "I understudied Juliet. How about her side of the pas de deux in the first act?"

"Were you ever called up?" I climbed the rock and sat.

"No. The cow was indestructible."

She continued her stretches for a few minutes while I soaked up the setting, and then she hummed the first few bars and began. I gazed down at her, basking in this classic lap dance: plié, demi-plié, arabesque, jeté; she swept through the classical moves and positions, humming the orchestration the while. When she had finished, she curtsied, and the firm sand of the tiny beach was scuffed throughout with the marks of her performance. A wave tumbled between her calves and swept the beach clean.

I stood and clapped and we made eye contact and held for a long, long time.

"I wonder, by my troth, what thou, and I did, till we loved?"

"Oh Jem, you jest surely. You think I wouldn't know 'The Good Morrow.'" And she swept on through one of Donne's best:

"Perhaps we sucked on country pleasures, childishly? Or snorted we in the seven sleeper's den? And I . . ." She frowned. "Line, please."

"'Twas so; but this all pleasures fancies be," I prompted.

"If ever any beauty I did see," she went on, and we both finished the stanza:

"Which I desired, and got, 'twas but a dream of thee."

I jumped down and ran to her and swept her up and carried her to a wedge of warm sand between the rocks. She wrapped herself around me and we lost ourselves in each other until I made to turn her and she sprang over eagerly on to her chest and gave a sob of anticipation. I straddled her shoulders, facing her bottom, and encouraged her pelvis higher. She arched her back with that brilliant flexibility that only those long trained in the supple arts can manage. I dove into the canyon of her buttocks, rasping my tongue along the bed, pausing to nibble briefly for the first time at the forbidden pucker, delighted by her snatched whimpers of shock and abandon, then traveled the perineum to land at the petals, and drove my tongue deep into the folds while angling my fingers between her thighs from below, and then flailed all extremities in the moist salt at the hood of her cunt until she wailed her climax to beach, wave, cove. Still shuddering, she turned onto her back and I encircled her waist and snatched her up so that her toes groped in vain for the sand and plunged my lips into her and she twisted toward my center and loosed a brief lament of lust and abasement before her mouth and throat engulfed me and we both hollered release to the entire, uncaring state of Michoacán, and our world past and yet to come.

17

The Hotel Las Golondrinas on Calle Tinico y Palacios in Oaxaca had a room reserved in my name. The unforgettable journey, which would prove, all things reckoned, to be the best of my life, was over and I was forced to confront the glib reality of earning a dishonest living.

Wiz and Crisp had told me to wait to be contacted by the people of Flaco Miguel, whose mugshot, in May 1982, would grace the cover of *Newsweek*. Flaco owned the hotel, so, assuming the staff knew that we were there courtesy of the hombre himself, I wangled an upgrade to the honeymoon suite.

Three days after our arrival we were passing through the lobby for the *paseo* and dinner when the desk clerk called out:

"*Señor! Un mensaje para usted.*"

He handed me a card with a telephone number on it. I tucked it in my pocket.

Next morning I made the call, and soon a small man in a shabby suit arrived in the lobby. The desk clerk nodded for me to follow him, and without a word we walked to the car. We drove through the busy streets and into the north outskirts, where we pulled up to the gates of a hacienda. A man with a rifle held across his chest exchanged a word with the driver, and swung the gate wide.

We parked in front of a vine-draped hacienda. I walked up to the massive zaguan door assailed by a barrage of emotions: anxiety tinged with terror, terror spiced with intrigue. It isn't every day one gets invited to the home of one of the major gangsters in the Americas. The door opened before I reached it, and a man in jeans and a leather jacket held his hand up to me.

"*Disculpe, señor.*" He gestured for me to lift my arms and I noticed the straps of his holster. He frisked me carefully from shoulder to toe. He searched the bag, passing the seeds without pause; his charge was to protect his boss, not meddle in affairs. Satisfied, he beckoned me in.

He led me through a high-ceilinged foyer featuring a sweeping staircase, and gestured me into a large, dark room. Bookshelves lined one long wall. On the other side, which was split by a chimneybreast, an array of Mexican art was displayed that defied belief. A huge study of Orozco's infamous Prometheus mural, which graces the Pomona College dining hall, and an oil of his portraying a jaguar and an eagle. Pre-Cubist fruit and post-Cubist figures by Rufino Tamayo. There were a couple of surrealist pieces by, I think, Guillermo Meza. Some Rivera, of course. And the monkey peering over Kahlo's self-portrayed face, could it be the famous . . . surely not! I approached more closely to check it out, when a voice from a winged leather chair startled me.

"*Conoce usted nuestros pintores mexicanos?*"

I swung around to face the speaker.

"*Algunos. Más o menos,*" I answered timidly.

He held out his hand but did not rise. I took his hand and squeezed as gently as he did.

"*Sientese, por favor. Cuál pintor es su favorito?*" He pointed to the couch, then called out. "Roberto!"

"*No tengo bastante*, uh . . . knowledge." I groped for the word

"*Conocimiento.*" Another man entered the room. He was middle-aged and wore corduroy trousers and a button-down shirt. He had an avuncular manner, reminiscent of the masters at my school.

"Hello, Jeremías. My name is Roberto. I see you speak some Spanish."

"A little. And very poorly," I replied.

"I help Miguel with translation."

I sat and studied the famous criminal while he and the translator spoke. He had a lean, sallow face. There was a distinct sheen to his eyes as if he lacked sleep, and there was a twitch in his eyebrow; I wondered if the great man had a tic. He wore an olive silk shirt and a gold chain. His trousers were neatly creased and a pair of tasseled loafers gave him a preppy touch.

"*De dónde viene?*" Flaco asked after we had all settled.

"*Inglaterra,*" I said in my nervousness, unsure what he'd meant by the question.

"*Muy lejos.*" He snapped open a little silver box. "*Pero dónde vive en este momento?*"

"In Arizona."

He dipped a tiny spoon into the cocaine and held it out to me. My resolution to cry off this insidious stuff wavered. Would I offend the man if I declined? Would he think I was a pussy, or worse, a narc? All sorts of dreadful thoughts of what could befall me flew through my brain, but I held up my hand.

"*No quiere el perico?*" He seemed more surprised than offended.

Presumably people seldom refused free coke, and perhaps never from the master smuggler.

"Not while I discuss business," I said.

Flaco smiled at the translation, snorted the powder, and asked, "*Que clase de negocio hace?*"

I began cautiously, choosing my words carefully, attempting to sound confident, and giving the translator full sentences at first, until I sensed a little impatience on Flaco's part and shortened the explanations.

I explained how the market was changing in the States; how smokers were switching to "green" marijuana; how if he improved his curing and pruning methods he could substantially increase the price north of the border; how Crisp (and here he smiled, as if remembering the pilot fondly) had sent me down to educate the growers and pruners; and lastly I explained that there was a new strain from the other side of the planet whose growing season was almost half that of the sativa and whose smoke was more potent, and that many seasoned dopers were taking to it. To emphasize my point and, I hoped, my credibility, I showed him the bags of indica seeds.

He studied them closely. I held a few sativa seeds in my palm by way of comparison.

"*Muy grandes. Y fuerte?*" He kept the words simple.

"*Sí,*" I said. "*Esta planta tiene huevos grandes.*"

He laughed at that and the toady interpreter followed suit.

"*Cuántos meses para esta semilla?*" asked Flaco.

"*Tres,*" I said.

"*Tres!*" Flaco had been involved in the growing of *mota* long enough to know the advantage of having the grass in the ground for roughly half the time the native strain required.

He spoke at length to the room and the interpreter nodded along.

"He wants you to go up into the mountains tomorrow and meet his chief *jardinero*. Show him how to prepare the grass for export. And leave him the seed for next year's crop."

"Good. *Tengo mi mujer conmigo.*"

"*No importa,*" said Flaco.

"And who will pay me for the seed?" The translator relayed the request. Flaco's head twitched in my direction. I felt a pang of fear. Things had gone well. Had I ruined it with my chutzpah?

"*Cuánto cuesta una semilla?*"

"*Un dolar cincuenta.*" I figured a dollar fifty a seed was a fair price in the U.S.

"*Y cuántas semillas hay?*"

"*Quince mil, más o menos.*"

He considered for a moment.

"*Veinte mil?*" Twenty thousand would be a nice contribution to our traveling fund. He looked at me and I held the eye of a man who'd made a thousand deals of illicit contraband in his time and maybe ordered the deaths of some who'd stood in the way of his rise to the top of his trade. I couldn't shake off Dylan's words: "I stared into the vacuum of his eyes and said, 'Do you want to make a deal?'"

"*Veinte mil.* Okay," I said.

He laughed. "*Paga el inglés.*"

It was obviously chicken feed for him. I cursed myself for not asking more.

"*Y ahora quiere perico?*" He held the spoon out and this time I felt honor-bound to accept.

Next morning Emma and I were met in the lobby by Flaco's sad driver, Enrique. We pitched our gear into the trunk of the car and climbed gingerly into the back seat to be driven to the place where Flaco's men grew and prepared enormous quantities of grass for export to the United States, and where I would have to change the way his crew had prepped contraband marijuana for generations.

Cloud hung low around the mountainsides that day and we swung through the curves, now in bright sunshine, now in dense fog. It was market day and people—mostly women, Emma observed—tottered through the mist toward the city carrying loads in time-worn manner. The broad, olive-skinned faces of the Zapotec women were often topped by large bundles; brightly-colored shawls draped their shoulders; red sashes cinched their white dresses at the waist. Men walked with them, but many rode donkeys; some were on horseback.

After a silent few miles, we pulled into a village and turned off the plaza by the church onto an unpaved road. As we lurched down this track, a gunman appeared from the undergrowth and held his rifle high. We came to a halt and the man peered in the passenger side. Enrique spoke rapidly and gestured back to us. The man passed the rifle muzzle across the window and looked in at us, pausing much longer on Emma than on me, then gestured the driver on. We negotiated some more ruts and potholes and finally swung into a compound: an older house with a small courtyard, and, across from it, some cinderblock barns.

I wondered what on earth we might encounter in this villains' lair. Bougainvillea vines clung to the posts of the portal that surrounded the courtyard. Costa's hummingbirds darted between the flowers. A bucket dangled on a wire under an ancient capstan in the middle of the small lawn. Under the portal, three men ate their midday meal.

"*Buenos días, señora.*" A stout middle-aged woman approached Emma, carrying a tray of food. "*Tiene hambre?*"

"*Tiene hambre?*" Emma repeated before comprehension flashed across her features. "Am I hungry? *Sí, sí. Tengo mucho hambre,*" she replied proudly.

The men rose and the woman made brief introductions. One of them wore a military uniform, and I noticed a modern rifle propped against the adobe wall. Was this one of the famed Federales, whom the Yanks always spoke of with fear? We sat and ate and listened to the men make jokes, which of course we did not understand, but I caught the words *guapa* and *güera* a few times and thought to myself, yes, she is beautiful and blond, and keep your stinking gangster hands off.

After the meal, the housekeeper showed us to a simply furnished room off the courtyard and announced that it was time for siesta.

"Tough life being a crook," I said, after she had gone, and stooped to sweep Emma onto the bed, but she held my shoulders.

"Are you sure we're safe here, Jem?" The creased forehead showed her fear.

"Having second thoughts?"

"Not exactly." She peered nervously through the window into the courtyard. "But—we are in the belly of the beast."

"Wiz and Crisp swore that everything down here was kosher."

"I hope they're right." She turned back, and a few days later I would reflect miserably on her doubts.

Later in the afternoon we strolled into the courtyard and across the yard to the barns. The rifleman tilted his chair back against the barn wall and watched us approach.

"*Buenas tardes,*" I said. He replied in kind.

I stepped into the barn and surveyed an amazing scene. At two lines of tables, perhaps fifty people sat working on the weed. Branches of marijuana lay in the middle and the workers tossed the pruned buds into large wooden troughs. I walked between the tables, aware of the silence I had caused. Emma followed. As I was looking into one of the troughs, a man spoke.

"*Buenas tardes.*"

"*Buenas tardes.*"

"*Soy Tomás.*"

"Ah, *el jardinero. Somos Jeremy y Emma.*"

"*Bueno.*" His tone was curt, and I anticipated resistance to our role as the bringers of new methods. "*Listo para trabajar.*"

"*Listo*. Ready for work."

"*Sí*. What do you think of our *mota?*"

I picked a few buds from the trough. Most were light brown, some dark green; they were pressed and looked as if they had been dried in a heap. Most of the buds had a few seeds.

"*Muy bueno*," I lied. "*Dónde está el lugar para* . . . uh . . . drying . . . *secando?*" I stumbled through my pidgin Spanish in an effort to soften his tone.

"*Ven.*" He led us to a smaller building, where shelving covered much of the walls, like a battery chicken farm without the chickens. Each shelf was stacked with piles of grass in various stages of curing. The smell was powerful, and though I detected the base scent of our Mad Jag it was overpowered by the mustier smell of overgrown and over-cured weed. Tomás was making an effort to improve the quality of his product, but his methods were still primitive.

The crucial time for any marijuana, any crop, was harvest. If the plant was not cared for the moment it was cut and over the following days, there was no chance of it reaching the standards that smokers in the States were demanding.

"*Hay mota en la tierra?*" I asked.

"*Sí,*" Tomás replied rather cagily.

The three of us walked down a jeep track for about a quarter of a mile, then turned onto a footpath through the oaks and down a south-facing slope. On a narrow terrace cut into the slope was the last patch of this year's grass. Emma and I walked among the plants, sniffing the buds and delighting in the aroma. Here was the source of the Mad Jag, the brilliant, powerful weed that was presently blowing minds and winning accolades in the States.

I checked the colas and saw that the seed bracts were swollen and rich with resin. I twisted a bud gently in my hand and held it down for Emma to smell. She sighed and smiled at Tomás and he grinned back. Nothing like a fair lady to melt a desperado's heart.

"*Tomás, tiene una otra . . .* uh . . . *lugar para secando,*" she asked.

"*Por supuesto.*"

Tomás showed us an old stable, and we spent the evening rigging a spider's web of wires and string under the beams. We drove a pickup back to the terrace and cut a load of the willowy sativa.

"*Es muy bonito,*" I flattered the *jardinero* as I gathered armfuls of the weed and laid them gently in the bed of the pickup.

"*Muy bonita,*" Tomás corrected me with a grin.

"*Claro que sí.*"

We drove the load back to the stable and Emma and I carried the plants in, a few at a time, and hung them over the lines. We exaggerated the care we took and showed Tomás how to pull the leaves over the buds to help the cure. By last light, we had the barn full of hanging plants.

A couple days later Tomás chose a crew to work with us in the stable: four cheerful women and six men who started out moody but warmed to the task. The buds of this crop were full and pristine and our workers chattered away in Zapotec, holding the colas up in admiration. Their fellow workers visited to check out the *nueva mota verde*, intrigued by the care that was being taken by the *equipo especial*.

We insisted on packing the market-ready product in boxes. Tomás resisted this request as he claimed, quite logically, that it would mean less poundage on the plane, but we held firm. Over the days the pile of boxes grew, and soon we were close to having a thousand pounds of market-grade green sinsemilla ready for transportation. I was ready to call Wiz and arrange for the flight when the *mierda* hit the fan.

The bust came not at dawn, as it would in the States, but during the siesta. I was woken by the muzzle of an automatic weapon being prodded into my chest. Emma yawned, then let out a startled scream. We were forced to dress with the Federales peering at Emma. Outside we heard shouts, and then in the distance a rifle shot rang out and Emma grabbed me. Another couple of shots shattered the afternoon and Emma clung to me as a soldier grabbed me by the arm and flung me forward.

Outside the courtyard, three military trucks were parked in line. We were hustled to one of them and ordered in. Many of the pruning crew, mumbling and crossing themselves, sat on benches on either side. Once it was full, two of the Federales slammed the tailgate. We bounced away down the dirt road.

Emma whispered, "I thought you said Flaco Miguel had the authorities in his pocket?" Her eyes were moist and her brow knotted.

"That's what they told me."

"Will we be separated?"

"I don't know, love."

"I'm frightened of what they might do to me." Her face was gray, the whites of her lovely eyes bloodshot, the frown lines of her brow deep and shadowed.

"Don't worry, Ems. Nothing's gonna happen to you. The guys in Arizona'll find out about this and have us out in a flash." I spoke boldly, but I had my own fears.

We turned into the plaza of the little town and the truck backed up between two buildings. The soldiers dropped the tailgate and shouted something. The men jumped down. I stayed put until a Federale holding a pistol saw me.

"*Y usted. Gringo. Vamanos!*"

I hung back.

"*Vamanos!*" He waved the pistol.

"*Y la mujer?*" I hesitated at the tailgate.

"*La mujer está segura con nosotros.*" The guy leered at his compadres and slid the barrel of the pistol up and down his palm. I felt something flash across my vision and before I could control my fury I had leaped from the bed of the truck and lashed a kick at the man's head. My shoe caught him in the chest and we both crashed to the ground. I gained my feet briefly before the blows rained in and I heard Emma shriek my name before a blunt weapon dented my cranium.

18

The pain woke me. I held my head in my hands and forced my eyes open. I was lying on a hard dirt floor staring at the ceiling of a small room. Beside me, on two bunks and the floor, lay other men. I closed my eyes and the horror of where I was and what had happened swept over me.

Dear god alfuckingmighty. No no, oh Jesus no. Where was Emma? What had happened that Flaco Miguel hadn't been able to protect us? And what would my father and the rest of the family think when they heard about this? I sat up and backed against the wall, and took stock of the situation. There were six men in the small room and through my haze of pain I didn't recognize anyone from the marijuana ranch.

There was a bucket against the wall.

"*Agua?*" I croaked to the man closest to me.

"*Sí.*" He stared at me through hollow eyes.

"*Potable?*"

He shrugged.

My throat felt like 80-weight sandpaper. In the pail I found an earthenware cup. The water was brackish; with what I didn't dare think, but I had to drink.

Had the Federales been forced to bust the operation? Had Flaco Miguel been busted? I had heard of dope smugglers tossing bones to the authorities now and again to allow them some publicity while they took a hefty backhander to turn a blind eye to the major operations. Were we the juicy bone flung to the government dogs?

I shivered on the dirt floor until dusk, when there was a noise outside. There was a slot in the door under a barred window. Trays of food were passed in. I grabbed the bars and yelled.

"Let me speak to someone. I have some money. *Tengo dinero.*" The jailer walked away and when I turned back to the men in the cell, I immediately regretted what I'd said. Six dark faces stared at me over the beans and tortillas.

"*El dinero está afuera,*" I blustered, and made a gesture that was intended to indicate anywhere but here. I shuddered and catnapped through the night and awoke with a start to discover one of the men trying to tear the heel off my shoe. I scrabbled with him, trying in my lousy Spanish to convince him that I had no money on me.

I lay for four days in that foul incarceration until my spirits were at such an ebb that I began to fear for my sanity. Christmas was only a couple of weeks away; would I still be here then; could I be in here for years? Desperation and remorse overwhelmed me.

On the second day I had heard a low grunting coming from another room. I crouched to peer through a low door. The men around me made obscene gestures. The sight of the deranged creature sprawled on the fecal-carpeted floor of his foul oubliette beating his dick while observing his arsehole via a sliver of cracked mirror haunts me still

I worried about my heart. It had already skipped a few beats while I lay in this vile place. But my worst fears were for Emma, and that what might happen to her was my fault. On the afternoon of the fourth day the guard came to the door and shouted through the bars.

"*Oye, güero. Venga aquí.*"

He swung the door wide and I almost ran out of the cell. I didn't care if I was going to a firing squad; the relief of getting out of that place was tantamount to a death-row reprieve. The guard waved me ahead of him and we walked down a dark passageway. He unlocked a door and led me into an office.

"*Buenas tardes.*" An officer sat behind a leather-topped desk. "I am Capitán Costillo." He held out his hand and I felt like refusing it, but thought better of it. Beside him stood the Federale whom I'd kicked.

"*Señor Inglés.* There are some very serious charges against you."

"What are they?" I nodded to the soldier, who remained po-faced.

"Cultivation of marijuana. International smuggling. Assault of an officer of the federal government."

I said nothing.

"*Muy serio. Es posible que usted pase veinte años en prisión.*"

Twenty years! Holy Christ. But the fact that I was here and he was talking to me gave me some hope. I waited for the bite.

"Of course, *quizas* it's possible an arrangement."

He made the universal sign, rubbing his thumb on the pads of his first two fingers.

"There are many expenses, much paperwork, involved with your case. Also my soldier here, he is badly injured by your, how you say, *violencia*. He cannot work and his family must eat."

I nodded along with his bullshit.

"If you would like to help us with these . . . costs." He angled his head slightly and held my eye. "You could be free to go, *ahora*, now."

"*Cuánto?*"

"*Diez mil.*"

"*Diez mil! Y mi mujer?*"

"*Lo mismo.*"

"Twenty thousand U.S. That's loco."

"Of course, if you prefer to continue to stay in our fine rooms, Guillermo can take you back." He snapped his fingers. The soldier stepped forward.

I held up my hand. "How will it be arranged?"

"Do you have the money?" he countered.

"Maybe."

"Where?"

"In Oaxaca."

"We will drive you and your mujer to the Ciudad de Oaxaca. You pay. You and your mujer are free to go."

"No more arrests? No bullshit at the airport?"

"Señor, I give you my word." He held his hand across his chest.

I trusted him about as far as I could kick his skinny arse, but my choices were slim.

"Okay." I crooked my arm. "But you don't get a peso till my woman is here. And she better be untouched."

"Señor Inglés, you offend our Oaxacan hospitality. *La mujer está segura.*"

"I've heard that song before." I stared at the Federale.

"*Mande?*" The capitán glanced between us.

"*N'importa,*" I said, "*Vamanos.*"

"*Tranquilo,* Señor Inglés." He dialed a number on his rotary phone and spoke rapidly and I picked up a few words: *coche, ciudad, güera inglés.* The *capitán* completed his call and we all walked out of the wretched village lockup into the bright sunshine. I stood for a moment, eyes closed, letting the sun and fresh air wash over me.

I reflected on the *mordida*. Twenty grand! It couldn't be coincidence. Flaco Miguel had stitched me up. He'd got his knickers in a twist over my asking payment for the seeds and set up this whole scam to show me who called the shots in his manor. Even though I had seen the pruning crew swept up in the bust, I had seen none of them in jail. Had he told the soldiers to put on a good show, then had the crews sent back to work? We pulled up to the Hotel Las Golondrinas and I guided them to the car park.

I walked over to the VW van, opened the doors, and turned to them.

"*Dónde está mi mujer?*"

"*Ella está aquí, señor.*" The *capitán* turned his hand out and I searched the cars in the lot until I caught sight of her silver pageboy cut and saw her brave wave and wanted to dash over there and grab her and beat the bejeesus out of the men who held her.

She held her head down until she got close, then looked up and ran the last few paces to me. I held her as she sobbed on my shoulder and I apologized and apologized.

"*Señor. El dinero, por favor.*"

"Jump in." I slid the door open and Emma threw herself inside. I reached in to the fridge and pulled out the Budweiser cans, unscrewed the bases, took out the rolls of cash I'd exchanged for the seeds, lobbed them to the *capitán*, and jumped in the driver's seat and drove away from the hotel of the double-crossing Flaco Miguel.

I drove hard, following signs for the airport, to the outskirts of town. I picked a side road and pulled to a halt in a grove of pines, and flung myself in beside Emma, who had curled under the covers of the bunk. I clasped her to me, but she held her arms across her chest.

"Ems, are you all right? What did they do to you? Tell me." I held her head up; her eyes were glazed, distant.

"I'm okay, I suppose." She stared past me.

"Did the soldiers . . . try anything?"

"They tried. But the other women protected me."

"Bastards. I'm so, so sorry that all this happened."

"Yes. So am I." She sat up. "I could murder a cup of tea."

I popped the roof and started a brew.

"If I'd had to stay in that filthy hole another hour I doubt if I could have managed it. I've got to get the stench off me." She took off her clothes and began a French bath at the little sink. I turned away as if we had never been lovers.

"And those poor women who'll be there for god knows how long! Oh Jesus." The tears burst forth and she slumped down on the bed and I tried to hold her, but she was inconsolable and shook me off and wept bitterly into her hands.

I felt my own tears welling—not just from the memory of my own experience in the jail, but at the thought that I had given

Emma the most terrifying experience of her life and that she held me responsible.

I stepped out of the van, closed the door quietly, and walked among the trees trying to find some comfort in the things I'd yearned for in the cell: the smell of the pines, a cold breeze, a cloud-flecked sky. A flash of crimson in the lower branches might have been a red warbler, but the sighting brought none of the usual delight.

"I'd like to get a flight out of here."

"Where to?"

She tucked her sweater in and zipped her pants and my usual pang of desire at watching her dress was shut down by despair. "To the States. See if my husband will have me back."

I felt a blow in the diaphragm and gasped at the bleakness ahead.

"Okay. I was headed to the airport."

We drove silently, and while she packed a bag I went into the airport and found a telephone. After a false start, I got through to Wiz.

"Hey, man. How's it going down there?" I envisioned his cheery face, the mustache jutting out as he grinned, his head nodding with excitement at hearing from me.

"Crap," I said. "Emma and I just got out of jail."

Silence for a moment. "Emma? What's she doing with you?"

I sensed the reproach. Wiz hated scandal.

"I think you better phone your man. I suspect that the deal is off," I said.

"We'll see. Did you get a load prepped?"

"Just before the Federales kicked my arse and threw me in the slammer."

"Jeez, too bad. Did you hand over the seed?"

"Yes. I handed over the fucking seed. And got a rifle butt in the head for my troubles," I snapped.

"Easy man, it'll all work out." His voice softened an octave. "You better call Dali. His crib got burglarized."

Oh, for Christ's sake. When sorrows come, they come not as single spies, but in fucking battalions. "Right. I'll call him." I could barely croak out the words. "I'll be back in a week. We'll talk then."

"Far out. Drive safe."

I hung up and slumped against the wall and gradually slipped down to the floor, my head between my knees. Everything was collapsing: the smuggling, the selling of the Mad Jag, the affair with Emma. I looked up and saw her walk purposefully across the terminal. Back in the public eye, she seemed to have regained her composure, despite or perhaps because of the incarceration: the fine posture born of years of disciplined deportment, the offset camming of buttock and breast, the toss of blond Barnet Fair. Beyond her I saw men and women waiting for flights follow her path across the floor and I felt as if a part of me were being ripped away.

I joined her at the counter and counted out the notes for her ticket to LA. She showed her passport and there was a moment of panic when the ticket clerk looked at the name and turned to her supervisor. But after a quick consultation the woman handed everything back and we walked away to the gate.

"Don't you want some coffee?" I wanted to hang onto her for a few more minutes, a few more decades.

"We're boarding soon. You don't have to stay." Another blow; I was being dismissed. I wanted to scream, I wanted to grovel at her ankles, to clench her shoulders and glare into her eyes and yell at her and the entire teeming terminal that it shouldn't end like this, that we had shared something rare and precious on the beaches of Michoacán and Baja, that I was terribly sorry about her suffering in jail but I had gone down too and it wasn't fair of her to hold it against me, she had accepted that risk; but nothing would come out other than:

"I'll see you in Arizona then?"

"Jem. I'm married, to a friend of yours. I have to find Geoff. See if he'll take me back."

"It was just a quick fling then, all along." I pulled her shoulder round to make her face me. There were tears in her eyes and she shook her head and the platinum curtains stroked her cheeks.

"Thank you." I choked out the two words and tried for three more, the three that are most difficult to say, three that I'd never uttered in my life; but they wouldn't come. She turned on her heel.

I watched her back until she disappeared and then began a journey of such bitter abandon, of such salt-eyed mania, of such fatalistic, abject despair that I still look back on that devil's drive up the murderous roads of Mexico and find it hard to believe how the fuck I failed to wind up another tarp-flung, blood-tainted statistic in a roadside ditch.

19

Despite my best efforts to splatter my sniveling visage across the hood of a bus on a dark road in Mexico, I made Dali's drum a week out from Oaxaca. I crept into the studio and he swiveled on the stool and with a yell of "Stylor, you dog!" coiled me in a wicked embrace. I nearly burst into tears but kept it together.

"Jesus Christ, man, how the fuck are ya? We heard you were rotting in a Mexican jail?" He held me at arm's length. "Goddamn, it's good to see you safe. You look burned out on the trail, man. Look like you could use a toke." He released me and turned to the tray and began crumbling a bud.

I gave a brief rundown of my recent adventures while he skinned the jay and stared wide-eyed.

"So, how are the sales going?" I asked.

"Fantastic, man, People just can't get enough of the m.j. Specially after we got the award."

"What about the break-in?"

"They just took the stereo. Probably some punks."

"It was nothing to do with you selling the gear?"

"Who knows? You can't worry about these things, Jem boy." He pulled an old cigar box from a shelf under the easel. "Stilt brought down ten pounds total. I'm working on the last box so I'll settle for the eight right now, okay?" We counted the twenties and fifties together and my spirits rose a notch.

We went to the kitchen and Dali swept up his daughter and sat her on the cable-spool dining table and began laying settings for dinner. I went to the phone in the living room, sat in the low basket chair, and dialed Wiz's number. I soaked up the familiar room, Dali's outrageous, brilliantly-colored art, the plants, the LPs stacked under the stereo system, the low coffee table covered in books and *Rolling Stone* mags.

"Hello."

"Hey, it's me."

"You're back. Welcome home."

"Did you talk to the thin man?"

"Yes. He said you did a great job. Tomás and he are excited about adopting the new methods. They're chomping at the bit to see how the Asian ladies turn out."

"And the package?"

"It'll arrive soon."

"Is that so." I could scarcely believe my ears and wanted to say something very rude about Flaco Miguel and his methods, but held my tongue. I wanted to quiz him about the bust, but knew it contravened protocol to broach subjects like that over the phone.

"You're coming up here soon."

"Tomorrow."

"See you then." Click.

"Well, I'm buggered," I said, and explained to Dali and Fiona that despite everything that had gone down in Oaxaca we were still on to bring in the load. Fiona told me that I was mazed and we sat and ate roast chicken and scalloped potatoes and I played "I see you" with Sophie around the flower vase and grinned at mine hosts and learned the true meaning of the term "comfort food."

My excitement at coming back to my old haunts was tempered by the realization that I was heading back into the spider's web and, lurking at its edge, his pink Mormon paws monitoring the strands for the slightest sign of Wiz or me or any drug-dealing scumbags, was the ominous bulk of Willard Farr. But luring me into his domain was the far more compelling figure of a young woman, who, as far as I was concerned, could recite Donne and the metaphysicals as well as Dame Judi Dench, could fling an arabesque jeté alongside Dame Margot Fonteyn, and could rival Linda Lovelace in the oral traditions.

I found her at Michèle's place in the gulch. Outside, I saw Wally's Oldsmobile. The dark-stained wooden house was set below the road, which cut across the steep hillside. A rickety footbridge led to a wraparound porch. From the road I could see Michèle in the kitchen and beyond her, sitting at the dining table, Wally and Emma.

I felt a stab of nerves as alarming as seeing a truck out near the canyon or a sheriff's vehicle in my rear-view mirror. What would be my reception: the ice of the Oaxacan airport or the heat of a Michoacán beach? Before I could change my mind and turn away, Michèle spotted me, gave a shriek, and ran onto the porch. We met in the middle of the bridge.

"Jem, Jem! *Tu es arrivé. Tu es en sécurité!* Wally, Ems, *c'est Jem!*" And she flung her arms around me and gave me a smackeroo on the lips and dragged me inside. Wally walked from the table, held out his hand, paused for a mo, then pulled me into a back-slapping embrace. But Emma stayed seated and I felt my hopes sink. At last she stood and came to me and held my shoulders as the others fidgeted, and she held my gaze with those azure eyes, then hugged me close and led me back to the table and made me sit beside her and held my hand under the table and the world turned again.

"Canny drive?" asked Wally.

I nodded and grinned and we chatted and sank a few brews and Emma squeezed my knee occasionally and after a while, as the shadows crept up the cliffs above Sedona to the east, Wally suggested we adjourn to the bar. He and Michèle drove while, at Emma's suggestion, we two walked. She tucked her arm in mine, as she always did, and we climbed in silence, panting, for the first few blocks before she spoke.

"Geoff's in town."

"So I gather."

"He wants me to go to Oregon with him. He says I'd like it there."

"Very green and lush, I've heard," I said. "Are you going?"

"What are you going to do?"

"I'm going to New Mexico. Look for some land. Build a house maybe."

"They say it's lovely there. Adobe houses, high mountains, Indian pueblos, right?"

"Yup, lots of history, good food, great skiing."

"I'm coming with you." She broke the silence. "I wasn't sure until this evening. But seeing you again . . ." She stopped walking and leaned back against a fence. "I've missed you tremendously." She paused. "But the whole Oaxaca jail. It was so terrifying. And I blamed you. It wasn't fair. I'm sorry."

She pulled me against her and we kissed, and there was no caution, no hesitation, no doubt; we melded into each other's lips and mouths with all the disquieting drive of our affair.

She held me away and I stared at her face and felt a surge of joy that, falling as it did after the long journey of such bitterness and uncertainty, matched any I'd felt in my life to that moment.

"When are you going?" she asked.

"In the morning."

"I'll meet you out on the road to the Daisy Hotel at first light." She turned and we walked on. "But I'll have to tell Geoff."

"Yes, of course."

"He won't like it."

"You don't say."

We walked up through the town and my steps were light with the reconciliation, yet weighted by Geoff's looming presence. We joined Wally and Michèle at Paul and Jerry's bar.

Back at Michèle's house, we'd barely settled at the kitchen table when we heard Geoff's truck skid to a halt and I went out to meet him and the fight took place.

"Don't think you're fucking off with my missus, Stylor," he barked. "You've done your dash with her."

He came on hard, swinging wildly, backing me against the porch rail. I avoided a wild blow but he grabbed me and threw me down. Emma and Michèle ran from the house and calmed the fight for a moment. But when my guard was down, he gave me another hard sock in the mouth and I ended up in the cactus, and it was my turn to be enraged and I pinned him until the others dragged us apart.

"Stop! Stop it! Both of you," Emma shouted, and we both turned to face her, flushed and angry in the moonlight. "It's no use, Geoff." Her voice had an air of sadness. "I've decided to go with Jem."

Wally edged between us, sensing more trouble. I tensed, expecting Geoff to have another go at me, to grab me again, to swear to kill me as he had when we were making the run along Mimbres Canyon Road with the crop, but he simply slumped against the railing. Michèle took him by the shoulders and led him across the bridge. Wally stood looking at Emma, who swayed slightly as she breathed heavily through a clenched hand. Then he turned to me, glared for a moment, shook his head, and turned away to the house.

I drove away and went down to the road that led around the curve in the land and out to the promontory where the Jerome Mining Museum hung above the valley and on the hill stood the huge dilapidated ruin of the Daisy Hotel. I spent a restless night in what might be described as a contrived agony of indecision. As many times as I thought of the pain I was causing Geoff, I was reminded of the unfathomable pleasure Emma and I found in one another, and not simply in the sack. Here was the first woman in my life in whose company I was not merely at ease but with whom every moment was a delight to be treasured. If I could wrestle her away from Geoff for while longer, I would do that. In the back of my mind, though I was loath to admit it, was the biting knowledge that our affair was doomed; that there were more Oaxaca airport days ahead; that Emma, when faced with the decision, would resort to the status quo.

Thus, as I sipped a cup of cha and watched a fair lady walk toward me along a Jerome street on the morning of the winter solstice of 1980, I felt little remorse and a lot of keen anticipation. I was headed to Santa Fe and Taos with my lover, and on the way we would stop off and unload a planeload of Mexican grass and make a shedload of dosh. The jag was still on. *¡Vamanos!*

20

We made the village of Christopher Creek under the Mogollon Rim by the afternoon, and took a cabin at the Creekside Steakhouse and Tavern. I tucked Emma, exhausted from a night of heated discussion with Geoff, into bed.

I slipped quietly from the cabin and took a long walk through the forest. In the late afternoon I dropped back to the lodge, found a pay phone, and dialed Wiz's number.

"We're on," he said after the platitudes. "Tomorrow. We'll meet at the Hand Pumps at eleven."

"We'll be there."

Could we really pull it off? Was our jail time in Oaxaca indicative of some breakdown in the security of Flaco Miguel's operation? While in the valley I had spoken to both Wiz and Crisp about the bust, and they had both assured me that it was as I had guessed: a test of my resolve.

And did I have any qualms about smuggling marijuana? Absolutely none. Since my first experience of the product of cannabis, a joint of Old Holborn tobacco and Lebanese blond at a party to celebrate our A-level results on a beach near Exmouth, I had had no doubt about the value of the drug. My initiation was spiced by a certain Alison Maynard leading me away into the dunes to drape her slender figure across my loins.

The discovery of dope by no means meant the replacement of alcohol. Dope became the secretive pleasure, often shared late at night with friends amid ribald laughter, or alone on a soaring walk across the Devon clifftops, looking down, if blessed, on the russet shoulders of a hovering kestrel or, exquisitely, with a lover savvy to the piqued sensitivity of the nerve endings, or, best of all, with an initiate swept away, breathlessly, a little confusedly, but none the less memorably by her first high in my arms.

The moral implications of growing or smuggling pot presented no quandary. The branding of my trade as narcotics trafficking rankled somewhat, as it was utterly inaccurate. As growers we thought of ourselves as modern-day moonshiners preparing a product that, like the booze of the twenties, was merely in a temporary state of prohibition. Never did we imagine it would be the best part of four decades before the authorities shared our view.

Emma sat up in bed when I got back to the cabin.

"It always surprises me when it's you, not Geoff, coming in."

"When doesn't it surprise you? In the sack?" I snapped, more sharply than I intended.

Emma put her palm to her mouth, as if regretting the statement. "Jem. You know who I prefer to see."

"For now, I do." I felt myself pursuing the tension almost against my will. The realization of the obviously finite timeline of our affair brought out my mean streak.

"I want desperately to be with you." She stepped from the bed in her undies and T-shirt.

"But you've got the best of both worlds. A lover and a husband, at your beck and call."

"That's not true." She made to hold me but I turned away. "Geoff told me not to bother coming back if I left with you today."

"Please Emma. Spare me the angst." I held her eyes. "We both know Geoff quite well."

She sat on the bed, her hands between her knees, lifting and lowering her head.

"I know you too, Jeremy."

"What's that supposed to mean?"

"Since I've known you, I've never seen you go steady."

"And?"

"I'm not sure I can trust you to do so now."

"Thanks a bunch." I chopped the words out, though I knew my history lent weight to her argument.

"I just don't know how serious you are about all this. About me." She looked up. "Arizona's brought out something in me I didn't realize was there, a capriciousness, a little lunacy. At the same time, I need something to hang on to, something reliable."

"And that's Geoff?" I said to the mantelpiece.

"It doesn't have to be, Jem." Her words hung there; I tried to reply but the sentence was stalled in my throat, stalled by an ingrained unwillingness to commit, stalled by the conviction that she could not leave Geoff, stalled by my concern, however conflicted, for my mate. The silence lurked in the cabin like FX smoke in a studio.

"Tomorrow's the big day." I finally broke the tension.

She stared at me for a long time before reacting to the change of subject.

"Oh lord. I'd forgotten about unloading the plane." She clenched her jaw and neck muscles to show her nervousness. "I suppose I'm ready."

"You don't have to do it."

"Geoff and I talked about it while you were gone. He said it was up to me. As long as you're certain there'll be no monkey business this time?"

"Absolutely certain. Wiz and Crisp have both been down there since we got put in the pokey."

"Are you sure they can be trusted?"

"It was Flaco putting us to the test. And he was a bit put out by me charging for the seed. It's partially my fault."

"You weren't to know that. It was just business."

"Wiz said Flaco didn't know we were in jail so long. He's promised to make it up to us."

"I'm not sure that's possible." She was thinking back to the dreadful jail, the wretched women in there for god knows how long.

"It's up to you, love." I held her look for the first time since I'd got back to the cabin.

"I would like to see it through. After all, I was quite intimately involved with the process, as well as with one of the participants." She smiled and held me tightly. "Now, will the handsome villain take his ingénue, whom he's lured into a life of crime, for one last supper? She's ravenous."

"Of course. But first we have to get our escape packs ready."

"Escape packs?"

"A pack with the essentials for a getaway. If the law comes down on us while we're unloading the weed, we might be able to leg it. And I fancy my chances in the woods against those guys."

In a Kelty daypack I stuffed a space blanket, nuts, dried fruit, a flask of tequila, a small torch, extra clothes, two cigarette lighters, a water bottle, and a couple of topo maps of the rim country. Emma watched me, then followed suit with a pack and supplies I'd brought for her.

After dinner we had a brandy at the bar, chatting cautiously with the cordial barkeep, who quizzed us with the standard questions and gave us the lowdown on the area, of which I claimed ignorance. The temperature had dropped below freezing when we left the joint, and we huddled close on the walk to the cabin. We stood on the porch and had a post-prandial puff of the m.j., our breath mingling with the smoke to form brief trumpet clouds in the dry air.

Emma shuddered and dashed inside and I ran after her and stoked the fire into a blaze and turned to see her emerge from the bathroom in the white teddy that was to become the talisman of our affair. Lace-trimmed and cut high on the hips, and cropped low on the bodice to allow easy access, it had the effect of a physical blow on me. I groped behind me and grabbed the mantelpiece. She pranced across the room, threw a couple of arabesques, and toppled against me.

We kissed deeply till I squirmed.

"What's the matter?" She looked at me in alarm.

"My jeans are about to burst into flames," I said, and jumped away from the fire, trying to hold the material away from the backs of my thighs. Emma laughed and unbuckled my strides and pushed them and my underdogs down my thighs. I stepped out of them and threw off my shirt.

She kissed me, but not with her usual ardor, cautiously, as if exploring some uncharted experience, her lips barely touching mine. Our sensory perception from the Mad Jag buzz was so acute that the slightest nexus of contact was utterly absorbing. She trawled her upper lip slowly across my throat and I arched my head away, the tension quivering between agony and fantasy.

I watched her tongue emerge like a maggot from a carcass, and the image, far from dampening my zeal, heightened it. She allowed the soft underside of her tongue to drape itself across my chest to a nipple, where she paused to close her teeth, and made me snap my jaws in terror and delight.

I begged in deafening silence for the obvious progression and though she made me tremble in a misery of anticipation she did not disappoint, sliding slowly to her knees, tongue and teeth snailing across my gut, while I gazed, moon-eyed, at the trail of saliva.

Finally, her quest reached its grail, and she nibbled interminably at my bobby's helmet before, with one steady, inexorable motion, she sank her lips to the base of my old man. I didn't gasp. I yelled my appreciation and surprise. In a dozen years of shagging around I had certainly become familiar with the pleasures of a willingly delivered b.j., yet no girl had ever come close to the engulfing that Emma had just achieved.

Strangely and wonderfully she held still, her teeth gnawing gently at the base, while a substantial portion of my dick was firmly entrenched in, and beyond, her pharynx, which gave a soft, peristaltic pulse accentuated by the vibrations of the long notes she crooned. Amazement led to extreme excitement and despite her stillness I found myself surging toward release. I tried to prolong the elemental bliss of the moment: the little romantic cabin; Emma's gorgeous, tanned figure, kneeling, splay-thighed; the warmth and crackle of the fire, and all enhanced by the tactile transport of bliss from our brilliant weed; but I was powerless to stave off the stimulus of her stationary esophagus and came with a chorus of yelps. The potent combo of the peaking of the cannabis high and the unique sensuality of Emma's oral technique gave me a shuddering climax I had never experienced before and have not since.

After several gulps her lips slid carefully up my length, paused to suckle briefly at the head, then popped off the tip. She let out a long sigh and stared up at me wide-eyed.

"When . . . how?' I slumped to my knees; my breath came in gasps. "When did you learn that?" It was certainly an inadequate comment on such a mind-blowing moment, but my thoughts were clouded by the drug and by the stunning pleasure of the unique fellatio.

"I didn't. Just thought I'd give it a bash."

"Bash away any time." I answered pathetically, drew her up and grabbed her shoulders and kissed her mouth; as her tongue cleft my upper palate I tasted the salt of my seed.

21

The Hand Pumps of the meeting place were gravity-fed gas pumps set in front of the general store and feed bin of a tiny town that will remain nameless. Wiz's Volkswagen Thing, the rugged little car he'd bought for the AZ back country, was parked in front of the store. Nobby was sitting in the passenger seat, polishing his glasses. He put them on, focused on me, and slowly lifted his thumb. A large panel van was pulled up to the pumps, and a stout old boy in bib and brace overalls was cranking the pump.

"Eight gallons, you said?"

"Right," said Three Hawks and winked at me as the old feller pumped a couple more times to take the fuel level beyond the mark on the glass. He lifted the handle from the slot and clenched the trigger. We all watched the gas gurgle from the sleeve.

"Simple yet ingenious." I tried my best Sidney Greenstreet and failed. Emma raised her eyebrows and shook her head. The old feller slanted a look my way and said, "Last I heard, gravity still works." He lifted the nozzle. "You need gas?"

"No thank you," I said, and realized in my nervousness I had said too much. Wiz and Dali came out of the store and we exchanged twitchy nods. They got in the Thing and drove away. Emma and I followed as Three Hawks paid. About a mile up the dirt road, Wiz pulled off into a clearing amongst the junipers.

"Okay." Wiz was jumpy. "Leave your vehicle here, Jem. You and Emma can ride up there in the cargo van with Three Hawks. Dali will drop me at the strip and then drive back and disable the VW in the road in case anyone drives up while we're unloading."

"What do we do if there's a bust? Every man for himself?" I looked around the group.

"I gotta a C-note says I'll beat you all to the treeline." Three Hawks rattled his teeth a couple of times.

"Everyone looks after their own hide." Dali looked very serious.

"Don't vorry so. All vill be gut." Nobby was rolling a cigarette with the air of a professor about to deliver a lecture to his students.

"Look, nobody's gonna get busted," said Wiz. "Everything will be cool. Just listen to the radios and stay alert. I'm the only one who talks to Crisp. And everyone be aware of the props."

He held his hand in the middle of the group and we followed suit, laying our hands on top of his, grinning sheepishly, like a freshman basketball team.

"For the Mad Jag," said Wiz, and we all repeated it self-consciously and swung our hands down and went to the vehicles and away to our fates.

The strip served several large ranches in the vicinity and was long enough, Crisp said, to land his twin-engine Cessna 414. At the west end, concrete blocks served as tie-downs for small planes. At the east end, a faded orange windsock sagged from a staff.

We completed a radio check, then the smuggling business turned out to be much like the film business: hurry up and wait. Dali drove the VW away and we heard the engine stop in the valley to the south. Wiz stood fiddling with the walkie and glancing occasionally into the sky. Nobby strolled to the trees and sat back against the bowl of a juniper, smoking, his face tilted up to the sun.

I suggested to Three Hawks that we make a drive of the perimeter, though it seemed a fairly pointless exercise since unless the DEA was staffed by complete cretins, they would surely not be visible to a cursory look. The Apache drove the cargo van slowly down the runway; Emma sat in the passenger seat and I crouched on my haunches between them. When we reached the windsock Three Hawks stopped, pressing the brake hard and pitching me forward.

"These brakes snatch a bit." Three Hawks giggled, patently nervous. "I better watch 'em on the highway."

"Are you driving this van all the way to Chicago?" Emma asked, as the three of us walked toward the dropoff at the end of the gravel.

"We're going to transfer the gear to a Winnebago. Then me and my woman will take it cross-country."

The landing strip was built on a little mesa and at this end the land dropped away steeply. We poked about in the trees for a spell. A jackrabbit burst away from under bear grass at Emma's feet and we all jumped back and grinned at one another. We made a couple more stops to scour the perimeter bushes, then went back to the west end and hung around the van pitching pebbles, chatting, while the tension built.

Emma heard the plane first. I saw her cock her head and hold her finger up and then all three of us were straining to listen. The drone became unmistakable, and she clenched her jaw and neck muscles and bared her teeth without smiling as if to say, "Too late to back out now!"

"MJ, come back." Wiz tried to raise Crisp over the airwaves. There was a silence that seemed interminable.

"MJ, come back." No response. What if it wasn't Crisp? Maybe it wasn't even our plane. Maybe one of the goddamn ranchers was actually using his strip at this moment. Had someone been nabbed down in Oaxaca and the DEA had got their own pilot on board and he didn't know the code so was staying shtum?

"MJ, do you read me? Over."

"Clear as a Sedona sunset." Crisp's voice, unmistakable through the static, came through the walkies. On the far side of the strip, Wiz made a circle with thumb and forefinger. Nobby rose stiffly from beneath the juniper and trod out his fag.

"Are you coming in from the west, over?"

"Affirmative. Coming in from the west."

"Copy that." Wiz waved at us. "You guys should drive down the other end." He yelled and we scrambled into the van and took off down the runway; my heart pounded my ribs and I gripped Emma's shoulder and she put her hand on mine and clenched it.

"*Yataheh*, motherfucker!" Three Hawks gunned the van.

Soon we were doing seventy—seventy miles an hour down a gravel runway to meet a planeload of grass that my lover and I had prepared and suffered for in the Sierra Norte and in a quarter of an hour the dope would be in this van and Three Hawks would drive it off and we would be clear of risk and, and . . .

I slapped the Indian on the shoulder and looked up and saw in the windscreen, as we hurtled toward the end of the runway, nothing but the nose of the plane—the classic movie shot, the aircraft rising into frame on a long lens.

"Holy fucking Custer," yelled Three Hawks and braked hard, and the van slewed to the left toward the trees as the landing gear of the plane whistled overhead and Emma and I ducked instinctively.

"He must have flown around the mesa," I said foolishly.

"No shit, Sherlock." Three Hawks flung the van into a U-turn in the gravel. Unable to avoid the detachment that seemed to take over in these situations, I felt myself looking down on this comedy of smuggling errors as we raced back up the strip in pursuit of the plane.

"You nearly rammed the plane, guys. Go easy," Wiz's voice barked over the walkie.

"Didn't he tell us to go down there?" Three Hawks shook his head as we approached the plane, which was turning sharply to face us. It came to a halt and we stood by the van and saw two men climb from their seats, open the door in the fuselage and drop down onto the gravel. Crisp came first, a grin on his swarthy face. There were handshakes and hugs all round. Then I saw the second man: Tomás, the *jardinero*. I grabbed Emma's shoulder and we ran forward to meet him. We had grown very fond of the stocky Zapotec, and, I felt, he of us.

"Tomás!" We embraced warmly. I held him by the shoulders, "Did you get out of jail okay?"

"*Sí*." He held his head down, ashamed, confirming what Emma and I had suspected and Crisp and Wiz had confirmed: Flaco Miguel had stitched us up. "*Lo siento*, Jem. I am very sorry."

"Ah, *n'importa*." But I felt the anger rise again and looked at Emma. Her face hardened for a moment before she said, "It's lovely to see you here."

Then I noticed the plane was moving, swiveling toward us around a locked wheel while the engines idled and the wicked props whirled slowly. I yelled and ran to grab the starboard wing's leading edge. We all held the plane while Crisp jammed a rock under the tire.

"Back the van up, Three Hawks," Wiz yelled and jumped in the plane and began lobbing down the boxes. The men formed a chain and Emma stacked. I caught and lobbed boxes and occasionally glanced up and down the runway and tried to remember the cloud formations, the angle of the sun, the expressions on my fellow villains' faces, the smell of the piñon trees.

"I got a bogey drivin' up." Dali's voice came across the airwaves as we threw the last of the boxes in the van.

"Hold him. Mission almost accomplished," answered Wiz and ripped open the last box. "Let's have a quick look at the quality here. See if Stylor earned his cut."

We gathered in an expectant huddle as Wiz slashed the trash bag open and pulled a handful of buds out and held them across his palms.

"Wow," said Three Hawks. "Just like home-grown green."

"Far out, man," said Wiz, and grinned at me. "This is primo. We're gonna move this shit lickety-split." He held his hand low and I gave his palm a slap.

"*Cuánto es aquí?*" asked Emma.

"*Cuatrocientos cincuenta y ocho kilos*," said Tomás.

"A tad over a thousand pounds," Crisp said.

And we all stood, nodding happily round the circle, six very diverse people, who'd jointly pulled off this blag, smiling smugly, realizing we'd not just pulled off a major part of the fric-frac but had tapped a very rich vein that we could continue to mine. It was a moment that I, for one, would have liked to have held for a long while: looking down at the beautiful original Mad Jag buds, surrounded by those decent folk on a landing strip in remote and lovely northern Arizona on a bright midwinter noon. But business pressed.

We took our leave of the airmen and watched the plane lift away. Emma and I jammed into the front seat of the van and we brazenly drove down the road, jumping out to help Dali push the "broken-down" Thing to one side as a couple of tourists, looking lost and bewildered, watched us all drive away.

And drive away we did. Three Hawks to Chicago, without incident, to deliver the load; Wiz and Dali back to their family lives; Emma and I across the high plains to Taos to further our fabulous, cursed affair.

Taos touched us both. We walked the narrow streets on crisp mornings under cobalt skies; huddled together under porches and watched snow flurries and crystalline showers dance through lambent sunshine; sniffed the pungent piñon smoke from kiva fireplaces; skied the steeps with names like Longhorn and Lorelei; drank Coronas on the deck of the St. Bernard hotel; and made very naughty love in the Manby hot springs at the base of the huge gorge of the Rio Grande while a bald eagle watched, like some regal voyeur, from a snag. On Christmas Eve we walked up to the ancient fortress of Taos Pueblo, where wraith-like figures swathed in pale robes dotted the ramparts, and we stood by the ice-bound stream to watch the pagan and pious procession wind among blazing bonfires of black-smoked pitch-wood—as if we'd been flung back in time a millennium.

One afternoon we chanced on the ranch where D. H. Lawrence had lived, and where his remains lay. Emma read from the great man.

"In the magnificent fierce morning of New Mexico, one sprang awake, a new part of the soul woke up suddenly and the old world gave way to the new." She skipped a few lines and read again: "the sage-brush desert sweeping gray-blue in between . . . the vast amphitheatre of lofty, indomitable desert."

She lowered the book. "There must be worse places to spend eternity," she said, and gazed out over the vastness. "Do you think we can see as far as Arizona?"

"Doubt it. Maybe to the edge of the Navajo Nation."

Silence, for a moment, before she said, wistfully, "It's stunning here, Jem."

"But you've got to go, right?"

"I spoke to Geoff last night. He's given me an ultimatum."

"And?"

"Come back now, or not at all."

"Hang on a couple of days and I'll drive you back."

"You lads have another load coming in?"

"We do. Wanna help again?"

"I think I'll pass this time." She stared out over the void.

Wiz indeed had another load of Flaco Miguel's weed, cured and prepared, ready to ship in from Oaxaca, and I had to head back to Arizona to help with the unloading. Over the next two days the high plains slipped away under our wheels and soon we approached the rim country. Wiz had told me that his offer on his beloved ranch, his escape, which he'd raved about all year, had been accepted. It seemed as apt a place as any to play out the last scene of our charade.

The route to the ranch passed through the town we called Hand Pumps and then veered north through the juniper country on a rough dirt track. Finally we crested a ridge and were able to check out the object of Wiz's long obsession.

From the northeast a creek wound through an avenue of sycamores and cottonwoods into a clearing of several acres hewn out by early homesteaders. Wooden barns and a clapboard two-story house enclosed a sheltered quadrangle set above the flood plain.

"Wow." Emma shook her head in awe.

"Now I understand why he dreams of this place." I leaned against the front of the van staring down at the idyllic ranch, and thought of Sterling Hayden in *The Asphalt Jungle*, yearning for his place in the country; it didn't cross my mind that Wiz would meet the same fate as Hayden in that movie. We spent a celibate night in the sparsely furnished house. In the morning, after breakfast, amid the tension, I pretended to read.

"Feel free to leave any time." I caught her eye.

"I really should be getting back."

"Yes, you really should." But I cursed my sarcasm as I lobbed the keys onto the kitchen table. She was taking my camper van back to the valley and Wiz was delivering the VW Thing to the ranch house for me to use to block the road.

"I'll pack, then."

I watched her over the book as she climbed the stairs, then slowly closed it, walked out to the porch, and began the melancholic gaze that would last for much of the following decade.

She came outside and put her bag in the back of the van, slid the door shut, and stood staring in my direction. I walked over and held the driver's door open for her. She leaned against the seat and drew me to her and tried to kiss me, but I held my head aside.

"So," I said weightily, "you will certainly go down as the best fortnight's fuck I ever had."

She grabbed me by the temples and stared angrily into my eyes.

"Don't you ever think of me in those terms!"

"What choice have you left me?" I stepped away. She continued to stare at me, tears pouring down her cheeks.

I closed the door a few degrees. She swung her legs in and gripped the wheel, her head lolling. I shut the door and walked up the porch steps to the house and thence up the stairs and closed the door and toppled onto the bed.

22

On the morning of the third day following Emma's departure, Wiz arrived. My partner held his arms in an expansive gesture. "Whad'ya think?" The smile was unashamedly smug.

"Not too shabby." I grinned back. He proudly gave me a tour of the ranch, the peach and apricot orchards, the corrals and barns, the ravine downstream where the creek coursed over a lip to form a pool deep and wide enough for a swim.

We walked back into the barnyard as Stilt drove in and unwound his linear frame from the jeep. Wiz grabbed a satchel from the Thing and we went into the kitchen and sat at the little dining table. With a bright smile plastered across his face, Wiz unzipped the bag and upended it. The bundles of cash spilled across the tabletop; Stilt and I had to spread our arms to dam the flood of lucre.

"Two hundred and seventy-four thousand, one hundred and sixteen dollars." Wiz sat beside Stilt, and the sight of these two solid guys grinning at me over the stack of cash, mine, all mine, was enough to color even my black spirits.

"Your college pal came through," I said. "Nothing like a good education to get you set up in life."

They laughed.

"Fancy sharing the numbers?"

Wiz studied a handwritten sheet. "Because of your contribution in Oaxaca, Flaco gave us the awesome price of one seventy-five a pound."

"And to compensate for throwing us in the slammer?" I cocked my head at Wiz.

"You shouldn't have charged him for the seed."

"Wish I'd known."

Wiz ignored this. "The load weighed out at four hundred and fifty-eight kilos, just over a thousand pounds. Flaco rounded it out to a thousand so we owed him one hundred and seventy-five grand."

"And how much did you get out of your mate in Chicago?"

"He was so stoked by the quality he figured it must be homegrown sins."

"And you did nothing to quash his misconception." Stilt looked from me to Wiz, the honest crook who prided himself on being on the level with all his business buddies. But he kept his head down, and I realized that even his principles had limits.

"One thousand and fifty per pound."

"Nice margin." I whistled.

"Much of the credit due to your odyssey to Oaxaca." Stilt turned his hand out toward me.

Wiz pressed on. "One thousand and seven pounds multiplied by one thousand and fifty comes to one million, fifty-seven thousand, three hundred and fifty bucks."

"Jesus! What does a million look like?"

"Sweet." Wiz was grinning widely again. "Total expenses were the one seventy-five purchase price, fifty K to Three Hawks for the drive, five each to Emma, Nobby, and Dali for the unloading, that's two hundred and forty, which leaves a profit of eight hundred and twenty-two grand, three hundred and forty-five dollars."

"Split three ways equals two hundred and seventy-four thousand, one hundred and sixteen bucks?" I looked at them and they nodded again.

"How do you intend to invest your dividend, young man?" Stilt, who liked his dough as well as any man, was patently envious of my substantial cut.

"On a fuck of a jag."

Stilt laughed loudly but Wiz, who never really did cotton onto my poxy attempt at a Cockney wide boy's humor, narrowed his eyes in bewilderment.

"How about you?" I asked my partner.

"A good chunk of change has gone down on this place."

"And the rest of the dough?"

"Crisp and I bought a plane."

"You're investing heavily in this scheme."

"Money's round . . ."

"Meant to roll," Stilt and I chimed in together.

"What sort of plane d'you buy?"

"We got a helluva deal on a De Havilland Twin Otter. Crisp has connections with some dudes in Tucson. Two thousand-pound payload."

"Christ. We—should I say, you—can fly in a ton a time now."

"Whad'ya mean, you?" Wiz looked genuinely concerned.

"I've been giving this game a lot of thought," I said.

"You're not quitting, man? We've got a dead cert set up. We've tapped a main line. You could make a couple of million by the fall. Be set for life."

He stared hard at me. I looked at him and back at the bundles of cash that we had stacked according to denomination.

"Things have been a bit hectic recently." I caught his eye and I knew he knew I meant the affair. "This here's a lot of scoots for a Devon farm boy. I think it's time to call it quits, get up from the table while I'm ahead."

"Shit." He shook his head sadly. "I was hoping you'd go down to Oaxaca in the spring and help Tomás plant the skunk. Flaco says he owes you one. I'll fly you down in the Otter. C'mon, man."

"I've still got a bad taste in the mouth from Oaxaca. And Emma was this close to being raped by the soldiers." I held my thumb and forefinger close, then snapped my fingers.

"Maybe you should've kept her out of that mission." Wiz stroked his beard, looking intently at me.

"Send this man. He knows the game." I turned my palm out to the lean fellow, who tilted his chair back against the wall.

"Not me, doctor." Stilt smiled. "My better half has my testicles in a sling already over these minor involvements."

"I need a break, Wiz." I held his gaze. "Sooner or later I'm going to run into Willard Farr and I'll be up shit creek."

"Well, at least you'll help with this next load, yeah? I'm flying the Otter down there this afternoon. Then back tomorrow afternoon."

"You're flying?"

"I'm itching to try the Twin Otter's STOL reputation."

"STOL?" Stilt asked.

"Short Take Off and Landing." Wiz stood and looked at me. "Are you in for tomorrow?"

"If you need me, sure." I stood also.

There was a moment of distinct awkwardness between us. I felt as if I had failed him somehow; this marvelous bloke had, just a year ago, offered me an entry into as justifiable a life of crime and as decent a set of crooks with which one could rationalize involvement in a criminal enterprise. But the growing had been one thing: exciting, contemplative, forgivable in my view, a pastoral victimless crime. The smuggling was far too dodgy, too many unknowns, too many links in the chain, any one of which could snap or be broken at any time, and one of which was being broken at that very moment fifteen hundred miles south of us, in a dark room in a Oaxacan jail.

Wiz held out his arms and we embraced. He clenched my biceps in his big hands and held me with those searching adobe brown eyes.

"It's been real, man." He smiled and pursed his lips. "Let me know if you change your mind. You could soon be a very rich dude."

"I already am. Thanks to you." I reached my arm across his shoulders and walked him on to the porch. Stilt and I shook hands, and I watched them drive away in the jeep while down in the dark room in Oaxaca Tomás was being pistol-whipped by a Federale, his family was being threatened, and our plans were being exposed—thus putting our freedom and, without exaggeration, our lives in jeopardy.

Next morning, I drove the VW Thing to First Arizona State Bank in Payson, and stashed a quarter of a million dollars in a safety deposit box. It finally dawned on me as I drove away from town back toward the rim and the turnoff to Hand Pumps—a quarter of a million bucks! Jesus wept. We'd done it. I'd done it. There it was: a house, a business, a yacht, whatever I fancied within the bounds of my farmer's son dreams; there it was, stashed, safe, in the rattle 'n' crank with only the key as evidence and the name of Duce Daley Tosser on the registration form—untraceable by DEA, sheriff, INS; no other wanker but me could get at it. I clenched the key in my pocket and grinned. If it hadn't been for that fucker Flaco slinging our sorry arses into the slammer, the whole scheme would have been a breeze, pie, gravy, cake.

Such thoughts kept me amused as I made the turn from the highway onto the long dirt road to the little town. After a quarter mile or so I pulled off into some trees to drain the dragon and, had I looked more closely at an old pickup passing by, I would have recognized that the plaid-shirted ranch hand riding shotgun had the square ruddy jaw of Sheriff Willard Farr.

We met in Hand Pumps without acknowledgment, then rendezvoused down the road as before. We were just four this time: Dali, animated and psyched; Nobby, the wonderfully quirky Swiss, rolling a cigarette, calm, no big deal; Three Hawks grinning, wisecracking.

I followed the van in the Thing to where the road narrowed before a little bridge. I pulled it onto the bridge and flipped the hood, snapped open the clips on the side of the distributor, and took the rotor arm off its spindle. I hung around, then with a start heard barks from the radio as Three Hawks attempted to raise Wiz. Finally I heard the plane and it was then that the morning movement became irresistible. I grabbed my pack, which held the t.p., and dashed into the trees to answer the most opportune peristaltic urge of my life.

No sooner had I crouched to strain for the pony and trap than the pickup that I had not seen pass me earlier swung around the corner and blazed to a halt. Willard Farr forced his massive frame through the passenger door and began yelling into his walkie while his fellow flatfoot ran to the VW.

"Take 'em. Hit 'em. Soon as they land that plane. We got a veehickle blocking the road." He flicked the farmer's shirt back and pulled his gun from the holster on the belt of his jeans. The other officer wrenched the door of the Thing open, loosed the emergency brake and strained to shove the car aside.

Willard Farr scanned the slopes on either side of the draw, and as I crouched, in extremis, his gaze crossed the piñon in front of me. I reflected later that it was good job I had my kecks round my ankles at that moment, as the sight of the lawman staring in my direction from less than twenty yards might well have caused me to soil them. The deputy had by this time cleared the Thing, so Farr took one last glance around and hauled himself back into the cab of his truck.

Jesus fuckin' Christ. This was it. We were nabbed, dead to rights, and the boys were exposed up on the strip. I scrabbled for the walkie and began to yell into it while I finished the biz and hauled up my jeans.

"Dali, man, Three Hawks, Nobby! We're busted, busted. Wiz, Wiz, touch and go, don't land, get the hell out of here."

I ran up the hill toward the mesa, gasping with terror. The plane's engines, which had lowered to a drone for the landing, roared to a deafening pitch as the pilot gunned the Twin Otter down the runway. Shots rang out. At the east end of the strip, I made out two agents in camouflage, crouching and firing. The plane flashed by and was airborne. Wiz was making it!

But the Otter wasn't gaining height and the flight was wobbly. The DEA agents must have damaged some of the gear, or hit Wiz, I thought, as I cut across the slope to keep the plane in view. The Twin Otter flew like a vulture, wings yawing as if riding a strong breeze, then it banked hard to the north and blasted into a scrubby hillside. A livid plume sprang from the wreckage.

Fucking hell. No. No! These bastards had killed Wiz and, I thought at the time, Tomás. No one could survive that crash, let alone the fire. I stifled a scream and dropped to my haunches as the horror of it sank in. Shouts from above snapped me out of it. Panic-struck, I started to haul ass down the slope—anywhere away from these swine. But I couldn't just abandon the rest of the firm. I skirted the mesa and came around to the north side and crawled to a gap in the trees at the edge of the gravel. The two agents who had shot down the plane were running hard up the strip. At the west end I could see Dali and Nobby splayed against the rented van, their arms high, as one of four men frisked them. Where the hell was the Apache?

I slipped through the trees until I was as close as my shrunken cobblers allowed. Willard Farr stood behind Dali.

"Where are your partners?" he shouted. "Who was with that vehicle on the bridge?"

"What vehicle?" Dali's voice was muted but firm.

"We know who you're dealing with in Mexico." Farr waddled to Dali's other side, holding his pistol low. "We need to find out who your people are on this side of the line. Who's your buyer?"

"I haven't a clue what you're talking about." Dali's head lolled between his raised arms.

"Don't play dumb with me. We've had your people under surveillance, feller. Give us some names, it'll go better for you when you're up in front of the judge." Farr moved closer to Dali, speaking so quietly that I had to strain to hear his words. "Who are the rest of your gang? Where is that goldarned limey I missed corraling a couple of months back?"

"I've no idea what you mean," Dali repeated. "We were just up here taking a drive. My pal here just came out from Europe and I was just showing him around. And then you guys rush us. I don't know . . ."

But he couldn't finish as Farr brought the pistol butt down hard into his kidneys and the big artist slumped forward against the van. I started to crawl back, away from the scene, and the last thing I saw was the fat sheriff raising his gun and I heard another groan before one of the agents stepped forward and took hold of Farr's raised arm.

Shit, fuck, bollocks, I swore silently, and took off at a dead run down the slope and into a rough arroyo. I raced along, my senses reeling from what had gone down. Wiz and Tomás dead in the plane crash; Dali and Nobby, facing a thrashing from a vindictive sheriff who'd been looking for vengeance since I had slipped his noose back in November, a sheriff now even more furious after this cockup of a bust—no dope, or at least very little that could be salvaged from the burning wreck, to parade to the press, only two drug traffickers in custody and the repercussions of a crashed plane to handle.

In the distance I heard the cursed chop of a helicopter. They must have had it stashed close by just in case! I cinched the waist and sternum straps of the pack tighter and quickened my pace again. Then I rounded a bend in the wash and skidded to a halt in terror as a man stepped out from behind a tree. I had begun to scrabble up the slope before I recognized Three Hawks.

"Three Hawks. Jesus wept. You scared the piss out of me." I slumped down on the bank, lungs shuddering, temples pounding with fear, rage, remorse, too many sensations to get my head around.

"C'mon over, man." Three Hawks beckoned. I stood, feeling shaky, and joined him in a little cave formed by an overhang of sandy rock and the small piñon. I slumped down and tried to keep it together, but it was all too much to grasp.

"Easy." Three Hawks put a hand on my shoulder.

I shook my head to stave off collapse, dragged a sleeve across my eyes, and looked at the wine-dark face and the lowered eyes.

"What a balls-up," I said, and he shook his head. Although his expression was blank, I knew he was more gutted than I. He had known Wiz for years and they were close.

"How the hell are we going to get out of here?" I pulled the water bottle from my pack and offered it to him. "Place will be covered with fuzz in a tick."

"Best lie low for a few days. Here in the back country." He took a sip of water and passed it back. "Then drop toward the Salt River, stay off the roads."

"Right. Then we can phone for a ride. Stilt'll come and get us." I began to feel better as I drank. It would be fine to have someone to lead the escape, someone like the Apache who knew the country as well as any.

"We need to split up." His voice was cold. I turned to him, but his face stayed set.

"Why?" I felt another surge of fear.

"Better chance of making it alone."

"Nothing to do with the sheriff mentioning me, eh?"

"What the fuck did you do to him, man?" Three Hawks looked at me for the first time. "Why is he jonesing so bad for your ass?"

I told him of my escape at the Fruitown café in the fall and the run through Mimbres Canyon with Geoff and throwing the innocent four-wheelers to the deputy while we got away.

"Jeez. No wonder he wants your butt in jail. You cost him the biggest bust of his career. And now this one's gone in the crapper."

"But he's got Dali and Nobby in the pen and will do god knows what to them." I ground my teeth. "Pity we can't teach the fat arsehole a lesson."

The Apache slowly swung his face toward me again, and we nodded gravely at each other. Twenty minutes later we were working hard up the slope of the main canyon and there was a purpose to our struggle—a wild, desperate, forlorn intent, but a purpose nonetheless. The helicopter startled us, clearing the ridge and canting toward the plane wreck. Three Hawks flung himself into a brake of manzanita, but I was in the open and dropped where I lay. The chopper passed overhead and I waited a moment before I heard Three Hawks scramble from cover. At the ridge we turned and watched the helicopter land and disgorge four men, who ran to the wreckage and began to work on the fire. I watched for a while before Three Hawks snatched my arm and we took off down the long slope into the canyon where we knew we would cross the road: the road which led from the airstrip, the road which would bring the vehicles with the agents, our mates, and the sheriff.

We plunged headlong down the manky terrain. We saw the road, skidded to a halt, and picked a spot near some live oaks from which we could spring our madcap plan. The first truck soon came. It was a large fortified van, a paddy wagon. Dali and Nobby must have been sitting in misery in the back. We stared bleakly at it, but there was nothing we could do against several armed agents and a well-secured prison vehicle. We let it pass. Next there was a sheriff's four-by, and I peered intently through the glasses, trying to calm my heaving chest, looking for the bulk of Willard Farr, but he wasn't there. Then came the beat-up Chevy pickup truck, with Farr alone in the cab.

"It's him. Let's go," I said, and we slid down the roadside bank and stood panting in the bar ditch.

Three Hawks took his knife from the leather pouch at his belt and looked at me hard.

"You really wanna do this?"

"For fuck's sake just get on with it!"

He grabbed my jaw and turned my head away; then, gripping the knife handle in his fist, pressed the point through the skin just above my left eyebrow. I flinched and gritted my teeth as he slashed across my forehead and the claret gushed and I had to clench my eye shut.

"Jesus. You didn't have to scalp me."

He smeared gore across my cheeks as we heard the truck nearing the bend.

"Your own mother wouldn't recognize you." He locked his eyes on mine. "Give the porker one for me, man."

"I will. See you back in the valley." I nodded and slapped his shoulder. "Now go. Go!"

The Apache took off at a sprint, running hard toward the bend where Willard Farr approached. I began my staggering lurch, one hand held across the wound, hoping to Jesus I had the bottle to pull off this desperate scheme.

I heard the truck skid to a halt and glanced up as Three Hawks leaped up the bank, stumbling and plunging through the brush while Farr lowered his bulk from the cab and leveled his sidearm.

"Hold it right there!"

Two shots rang out, and I chanced a glance through my fingers up the slope and saw the Apache dash over the ridge in fine form, obviously unscathed. I fell against the hood of the truck groaning and heard the sheriff lurch around the open door.

"Goddamn Indian. He cut me. Sonofabitch." I held my right hand over the side of my face so the sheriff could see only the blood-smeared side. He was advancing cautiously, odd-looking in his rancher's disguise, the corner of the truck between us, his gun, dwarfed by two huge hands, trained on my chest.

"Spread 'em," he said.

"I'm cut bad, man," I protested, affecting a passable redneck drawl. "I need first aid. Why you drawing down on me?"

"Spread your arms on that hood." He stood stock still until I complied, then came cautiously around the fender and slipped his hands up and down my thighs and ribs while I continued my whining.

"What the hell is going on here, man? I'm just out for a hike and run into all this bullshit. A plane crash, helicopters. Then this crazy Native tries to fuckin' scalp me. I've lost a lotta blood, man. Don't you got a first aid kit in your truck?"

"Stay spread there. Turn your head to me."

I turned toward him and looked into his eyes. He lowered the gun, pointing it at my crotch, reached a hand to my brow and gave a brief nod.

"Whad'I tell ya, sheriff, the goddamn . . ." I began, and then time stood still while his face hardened as he recognized my blunder. I sensed rather than saw the pistol muzzle rise. I slashed down with my left hand and turned my shoulders a fraction and with all the fatalistic misery of my doomed affair, all the volcanic release of years of pent-up pacifism, all the blind hatred of uniformed authority, I clocked the sheriff of Gila County with as mean a Kirby kiss as I could muster.

My forehead cannoned into the bridge of his nose and, as the cartilage crumpled against his face and his cheekbone caved into a depressed fracture, I reflected on one of the few advantages a man of five foot eight and 160 has over someone six foot four and 280: the brow of your head is level with the middle of his face. The gun exploded and fell away as I brought my knee up into the big man's groin, and then any advantage I had was gone as his massive arms curled around the small of my back and I was lifted like a rag doll and the breath was crushed from my lungs. His strength was paralyzing; he slammed me against the angle of the truck hood and I felt a rib go. I screamed and bit into his ear. He let out a gasp and twisted away, leaving a piece of gristle in my teeth, then turned his mouth on my throat and clenched his huge jaw. I felt as an antelope must in the grip of a lioness. I was smashed repeatedly against the truck until my wind was gone, and I was about to pass out when my foot caught the bumper. With all I had left, I kicked away from the truck. The sheriff staggered back to the edge of the road, seemed to regain his balance, and we twirled like Gormenghast's Flay and Swelter in an absurd deathly jig until, like lovers in a suicide pact, we pitched over the brink.

The only thing that saved me from a life in a wheelchair as we went arse over tit down that cactus- and rock-strewn slope was my pack. Every time the sheriff's weight crashed on to me, it seemed as if my torso was flattened, and I'm quite sure that only the thin cushion of the gear in the pack spared me a broken spine. Time was suspended and sound distorted, as they are in moments of extremity. I remember floating toward the wicked bloom of a bayonet agave, powerless to determine who would take the brunt of its spiked defense. Two of the poisonous spears stabbed me in the thigh and shoulder, but Farr got half a dozen in his back, and as we careered away down the slope one broken barb thrashed from his temple. A rock barred our descent, and I saw and heard the sheriff's skull crunch into the granite with a satisfying thud, slowing our pell-mell plunge. We skidded sideways and came to a halt in the bottom of the draw.

His arms were still in a death grip across my back as he lay motionless beneath me. I sprawled on top of him for minutes, like a spent lover, a calf on a mother whale. Then the pain began, and I groaned and forced myself up, gasping from the agony in my chest, surprised I could move at all. I pried his hands loose and kneeled beside him, wondering if he was dead. I certainly hadn't meant to kill him. Murder of a law enforcement officer in the line of duty wasn't a charge I relished facing in this Mormon enclave. But his chest sank and rose and I sighed a hiss of relief.

I rose shakily and stood astride the colossus, like Patroclus over Sarpedon, and clenched a fist and curled my upper lip. But the sound of a truck approaching spoiled my moment of unwarranted triumph. With the gait of a cripple, I stumbled away down the wash.

23

My recollection of the five days and nights it took me to drag my arse through the Mazatzal Wilderness to Mad Jag Canyon from Willard Farr's comatose carcass is clouded not just by the rust of time but by the onset of delirium as the journey took its toll. Sleeping or, more accurately, shuddering through the night, in the high desert in winter, wrapped in the comfortless silvery fiber of a space blanket, will not improve one's strength or spirit. Lack of food and the pain of my injuries sapped my reserves. Moisture from *tinajas* and snow and the scant food in the escape kit kept me alive, barely.

All my ribs seemed to be cracked and the coughing worsened. A bout of hacking would leave me curled fetally on the desert floor, sniveling. The stabs from the agave swelled into festers. The cut on my forehead throbbed. I cursed Three Hawks, only to scold myself in my madness, remembering how he'd run the gauntlet to give me a crack at fatso Farr.

Viewed from above, my passage across the last mesa to the rim of Mad Jag would have resembled that of a snail in speed and line. A front had moved in and snow flurries draped the higher ground in an icy stole. I made the cliff edge and slumped down in the snow staring into the familiar terrain, striving for the drive to negotiate the treacherous descent and make the haven of our camp. The distant whock of a helicopter drove me on. I'd heard them almost constantly during my flight and knew they were after Three Hawks and me. The bust had netted Dali and Nobby, and no doubt the sheriff's department and the DEA were crowing to the press. Privately, though, senior law enforcement would have seen the operation as a disaster. APBs would have been posted for the two fugitives. Grimly aware of the price on my head, I made my way toward our lair, on edge for a DEA trap even in my fevered state. But the threat came not in human form.

My exhausted, staggering progress came to a halt against a boulder in the streambed. I fell across the cold stone and watched flecks of snow settle and transform to blooms of moisture in front of my blurred vision. Feeling buoyed by the closeness of the camp, shelter, a sleeping bag, fire, and food, I painfully raised myself for a last effort when I saw the jaguar.

After all this agony, and so close to home, was I to end up prey to the mad jag? He sprawled amongst the rocks on the creek bank, watching me. I shrank back in terror and misery. There was no way to slip past him, and it would have been pointless anyway. In my parlous state, he could finish me off with a single cuff of his giant paw.

I slumped down against the boulder, my arse in the stream, oblivious to the cold water, beaten, done, resigned.

I stared at the huge cat for a time my delirium could not compute. I wondered if I was dreaming. Was this the nagual that Wiz said Don Juan spoke of? An apparition. A trick of my failing mental equilibrium.

He didn't move. Was he waiting for me to attempt to crawl past him?

I lay in the streambed, slipping in and out of consciousness, until the evening cold roused me. I realized that the jag hadn't moved since I'd first seen him. There was something odd about his inactivity. Surely he could sense how weak I was, how easy a kill I would be?

With the last vestige of strength, in an agony of fear, I dragged myself to my feet and began to lurch forward. I knew I would not last another night in the open, so it was die either at the mercy of the jaguar or from the winter cold. As I stumbled across the stones, he still didn't budge. I came closer. I stood looking at his face and realized that his eyes were blank. Was he dead? I saw a tremor in his chest, and realized he was alive but in sorry shape, worse even than I. I crept closer—no response. I stood next to him and his eyes flickered. The poor old sod had come to his last bitter season.

I knelt beside him; he tried to turn his huge head my way, but failed. I reached forward in slow motion to stroke the dappled shoulders. I stared down at him and welled up, feeling empathy for the old cat, as I too was approaching an end; then I realized his demise might abet my salvation.

I slipped my Buck knife from its sheath. Our jaguar, the presence that had scared us, spared us, and watched over us through our intrusion on his territory, was near death. If I killed him now in order to eat his parts, would I be performing an act of compassion, or one of desecration and thus bringing more ill luck on us? No—I reasoned that he'd chosen to crawl there to die, to offer himself as a final gift.

Very, very carefully I lifted the massive front paw. No resistance. I pressed the limb back, exposing the paler coat of his underparts. And then, with a stomach-churning slash, I brought the blade of the knife across his throat. He thrashed briefly. I lurched back, fell, and passed out.

I came round to the muted sounds of the snowstorm, the scent of sycamore leaves, the tremble of creek water, the agony of a stone between my shoulderblades. Beside me, one paw held against my chest as if in supplication, lay the dead jaguar.

I pulled myself up and stared down at him for a long while. Then, with all my remaining strength, I turned him over and fell across him, gasping. I sawed down the length of his stomach with the point of the knife. Blood poured from the still-warm flesh; I lapped at it. Nausea swept over me and I hawked. The stench of his entrails made me recoil. Reaching in to his guts, I identified what I reckoned to be the liver, kidneys, and heart of the old cat. I hacked them loose and rolled the jag back onto his side.

I gathered up the offal, gore soaking my clothes. Lacking the mettle or the strength for any further caution, I stumbled through the last turn in the creek and staggered into camp.

I gathered some firewood, dug the matches from the waterproof can, and kindled a blaze. Soon the fire took and I groveled over its heat, slicing the organs ineptly into a skillet and delighting in the spit and crackle as they hit the metal. I ate cautiously at first, knowing that the richness of the meat would sit oddly in my empty guts. But the bliss of the first few bites overcame any caution and I wolfed down the jaguar's seared organs. I slumped over the fire, gripping the stones in my filthy, battered hands, luxuriating in the heat after so many nights of biting cold. The nausea came but I fought it, forcing myself to swallow the bile that came up my throat. I'd hit some atavistic nadir, some throwback to an animal state. Perversely I grinned down at the fire, basking in the strength surging through me from the meat and the warmth, listening to tears and sweat and phlegm hiss in the flames.

I lurched into the tent, pulled the two sleeping bags from their duffels, and froze in amazement. Neatly laid out in a line on my bedroll was the array of necessities that Wiz always left me: a snakebite kit, two new AA batteries, a flashlight, and two tiny glass bottles, one containing cocaine, one containing Demerol.

What the hell! Had my partner been down here since Nobby closed up the camp and garden for winter? The Swiss had said he wanted to say goodbye to the place where he'd spent more time than any of us and had volunteered to bag up the shake, bury the pump, and do his best to make the place animal-proof during the cold months.

When had the crazy pilot come down? He never did like the hiking much, so he would not have made the grueling trek just for sentimentality. Was it possible that he had not been the pilot of the crashed Otter? Had something happened in Oaxaca that prevented him from flying? Had Flaco Miguel replaced him with one of his other pilots? Had Wiz taken a commercial flight Stateside and come looking for me after the bust? Was he lying low in the Mazatzals?

Such a tsunami of emotions assailed me, as I burrowed into the womb of the down bags, that the mellifluous song of the canyon wren warbling down the scale from the creekside proved the last straw for my shattered psyche. I sobbed myself to sleep.

At first, I had had to force myself to eat and often followed a few mouthfuls with a Technicolor yawn. But soon my guts settled, my appetite returned, and I opened cans of food I'd dropped from the plane four months back, scarfing them up with half-arsed pancakes concocted from an old bag of flour and fried in the skillet. I swilled the lot down with cups of rosy lea.

It was a couple of days before I gained strength enough to do the right thing by the jag. One crisp afternoon I walked across the creek to where the carcass lay on the stones. I had considered lopping off a limb to supplement the tinned grub, but when I saw his coat coppered by decay, his eyes dulled by age and death, I could not bring myself to defile him further.

I chose a place against a head-high boulder to build the fire and spent the afternoon gathering wood. By early evening I had built a bonfire. Using the lip of the rock as one support and two cedar trunks as the other, I lashed up a frame to support the weight of the jag over his pyre.

Crouching on all fours by his stiffened remains, I burrowed my head under his split guts and levered his bulk on to my shoulders. Straining every sinew, I managed to rise to my knees. His weight was frightening. I crawled toward the rock, his limbs dragging through the creekbed. Every inch was a battle.

I slid the corpse from my back and rolled away, gasping and shuddering from the effort. After my breathing settled, I struggled to my feet. I had laid two poles of sycamore against the top of the rock to form a ramp. Holding the jag's legs by the limp paws, I maneuvered his mass into position. Then I grabbed a couple of preselected juniper limbs and levered the carcass up the ramp to the top of the boulder.

Finally, I climbed to the top of the rock and with a couple of uncoordinated rolls forced the corpse onto the rickety frame. A front had moved in and a cold drizzle was now interspersed with sleet—a good day for a funeral.

I attempted incantations that Three Hawks might have intoned but failed to give them gravitas, so I resorted to a bastard version of Blake's "Tyger." I stooped to arrange my jaguar's fearful symmetry, then climbed down and lit the kindling.

The fire was slow to catch with the wood winter-damp. At last it caught. Flames searched upward. The heat forced me back. I sat on the opposite bank as the stench of scorched hair and flesh wafted through the canyon. I was still there when darkness had swallowed the creekbed except for the embered glow from the fire, and nothing remained of the old mad jag save a few blackened bones.

A week later, I climbed reluctantly out of the canyon. I made the climb in better time than I'd hoped, and realized I was almost back to full fettle. When I heard a vehicle grinding up out of Relic Canyon, I slipped away through the scrub and skirted the road for a few hundred yards. A pickup passed beneath me, and then another approached from the north.

I sat for a while on an outcrop until the sound of another vehicle starting the long climb from the creek set me off again. The vehicle emerged into view and I felt a surge of adrenaline. I snatched up the binoculars and trained them on the van, the orange VW van, Geoff and Emma's van!

The van swung out of sight for a few curves and then reemerged. I held the glasses steady and felt a rush of pleasure as I made out Emma's blond fringe. And there was Geoff in the passenger seat, a serious pall clouding his face.

I was held in a moment of indecision. If I took off immediately, I might make the road before they passed and I could surprise my old friends, play the roguish fugitive whom no one had seen for three weeks and whom no one knew was alive.

But I held back and the moment was gone. I knew I had let it slip in favor of another. I tracked the van as Emma drove up the side road and out across the mesa; clearly she was taking Geoff out to the canyon edge so he could hike down to start the preparations for his year with Stilt. I dropped down to a place where I could watch it return and from where I could cover the turn north toward Fruitown or, more likely, back in the direction it had come, toward the hot springs.

The half an hour of waiting was spent in turmoil. Since our bitter parting at Wiz's idyllic ranch I had tried, unsuccessfully of course, but strived nonetheless to rationalize the loss of Emma. So much had happened: the quarter of a million bucks, which, along with over 150K from the growing gig, would change my life; the bust, the plane crash, and the fight; the grim ordeal of escape and the slow recovery in the canyon. All this had helped to cloud the memory of our ill-fated affair and I had begun to steel myself for the future without her. But now our paths had crossed again and I knew I lacked the resolve to watch her drive away.

She surprised me by turning up-canyon toward Fruitown, and I had to dash across a ridge. Down at the roadside, I came breathlessly alongside her window. She snatched the wheel and the van lurched away, and she kept going until I shouted her name. She came to a halt and covered her cheeks with her fingers and stared at me without recognition.

When I approached the window, her eyes widened and she shook her head and stared; then she flung the door open, stepped into the road, and gave me a stinging roundhouse slap across my cheek.

"You frightened the bloody life out of me, you bastard! Where in god's name have you been? I was . . . we were all so worried!" She clenched her fists and drummed on my chest.

"I'm sorry, I was in the canyon, I had to lie low . . ." I held her wrists.

"How the hell was I supposed to recognize you?" She twisted the wing mirror. "Look at yourself."

Like a scolded schoolboy I peered at my face. A purple welt ran above my left eyebrow; a three-week beard, tinged with ginger, did not disguise the junkie's sunken cheeks. I had lost over a stone during my ordeal and was down to a skeletal 140.

"Lord. I do look a bit ropey."

"A bit ropey! You look like you're on a short exeat from Auschwitz." She allowed a flicker of a smile to cross her face.

"That bad, eh?"

"Oh Christ, Jem. We all thought you were dead." And she grabbed me by the shoulders and, with a sigh, sank against me.

I held her firmly and tried a laugh, but it was choked by her reaction to seeing me.

"You are a useless sod." She stood away and smiled. "But I am glad to see you."

"Feeling's mutual. Now, shall we get out of here? You may not want to be caught on this road with a man on the run."

We piled into the van and took off. I asked her to take me to Payson; she plied me with questions. I told my story and stared at her as she drove and tried to keep my cool.

"Anyone heard from Three Hawks?" I asked.

"Yes, he holed up in the Mazatzals for about ten days before slipping back to the Valley."

"Great." I smiled. The Apache had made it out. Not that I had had many doubts. He was as fit as a butcher's dog and knew the terrain as well as any.

I entered the bank in Payson very cautiously. The clerk gave a cursory glance at my disheveled state, ushered me into the safety deposit box room, and departed. I stuffed the quarter million in cash into the backpack and walked briskly out of the building and across the car park, expecting any minute to hear a shout. But none came, and we were soon heading west through the pines toward the Verde Valley and Stilt's hidden home.

The towering figure grinned when he clocked me and folded me in his arms, and said to Emma, "What, my dear, are the three things that will survive the apocalypse?"

As she pondered a smart reply, Stilt said, "The cockroach, Keith Richards, and this scurrilous reprobate."

We sat at the kitchen table and drank homemade lemonade.

"You certainly gave the sheriff a few bruises." A satisfied grin crossed his face. "The English David takes down the Mormon Goliath."

I couldn't resist a smug smile.

"Any idea on who gave us away?" Emma leaned on her elbows.

"Crisp said someone got incarcerated in Oaxaca and turned queen's, as you two would say. A fellow by the name of Tomás, as I recall."

"Tomás," repeated Emma.

"That explains a lot," I said. "Do you know if they got any evidence from the wreck?"

"A story in the *Verde Independent* claimed a ton of grass with a street value of five million."

"Five million! Wish we had their buyers," I said. "What about Dali and Nobby?"

"The judge in Globe has taken a draconian approach to our colleagues. Bond was set at half a million. Perhaps because the sheriff's operation was such a fiasco."

"We need ten percent of the bond, right? Fifty K to get them out on bail?"

"That is correct."

"Obviously I can't go to Globe. Will you?"

"Of course."

We counted out fifty thousand.

"Good man," he said. "You know you may not see this again."

"I owe them. And here's a little something for you." I put five thousand more on the table.

"No need." He made to push it back.

"Let's say that's a bonus for stashing the crop," I said, referring to the boxes of the immaculate Mad Jag grass in his garage.

"Thank you." He gave a little bow of his head, put the five and the fifty in a brown grocery bag.

"Damn glad you made it out, Sherlock." He patted my shoulder as we all stood on the porch.

"Makes two of us." I looked up at him, a foot taller than me, give or take. "Coming up to Jerome for a farewell drink?"

"Think I'll pass. Willard Farr may have planned a warm reception for you." He smiled. "Where do you intend after that?"

"Thailand's always intrigued me. There's no extradition policy with the U.S."

"Bangkok. Phuket. Wiz used to go there for R and R when he was in Nam." He glanced away at the mention of the name. "Damn, I shall miss that man."

"You may not have to." I looked intently at him.

"I beg your pardon?"

"You know how annoying his obsession with tidiness can be."

"It drove me to distraction. He made OCD sufferers look normal."

"You remember how he'd always leave a neat line of stuff on the sleeping pads?"

"I do. As if he couldn't trust one to take care of oneself." Stilt gazed into the distance at his wistful memory of the Wizard of the Rim.

"Like having your mum in the canyon!" I said, and we all laughed. "When I finally crawled into the camp, there was the same line of gear laid out perfectly as only he would."

"Really?"

"Perhaps Nobby did it when he closed the camp. Just to take the piss, as it were. Ask him, will you?"

"I certainly will." He laid a lean arm across my shoulder. "Write me from Thailand. Perhaps I could slip away for a short trip."

"You might like it down there. There's Thai sticks. Five for a buck, I hear. And they like their men tall." I grinned up at him.

"I hear there's the odd pretty girl." He nodded to himself.

"Oh, you men." Emma walked to the van. "Stop your dreaming. Stilt's a happily married man."

I waved as we drove away and watched the heron-like figure as he leaned on the rail, and knew I would miss him as much as any of these lovely villains. We drove in resigned silence across the valley and through the switchbacks to Jerome.

You're looking very bonny, Ems," I said as we parked next to the Spirit Room. "This desert living agrees with you."

She turned, held my eyes for a second. "I'm pregnant."

The words hung between us like a tethered zeppelin.

"When did you find out." I had ashes in my mouth.

"Three weeks ago. I missed my monthly. I took the test."

"And who do you think . . ." I stared out over the valley. The massive cream and red cliffs above Sedona rose into the late desert twilight.

"I don't know, Jem, and I don't care." She said it firmly but without flippancy.

"I bloody well do," I snapped. "You're going to have it?"

"Yes, of course I'm going to have the baby." She leaned toward me. "Is it so awful for someone to love two people at the same time, Jeremy?"

I dodged the question for which I had no answer. "Does Geoff know?"

"Of course he bloody knows."

"And?"

"I don't think he could care less. Despite everything, he's still very fond of you."

"Spare me the sanctimony." I swung out of the vehicle.

"That's not fair," she said.

"You're right. That's not fair." I took her arm and slipped it through the crook of mine and we walked the streets of Jerome together for the last time.

Emma led me to her marital bed, disrobed coquettishly to show the gorgeous figure, swollen a lovely increment from the taut dancer's form by the onset of her pregnancy, slipped astride me and moved confidently to her keening climax, which held, it seemed, elements of both bliss and regret.

We lay for a long while entwined before we stirred. I reached for my backpack and took out some rolls of dough.

"I don't think Geoff should chance growing this year." I counted out the bundles.

"What are you doing?"

"You helped earn this. In Oaxaca."

"But you'll need it. Down Under, or wherever . . . for your business."

"There's a few quid left. Besides, you've a family to think of now. Geoff wants to build a house. This'll get you started. He won't have to risk growing."

"I may occasionally act like a member of the oldest profession, Jeremy Stylor, but I prefer not to be thought of as a prostitute."

"You can take consolation in commanding the highest fee of any whore in the world. Here's fifty thou."

"Christ, Jem, I can't take that much."

"Yes you can."

"It's far too much."

"It's not." I held her cheeks in my palms, and locked the turquoise eyes. "I've been selfish this year, Emma. With you. With Geoff. Given you both a lot of grief."

"It was our choice. We knew the risks."

"But I feel responsible for you lot. I came here first. Got involved in all this. Dragged you over here."

"Codswallop. We came because we wanted to. To see America. The great wide West. 'O, my America, my newfound land.'" The Donne line, and my memory of the last time we'd shared it, in Oaxaca, lightened the mood briefly.

"Maybe if I'd been more cautious . . . Maybe if we hadn't gone to Oaxaca, Wiz would still . . ." I tailed off.

"You mustn't think that way, Jem." She held my face now. "If it hadn't been you and me, he'd have found someone else."

"I suppose. But god, it's all gone pear-shaped." I lowered my eyes as I felt a loss of control. "I'm going to miss you. All of you." The tears came and she pulled me to her and held me tightly.

"It's not your fault. Don't blame yourself." But we both knew that my tears were not shed purely from remorse.

I pulled myself together and pushed the wads of cash to her.

"If you're certain." She looked at me.

"I'm certain."

"It would be a great relief if Geoff didn't have to spend the year in the canyon. I shan't have to worry about the jag gobbling him up."

"No one will have to worry about the jag anymore, Ems." I told her of the great cat's demise and the funeral pyre.

"The poor old fellow." she said, and then crossed the room to stash the cash in a drawer.

A couple weeks later I was in Taos, closing a deal on a lovely plot of land where I would build my house and be based for much of the time left to me, when the phone rang.

"Dude, what the eff?" Dali's patter had me smiling.

"You're out of the slammer! Great."

"Thanks to you, man. I owe you big time."

"Not a penny, mate."

"You're a good man, Style. Don't listen to what those folk say behind your back."

"Always the comedian." I chuckled.

"We're doing a sweat. You wanna drive over and join us?"

"Damn straight."

At dawn three days later, I negotiated the dirt roads to Crisp's sweat lodge beside the stream. I recognized the vehicles parked among the sycamores, and with some nervousness and a thrill of anticipation threw off my threads and ducked under the blanket. Three Hawks was chanting softly. A hand grabbed my wrist and pulled me gently down and I made out Nobby's profile. He turned to me and his teeth sprang like fireflies into the gloom. I smiled back. Next to him crouched Stilt, his long spine bowed to the confines of the lodge; he pursed his lips at me. Another large frame betrayed Dali; his bright forehead rose and fell in acknowledgment. There was a space between him and Three Hawks and as the Apache's chants rose to a pitch and morphed into the beginnings of a wail, I realized that we were to be privy to the death song of his tribe and knew now for whom the space was left. His voice gathered tenor and swung between heart-wrenching howls and somber ululations.

Nobby and I were pressed together, comfortable with the contact, and as the dirge intensified I felt him shudder with the first spasms of loss and soon he burst out and I felt unable to curb my emotions for the presumed loss of our great friend, and for all that had gone down in this frenetic year, and for my impending banishment, and I too wept as Three Hawks's song rose in a crescendo of lament; I wept also for the great tribe of the Apache, a couple of hundred of whom had held the United States Army at bay barely a century past, in this gorgeous barren land which I'd grown to love and had now lost through my own lust and greed and violence as the Apache had lost their homeland to the lust, greed, and violence of manifest devilry; and I wept as Cochise had wept, after the army had hanged half his family, for the loss of a way of life in which a man won stature through the permanence of his bond, the generosity of his spirit, and the savagery of his close combat, and lost it through duplicity, cowardice, and greed, niceties of character displayed by many of the so-called civilized men of the time.

The heat, the song of mourning, the pathos of it all became too much. I ducked out and stood in the cool morning air and realized it was finally over. All was done and dusted. I donned my clothes and drove away.

As one with little credence in any form of afterlife, I did not spend the intervening twenty-one years in self-imposed purdah. Life is too long, as one wag says, to spend half of it wallowing in self-pity, pining for the partner who turned me down.

Occasionally I contemplated hastening the end. As I steered my ketch through the southern ocean I would see her face in the brief green effulgence of the tropical sunrise, and would contemplate the simplicity of stepping off the transom to watch the yacht sail away.

Music offered its ephemeral balm. Delibes's "Duo des Fleurs" could lift the spirits for a spell. Like Joni Mitchell, I had many blue motel rooms without finding her refuge of the road, or her comfort in melancholy. I often drank Scotch whisky all night long, yet failed to take Steely Dan's advice and die behind the wheel. And there was far too much Tom Waits: a battered old suitcase to a hotel someplace and a wound that would never heal.

I blundered on through the eighties and nineties, seeing the great hope of our age of enlightenment, conceived in the late sixties, born in the early seventies at Woodstock, suckled on *Dark Side of the Moon* and weaned on Band Aid—I watched that zeitgeist slowly strangled in its infancy by the stultifying regimes of Thatcher and Reagan.

Women there were, of course, but the solace of sex was ruined by the curse of Emma's memory and I lost count of the times these affairs ended in an angry condemnation of the "cold Englishman." My passions became confined to solitary pleasures: watching a Stellar's sea eagle plunge into the Arctic Ocean, sitting alone among tens of thousands to see Maradona weave his way through the Independiente defense in the cacophony of La Bombonera stadium; the muscle-freezing rush of leaping from a plane over the blue mountain hinterland behind Sydney; freeing the Zig-Zag pitches, fifteen hundred feet above the deck on the northwest face of Half Dome.

But despite the passing of the years, despite the determination to expunge the bliss of her memory, the desperation to find another lover, another love, I approached middle age resigned to spending the rest of my days in the knowledge that I would never replace the lovely lilt of her Yorkshire vowels, the thrilling sheen of her smile, or the shuddering rush spurred by the double-barreled promise of her upthrust pelvis.

24

By the time the nurse had rushed to the bedside, Geoff's choking had passed and his breathing had settled to a brisk rasp. I sat listening to his rattling breath for perhaps an hour, then stood.

"Stench of impending death getting to you, Stylor?" One eyelid had slid open.

"Just stretching my legs."

"Feel free to fuck off anytime."

"Decent of you."

"Don't know why Ems asked you to stay."

"Perhaps she thought you'd kick the bucket easier with me here."

"Bollocks." The one eye drilled me. He strained to drag himself up on the pillows. I reached to help him, but he brushed me away. There was a long, awkward moment before I sat back down.

"Couple o' laughs we had out there in the ol' U.S. of A." He caught my eye.

"Got that right." I held his.

"Thought you were gonna write about it." His stare intensified, sensing he was treading on a corn. "Typical Stylor. Big plans, little delivery. What happened, Hemingway?"

"Bollocks." We locked eyes again, and there was a flare of the old harmony. Then another pause while we harked back half a lifetime to the adventure that had been the defining experience of our lives, and had torn us asunder. He tried a smile. "I never could decide whether to curse or thank you for dragging us into all that. We certainly made a few quid though, eh?"

"Couple o' bob, yep."

"That cash you gave Ems." He stalled, then pressed on. "Never did thank you for that. Got us started. Primed the pump, as it were. Helped us build that gaff."

"Ems had earned it," I said, and immediately regretted the implications.

He glared at me but let it pass.

"What d'you do with your stash?"

"Pissed it away in Thailand."

"At least you held on to that land in Taos."

"Umm."

"You built a mud house there."

"Adobe."

"Right." His face softened. "I'm glad we went over there, Style. To Arizona. We loved it there, 'specially Ems. We often regretted coming home. It was the end of things over here. By the time Emma and I and Matthew got back to England, in the eighties, it had all gone in the netty."

"Across the board, I always figured."

"The sixties set it all up for it to take off in the seventies."

"Sixties for the famous, seventies for the infamous," I said.

"Right." His face gathered a touch of the old luster as he warmed to one of our favorite themes. "And we were in the thick of it, weren't we mate? We didn't go looking for the heart of Saturday night. We took it with us."

I chuckled at the metaphor and the memories.

"It was our crowd, Geoffrey pal." I grinned at him. "Remember how Fat Eric would whisper in your ear when we went into a joint: 'Find the fulcrum of the room, mate, and we'll take the fookin' place over.'"

"Right. And Murphy and Tel would start their routine, and soon have the place creased up."

"And the Bullet would drive us in his old post office van."

"Warp factor seven, Cap'n! I canna hold 'er." His voice broke as he strove to shout the remembered line. And we both laughed at the memory of the bald-headed madman flinging the rattle-trap van into the dark tunnels of Birmingham at eighty miles an hour while Fat Eric roared from the passenger seat and swigged some hideous Polish firewater and Wally skinned up a spliff, cursing the Bullet's driving, and Tel pressed on with some daft joke, and Geoff and I braced ourselves against the van walls and laughed and prayed.

He chuckled. The cough started again from deep in the skeletal chest and his torso convulsed until his eyes watered. I reached for him tentatively and held him until he stilled, and this time he pulled me to him and his head fell on my shoulder. I felt him break and tears dampened my neck. We clung to each other in a long moment of—what?—regret, forgiveness, a silent remembrance and mute conclusion of all the love and adventure and hatred and competition that had passed between us during the brilliant decade we'd spent together.

After a while he lifted his head, but held my shoulders.

"If you can find it in you, Style, take care of Ems and the kids for a while, there's a good mate. You made her very happy once. See if you can do it again. I just want her to be happy."

"Sure. I'll change my flight."

"I've taken care of them, financially. Emma needs . . . Well, you know Ems." He let the words hang for a moment.

"Yes," I said, holding his look, "I know Emma."

"The kids could use a little paternal guidance." He cocked his head and I sensed an intimation I couldn't grasp. "Matthew especially. Worries me a bit. He can get himself into a bit of state, you know." He lifted himself up a touch. "Ever noticed what a stocky lad he is? Anthropoid, as you would say, simian perhaps, bit of an apeman, not unlike . . ." His voice tailed off.

The shock ran through me.

"Know what I'm getting at, Style?"

"Yeah. I guess I do."

"We've never done DNA testing. But . . ." Again, the little cock of the head.

"I'll do what I can." I nodded dumbly.

"Thanks." He gave my shoulders a feeble clench, then slumped down into the pillows. "God, man, I'm shagged. And I've had a skinful of festering in this fookin' dosshouse. I'll be glad when it's all over. I don't know if I can bear to see Ems and the kids again. It kills me to see them so upset." He shuffled down into the sheets.

"Think I'll have forty winks." He closed his eyes. "Thanks for dropping in. It was good to see you." One eye opened. "You old cunt." Then a glimpse of a smirk.

I sat by the bed as he quietened and his breathing leveled. I sat there for a long spell, grasping the implications of his words. Was I really Matthew's father? Should I feel remorse for missing out on bringing him up? Wouldn't they have told me years ago? But no, what was the point? They just pressed on the way people do, especially the English. Carry on regardless, living lives of quiet desperation.

I looked at Geoff snoring softly. Then I stood and reached under his head to slip the pillow out. He stirred briefly and I waited for him to settle before I pressed the pillow firmly to his face. He fought, and one hand came up and clenched my wrist weakly, before his body gave a spasmodic thrash and he lay still. I kept pressure on the pillow and finally released my weight and strove to keep my gasps quiet.

I lifted his head, replaced the pillow, and gently eased his head back down. I studied his face—the sallow cast to the cheeks, the dull sheen of his green irises, the nicotine-stained teeth—until moisture clouded my vision. With a nervous sweep of my fingers, I closed his eyelids. Then I sat for perhaps an hour, my mind whirling over the years past and those to come, before I slipped quietly from the ward.

A few weeks later, I sat nervously in a pub awaiting Emma. I watched the Brummies having a pint or six after work and saw their heads shift and the odd elbow nudged and knew she had arrived.

"Dry white, please," she said, in answer to the obvious.

"Large or . . . ?"

"I think I'll need a large." And that smile, that smile that had launched a thousand of my tears, graced her face and key-lit the room.

I returned with the wine and we both stared ahead in silence, and drank, and then turned together and spoke at the same time. We both laughed, and looked directly at each other for the first time since that Arizona night long ago. We held each other's gaze. Finally, she turned away.

"How are people in the States reacting to the Twin Towers?"

"You know the Yanks. Shock, horror, an inordinate amount of hand-wringing, an utterly disproportionate display of patriotism."

"Well, at least the Americans have the world's sympathy for the first time since the war."

"*Nous sommes tous Américains, aujourd'hui.*"

"*Bien sûr.*"

Silence fell over us again.

"How's Taos these days? Do they still have that amazing ceremony at the Pueblo at Christmas Eve? With the bonfires and the rifle shots and the women chanting?"

"They do. But instead of the couple of hundred locals standing round the fires when you and I were there, there's now a couple of thousand."

"I'd love to see it again. Even with the crowds."

"You'd have a place to stay."

"You've built a house there, I hear."

"I have. In the mountains, great views. Four bedrooms."

"We'd only need one, Jem." She took my hand and folded it in both of hers. I looked at her intently.

"You look marvelous, Ems. Custom and age don't seem to have withered you much. Must be the soft English air."

"You've weathered the dry desert country well yourself." She ran her fingers across my temple.

"The lines run deeper. And there's a hideous crow's foot about here." I put my right hand across my ribs and she gave a little whimper and leaned toward me and we locked looks in the manner we had often done those decades past so that the other's eyes became one.

"My face in thine eye, thine in mine appears," she said.

I tried the next line. "And true plain hearts do in the faces rest," then faltered and held her gaze till I felt the smoke in my eyes and added quickly, "I don't think I can manage any more of 'The Good Morrow' just now, lest I make a fool of myself."

She brushed the corner of her eye.

We drove to her house, a fine old three-story terrace. The telly was on in the living room; she beckoned me in.

"Matthew, this is an old friend, Jem Stylor."

He turned and I felt a surge of disquiet. The dark brown eyes were piercing, I thought, in my sinner's paranoia.

"We met at the hospital." He turned back to the tube.

"I'll get ready," said Emma, and her eyes swiveled me to a seat. Matthew and I watched the football match in silence until Tony Adams scythed down Lee Hendrie on the edge of the Arsenal box.

"He never touched 'im," I called out.

"Yes he did. Clearly fouled 'im." The young man craned forward for the replay. "Look. Tripped 'im. Typical Arsenal."

A thousand other similar moments with his father and my father and hundreds of others with whom I'd ogled football or rugby came to mind.

"You a Villa fan?" I said, and realized I'd made a foolish mistake even though Villa Park was only a couple of miles away.

"Wouldn't cross the road to see those wankers," he said, but I knew he'd grown up watching them with his dad, and held the English football fan's weird disdain for his favorite team. I studied his face for a while, noting the small nose, the thick lips, and the beetling brow, and concluded that yes, I suppose, he could be, maybe . . .

Emma entered and stood between us. I remained seated, savoring the remembered comforts of an English winter evening, a good footie match, a crusty companion and the fact that he might be very closely related. I stood and took a pace toward his chair.

"Matthew." Emma's tone turned her son's head, and he stood reluctantly and took my hand. I heard a little gasp from Emma at the similarity in height and build.

"I think the Gunners have got it," I said, in the needling manner of English football fans.

"No chance," he said, declaring his true loyalties, and grinned. I held his hand a second longer than was customary, and he flicked his head quizzically and pulled his hand away.

"We're going for a curry." Emma broke the tension. "Want to join us?"

"No thanks." He sat.

"Nice to meet you," I said.

"You also."

The walk to the balti house took us through dark streets alongside a golf course. Emma slipped her arm through mine and I clenched my elbow to hold her close.

"Matthew seems a nice lad," I said feebly.

"*I* think so." She gave me a questioning glance but let it pass.

We exchanged pleasantries and walked on in silence, the atmosphere delightfully easy yet electric with anticipation. I slipped my arm around her waist and she tucked her head on my shoulder. I turned to lean against a low wall beneath a hedge and she came against me and there was no restraint and our mouths met and her hips sawed across mine and her tongue scalded my palate and I was flung back through my life, past the time we had first necked against the rock in the Mad Jag garden and across countless similar encounters in the seventies and back to freshman college days when the gorgeous Marlene had squirmed against me behind the physics lab and had cupped me in her little Welsh hand and back farther still to my teens and my first kiss with Martha in a Devon hedge at a Kinks concert the day, the only day ever, the footballers from our Albion valleys beat the world at the game we invented, and I felt a surge of renewal, rebirth, and was born again, borne across those dark decades and back again to realize as we clung together in that hedge that passion could endure, that time could not destroy such a potent mutual desire, that lust, and perhaps love, were impervious to age.

"Oh Jem. It's too soon." She tailed off and thrust my chest back with her palms.

At the Indian, we recalled the wild days in Arizona. When a lull in conversation came, she reached into her purse and pulled out a scrimshawed mastodon horn carved beautifully, a couple decades earlier, by Craig in the Jerome gulch.

"Geoff made me promise to give it to you." She passed it to me. "It has a base that you can unscrew and a tiny pipe, which . . ." She smiled. "As if I need to tell you. You were friends with Craig yonks before Geoff and I crossed the pond."

After dinner we returned to her house where I slept demurely in the attic bedroom. The following morning I drank a cuppa with her and kissed her on the doorstep when she left for work and promised to call, then drove in a dazed euphoria to my mum's in Devon.

I parked in front of the little cottage and saw her rise from the chair. As always when I first saw her faded auburn hair, her pale powdered cheeks, her strong small frame, and having suppressed the tears over the recent trying days, I fell apart like a Korean watch and sobbed on her shoulder.

"You are a daft ha'p'orth." She held my face in her hands.

We had tea in the little conservatory and talked about New Mexico and my brothers and her grandchildren. Soon I excused myself and set off for a long walk, through the village, past a terrace of thatched cottages, and then along a public footpath that led me past a farmyard. A steep way crossed a stile and climbed a kale field along beech hedgerows to an old hay barn. I sat on a bale, examined the mastodon horn, then eased off the black jet base, turned the horn over, and spilled the little bud of the Mad Jag grass into my hand.

Holding the horn at either end, I swiveled the two pieces on the beautifully crafted pivot to expose the tiny bowl of the hidden pipe. A gentle crumble of the dried flower brought the gorgeous, unmistakable aroma of the famous weed to my nostrils. I fingered the grass into the bowl and tamped it carefully with a thumb. Cupping a match in my palm, and covering and opening the little carburetor hole disguised as the eagle's eye, I drew deeply on the smooth smoke.

Ten minutes later I strode, nay floated, along a path that skirted a tangled hawthorn hedge high above the Devon valleys. I paused to lean on a gate next to a gnarled oak and leaned into the breeze as my eyes watered from a potent combination of the fabulous, invigorating cannabis, the stiff salt wind belting in off the North Atlantic, and the blissful anticipation of a reconciliation with a woman about whom I could prattle on ad infinitum but of whose charms the reader, having hung in this far, is well informed.

I wafted down a damp bridle path as a pair of buzzards screeched and soared overhead. The slurred shriek of the buteos was so similar to their American cousins that I was flung again to the canyons of the Southwest, and when a cock pheasant sprang from the bracken with a hoarse cry, I closed my eyes and recalled the roar of the old jaguar who had lent so much to that *annus mirabilis*.

"I've changed my plans, Mama," I said at dinner. "I'm going to stay in England for a while."

"That's wonderful, dear." She beamed at me. "Another slice of treacle tart?"

Gratitude

To Allegra Huston, whose superb editing was essential in thrashing a dodgy first draft of a first novel into a readable book.

To Liz Burns for early encouragement, excellent plot and character suggestion and thorough proofing.

Acknowledgments

Alison Tomlinson
Ben Slator
David Hardy
Richard Johnson
Simon Bell
Jim Bergstrom
Doug Wade
Wally Coates
Lara Santoro
Pamela Keir
Bobby Bergstrom
Chip Eyrie
Hans Scherrer
Curt Pfeffer
Sean Murphy

And to my darling partner and muse of thirty-five years, Leah.

Cockney Rhyming Slang

As a young man working in the theaters of London I was, at first, utterly confounded by the snapped commands and frequent abuse I received from the old stagers manning the backstage areas, because much of it was couched in Cockney rhyming slang. There is some dispute as to the origins of Cockney rhyming slang, but little doubt about how it developed into a popular vernacular. In 1829 Sir Robert Peel, Home Secretary and later prime minister, started the first professional police force in London. As a result, the costermongers and street merchants of East London, who operated on the fringes of the law and often blatantly on the wrong side of it, started a "secret tongue" in order to conceal their intentions from the authorities. Usually, either a two-word phrase or a "this and that" combination rhymes with the word the phrase conveys; and often only the first word is used. So "Get up the apples sharpish, young china" translated roughly to "Mount those stairs quickly, young lad."

Barnet Fair	hair
Bath bun	son
boat race	face
Bob Hope	dope
Bo-Peep	sleep
china plate	mate
creamed (cream-crackered)	knackered (exhausted)
cream crackers	knackers (testicles)
cufflink	drink
festivals	testicles
frog and toad	road
Johnny Cash	hash
Otis Redding	wedding
pony and trap	crap
rabbit hutch	clutch
rattle and crank	bank
Rosy Lea	tea
rub-a-dub	pub
Scotch mist	pissed (drunk)
septic tank	Yank
Sweeney Todd	flying squad (London police force)
zigzag	shag

The author in the Swimming Hole, Mad Jag Canyon, summer 1980. He lives in Taos, NM. This is his first novel. *Photo: Wiz*

Made in the USA
Middletown, DE
20 September 2024

60676441R00166